# Undoing

## L.L. Diamond

**Undoing**
By L.L. Diamond
Published by L.L. Diamond
Copyright ©2020 LL Diamond

Cover and internal design © 2020 L.L. Diamond
Cover design by L.L. Diamond/Diamondback Covers
Cover Art: *Anna Maria Dashwood, Marchioness of Ely* by Thomas Lawrence, courtesy of Art Institute of Chicago and CC0. *Cottage on Fire at Night* by Joseph Wright of Derby. Courtesy of Yale Center for British Art and CC0.

ISBN-13: 978-1-7342783-5-4

Other works by L.L. Diamond include:
**Rain and Retribution**
**A Matter of Chance**
**An Unwavering Trust**
**The Earl's Conquest**
**Particular Intentions**
**Particular Attachments**
**Unwrapping Mr. Darcy**
**It's Always Been You**
**It's Always Been Us**
**It's Always Been You & Me**
**Undoing**

To all my friends who I've made during our stay in England.
Whether we were online friends before and finally met in person or we
met for the first time here,
thank you from the bottom of my heart for making this time in my life so
amazing.

# Prologue

**Monday September 28<sup>th</sup> 1808**

Elizabeth reached a shaky hand up to knock on the hard, wooden door of her father's library. Her stomach roiled and twisted while she waited for her father's usually comforting voice call for her to "enter." What would he say? Would she have a choice in her future? This was a day that had certainly not ended the way she had planned!

Instead of soothing her, his call made her muscles stiffen further. She cracked the door, but rather than step through, she hesitated and peered inside before slipping into his sanctuary. Her lips curved at the sight of him comfortably seated in his usual pose behind his desk, his wire-rimmed spectacles perched upon the tip of his nose. How many times had she entered to find him thus? Too many times to count, if she gave it much thought. Perhaps the tumultuousness of the moment made his current situation surprising, though oddly soothing. Her palm pressed against her chest. Why would her hands not cease their incessant quaking?

"Aaah, Lizzy, I have been expecting you. I take it the duke has departed for London?"

"Yes, important business requires his immediate attention, but he indicated plans to return early next week."

Her father nodded and held out a hand towards the chairs on the opposite side of his desk. "You have come to discuss his proposal, then?"

Nodding, she took the offered seat and firmly clasped her hands in front of her. Hopefully, they would stop that infernal trembling soon. Why had she let this situation discompose her in such a way? "I do not know what to do, Papa. I attempted to refuse as politely as I could, but he would not hear of it. He insisted I take a few days to consider my options. He even suggested I seek your counsel on the matter."

Henry Bennet sighed, placed his book on the desk, and leaned forward on his forearms. His steady and intent gaze was a tell-tale sign— this would not be one of their more light-hearted discussions.

"You do know he discussed his proposal with me before he approached you."

Elizabeth nodded, her hands clenched a little tighter, and she swallowed down a sting in the back of her throat. Lord, but she hated that feeling. "Yes. He indicated he had done so. He seemed certain you would sanction the match."

After a quick bark of laughter, her father shook his head. "I merely agreed to explain the particulars of the discussion between him and myself. I never suggested I would force your hand." He peered over the rim of his glasses. "I will stand by your decision, regardless of your mother's tirades—though, if she learns of it, she will never forgive you for refusing a duke."

His prediction of her mother's antics prompted an exaggerated roll of her eyes, though her trembling had lessened considerably. "I find him amiable and intelligent, Papa, I do. Yet, I do not possess the depth of feeling I deem necessary to justify marriage."

The slight crinkle around his eyes disappeared along with the slight curve of his lips, and she took a deep breath while she waited for him to speak. Would he speak favourably and press her to accept the proposal or would he simply recount the conversation? "Many marriages have no basis in emotion but are as a result of other factors. You are not so young to be completely naïve to those alliances."

Elizabeth shook her head, still attempting to cease that slight infernal shaking of her knees. The duke's proposal had been unexpected, to say the least. One day, he was a welcome visitor to the neighbourhood who became well-liked and respected for his open countenance and manner. This morning, he became an unwanted and unwelcome suitor. Elizabeth had no appreciation for being caught unawares. His confidence in her acceptance also unnerved and disturbed her a great deal.

Before she could respond to her father's statement, he tapped his palm upon his book and stood to pace around the room. "As an exceedingly wealthy and titled man, he could have any woman he desired from the *ton*, any woman in possession of a significant fortune and superb connections, yet he has overlooked those women since he became of marriageable age. Instead, he wants you. Do you know why?"

"He claims to appreciate my intelligence and my lack of artifice."

Her father gave a brief tilt to his head and lifted his eyebrows. "I cannot find fault with his judgment. He has indicated he cares little for your meagre portion and is prepared to offer you a generous settlement, as well as provide ten-thousand pounds to be settled upon Jane."

Her eyebrows drew together. Only Jane? "I do not mean to sound ungrateful, but why not set aside portions for all of my sisters?"

"By London society's standards, most ladies are not out until seventeen, which makes your younger sisters too young at this time. Instead, he intends to bestow money on each of your sisters upon their seventeenth birthdays in the hopes it might curb your mother's desire to push them out at fifteen, as she did you."

Her hand clenched upon the arm of the chair. She had hated being out at fifteen. She had not wanted to attend balls or attract a suitor. She wanted nothing more than to ramble about Longbourn and read the books in her father's library.

Her mother's intentions, however, were not the current issue at hand. Instead, the question lay in the motivation of the duke's generosity. She shrugged, lifting her hands then dropping them into her lap. "I simply do not understand why he would go to so much trouble."

"Our family is of little consequence to most of society. We have no great fortune, a small estate, and no relations of standing. His generosity provides some elevation to our status. Though he is the origin, his gifts give our family an appearance of affluence we lack and should help ease your way into society."

She gave a faint huff. Why did it feel as though she were being purchased like a mare at auction? "A society I shall not join unless I agree to his scheme."

His eyes twinkled with humour. "True, but he is trusting you will say yes."

With a spring from her chair, she crossed to the window before turning in a swish of her skirts. "I enjoy a companionable friendship with him, but I maintain that I do not love him."

Again, her father peered over his glasses. "Companionable friendship is more than most people possess in marriage, Lizzy. I thought I was in love with your mother, but in the end . . ." He paused and pressed his lips together.

Her eyes darted back to his face. "You never loved Mama?"

A long drawn out exhale escaped him. "I earnestly believed my heart was filled with her when I proposed, but I do believe upon reflection, that my feelings consisted of no more than a mere infatuation. Your mother was handsome and different than the other ladies."

"How so?" she asked, stepping closer.

"Well, she was not the silly woman you know. She possessed a quieter, more demure manner. Your sister Jane oft times reminds me of your mother when we first met."

An unladylike noise escaped her nose before she could stop it. Mama? Demure and quiet?

He sighed and removed his spectacles, rubbing a lens with his handkerchief almost absentmindedly. "After we married, I suppose she began to reveal her true nature. Not all at once, mind you, but gradually, over the next few years, she transformed into the woman I now take refuge from in this library."

Surely, he did not mean . . .? "Are you saying I should marry him to avoid a life such as yours?"

"I am saying you should not reject him simply because your feelings do not extend beyond friendship. It could be a blessing your feelings do not run deeper. You will not suffer for it. You would have a husband worthy of your respect instead of one you revile."

She glanced out of the window at the branches of a nearby apple tree swaying in the wind. The branches almost lumbered from side to side they were so laden with fruit.

A weight had appeared to press upon her shoulders, much like the descriptions she had read of the mythological Atlas. She shoved the tree from her mind and returned to the duke. How could she accept him? Yes, he was amiable, but her agreement would be in opposition to the ideals she had always held dear.

"Did you know he owns the great house at Stoke?"

Her head whipped around, her eyes wide. "I heard in the village he was leasing. Aunt Philips claimed Uncle Philips brokered the contract."

"You should know better," her father scolded. "Your aunt would claim she heard it from the queen herself if people would believe such tripe."

Her lip curved upward on one side at the unfortunate yet accurate description of her mother's sister. "So, her claims have no foundation in truth."

"Not a one. Stoke has always belonged to the duke. He has let the place out in the past, but decided to inspect the property himself before allowing new tenants to take possession."

"But what has this to do with his proposal of marriage?"

"He offered Stoke as your mother's home when I am gone."

Elizabeth pursed her lips and crossed her arms over her chest. "You would be gone, and I would be the one to receive her moaning and groaning about the impossibly small drawing rooms." She shook her head with a lopsided smile. "No, thank you."

Her father laughed as he sat in his chair. "You would not be in the neighbourhood to hear her complaints, and Derbyshire is too far for her to easily travel. You need not read her letters."

"Oh, Papa," she said, laughing. "I am certain to hear her lamentations from Hertfordshire. You do know how she likes to go on."

He grinned and his eyes twinkled. "Yes, but she would no longer wail of Mr. Collins casting her into the streets upon my death."

She blew out an exhale, shifting the pages of a ledger upon his desk. How weary she was of a topic she preferred to forget. "You believe I should accept his proposal?"

Mr. Bennet's expression fell. Long discussions of her hopes and aspirations occurred often in this very room, yet the answer to her question was plainly written upon his face. "I do." His eyebrows lifted. "But it is not my decision to make."

A loud cacophony erupted outside of the door before it flew open to reveal a red-faced and dishevelled Mrs. Bennet.

"Elizabeth Adelaide Bennet! What did you do to drive the poor duke away?"

She closed her eyes as the sound ricocheted like a bullet from her skull down her spine. Marriage to the duke would have at least one positive aspect—escape from Francine Bennet.

"I promise to give it more consideration, Papa."

He sighed and pinched the bridge of his nose over his spectacles. "I am glad to hear it."

# Chapter 1

### Friday March 10th 1809

The London home of Lord and Lady Vranes was an absolute crush! Fitzwilliam Darcy, who heartily disliked balls and large social gatherings of any kind, navigated his way through the throng in a vain attempt to find a place to stand. After pushing between two rather rotund women standing back to back, a small, vacated area appeared, and he stopped to examine his surroundings. Perhaps someone of his acquaintance stood nearby? An insipid discussion of the weather was preferable to being alone when the matchmaking mamas targeted him for the kill.

Instead, a familiar name uttered in a gossipy manner teased his ear. He trained his eyes on the crowd. Had he heard correctly? He did not turn but latched onto the sniping voice somewhere behind him.

"He may be a duke, but he is surely nearing sixty by now. I have heard she is but fifteen! I maintain the alliance is positively scandalous!"

"Oh posh, Hattie! Firstly, from what I understand, she is seventeen. If she were from the *ton*, this would be her first season, so she is not so young. Besides, he is not the first older gentleman to marry a lady newly out, and he certainly will not be the last."

The first speaker had to be Lady Dudley, a well-known, relentless gossip. She was the epitome of the reason he detested most women of society.

"His choice is simply nonsensical. I introduced him to, and gave him every opportunity to marry my Ruth, but he never even glanced at her. He leaves town to visit a property in Hertfordshire—of all places—and returns with a wife. A wife, I might mention, that is barely of marriageable age!"

He grimaced and attempted to block out a mental image of her Ruth. As if his godfather would look once at Lady Dudley's homely daughter, much less twice. She was cut from the same mould as the mother—not to mention she lacked the slightest bit of wit and intelligence.

"Mrs. James Chapman called on me yesterday. Have you met Althea?"

He could not see the two ladies, so the other party must have answered with a nod. "She saw the new duchess at the modiste and told me she saw no beauty in her. Her face was too thin; her complexion had no brilliancy; and that her features were not at all handsome."

"She must have some accomplishments to land the Duke of Leeds."

"Well, I also heard she had *no* fortune!" Lady Dudley's companion gasped as a hand on his arm jolted him from his eavesdropping.

"Are you enjoying yourself, son?"

His father stood beside him, a mischievous smile on his face. He gestured towards a set of glazed doors, and they exited to the balcony, ensuring the door closed behind them. It was a cool and foggy night, and despite the heat of the ballroom, very few people sought respite out of doors.

"I do not know why Lady Vranes insists on inviting so many people. They simply do not have the room to accommodate a crush such as this."

"It *has* become stifling inside," Fitzwilliam agreed.

His father tilted his head as he studied him. "What interested you so about Lady Dudley's gossip?"

Fitzwilliam gave a bit of a start. His father rarely wished to know the subject of anyone's gossip. "She was discussing our cousin's marriage."

George Darcy laughed and shook his head while he glanced out at the small garden. "She held grand aspirations he would wed her eldest daughter. He finally marries, so she does her best to lambaste the victor."

Fitzwilliam furrowed his eyebrows and stepped closer. "I do not understand why he married. He has always claimed he would never take a wife."

His father shrugged and leaned against the railing. "To be honest, his news took me by surprise as well. They should be putting in an appearance sometime tonight, but you know your godfather; he strives to be fashionably late."

They both smiled as his father gestured towards the doors. "We should return to the ballroom. Thomas would never forgive us for missing his grand entrance as a married man."

Fitzwilliam sputtered out a laugh. "No, he, no doubt, expects us to stand to the front of the crowd and cheer." He preceded his father through the door only to nearly collide with Lady Tennant, who was accompanied by her daughter Lady Sarah.

"Mr. Darcy," the mother crowed. "How lovely to see you!" Reaching out beside her, she propelled her daughter forward until the poor girl stood almost inappropriately close to him. "I am sure you remember my daughter Sarah." Fitzwilliam stepped back and gave a quick bow.

"Good evening, Lady Sarah." He remained impassive. He could not give the young woman or her cloying mother any hope of success. Lady Sarah may have the connections and fortune some families desired, but he could not tolerate her vanity and insipid conversation. He would rather muck out all the stables in London than be in Lady Sarah's company.

The lady in question smiled and batted her eyelashes. By the manner of her expression, some inane sort of flattery would soon leave her lips. He gripped his hands and clenched his jaw in preparation.

"You have been sorely missed from the season thus far, Mr. Darcy," she said in a honeyed manner. Why did that tone never fail to pain his ears? "Will we see you promenade in Hyde Park sometime this coming week?"

Had she not considered the abundance of rain this past se'nnight? The sun had finally broken through the clouds that day, so the park was muddy and still quite cool, even to promenade. "The weather since we arrived in London has been too wet to venture to Hyde Park."

She smiled widely, and he restrained the urge to roll his eyes. Lady Sarah, however, had not conceded defeat and tilted her head as she took a step closer.

"Have you met the new Duchess of Leeds?"

He stiffened and began to stutter a response as a hand landed on his back. "Lady Tennant, Lady Sarah." His father pressed him away. "I must beg your forgiveness. I was taking my son to greet his cousins, Lord Carlisle and Colonel Fitzwilliam."

"Oh, of course," Lady Tennant simpered. "Although, I am certain Mr. Darcy will wish to secure a set with my daughter before he departs."

Fitzwilliam's eyes hurt as they bulged at her forwardness. He required a quick and clever retort—one that would not be considered rude. He had to hurry! A swift glance to his side found his father considering him with an amused expression, his eyebrows raised.

"Well . . ." he stammered, "a . . . a . . . dance with Lady Sarah is an honour best left to someone more deserving than I. Colonel Fitzwilliam, as the son of an earl, would be a worthier candidate. I shall send him post-haste to secure a set."

He pivoted on his heel and headed towards the card room. His father soon stepped beside him, chuckling. "That was a rather unfeeling thing you just did to your cousin."

Grimacing, he shrugged. "I happen to think Lady Sarah would be perfect for Richard."

"Poor man! Will you and Carlisle never cease to bait him? The two of you give him no quarter." His father motioned towards a table in the far corner where his cousin Nicholas Fitzwilliam, Viscount Carlisle, gestured them over with a wave.

As they approached, Fitzwilliam noticed Carlisle's younger brother, Richard, betting on the hand of cards he studied intently.

Unlike his brother, who would play in a seedy tavern if the mood struck,—and often did—Carlisle was not much of a card player and preferred smaller games between friends to the tables at a ball or his club. By Richard's stiff posture and hard expression this evening, he held a losing hand, as was his wont.

Carlisle rose and grasped George Darcy's hand. "It is good to see you, Uncle," he said before turning and shaking Fitzwilliam's. "You too, Fitzwilliam. Mother insisted I remind you to respond to her dinner invitation."

His father smiled and nodded. "I shall respond to their invitation on the morrow."

"I would be grateful," said Carlisle. "I do not appreciate being tasked as her messenger boy."

"Uncle! Darcy! You must join our game!" called Richard from across the table.

"It appears as though you should join us in the next room." George Darcy may not have issued a blatant order for his nephew to quit the game, but his tone and expression did not brook argument.

Richard appeared to recognise the indirect command since he set down the cards and rose from the table. "I wish you gents better luck than I possess tonight." He shook the hand of another officer, seated across from him.

Fitzwilliam grinned broadly and clapped his cousin on his shoulder, hitting his epaulette. "I came across Lady Tennant and her daughter, Lady Sarah, in the ballroom."

Richard groaned and his brother began chortling.

"I informed Lady Sarah you would be most desirous of a set."

With a grimace, Richard practically growled, "You are an arse, Darcy."

"I thought you said Lady Sarah is the perfect companion of your future life," said Carlisle, goading him.

Richard regarded him with a pinched expression. "No, I prefer someone I do not mind bedding for an heir."

"An heir?" Why would Richard require an heir? He had nothing a son might inherit.

His cousin smirked. "The earldom will need an heir one day, and since my dear brother seems unwilling to do his duty . . ."

Carlisle barked and slapped his brother on the back. "When I find the correct woman, I shall have no problem doing my duty."

His brother grinned. "Perchance, that woman might be Lady Sarah. If I happen to see her tonight, I shall ensure she reserves you a set. I think the last will do nicely." Before Carlisle could retort, Richard disappeared into the crowd.

"He has been insufferable tonight."

"You could have left him." Fitzwilliam spoke softly, acknowledging an acquaintance as they passed.

"Do you not remember what happened the last time I abandoned him at the card tables?" Carlisle spoke low so as not to be overheard. "He lost so much to Lord Alconbury's cousin they tracked *me* down for his debt. No one will extend him any type of credit these days."

"So you linger about to prevent him from ruining himself?"

Carlisle stared at the back of his uncle as they made their way towards the grand staircase. "He will lose too much to the wrong man one day, and it will break my mother's heart."

A hush descended upon the crowd as by groups they turned to the large oak double doors where the Darcys' cousin, Thomas Osborne, the Duke of Leeds, stood with his bride.

Having never laid eyes on Thomas's wife until that moment, Fitzwilliam studied her. Why had his cousin chosen this particular woman as his bride? She appeared to be young—very young, but something about her eyes offset her youthful physicality. Those eyes did not appear out of the ordinary at first glance. They were wide, brown, and doe-shaped; however, upon further study, their brightness hinted at an underlying intelligence. Her mahogany curls sat piled atop her head while an arched eyebrow accompanied a curve to one side of her lips. She found humour in some aspect of this evening's gathering.

"She is uncommonly pretty," commented Carlisle near his ear. "What think you, cousin?"

"I agree." Yes, she was certainly handsome, but handsome young ladies were not exactly a rarity within the *ton*. What rendered this woman so special? How did she convince Thomas to break his vow to never marry?

The duke led his bride to where Lord and Lady Vranes stood to one side of the room. After their initial greeting, Lady Vranes took the duchess's hands as they spoke quietly with smiling faces. The two ladies had obviously formed an acquaintance prior to this evening. They even appeared friends. If this young lady hailed from the country as many claimed, what could she have in common with a countess noted for her artistic eye? After a few moments, the duke turned and espied Fitzwilliam and his father. A smile overtook his face as he led his wife to where they stood and offered his hand to Fitzwilliam's father.

"George," he exclaimed happily. "It is wonderful to see you so well."

"One could say the same to you." His father accepted the duke's proffered hand.

The duke then gestured towards the young lady on his arm. "I would like to introduce you to my wife, Her Grace, Elizabeth Osborne, Duchess of Leeds. Elizabeth, I would like you to meet my cousin, George Darcy, and his son, Fitzwilliam." He grinned when he noticed Carlisle standing to Fitzwilliam's side, offering his hand to him as well. "And this is their cousin, Nicholas Fitzwilliam, the Viscount Carlisle."

The duchess curtsied primly, a warm smile on her face. "It is a pleasure to meet you. His Grace has told me much of all of you. I anticipate ascertaining if his descriptions are as accurate as he claims." While she spoke, Fitzwilliam found himself drawn into the glimmering depths of her unusual eyes.

The duke chuckled. "She would have you believe nothing I say."

"I simply find the differences between your descriptions and reality interesting." She released the duke's arm to clasp her hands in front of her. "For example, you claimed Worthstone to be a modest country home. I believe your exact words were 'It is truly not so grand as some may claim.'"

George Darcy coughed to disguise a chuckle. "She has you pegged, Thomas."

"I certainly doubt I understand His Grace so well, Mr. Darcy, but I am learning."

"Yes, well," the duke interrupted. "I happen to know Her Grace enjoys dancing, but I do not wish her to be subjected to every gossip's son or husband. Enough fodder currently exists for the rumour mill. Would you gents object terribly?"

"Since I presume you will be dancing the next with your wife," George Darcy turned to the duchess, "may I request the dance following your husband's?"

"I would be pleased to offer you the first set after supper, Mr. Darcy."

"Thus far Fitzwilliam has avoided dancing, but you will have to dance eventually." His father levelled a smug expression in his direction.

The duchess arched an eyebrow. "I would not expect Mr. Fitzwilliam Darcy to dance if he dislikes the activity."

"Nonsense." His father laughed and nudged him in the elbow. "He avoids the ballroom enough."

Fitzwilliam smiled tightly, the muscles in his shoulders taut. Would he be trapped dancing with a string of tiresome young ladies for the remainder of the evening because he aided his cousin? "I would be honoured if you would join me for a set, Your Grace."

"I would not wish you forced, sir."

Her eyes twinkled with humour. There had been rumours she entrapped her husband, and Fitzwilliam's stiff posture relaxed as he became more certain the gossip was nothing more than falsehoods.

He dipped a slight bow. "I apologise for giving you the impression I was at all displeased. I shall be honoured to dance with you."

Carlisle gave a sweeping bow. "I would be delighted to claim the set after my surly cousin."

"Yes, sir," she replied with a broad grin.

The music for the current set ended, and the duke turned to his wife. "If we are to dance the next, we should take a place in the line. I have no doubt people will ambush us along the way for an introduction."

Her lips pressed together tightly as she placed her hand on husband's arm. Was she nervous or displeased?

Fitzwilliam's father shifted to his side while they observed the couple wending through the revellers to the dance floor. They stopped once or twice, obliged speak to a few people lest they offend them, but soon, joined the line to dance the next.

"What do you think of her?" asked his father.

"She seems a pleasant sort. There is something about her eyes that renders her older than she appears."

George Darcy nodded. "I agree. She is a handsome young lady to be sure, but I suspect she is more than a pretty face. Thomas has never tolerated idiocy."

Carlisle elbowed Fitzwilliam in the ribs. "She will definitely liven up these old society families. They are not thrilled His Grace overlooked their daughters but will not snub a duchess, especially one as affluent and influential as Leeds. That alone will be enjoyable to watch."

"Your mother will be disappointed she missed tonight," said Fitzwilliam.

"My parents committed to an engagement long before Lady Vranes sent around her invitations. My father has long admired Leeds, and my mother has not been the only one inordinately curious about the new duchess. I am certain they will make her acquaintance soon."

After supper, Fitzwilliam stood to the side of the ballroom with the duke while his father danced with the new duchess. "You do seem well."

"I am," said the duke. "The physician still expresses concerns about my heart, but I have had no further episodes of the sort I had last year."

"I am glad to hear it."

Her Grace leaned in a little to speak to his father, which caused his father to laugh. The duke smiled. His father appeared to enjoy the duchess's company.

"I would be pleased if you and Elizabeth could be friends. She is witty and intelligent. I believe the two of you could have much to discuss."

Fitzwilliam's hands joined behind his back. "I shall do my best to make her welcome into the family."

"Thank you, Fitzwilliam." The duke bestowed a fatherly slap on the back and turned to watch the dance end.

His father led his partner to them, and Fitzwilliam stepped forward. "I believe our set is next?"

Her eyes held his as she nodded. "Mr. Darcy."

The duchess placed a graceful hand upon his arm, and he glanced down to where she touched him. Her hand gently rested upon his forearm, near the elbow, but despite his topcoat and his fine lawn shirt, the precise location of each finger could be discerned through the layers. He was unaccustomed to such a sensation. Why should her touch be felt so acutely?

Unwilling to offend her or Thomas, he lifted the corners of his lips a tad and proceeded to the dance floor. She watched him steadily. It would not do to show his disturbance of mind.

As the couples began to move to the first strains, the duchess continued to study him and did not cease her examination for the entirety of the first dance. Why did she stare at him so? And why should he care that she did? He had been the subject of scrutiny from a lady before, but still, the quiet observation for that long of a time made the first half of the set drag.

Soon after the second dance commenced, she glanced up and arched that same eyebrow she had earlier. "I enjoy how this dance matches perfectly to the melody of the music."

He managed a nod before the dance parted them but soon enough her hand joined his once more. He looked at their joined hands, both encased in white gloves as propriety demanded.

"It is *your* turn to say something now, Mr. Darcy—I talked about the dance, and *you* ought to make some kind of remark on the size of the room, or the number of couples." Her head tilted a bit to the side, and she waited for his response with that same arch expression. What was she about? Of course, the only way to discover her motives was to oblige her.

"I would be happy to discuss any subject you would like."

She sighed loudly as she rolled her eyes expressively. "Very well. That reply will do for the present."

The dance parted them. As he turned with another lady, his grin grew larger until the duchess's hand again joined his. "Do you talk by rule, then, while you are dancing?"

Her head turned to him, a slight curve upon her lips. "Sometimes. One must speak a little, you know. It would look odd to be entirely silent for half an hour together."

She was correct. He had never considered the notion since he spent most dances avoiding his particular partner. He smiled, shaking his head. "What think you of books?"

"Oh," she said with a grin. "I cannot talk of books in a ballroom; my head is always full of something else."

"And what might that be?" A teasing tone had crept into his voice.

She laughed then bit her lower lip with a large smile gracing her face. "Perhaps we *should* speak of books." The dance required them to part once more. When they came back together, their eyes met. "Have you read Sir Walter Scott's *Marmion*?"

"I have. You are a great reader of poetry then?"

"I enjoy poetry, dramas, comedies, and even a good novel from time to time. I have also been known to read histories, and books on science and nature."

His eyes flared for but a moment before he allowed one side of his lips to tug upwards. "So, you are a bluestocking."

"Hardly." She blushed and bit her lip. "But I do enjoy learning about the world around me."

"Well, I certainly cannot find fault with that."

"I should hope not." Her eyes took stock of those around them. "Too many look to find fault in our world. A diversion as uplifting and gratifying as reading should not be a fault."

"I did not mean to imply that it was," he said. Had he offended her?

Her eyes returned to him with one side of her lips uplifted. "I know you did not. I am merely making an observation. Forgive me if I sounded accusatory."

"Not at all. Since we have only just met, I did not wish for us to suffer a misunderstanding."

They turned and her hand rested atop his. "I have no wish for such a circumstance either."

With only a few moves left in the dance, they stepped back into their original place and the last chord of the music filled the ballroom. He bowed while she curtsied. Offering her his arm, he led her through the throng until Lady Vranes stood in their path.

"Oh, Lizzy," she said, grasping the duchess's hands. "I have just heard of a new artist—a woman. I hope to meet with her two days hence. Would you join me? I would dearly love to have your opinion."

"You hope to sponsor her?"

"Yes, I do. I have searched for a suitable artist—a woman—for some time. The *ton* will talk and whisper, but I care not. I have longed to give a woman the opportunity to prove herself."

"Then I shall be pleased to join you."

Lady Vranes clasped her hands before her. "Excellent. I shall send a note around tomorrow when I know the exact time."

After Lady Vranes bustled away, Fitzwilliam continued to lead her towards Carlisle for the next set. "You take an interest in art?"

"I enjoy art as I have little talent to show for drawing and painting. I admire the skill and dedication required to produce a painting or even a simple sketch. Lady Vranes has been quite welcoming since our arrival in London and become a valued friend. I enjoy her company, and I have learnt a great deal about art in her company."

"Lord and Lady Vranes are well-known for their collection."

"They are," she said. "My husband informed me of that straight away."

When they reached Carlisle, who stood near his father, Fitzwilliam bowed once more to the duchess before he relinquished her. "Thank you, Your Grace."

Fitzwilliam watched Carlisle lead the duchess away until his father startled him from his unknown reverie.

"What do you think of her?"

"She is intelligent and, much like my godfather, does not suffer fools gladly."

His father smiled. "I believe you are correct."

"Could he have married her because he took pleasure in her company?" He could not comprehend the duke's decision to marry at all, much less someone so young.

His father shrugged and glanced over to where their cousin was speaking with Lord Vranes. "I am unsure of the considerations which induced him, though I am certain he will tell me after dinner next week."

Fitzwilliam turned to him.

"He has invited us to dine with them." His father placed a hand to his shoulder and stepped closer to speak in his ear. "You will be labelled as rude if you do not dance with one of the eligible young ladies tonight." Disapproval laced his father's tone.

He frowned and shifted on his feet. "Is it wrong to desire more than what society dictates is proper?" he asked in a low voice.

His father squeezed his shoulder. "No, son. Of course not."

"I would like to abide my wife, Father. I shall not give false hope to any lady by dancing with her."

His father's eyebrows rose upon his forehead. "If you danced more often, you would not give any of these young ladies the impression you are interested in more than a dance." He gestured to Richard, who currently danced with Lady Sarah. "Your cousin dances often without inciting expectation."

He rolled his eyes. Richard did not excite any hope because no one wanted a penniless colonel—even if he was the son of an earl. His cousin sought a well-dowered bride, but most society families were aware of his excessive gambling. His father and mother still saw the entertaining little boy of years past. They did not see the reality of their son's situation.

By the end of the ball, Fitzwilliam had escaped without standing up with any eligible young ladies. He stood with his father, waiting for their carriage when the duke and duchess emerged from the front doors.

"George," called his godfather, happily. "I trust we shall see you next week for dinner?"

"We should be delighted."

"If Georgiana accompanied you to town, please bring her along. I am certain Elizabeth would enjoy an introduction. They would be fast friends—I am sure of it."

"Alas, she remained at Pemberley. We only planned to be in town for the month. I did not wish to disrupt her studies."

"Then you must bring her to Worthstone for Easter."

His father grinned widely. "I am certain she would be thrilled to join us. I believe she would also find great pleasure in making the acquaintance of her new cousin."

"Wonderful!" Leeds said in a booming voice. "We shall look forward to it."

His wife wore a small smile as she observed the conversation. "I anticipate making the acquaintance of Miss Darcy. I have been told of her many talents and accomplishments."

"We are hardly impartial," said Fitzwilliam. "We can only believe she is the best of young girls." He cleared his throat while he glanced at his father, who stared at him out of the corner of his eye with a peculiar expression.

"Well, here is our carriage," said the duke, shaking hands with both Fitzwilliam and his father. "We shall see you at dinner next week."

The Darcys both nodded and watched as the duke handed his wife inside. The door closed, and the horses pulled the equipage away and into the night. He finally met the duchess that had all of the *ton* in an uproar, yet he found himself no more knowledgeable of her than before their introduction. How could that be?

# Chapter 2

*March 17th 1809*
*Worth House*
*London*

*Dearest Jane,*

*I do apologise most heartily for my lapse in correspondence, but in my defence, I have not had the time to put pen to paper. We have regularly attended balls and dinners since our arrival in London, which has caused me to woefully neglect you, my dear. I do hope you will forgive me since I cannot do without your regular correspondence!*

*Despite the hectic schedule, I did manage an afternoon with my Aunt Gardiner and the children. My husband had business in that part of town, so he delivered me personally to our aunt and uncle's home during his trip.*

*How the children have grown! I so enjoyed their company. I have greatly missed Aunt Gardiner and her counsel, and I confess I quite enjoyed spending the day without the whispers and stares of society. The easy company at Gracechurch Street was just the respite I required.*

*Though I may sound bitter, I assure you, I am not. I have made a friend, Lady Vranes, who possesses an independent spirit I admire and strive to emulate. She scandalously befriends who she wishes and has included me in several outings to art exhibitions, which I have enjoyed immensely. She intends to sponsor a female artist—a Miss Geddes, who shows a great deal of promise with her portraits.*

*I penned a letter to Mama today. She has been upset at my lack of correspondence, so I do hope she has not been too* insufferable to bear. I reported the particulars of my presentation at court to the minutest of details. I felt it a pretentious absurdity, but I know she will recount every bit to the neighbours while Papa rolls his eyes. I do understand it is considered necessary to my new position, yet I am relieved the ordeal is done. The monstrosity of a gown was the most uncomfortable thing I have ever been forced to wear—truly a travesty!

Tonight, we expect the Darcys of Pemberley for dinner. Mr. George Darcy, the duke's first cousin on his mother's side, seems a gentleman in the truest sense of the word. I must say my husband certainly favours that side of his family. Although his hair has a touch of grey, they boast the same dark curls and certain aspects of their features are identical. I see a great resemblance—more than to the portraits of his father at Worthstone.

Yet, I digress. The Darcys are to come for dinner. I met them at Lord and Lady Vranes's ball, and they were amiable company. The elder, Mr. George Darcy, is very tall, and I believe a similar age to my husband.

His son, Mr. Fitzwilliam Darcy, is likely to be near five and twenty. I must confess, my dear Jane, the son intrigued me at our first meeting. He appeared out of sorts and very proud, but upon further examination, I believe my first assumption incorrect. As a favour to my husband, the younger Mr. Darcy requested a set, and after our dance, I am more inclined to believe his behaviour is merely reserved.

My husband says their estate is worth ten-thousand pounds per annum, so I imagine the gentleman is much sought after by the ladies. Could you imagine Mama's raptures should he find his way to Meryton? "Mr. Bennet, such a fine thing for one of our girls!" She would likely have you riding in the rain to take tea with his sister so you would be forced to spend the night!

*Dearest Jane, I do hope you are well! I confess to melancholy in the absence of your company! You must pen me a letter soon and tell me all of the latest news from Hertfordshire. Pray limit it to the news and not the gossip Mama so delights in.*

*Yours affectionately,*

*Lizzy*

The former Elizabeth Bennet considered herself in the full-length mirror. The last six months since the duke's proposal still rendered her speechless. How had little Lizzy Bennet become a duchess? Yes, her father would have accepted her decision should she have refused, but her mother proved relentless. The woman made it no secret the duke would soon propose and her daughter would be his wife—his duchess. Mama's only lament had been that he had neglected to choose Jane.

As a result, Elizabeth resigned herself to being the means of helping her sisters. Jane would have to dream enough for the both of them. Her elder sister would not be relegated to a marriage of convenience. No, Jane would marry for love, and nothing less. All of her sisters would have that opportunity if they chose. Her father had been made to swear he would ensure Elizabeth's wishes would be seen through to fruition, and she would hold him to his promise.

She turned to the side, smoothing her hand down the front of her white and sky-blue sprigged muslin. The fashion plate called it a "Costume Parisien," which would impress her mother, though she would bemoan the decided lack of lace.

However, Elizabeth selected each of her new gowns herself, so they pleased her. The dressmaker ensured she only chose from the latest fashion with clean lines that accentuated her figure, as well as sumptuous fabrics. This gown boasted a trim of matching sky-blue satin roses to complement the fabric. A strand of pearls was interwoven into her curls and perfectly matched the floral seed pearl earrings and simple pearl necklace her husband had given her from the family heirlooms.

Her abigail, Lalande, tidied behind her taking her day gown to hang. Elizabeth slipped her wedding ring, an almost lilac-coloured sapphire accented on either side with diamonds, onto her finger.

"Your Grace," said her maid in a thick French accent, "the Darcys should arrive any minute. The duke will expect you to greet them."

"Of course, thank you." With the ring secured, she departed and smiled at the footman stationed in the corridor.

"Good evening, Matthew. I hope you are well tonight."

"Very well, Your Grace. I thank you." He gave a slight bow.

When she and the duke first wed, she began learning her household duties at Worthstone, and the housekeeper at Worth House, Mrs. Grigg, now continued her education. Despite her mother's teachings, Elizabeth found herself woefully ignorant of how to run such a grand home, but her most valuable lesson had been to always treat everyone with kindness. The staff's patience proved greater when she cared for them as they did her.

As she entered the hall, the familiar hoofbeats and clanking of a carriage sounded from the front of the house, so she glanced to the footman at his post near the stairs. "Inform the duke our guests have arrived."

"Yes, Your Grace," he said, rushing in the direction of her husband's study.

Mr. Hughes, the butler, emerged from the dining room and opened the door to the Darcys standing at the front door. Her husband appeared by her side a moment later, a wide smile across his face.

"George!" Her husband strode forward as they entered. "I am so glad you could join us!"

Once Mr. Hughes and a footman helped relieve them of their greatcoats and hats, the gentlemen gave a quick bow. Elizabeth curtsied though the elder Mr. Darcy had already strode forward to shake his cousin's hand. After, her husband stepped towards the younger Mr. Darcy to welcome him.

"Fitzwilliam, I know I say this every time we meet, but you remind me so much of your father."

The younger Mr. Darcy had appeared so critical when they were introduced at Lord and Lady Vranes's ball. Outgoing would not be a word used to describe him—he spoke little and smiled even less. Was he shy or simply uncomfortable in crowds? Regardless of the reason, he proved a fascinating character study.

"Mr. Darcy," she said, acknowledging the father before she turned and nodded to the son. "Mr. Darcy, we are so pleased you could join us."

"Your Grace," George Darcy began carefully. "I hope you do not find me presumptuous, but I fear the evening will be rather confusing if you insist on addressing both me and my son as Mr. Darcy. Yet, if you call my son Mr. Fitzwilliam, I am sure he would search for Carlisle's cousin, the curate, nearby.

The elder Darcy, thus far, had been amiable and had not appeared judgemental when she had made his acquaintance at the ball. Most assessed her gown, or they took the opportunity to look down upon her without furthering their acquaintance. Mr. Darcy had been pleasantly different.

"We are family now, so I would not object to you calling me George as your husband does. I believe my son would also consent to you using Fitzwilliam."

His request for informality surprised her. The elder Mr. Darcy was nearly the same age as her husband, and she had yet to feel comfortable treating her husband in less than a formal manner. Both men were of a similar age to her father. She could never call her father Henry!

"I . . ."

Her husband laughed and placed a hand to the elder Darcy's shoulder. "I have explained to her that we have been like brothers since we were children and have always addressed each other by our Christian names. I also entreated her to call me Thomas while we are within our homes, but she will not hear of it. I daresay she will still call you Mr. Darcy whether you want her to or not."

Mr. Darcy wore a warm smile. "Well, if that is true, then I would prefer you to address me as you are comfortable."

The younger Mr. Darcy leaned forward a bit. One side of his lips curved, showing a dimple. "You may call me Fitzwilliam if it will make conversation less confusing."

"Thank you," said Elizabeth. "You are welcome to call me Lizzy, or Elizabeth, if you like. My husband uses Elizabeth, but my family has always used Lizzy. She glanced between the father and the son, who both nodded.

Her husband's lips pressed together while he smiled, as though he held in laughter. "Shall we move into the drawing room until dinner is served?"

Elizabeth's back and neck were so tightly strung they could have been plucked. She surveyed the table one last time before they sat down to the meal. Thus far, she and her husband had mostly attended dinners and balls at the homes of others. Tonight, she hosted her first dinner party. Whether it was her husband's family or not, what if something went amiss?

It was not until the end of the meal that she allowed herself to relax. The food had been prepared to perfection, Mr. Hughes had ensured the wines matched each course perfectly, and if her guests' appetites were any indication, the Darcys enjoyed the dishes she had requested.

The discussion veered towards various estate issues when the elder Darcy suddenly paused.

"We should apologise to you, Elizabeth. Farm yields and sheep cannot be interesting dinner conversation."

She grinned as she set down her utensils. "I was raised in my father's library, Mr. Darcy, and learnt at his knee. My mother, however, found my ability to discuss estate business unladylike. I learnt early on to listen and not comment outside of my father's company, but I understand the topic well enough. I do not remain quiet out of a lack of interest."

"During our time at Worthstone," said her husband, "Elizabeth, who enjoys walking, came in from a few of her rambles to inform me of a problem here or there she noted around the estate. In one case, it was very lucky that she did too."

Mr. Darcy's eyebrows lifted as he turned to her. "You should bring your wife to Pemberley, Thomas. I would be curious to hear her suggestions."

Her gaze shifted from her husband to Mr. Darcy. "I am unsure if my observations would help, sir. I am certain you are not in need of my counsel."

Mr. Darcy set down his utensils and leaned back in his seat. "If I am to believe the rumour mill, you are either from Herefordshire or Hertfordshire."

Elizabeth smiled and joined her hands in her lap. Identical whisperings reached her ears wherever they went—the modiste, the ball, the bookseller on Bond Street. "I am from Hertfordshire. My father's estate, Longbourn, is near the town of Meryton."

"A quaint property," said the duke. "I offered a few suggestions to Mr. Bennet before the wedding. I believe he can increase his income substantially if he implements them."

Mr. Darcy pivoted to face his cousin. "You have a property near Meryton, if I remember correctly."

Her husband nodded. "I do. The great house at Stoke was a part of my grandmother's portion. The property is not large, but I keep it in excellent repair. I rarely have a problem leasing it."

"Do you have any siblings?" Mr. Darcy's gaze returned to her, and despite the sudden return of her tight shoulders, she returned his look steadily.

"I do. I am the second of five sisters. My eldest sister, Jane, is one year older, while my youngest sister, Lydia, is twelve."

"Your youngest sister is of a similar age to our Georgiana," he said. "Georgiana could use a sisterly influence, particularly after being cooped up in a house with two grown men for so long. I know Thomas has told you of her, but I do hope the two of you will become friends."

Her bearing relaxed a great deal, and she could not help but beam. How dearly she missed Jane since her marriage! When her husband had mentioned Georgiana, the girl sounded lovely. Despite the difference in their ages, she hoped the young girl would accept her as, at the very least, a good friend. Moreover, Mr. Darcy had suggested they meet, so surely, he must welcome her to some extent.

"I would be honoured to make her acquaintance. My husband and I are hoping your family will pass Easter at Worthstone."

Mr. Darcy rested his forearms upon the edge of the table, and after a quick peek at his son, he nodded. "Fitzwilliam and I discussed the prospect after last week's ball. We would be delighted to spend the holiday with you."

Her husband slapped the table with his hand as he grinned. "Excellent! We shall anticipate your company. If Georgiana and Elizabeth become close, perchance you might allow your daughter to stay for a time. They will have the company of each other while we work with our stewards on the spring planting." He finished his last sip of wine and looked over to Mr. Hughes. "Hughes, the Darcys and I would prefer to drink our brandy in my study."

"Yes, sir," he replied. "Everything has already been prepared."

The duke stood with a large smile. "You have anticipated me again, Hughes. I believe I have become too predictable."

The stoic servant gave a small, uncharacteristic lift to his lips. "I do not believe so, sir."

Elizabeth and the Darcys followed her husband's lead and stood. The gentlemen all briefly bowed to her before they departed the dining room with Mr. Hughes following behind.

She turned to the footman. "Matthew, pray notify Mrs. Grigg that the dining room is empty and can be cleared and cleaned."

"Yes, ma'am." After a quick bow, he hurried from the room.

The gentlemen were likely to be a while, so she departed to the music room. Taking a seat at the pianoforte, she adjusted the music sheet of Bach to practise. She preferred the progression of this particular work to exercise her fingers before she began to play other composers. The Darcys might depart directly after their brandy, but if they remained, it would not hurt to be prepared since she might be expected to perform.

Once she finished the piece by Bach, she began to play a sonata by Scarlatti until the air weighed upon her in the most unusual manner. What caused that slight prickling to the back of her neck? As soon as she concluded the last measure, a glance towards the door revealed the younger Darcy staring in her direction.

Fitzwilliam stood and straightened his topcoat. "I believe now is when I entertain myself for a time while the two of you talk."

George Darcy laughed along with his cousin. "You have always been so generous as to allow us privacy when we are together, and I do wish to speak to Thomas alone. Thank you." Darcy watched Fitzwilliam as he headed towards the door.

"I am certain there is a book in the library to tempt me," said Fitzwilliam as he placed his hand on the door latch. Once Darcy ensured his son had closed the door, he turned to face the cousin he had known since infancy. "So, what possessed you, of all people, to marry?"

Thomas groaned and leaned back in his chair. "I knew this conversation would be a necessity, but I have not anticipated it."

"You knew I would wonder at your motivation," he said. "There is no possibility of you having any interest in this young lady, much less any other woman, so I *know* another reason must exist."

"Have you not heard of James's latest exploits?"

Thomas's nephew and heir, James Osborne, always insinuated himself into some sort of mischief, but what his cousin alluded to this time, Darcy had no idea. "I hear of many escapades that include your wayward relation, but I am uncertain of which scandal you refer to at the moment."

Thomas's fist slammed onto his desk. "And that is the problem! He gambles incessantly; the rumours of his frequent visits to brothels in the seedier parts of London are daily fodder for society. Not only will no respectable lady marry him, but he will ruin Worthstone and destroy everything I have worked so hard to build and maintain."

Darcy stood and stepped towards the fireplace, fingering a figurine upon the stone mantel. "I do not see this as a revelation, Thomas. Why, after all these years, would James suddenly prompt you to marry?"

"Do you not see?" The tone of his voice rose dramatically. "I can leave the properties not associated with the dukedom to Fitzwilliam, but what of those tied to my title? I cannot allow them to be ruined. You must see that I require an heir."

Darcy gave a bark of laughter. He could not be serious? "You, an heir? May I ask how you hope to accomplish that?" He leaned slightly forward and tipped his glass in his cousin's direction. "You tried to bed a woman once when we were at Cambridge. I took you to . . ."

"Yes, yes, I remember. I see no reason to rehash that humiliation." The duke propped his elbows on his desk, rubbing his face tiredly. "You are well aware my predilection lies outside of the female sex." He spoke in a soft tone and with a weary voice. "I have never made any secret of that with you, and despite my differences, you have remained my most trusted friend."

Darcy took a sip of brandy and shook his head. "Some young woman is married off each season under suspicious circumstances or some widow becomes with child and creates a scandal, yet you removed this girl from her family and friends. I do not understand why." In frustration, he scrubbed his hand across his forehead. "You have been married for months. She does not yet appear in the family way."

Thomas grimaced and straightened, gripping his hands into fists. "I will not pass off some groomsman or piano master's bastard child as my own." His lips sneered as he spoke, and his tone dripped with contempt. "I might be married to nearly any make of simpleton if I employed such a scheme."

"Yet somehow you thought Elizabeth would beget your heir?"

Thomas rose and poured himself another snifter of brandy. "I was in Hertfordshire when I received a missive detailing James's latest loss. Are you aware that he has run up a debt of fifty thousand pounds—fifty thousand! People continue to extend him credit because he is my heir. Let us not even discuss the duel he had with Viscount Grantley over that liaison with the viscountess. Thank goodness Grantley only received a flesh wound. God forgive me, but a part of me prayed James would lose."

He rose and stared through the window at the foggy street below. "I met Elizabeth at an assembly. I had not planned on attending, but I did not want to seem as though I was snubbing my neighbours." He exhaled heavily and returned to his seat. "Her mother, not the wittiest of women, pushed her oldest daughter in my direction—an exceptionally pretty girl, but too placid.

"I was not intrigued by Elizabeth until a few days later. While in the local bookshop, I overheard her and her father having a discussion. He was searching for a book on the latest farming techniques, which she knew well. From that moment, a plan formed."

Darcy sipped his brandy and sighed. "The problem remaining, Thomas, is that she is not with child, and one is needed for your plan to succeed."

His childhood confidante turned his eyes upon him with a glint Darcy did not recognise. "I hoped you would assist me with that minor detail."

George Darcy stared at his cousin. What had he said? He took two decided steps forward, put his hands upon the desk, and leaned forward. "Pardon?"

Thomas looked him directly in the eyes. "I hoped you would seduce Elizabeth and father my heir."

Dear Lord! He could not be serious! Why would Thomas believe him capable of such a deception? "Your scheme is for *me* to seduce *your* wife?"

"Yes." He dipped his chin, as though his affirmation required more emphasis. "I have never been much of an Osborne but more of a Darcy—even my father lamented that fact. We favour one another. Just think, a Darcy would be the heir of the Leeds dukedom."

"You are mad." Darcy raked his hand through his curly hair. "You *know* I have not touched a woman since Anne passed from this world. Our vows may have been 'until death us do part,' but I still feel unfaithful to even consider the notion. And that is just one reason. Elizabeth remains a child."

L.L. Diamond

Thomas scoffed and waved off his statement. "She is seventeen."

"She is close to five years older than Georgiana. I know gentlemen sometimes marry wives who are significantly younger, but I cannot bed what I consider to be nothing more than a slip of a girl." He began pacing once more. "Also, what happens after she carries your 'heir?' You obviously have not considered her feelings. She is young and might form an attachment to whoever beds her, leaving a tremendous risk for a prolonged affair. If that man were me, I would be forced to break her heart." Abruptly, he halted and levelled his cousin with a hard look. "You must also consider that she might reject the idea of being seduced."

Darcy paused to take a deep breath, he turned, and stared at the portrait of his aunt, Amelia Darcy Osborne, over the mantle. He had to calm himself. An angry discussion would achieve naught but wounded feelings.

Would Elizabeth be amenable to such a scheme? His first impressions indicated she would not. She behaved in a friendly and approachable manner, yet she remained well within the bounds of decorum—unlike other wives and widows within their society.

He pivoted back to Thomas, his voice more tempered. "In fact, I feel it a distinct possibility she would refuse. You also know I would never take any woman by force—ever. There is also the matter of the sex of the child, which is something you are well aware cannot be controlled. What if the child were a girl?"

"A daughter may not inherit the dukedom, but she could inherit all of my holdings but Cantwell Park and Worthstone, the only properties entailed to the title. As it is, I have already made Fitzwilliam the heir of every property I can."

Darcy could not prevent the glare he aimed at his cousin. "This was a foolhardy and selfish scheme you concocted. The only person you considered was yourself."

"I did try," Thomas said weakly.

"You tried? I do not understand your meaning."

"I went to her on our wedding night." Thomas's face was a brilliant red, and he would not maintain eye contact. "I attempted to

35

hold her close. I kissed her cheek." He shook his head adamantly. "It was wrong—all wrong. She did not feel right in my arms. Her smell was not appealing in the slightest. It would not work."

"Of course, she would feel odd in your arms. She is not a man!" Darcy said in a hiss. "The poor girl!"

"What do you mean poor?" Thomas's volume increased and his tone hardened.

Darcy held out his palms to face his childhood confidante. "You marry her, take her to a strange place, and thrust her into a society that does not want to accept her. Rumours abound of her relations in trade, which are spreading like a pestilence through the city. Carlisle told me yesterday of a gentleman at St. James Court who bragged he knew well the new Duchess of Leeds. He was all too pleased to speak of his knowledge."

"Sir William Lucas." Thomas dropped his head back and closed his eyes for a moment. "He means no harm, yet he is not the most intelligent or intuitive of men and will ramble on without any regard for what he says." His cousin's voice still contained a trace of anger. "Her uncle and aunt are fashionable people. I would prefer to be in their company than nearly all of the peerage."

Darcy shook his head. "*You* have brought her into all of this for a purpose. You have stolen from her the chance to marry a man she loves and have children—for what? Is she to be your companion? Or do you leave her to her own devices every evening after dinner, so you can keep company with Colin in your rooms?"

His cousin's face reddened, which answered his question without speaking. "Good Lord! You do! I always said it was convenient to employ your lover as your valet. She has no idea, does she?"

"I do understand your reluctance to help me, but what of Fitzwilliam? He is young and young men are often in and out of love." Was he holding his breath?

Darcy leaned back over Thomas's desk, close to his cousin's face. "Over my dead body. You will not so much as hint of the possibility. Do you understand me?" He pointed his finger in his cousin's face yet kept his voice moderated. They could not be heard outside of this room. "I shall not have him in love with a woman he could never have. He does not deserve such torment."

Thomas nodded and leaned back in his seat. "I apologise for asking this of you. I was mistaken. I hope you will still come for Easter. I truly believe Georgiana and Elizabeth could be great friends."

"We shall come." Darcy took a long gulp of his brandy. Perhaps it might alleviate some of that tightness in his throat. "I could not deprive Elizabeth of some shred of happiness in this life you have deceived her into."

Thomas rubbed his face. "Forgive me. I had no intention of offending you."

"I do realise that. Unfortunately, the person you should apologise to is your wife."

Thomas glanced up sharply.

"What did Colin make of this plan when you proposed it? You discuss all with him. You would not marry without asking his opinion."

His cousin winced. "He predicted your precise response, but agreed to support me should I try. He heard much good of Elizabeth during our stay in Hertfordshire. He did not wish to see her misled."

"You should heed his counsel more often."

After taking a drink from his brandy, Thomas swirled the contents of the glass, watching the liquid as it clung to the sides. "As you have said many times." He rested the glass on the table and held Darcy's eye. "I treasure your continued friendship. Despite who I am, you have kept my secret and remained my confidante. Many would not."

Exhaling heavily, Darcy sat and pinched the bridge of his nose in a futile attempt to ward off the headache attempting to take a firm hold. "I have no claim to being perfect." He dropped his hand back to his lap. "You are more my brother than a cousin. I could never bring myself to judge you or cast you aside. My heart would never allow it."

"You are the best of men, Darcy. I have always believed that."

"Yet, you expected me to behave with a callous disregard for Elizabeth's feelings."

Elizabeth was a lovely young woman, her physical beauty enhanced by her intelligence and open nature. She was easy to admire and like, yet she lived in this appalling situation through no fault of her own.

Thomas shifted and drew his attention. "I apologise. I hope we can get past this. I do not wish it to alter our friendship."

"Perhaps by the time we arrive at Worthstone, I shall find the ability to behave as though this never happened, but your expectations of me in this matter are something that I . . . I cannot. I do accept your apology. I only require time." Darcy rose from his seat. "I shall give no hint of our conversation after we leave this room."

His cousin stood and walked around the desk, stopping a few steps away from him. "You had to have suspected some scheme resulted in my marriage, yet you never gave any indication of it. Thank you."

Nodding, Darcy gestured towards the door. "Perhaps we should join Fitzwilliam. I believe we have left him to his own devices for long enough."

Elizabeth paused before she began the next piece. The younger Darcy stood just inside the room where he watched her intently. Why did he stare at her so?

"Are my husband and Mr. Darcy joining us?"

He startled from his reverie and shook his head. "I generally give my father and godfather some time alone when we visit. They have been friends for so many years. They share confidences they, no doubt, wish to discuss. My presence is welcomed, but I always provide them with some privacy."

Smiling, she stood and stepped around the pianoforte. "That is kind of you. I am certain they appreciate your consideration." He shrugged and glanced around the room. He was quite handsome, though something about how he watched her made it difficult to return his gaze.

"I shall ring for tea." After she pulled the bell, Elizabeth sat on the sofa, motioning to an armchair. "Will you not sit?"

"Yes, thank you," he said stiffly. After he took the seat, he glanced at the instrument in the corner. "You play very well."

She clasped her hands in her lap. Was he always so ill at ease? "I do not practise as I should. I understand from my husband that your sister is accomplished for her age."

"She is. My father has often brought her to town for the benefit of the masters, but one rarely finds her away from the pianoforte." Fitzwilliam glanced down to her hands and fidgeted a bit in his seat. "You should not discount your ability. You have a wonderful sense of expression my sister has yet to learn."

With a slight smile, she arched her eyebrow. "Youth is certainly her excuse. She will without a doubt develop more emotion in her music as she grows older and experiences more of life."

His eyebrows rose with another look at the pianoforte. "I had not thought of it in that manner."

He rarely held her eye for long, but when his crystal blue eyes grasped hers and refused to let go, her insides fluttered with nerves. Lord, the complaint sounded akin to one her mother might bemoan.

"My younger sister, Mary, enjoys playing the pianoforte and singing, but she has yet to perform with emotion."

"Does she play as well as you?"

Her cheeks warmed, and she bit her lip. "Mary practises diligently, though she does play with a pedantic style. Unfortunately, I do not believe any amount of practice can benefit her singing."

He barked out a laugh, and she smiled widely. He had such lovely dimples. His handsome countenance could not be denied. That irritating fluttering increased, making her look down at her hands in her lap.

"I love her dearly, but I hope she does not aspire to perform vocally when she comes out."

His low laughter continued. Hopefully, she had not said too much!

She bit her lip again as she struggled to meet his eye. "I hope you do not find me too dreadful for making such an uncharitable confession."

"Not at all," he said as his laugh subsided. "You surprised me. I had not anticipated you to be so . . . well, honest."

A maid bustled through the door and set a tea tray before her. Elizabeth set to work, preparing and pouring him a cup. "How do you take your tea?"

Once she had handed him his cup, he thanked her, and she sat back with her own, concentrating on the spoon as it swirled in the liquid.

"I understand you hail from Derbyshire like my husband?"

"I do. I believe you spent some time there before you travelled to London?"

She finally put the spoon on the saucer, taking a sip before nodding. "Yes, I found the peaks near Worthstone beautiful."

"I am rather partial towards them. I shall always prefer the peaks to other parts of the world."

She tilted her head as she studied the warm expression on his countenance. "I have no difficulty believing your declaration. It is your home."

"My godfather always travels to Pemberley and remains with us for a month complete during the summer. You will see more then to convince you Derbyshire is the most picturesque of places."

She beamed with pleasure as she sat forward. "He has not mentioned a trip to Pemberley. My aunt is from a small town called Lambton, which I believe is near Pemberley. She describes her home with such love. I have always wished to see it."

"Your aunt is from Lambton?" His voice filled with wonder. "Why, that is but five miles from Pemberley. We should be happy to escort you to the village so you can see it for yourself."

"That would be lovely. I shall send a note to my aunt first thing on the morrow. I shall want her to list the places she would have me see."

"You will have ample time before summer arrives."

He must think her silly, though he was being very kind.

"She has two young children. I never expect a hasty response, yet she rarely leaves me waiting. In this case, I would not have her forget something important."

He began to laugh again, and her cheeks became even warmer, if possible. He possessed the most wonderful laugh, deep and rich. One could not help but be cheered by the sound.

"I made the acquaintance of your aunt, Lady Matlock, at Madame Bonheur's, a few days ago. She assisted me in my selection of a gown for the theatre."

"I believe my aunt is often found at her dressmaker's." He attempted to sip his tea, but it was too hot, so he set it down on a table to cool. "Georgiana and I have enjoyed a close relationship with our aunt since our mother died five years ago. She often calls on her way to or from Madame Bonheur's shop."

"She is amiable," said Elizabeth. "I enjoyed her company very much. Your cousin, Viscount Carlisle, and his brother, Colonel Fitzwilliam, escorted her home."

"Carlisle and I have always been close—like brothers."

"You are not close with the colonel then?" She closed her eyes and clenched a hand. His relationship with the colonel was none of her concern. "I apologise if I am intrusive. I simply wondered when you failed to include him."

"Pray, do not make yourself uncomfortable. I understand. Honestly, Richard and I are strikingly different. He is not what he seems."

Her eyebrows furrowed. "His manner was all that was proper when I met him, yet I shall keep what you have said in mind."

"I am certain you will hear tales of him, but in the meantime, I implore you not to trust him."

Her eyes widened, and she set down her tea to clasp her hands in her lap. "I thank you for your honesty, sir. I promise to heed your warning."

Nodding, he had just opened his mouth to speak when her husband entered followed by Mr. Darcy.

"I do hope the two of you found something to speak of in our absence," said her husband.

Fitzwilliam turned in his seat to follow the entrance of the newcomers. "Elizabeth informed me of making the acquaintance of my aunt."

"Aah yes, I introduced them when I escorted Elizabeth to Madame Bonheur."

"You, in a dressmaker's establishment?" questioned the elder Darcy.

Her husband laughed as he took a seat beside her on the sofa. "I saw her to the dressmaker on the way to my solicitor's office. When my business was concluded, Lady Matlock was kind enough to offer Elizabeth to return with them.

"After my appointment, I travelled to the Lyceum. I have been told since the fire last month, the Drury Lane Company will be staging their productions there."

The younger Darcy sat forward in his chair. "I heard the same today at my club. Is it certain then?"

The duke gave a definitive nod. "Quite certain, I reserved a box for Friday next. It will be the opening performance of Shakespeare's *Twelfth Night*." He glanced over to George Darcy and smiled. "Would you and Fitzwilliam care to join us?"

Mr. Darcy looked to his son. "Would you care to see it?"

"I would," he said with a smile.

Her husband beamed. "It is settled then. We shall attend the play, and after, we shall dine here." He lifted his eyebrows when he turned to her. "Would that be agreeable to you?"

Her hands held one another tighter to contain the surge through her body that occurred when her husband announced their outing. "I believe it will be an enjoyable evening. I would be happy to plan a meal after the event." Now that she had hosted the Darcys once, doing so again should only make her more comfortable in the activity.

Her husband clapped his hands in front of him. "I shall send a note to the Matlocks and Carlisle. Perhaps they would enjoy joining us as well."

The prospect of entertaining an earl, a countess, and a viscount in one dinner made her head spin. At least, her husband had not simply thrust a full dinner party complete with peers of the realm tonight for her first attempt. Mrs. Grigg would need to be told before Elizabeth retired for the evening; preparations would begin when they met in the morning.

Once plans for the next week were finalized, the Darcys returned home, leaving her alone with her husband once more. As soon as the front door closed behind the Darcys, Mr. Hughes disappeared behind the door to the servants' passage, and her husband turned to face her. He took her hand and gave it a swift kiss.

"You planned a wonderful dinner. Thank you."

"I am glad you were pleased."

She stood stiff, unsure of what to make of him. His manner remained as friendly and engaging as when they first met, but he certainly was not what she expected a husband to be—not that she had much frame of reference beyond her parents. Her mother discussed marital relations prior to the wedding, but he claimed he was unable—not that she understood his meaning.

The entire situation begged one to question why he desired a wife in the first place. After he came to her room on their wedding night, he had implored her not to speak of his problem to anyone. To this day, she had not even confided the truth of her marriage to her aunt, despite how deeply she wished she could. Aunt Gardiner could have explained what Elizabeth did not understand.

"I wish to retire." He bowed over her hand. "Sleep well."

"Thank you," she said softly, while he disappeared up the stairs.

She notified a footman she wished to speak to Mrs. Grigg. Her conversation with the housekeeper took but a moment, so she stopped in the library to search for a book. Perhaps reading would help her sleep. *Twelfth Night* was found with ease, and she held it to her chest with both arms as she walked silently to her bedchamber where Lalande waited to prepare her for the night.

# Chapter 3

**Wednesday March 22<sup>nd</sup> 1809**

Elizabeth stepped out of the carriage with the support of her husband's hand and surveyed the building before her. The Lyceum was not as opulent as the Theatre Royal, but since the fire, the Lyceum was certainly grander than a pile of cinder.

"Have you never been here before?" asked her husband, offering his arm.

She shook her head but made certain her expression remained pleased. "No, I have not. My aunt and uncle have taken me to the Theatre Royal in the past, but my uncle did not seem inclined to attend an event here."

"Perhaps due to the variety of shows?" He glanced at the building and then back to her face. "For a time, it was used for a circus, then a concert hall, and last I had heard, Madame Tussaud displayed her wax portraits here."

Her chin hitched back a little. "Wax portraits?" How odd?

"Yes, they resemble sculptures."

They began to stroll to the large doors as a footman followed.

She laughed, glancing over as he watched her curiously. "I attempted to imagine my uncle in such an exhibit. He attends art exhibitions in order to keep my aunt happy. I do not think he would consent to a show featuring wax statuary. I do wonder if Lady Vranes would find them worthy of her time?"

One side of his lips quirked as he disengaged his arm within the doors for the footman to remove his coat before the servant stepped forward to take her cloak. As soon as their coats were carried away, they started towards the stairs.

They were only a few steps inside when her husband's name rang across the hall. "Leeds!"

"Aah, Sir Isaac," her husband replied. "I do hope you and your wife are well."

"Yes, we are quite well, as you see." Sir Isaac's wife strolled up, and her husband's arm tensed. "We heard you had returned to town," said Sir Isaac, "but it seems we have not attended the same soirees." The gentleman's air was jovial, but his wife was another story. She nodded to the duke upon her approach, then appeared to be interested in everything in the room but Elizabeth.

Her husband leaned slightly towards the wife. "Lady Beatrice, I would like to present my wife, Her Grace Elizabeth Osborne, The Duchess of Leeds." Lady Beatrice pursed her lips and crinkled her nose, appearing as though she had been made to drink dirty bathwater.

She curtsied as Elizabeth did. "Your Grace," she responded. She still never looked at Elizabeth's face.

Sir Isaac froze in place and swallowed hard. His head jerked to the side. "Ah! There are the Clarkes!" Sir Isaac glanced back to her husband. "Pray, forgive us, but we were to meet them here."

Her husband gave a curt nod. "Of course, we understand."

Elizabeth curtsied. "It was lovely to make your acquaintance."

Sir Isaac's head bobbed. "Yes, we were pleased to make yours as well. I hope you both enjoy the play."

She pressed her lips together to prevent a giggle until they were far enough away. "He reminds me of Sir William Lucas."

"Yes, they have much in common." His voice was lower than was his wont. "He is an agreeable fellow. I do not care to be in company with his wife."

"You did not appear pleased to see her."

"No, once upon a time, I protected Darcy from her schemes. She made no secret of her disappointment when his engagement to Lady Anne Fitzwilliam was announced. Lady Beatrice was the laughing stock of society for the remainder of that season."

"Why had she set her cap at Mr. Darcy, do you think?"

"Her father married her off to Sir Isaac a year following Darcy's marriage. Her father's estate and a few other holdings were sold not long after. His debts were severe. I believe she coveted George's wealth. The Darcys' reputation for managing their assets is well-earned."

She peered over her shoulder at Lady Beatrice, who smiled as she spoke to whom Elizabeth assumed was Mrs. Clarke.

"Your Grace, we are pleased to join you tonight." Elizabeth turned at the familiar voice, smiled, and returned Lady Matlock's curtsey. Lord

Matlock and Viscount Carlisle stood at the lady's side chatting with her husband, so Elizabeth removed her hand from her husband's arm to stand a bit closer to the countess.

"Your dress turned out lovely," complimented Lady Matlock. "I still adore the colour."

Elizabeth glanced down at her new evening gown. The rich apple blossom red velvet clung to her chest with a very high waist before it flowed down in long, elegant waves. A delicate lace trim adorned the top of each tiny puffed sleeve at the shoulder. The lady on the fashion plate wore a feathered monstrosity, but Elizabeth insisted on the excess velvet to wrap through her hair, fashioned like a Greek statue. A flower necklace of garnets graced her neck with matching drop earrings from the Leeds collection. Her mother would faint if she saw her.

"Thank you, I am pleased with the result. I appreciate your help in selecting the material at the drapers that morning. I had not noticed the bolt in the corner."

Lady Matlock gave her a motherly smile. "That colour suits your complexion and hair very well. I heartily approve of the wrap over the feathers."

A hand rested upon her arm, drawing her attention to the Darcys who had joined their group. "It seems all of our party has arrived. Shall we make our way to the box?"

Elizabeth nodded, and her husband led her towards the stairs, halting at the sound of someone calling Lady Matlock from behind.

"There you are, Mother!" Colonel Fitzwilliam squeezed sideways through the last of the crowd and stopped before Lady Matlock.

Elizabeth's gaze shifted to Fitzwilliam as he rolled his eyes to Carlisle. Carlisle closed his eyes and sighed.

The colonel took no notice. "Harrison said you and father had come to the theatre, so I decided to join you."

Lady Matlock coloured and opened her mouth twice before she could utter a sound. "B . . . but, Richard, we are here at the invitation of the Duke of Leeds."

The colonel showed not the least appearance of remorse or embarrassment. "I had not realised." His smile faltered slightly, but he

46

recovered without pause. "It is no bother. I shall return to the barracks . . ."

"Colonel, you are welcome to join us this evening," said her husband in his usual voice. "I am certain we have a seat for you."

The earlier grin instantly returned to the colonel's face, and he executed a quick bow. "I would be most grateful. I am so often at my duties. I rarely have a spare evening at the theatre with my parents."

Her husband merely dipped his chin before he resumed their way to the boxes. Fitzwilliam Darcy's assessment of his cousin must have been correct. Her husband surely indulged the colonel out of respect for Lord and Lady Matlock since her husband's tight expression certainly did not appear as though he was pleased to see the colonel.

Once they arrived at their box, the colonel offered to procure refreshments, excusing himself for a glass of wine. They had arrived early, which allowed them to visit with the other guests before taking their seats. Lady Matlock strolled over and took Elizabeth's arm, leaning towards her ear.

"I am terribly sorry Richard has imposed himself."

His behaviour had indeed been rude. Lady Matlock, however, had been a kind friend to Elizabeth, and she knew from experience one could not always control or influence their most unruly of relations.

"Please do not make yourself uneasy. He confessed himself that you did not invite him. I would not be comfortable if you were unable to enjoy the evening out of worry that you have offended us."

Lady Matlock took her hands and squeezed them firmly. "You are too kind. I fear I am too indulgent with him at times. You see, Nicholas—Viscount Carlisle—was actually the younger of a set of twins. His elder brother, Albert, died of a fever when they were but three."

How terrible it must be to lose a child! No one aware of her misfortune could blame Lady Matlock for her indulgence. Elizabeth pressed her hand to her chest to express her condolences, but Lady Matlock forestalled her by speaking first.

"I hope I did not upset you too terribly. I wished you to understand if I seem to indulge my sons from time to time. I was devastated when Richard joined the army rather than taking orders. I do worry for him so. I fear I give in to him far more than I should." There were tears in the countess's eyes, but she swiftly choked them back. "Tonight is for us to enjoy. I apologise if I rendered the mood melancholy."

"Not at all, Lady Matlock." Elizabeth squeezed the lady's hand.

"No more Lady Matlock. I should like you to call me Evelyn."

Elizabeth balked. She should address her as society dictated, should she not?

"I insist," said Lady Matlock.

"But . . ."

"I do hope we are friends. My friends address me as Evelyn."

Her husband and Lord Matlock joined them as Elizabeth nodded.

Lady Matlock released her hands to clasp hers in front of her. "I intend to pay some calls early next week. Would you care to join me?"

The duke grinned. "I think it is a wonderful suggestion, Elizabeth. You have received callers, but have not yet returned any of the visits."

The countess's adamant eyes returned to hers. "Then let us plan on Monday. I am willing to wager we have a few of the same names on our lists."

She could not refuse such an earnest offer of friendship. "I would be pleased to join you. But, if I am to call you Evelyn, you should call me Lizzy."

The colonel's voice heralded his return, and he stepped forward with his brother and the younger Mr. Darcy hovering nearby, which unsettled Elizabeth. Mr. Darcy wore an odd expression that made the hair on her arms stand on end, and whenever she happened a glance in his direction, he stared at her. What could he mean by such behaviour?

A bell signalled the performance would soon begin. Her husband steered her towards the first row of chairs, seating her beside Fitzwilliam, yet her husband did not sit to her opposite side. Instead, he took a seat almost behind her at the end of the row. He smiled at her, and she returned the gesture. Lady Matlock took the chair to her right with Lord Matlock to the opposite side of his wife. This was non-sensical. Lord Matlock sat beside his wife, but her husband was seated on an entirely different row? Would she ever understand him? He remained as much of a mystery now as when they first wed.

Fitzwilliam tensed when Thomas seated the duchess to his right and peered over his shoulder as his godfather took his usual seat—to the back and at the end. As Fitzwilliam diverted his attention back to the stage, his eyes met those of the duchess, and he involuntarily gripped his legs. Why did he respond in such a way whenever she was near? The sensation disturbed him, to say the least, but never failed to be present whenever her wide eyes held his.

In an effort to settle himself, he leaned towards her. "Have you previously attended the theatre in London?" Despite that strange sensation she caused, her conversation oddly calmed him. Perhaps it would now as well.

"Yes, with my aunt and uncle." Her eyes twinkled just as they had when she last spoke of her relations.

"The aunt who hails from Lambton?"

"The very one." She responded in a quiet yet higher tone. "I am particularly close to them. Before my marriage, I spent a prodigious amount of time with their family."

"I do not believe you mentioned your aunt's name when we discussed her last. I am curious to discover if I have ever made her acquaintance."

"Her father, a Mr. Harold Price, owned a small estate called Grovewood. My aunt was his only daughter, Miss Marianne Price."

He startled in astonishment. "I remember Mr. Price. I believe he passed on some time ago."

"Yes, it has been about ten years now. My aunt married my uncle the year prior to her father's death."

"I met Mr. Price a time or two, but he did not have a daughter with him. He was a friendly man. I would imagine my father possessed more of an acquaintance with him than I."

The beginning of the first act diverted Elizabeth's attention. She smiled one last time before she became absorbed by the performances of the actors on the stage. His eyes roved around the theatre. How few people truly watched the play. For many, the theatre was merely a place to hold a social gathering. People conversed and watched the other spectators as though they were the performance.

Tonight proved no different. A few women attempted to discreetly point at the duchess and stared while they gossiped behind their fans. Fortunately, Elizabeth took no notice of their gaping, and instead of watching the performance, Fitzwilliam became engrossed in her responses. His lips twitched up at her melodious laugh—even from the side, joy radiated from her countenance.

All passage of time was lost as he studied every nuance and feeling that crossed her face, so the interval surprised him. Had anyone noticed his stares? He cast a quick eye around the theatre where everyone chatted amiably, but no one appeared to be paying him any mind.

None of their party wished to mingle with the crush in the lobby, so the duke's footman fetched wine while their group conversed. The duchess and his aunt were deep in a discussion of the first act while he pulled his eyes from Elizabeth to search the theatre for those of his acquaintance.

Behind him, his father and godfather debated the latest politics. Richard attempted to interject his ill-founded and risky opinions into their conversation while Carlisle vehemently disagreed with his brother. The two rarely agreed on much, and Richard abhorred being proven incorrect. Fitzwilliam avoided many of their arguments since Richard became a most unpleasant companion when bested in an argument or fencing.

Instead, he eschewed the conversation between the men in favour of the ladies' observations. Like a moth to a flame, his ear singled out Elizabeth's voice—Elizabeth's laughter. Why did she draw his attention so?

Despite the fact he should have ignored Elizabeth and watched the actors on the stage, he passed the latter half of the performance as he had the first until she turned towards him and jolted him from his reverie.

"Did you enjoy the play?" Her every feeling and emotion was visible to anyone who cared to look. Unlike most of the jaded women of the *ton*, the duchess was without artifice. She was exactly who she appeared to be—a full of life, joyful young woman.

"I did. Very much." He swallowed the bile rising in his throat. Why could he have not met her before his cousin? Marriage was not a necessity for him—not yet, but he would have made an exception for one such as her.

"Are you well, Fitzwilliam?" He shook himself from his startling discovery to her eyebrows dipping in the middle and an ever so slight downturn of her lips.

"I am," he said. "I apologise."

Her eyes searched his. "I suppose I shall have to accept your answer, but I believe something is indeed amiss."

"I have a matter which preoccupies me lately. I did not intend on letting it intrude this evening." His words were true enough.

"I hope it is nothing serious?"

He shook his head. "I do not believe so. No."

They both jumped when everyone rose around them, making them rise and follow as their party departed the theatre. As planned, they reconvened at Worth House in Mayfair for supper.

Thomas and Elizabeth arrived before their guests, so when the entire group entered the dining room, a place setting was already set between his father and Lady Matlock for Richard. Her Grace sat at one end of the table with his aunt on one side and Fitzwilliam on the other. He sighed in relief at the seating arrangement. Richard was not seated beside the duchess. Either she had heeded his warning, or Thomas had protected his new wife. He could not be sure which.

Despite his younger cousin's constant bragging, the meal was pleasant. He, his aunt, and the duchess were often engaged in conversation. Some men might find the prospect of conversing with two women to be a chore, but these two exuded intelligence and discussed most topics with a keen perspective.

After the meal, the men remained in the dining room for brandy and cigars while the ladies adjourned to the withdrawing room. The duke mentioned an article in the paper on the latest in the Peninsular wars, which drew out an hour-long discussion with ease.

As the men entered the withdrawing room, the ladies were in an in-depth discussion of a particular piece of literature, which prompted the duchess to stand. "I shall retrieve the book, so you may borrow it. I believe you will take great pleasure in the lyrical feeling of the poet's work."

"Lizzy," interjected Lady Matlock, "why do you not send a servant?"

The duchess blushed and bit her lip. "I know precisely where I left it. I would locate it quicker than a footman or maid sent in my stead. I shall return directly."

She hurried from the room as the duke chuckled.

"Elizabeth is not one to rely on the servants for small tasks she can accomplish herself. She does send a maid when ladies call, for I have witnessed them scurrying about to fulfil her request, but I believe since we are in such comfortable company, she is relaxed and more herself."

His aunt beamed with pleasure. "I shall take her manner as a compliment, then."

Fitzwilliam began a conversation with his aunt, but as he took in his surroundings, he noticed his younger cousin was not in the room. He leaned towards his father.

"Where is Richard?"

"He lagged behind with the chamber pot." Fitzwilliam glanced at the clock. That chore did not require a quarter of an hour.

He placed his hand upon his aunt's arm. "Will you excuse me for a moment? I wish to go check on Richard. He should have joined us by now."

"I wondered where he had disappeared."

As he rose, she grasped his hand. "If you happen to find Her Grace, please tell her I shall send a servant to purchase the book on the morrow. She has no need to search for it."

"Yes, of course," he responded quickly before exiting the room. The empty dining room showed no sign of Richard. He must have departed some time ago since the servants seem to have already cleaned the room from dinner. As he passed through the hall, he questioned a servant, who pointed him in the direction of the library. The door was ajar. As he drew closer, voices filtered through the opening.

"I asked you to leave!" said Elizabeth in an authoritative tone.

Richard chuckled. "Perchance, I do not wish to leave. I believe I should like to remain here with you."

"You have insulted me in every way imaginable. I *will* summon a footman if you do not remove yourself from this room directly." At a rustle of skirts, Fitzwilliam peered through the door. The duchess strode towards the bell pull, but Richard overtook her without difficulty.

"Now, we do not require a footman," he said in a crooning voice. He applied a hand to her arm. "I swear to be better than that prune of a husband you wed." He attempted to push her back towards the shelves, but she slapped him across the face. He grasped her wrist, preventing her from striking him again. "That was not ladylike."

"I find it doubtful you associate with many ladies," she said through her teeth.

Fitzwilliam's hand reached forward, and he pushed open the door. Both pivoted around to face him, nearly Elizabeth's entire being sagged against the bookcase, but Richard's lips twisted into an ugly sneer. He dropped her arm and backed a step away.

"Your Grace," said Fitzwilliam in as even a voice as he could manage. "My aunt wished for your return. She intends to purchase the item you were discussing."

Elizabeth shifted a few steps to pick up a book from the table. "I found it. Unfortunately, I was detained." Her voice trembled as she clutched the book to her chest. As she neared, she glanced back at Richard then back to him. "I did not . . . I would not . . ."

"I overheard enough before I entered."

His cousin let out a bark of laughter. "Why does it not surprise me that my prude of a cousin, who never even partakes at pushing school, is the addle-plot?"

"Only you would be so stupid as to pursue Her Grace in her own home during a dinner party," said Fitzwilliam. "Did you think her disappearance would go unnoticed, or yours for that matter? This is not exactly a crush of a ball." He turned back to the duchess, whose wide eyes flitted between them both. "Pray return to the others."

Without a word, she hastened from the room. Richard attempted to follow, but Fitzwilliam grasped his arm before he could pass.

His cousin jerked away. "Unhand me! I am returning to the party now that you have spoiled my fun."

"You will leave, and you will not speak to the duchess again."

An incredulous laugh burst from his cousin. "Why? Because you have decreed it?" Richard studied him for a moment and smirked. "You want her for yourself."

Fitzwilliam shook his head. "She is the wife of my cousin. I would not dishonour either of them by attempting what you have tonight. She is not one of those society wives who weds a man for his money and takes a lover."

"I do not require her to take me when I can take her." The conceited grin upon Richard's face angered him beyond reason. His cousin's words were often bluster, but this was Elizabeth he spoke of.

He grasped Richard by the lapels. "You will not force your company upon her or touch her again. She does not wish it. Do you understand?"

A hand to his shoulder kept Fitzwilliam from slamming his cousin into the nearest wall. "I shall remove him. Do not give him reason to seek revenge. You are aware of what he is capable."

The same disgusting sneer graced Richard's face. "You should listen to my brother. I do have the connexions to ruin you and the little bunter who calls herself a duchess."

"Give everyone our apologies," said Carlisle as he hauled Richard over by his uniform coat. "Richard is unwell. I left to see him home."

Fitzwilliam studied Carlisle. "How did you know?"

"Her Grace appeared terrified and anxious when she returned. I followed my instinct, which always seems to lead to Richard." Carlisle flicked his head towards the door. "You should return. More than enough time has passed since the duchess returned."

A quick glance at Richard revealed he was not the least bit intimidated by the two of them, and Fitzwilliam sighed. "Just take him home. I shall make your excuses."

# L.L. Diamond

Carlisle nodded and dragged his brother through the hall to the front door where a carriage was soon heard pulling away from the house.

When Fitzwilliam returned to the withdrawing room, his eyes immediately sought those of the duchess. He needed to ensure she was well. She laughed with Lady Matlock, but her usually vibrant eyes seemed dimmed and less open than before Richard's ill-planned proposition.

"Would you happen to know why Elizabeth returned so ill-at-ease?" Thomas stood behind him, when he turned, his expression inscrutable. He regarded Fitzwilliam with lifted eyebrows and a set jaw.

However, Fitzwilliam did not allow his cousin's posture to disturb him. "Carlisle asked me to beg his and his brother's excuses."

Thomas straightened and stepped closer. "I take it the colonel behaved in an inappropriate manner while under my roof?"

He peered around the room. All were occupied with a conversation. It would not do to be overheard. "He did, sir, though I interrupted him. Carlisle happened upon us a few minutes later. He insisted Richard depart with him."

Thomas's jaw clenched and his hands fisted at his side. "I must speak to your uncle tomorrow. His youngest son will not be welcomed in our presence in the future." His head tilted closer. "He truly had the temerity to proposition my wife in our home?"

A nod was the duke's only answer.

"The duddering rake," said Thomas as he seethed.

"I believe we should return home." Lord Matlock stood and offered his wife his arm. "We must thank you for a lovely evening, Leeds."

His aunt surveyed the room. "What of Nicholas and Richard?"

"Carlisle escorted Richard home a short time ago," said Fitzwilliam. "I would imagine he intends to send the carriage straight back. The drive is not far."

Lord Matlock furrowed his brow and opened his mouth, but the duke forestalled him. "We will speak of it tomorrow—if you have time to receive me around two?"

55

The earl sighed. After sharing a quick look with Lady Matlock, he agreed. His wife's response, while not as pronounced, was weary. Despite her love for her younger son, her slightly upturned lips turned down with her posture giving an almost imperceptible droop.

Once the door closed behind the earl and countess, the duchess let out a long exhale.

"Are you well, Elizabeth?" asked the duke.

Her steady gaze shifted to Fitzwilliam. "You informed him of the incident in the library so soon?"

"Your manner made it evident something occurred. I had not the time to give him particulars."

His father stared at them incredulously. "Are you implying Richard attempted something towards Elizabeth here? Tonight?"

Elizabeth grimaced and rose, pouring herself a small glass of brandy. "Yes, the situation was distressing and unfortunate. I must thank you, Fitzwilliam, for your timely intervention."

He shook his head adamantly. "I should have made my presence known sooner. I found myself so stunned by his behaviour I am afraid I listened for a moment before I entered." The encounter was recounted in its entirety for his cousin and the elder Darcy, but Thomas showed no sign of shock.

"I cannot comprehend why you were stunned." Thomas regarded him with a curious expression. "Colonel Fitzwilliam is well-known for his deplorable tendencies. Tonight's escapade was not out of character. I hoped he would show *me* more respect, especially after allowing him to intrude on our evening, but I shall take that up with his father tomorrow."

The duchess's eyes bulged. "Oh! Please do not embarrass Lord and Lady Matlock."

"Calm yourself, Elizabeth," her husband soothed. "I shall do what I must to ensure your safety. The colonel will not be welcomed at Worthstone, Worth House, or any of my properties for that matter."

She closed her eyes and took a seat. "I do not wish to lose my friendship with Lady Matlock. She and Lady Vranes have been the only genuine ladies to befriend me this season."

The elder Darcy stepped forward. "Lady Matlock will be embarrassed, yet she will not fault you for her son's actions. She is aware of the gossip surrounding him. He is far too notorious for all of it to be false."

The duchess rose from her chair. "Forgive me, but I believe I should retire. I fear a dreadful headache is forming from this unpleasant business."

"We understand," consoled Fitzwilliam's father. "I hope you will feel better in the morning."

Her shoulders dropped. "I believe I shall be relieved when I hear from Lady Matlock."

Her Grace strode over to Fitzwilliam and grasped his hands. "I must thank you once again. I do not know what I would have done without your intervention."

He stifled a gasp at the burst of current he received from the warmth of her hands. "I was glad to be of help, Your Grace."

"I thought we agreed I would address you as Fitzwilliam, and you would address me as Lizzy. You have started to call me Elizabeth on occasion, which is a vast improvement on Your Grace. I understand why we should adhere to formalities at a ball or before strangers, but we are in family company here, are we not?"

"We are indeed," said his cousin.

Fitzwilliam stared into her wide, doe eyes for a moment before he smiled. "Then, I was glad to be of help, Lizzy."

She grinned. "Much better."

# Chapter 4

*March 25th 1809*
*Grosvenor Square*
*London*

*My dear Lizzy,*

*Words cannot express my mortification at the behaviour of my son the evening we attended the theatre. His insinuation of himself into our party in itself was rude and inappropriate, but to treat you so abominably in your own home—I am appalled. I have always been aware of the gossip that follows him, but until now, I confess to having had a difficult time accepting his faults. With his treatment of you, my dear friend, I can no longer ignore his transgressions.*

*My husband has withdrawn all financial support from Richard, restricting his activities until he departs for the peninsula in April. We have no assurances of how long his regiment will be gone, but his absence for the remainder of the season should provide you some comfort.*

*I hope this situation has not affected our friendship as I greatly anticipate our next shopping trip.*

*With fondest regards,*

*Evelyn Fitzwilliam*

Elizabeth sighed and placed the letter on the escritoire. Colonel Fitzwilliam was no longer a child and would likely take umbrage to his parents' curtailment of his activities. As long as he was abroad, his presence would prove to be a non-entity. A great sense of security would be found in his absence.

She picked up the next missive, breaking the seal and unfolding the pages.

*March 26th 1809*
*Longbourn*
*Hertfordshire*
*My darling daughter,*

A laugh bubbled from her lips at the address. Until her betrothal, Elizabeth had been her mother's least favourite child. This appellation was still very new and never failed to entertain her.

*I have just returned from calling on the neighbours to read them your latest letter. Friends with a countess, boxes at the theatre—how grand it all sounds! I have such flutterings when I consider your life now. I am in raptures at every detail!*

*This Mr. Darcy and his son sound very promising. I believe you mentioned the elder Mr. Darcy is a widow, and his son is still a bachelor? What a perfect opportunity for one of your sisters! You must invite Jane to Worthstone for Easter to meet these men. She is bound to attract one of them! The son would be a better match since he will inherit the estate. We would not want Jane to be thrown into the hedgerows if this Pemberley is entailed like Longbourn. That would not do at all!*

*I have made mention to send Mary or Kitty along, but your father is adamant that Mary is no longer out in society and none of your sisters will be out until they are seventeen! You must write to him and tell him how ridiculous this scheme is. They will not attract suitors confined to Meryton as they are. They must visit you if they are to ever marry well. What good is a duke for a brother if he does not throw them into the paths of other rich men?*

*Now, you have yet to indicate you are with child. Need I remind you, the duke requires an heir, Lizzy—and a spare if you can manage his attentions for long enough. Since you should now be familiar with exactly how unpleasant marital duties are, I have no need to dissemble. You must allow him to come to your bed as often as is required. Endure what you must to do your duty. Once you are with child, you may feign a headache if he does not leave you alone. I shall be most displeased if you are not expecting by Michaelmas!*

*Your mother,*

*Francine Bennet*

Elizabeth groaned softly while she folded the letter. Being a disappointment to Francine Bennet was nothing new. As a child, she tore her stockings or scraped her elbows as she played outside. Her father would laugh, kiss her injuries, and send her to repair her appearance before the matriarch of the family laid eyes upon her dishevelled state. Inevitably, her torn stockings or a slight rip to her gown would be brought to her mother's attention and her attempts to right herself in time would be for naught.

Yet, the dishevelled little girl who desired her mother's approval no longer existed. Instead, she sought the approval of her father, her husband, Lady Matlock, and for some strange reason, the Darcys.

Mr. Darcy to some degree, but Fitzwilliam especially, garnered her thoughts. His opinion had become paramount while she planned their visit for Easter. What room would he prefer? Did he hold a preference for certain foods?

But why? Why should she care so much for one guest over another? The answer eluded her time and again, so she ascribed it to the desire to grow their fledgling friendship. After all, she had no other friends who would visit. She would be just as solicitous of Lady Vranes should she stay at Worthstone.

The clock in the hall chimed the hour, announcing the time to all within hearing. The windows to her side faced the front of the house, revealing the melancholy weather. Worthstone possessed a beautiful park, natural and in possession of a myriad of flower gardens she adored meandering through. Today, however, dingy, grey clouds blocked the sun and had all day, though no rain had fallen as of yet. The weather was simply too dreary to lift one's spirits, even the daffodils bordering the rose garden appeared dull.

The Darcys would arrive at any moment, so she could not walk out regardless of the weather. That is, if they had departed as planned from Pemberley that morning.

Mrs. Hamilton, Worthstone's housekeeper, entered through the open door and dropped a curtsey. "Your Grace, the guest rooms are prepared and the fires lit in preparation for the Darcys' arrival. I have water ready to be warmed in the event any wish for a warm bath, and Cook says supper will be served precisely at seven o'clock."

"I worry I have missed some small detail," she said, tapping the letter to the oak surface.

The older servant smiled and shook her head. "You have nothing to be concerned over, ma'am. I have checked and double-checked all your preparations. Naught is amiss. I daresay you covered every contingency."

Mrs. Hamilton studied Elizabeth for a moment. "I shall bring some tea to help calm your nerves, perhaps with a bit of brandy . . ."

A horse neighed from the front of the house. A glance to the windows confirmed that a handsome coach had arrived before the front portico.

She stood and shifted from behind the small writing desk. "Pray send tea to the blue drawing room but without the brandy. I would prefer to keep my wits about me."

The housekeeper gave a curt nod but smiled. "Yes, ma'am."

Elizabeth carried her mother's letter to the fireplace where a low flame still burned in the grate. She tossed it inside, ensuring it lit before she stepped to the corridor. Footsteps echoed from the grand hall.

"The Darcys have arrived," said her husband as he entered.

"Yes, I heard the carriage and was about to join you." After placing a hand on his proffered arm, he led her to the front door where their guests entered, shedding their hats and coats into the arms of waiting servants.

Her eyes first set upon the son. He appeared well and in good spirits much like his father and the young girl on the elder Darcy's arm. In appearance, she favoured both father and son— dark hair, blue eyes, and tall in stature. She wore a warm smile while she gazed upon Elizabeth though she remained close to her father.

"George!" Her husband extended his hand, which Mr. Darcy accepted heartily with a slap to her husband's shoulder. "Fitzwilliam, I hope you are well." The duke shook hands with the younger Darcy before taking both of the girl's hands. "My, you have grown, Georgiana."

Miss Darcy hugged her cousin, holding his shoulders as she stepped back. "I am pleased to see you, Uncle Thomas."

After bowing to Elizabeth, Mr. Darcy beamed with pride, placing a hand to the girl's elbow and steering her forward. "Elizabeth, I am pleased to introduce you to my daughter Georgiana. Georgiana, this is Her Grace, the Duchess of Leeds."

Georgiana executed a graceful curtsey. "I am happy to make your acquaintance, Your Grace."

Elizabeth grinned and reached out to take the girl's hand. "And I am pleased to make your acquaintance as well, Miss Darcy. Only, I insist that you address me as Lizzy. I have told your brother and father to do so, but I am still called Elizabeth for some strange reason."

The girl glanced to her father with wide eyes, and he gave a laugh. "You call my cousin Uncle Thomas, so why should her invitation come as such a shock?"

Georgiana shrugged in such a girlish fashion it only endeared her further. "I suppose I did not expect her to be so . . ." A long pause followed, and she clasped her hands together.

"Please continue," said Elizabeth. "I promise not to be offended."

"Forgive me, but until we met I thought you might be like Miss Bingley." Georgiana stepped closer to Elizabeth. "Miss Bingley is the sister of one of Fitzwilliam's friends. Had she wed Uncle Thomas, she would insist on being addressed as Your Grace or Duchess."

The elder Darcy began to laugh. "I agree, but in the future, it may be best if you do not express why you are surprised."

Her husband smiled while he drew Georgiana into a hug and patted her upon the back. "I agree with your assessment of Miss Bingley, so I *am* offended." He drew Georgiana back by the arms and spoke with a grin while gazing at her face. "I believe your father and brother are safe as well—even should she force the matter."

Georgiana giggled and turned to Elizabeth. "Have you made Miss Bingley's acquaintance?"

"No, I have not; although, I have heard tales of her, and gossip which originated from her tongue." Elizabeth spoke in a dramatic manner much to the amusement of her company.

Her gaze returned to Fitzwilliam. As was his wont, he watched her steadily. She might have worried that he looked to find fault, but the slight upturn of his lips belied any threat of censure. "Fitzwilliam, I am pleased to be in your family's company again."

He bowed over her hand. "And we are happy to be in yours."

She bit her bottom lip and took care not to tear her hand away at the odd jolt that always seemed to accompany his touch. "Tea should soon arrive in the blue drawing room. Would you care for refreshments, or would you prefer to refresh yourselves after your travel? Mrs. Hamilton has anticipated your arrival by ensuring bath water would be available should you desire it."

Mr. Darcy gazed down in silent question to his daughter, who shyly peered back at him.

"I should like to have tea with the duchess before I am shown to my rooms." The young girl turned to Elizabeth. "Would that be acceptable to you?"

Georgiana's manner was hesitant and quiet. At that moment, the youngest Darcy captured Elizabeth's affection without reserve. She missed her sisters more than anything, and this young girl would be the same in Elizabeth's affections.

"I would be pleased to join you for tea. I should dearly like us to become better acquainted." Elizabeth looped her arm through Georgiana's, leading her in the direction of the small drawing room. "I am accustomed to living with my sisters, and I have missed their companionship. I hope you do not mind if I occupy a great deal of your time while you visit."

Georgiana nodded vigorously. "My father gave my governess the holiday to spend with her sister. I had wondered how I would occupy myself, so I would be pleased to spend time with you."

"Then it is settled!" said Elizabeth. "Tonight, over dinner, we shall discuss our plans for the morrow, ensuring we save needlework and books for when it rains."

Her husband's amusement could be heard from behind, and she glanced around. "Do you find my plan humorous, sir?"

"Not at all, Elizabeth. I think it a brilliant scheme."

The maids were arranging their tea when they entered the drawing room, so Elizabeth set to work serving everyone while Georgiana insisted on being of aid. The girl was good natured and sweet, bringing a certain calm to Elizabeth's soul. Amiable company for a fortnight was just what she required.

Georgiana did not stay for long after she finished her tea, but rather than request a maid to show the girl to her rooms, Elizabeth did the honours herself, only returning to the drawing room after she ensured Georgiana was in the capable hands of her maid.

When she sat in a chair close to the fire, the younger Darcy moved nearby and set his cup on a side table.

"Thank you for being so kind to Georgiana. She is reticent with strangers. I confess we hope your outgoing nature will inspire her to be less restrained."

She shook her head while she stirred a fresh cup of tea. "Please do not thank me for something I am happy to do. I have truly missed the company of my sisters, which has made me eager to make Miss Darcy's acquaintance. She is a lovely girl, and I shall be pleased to call her friend."

"Most women of our sphere do not befriend a young girl unless they find some benefit for themselves. Miss Bingley, for example, sings Georgiana's praises and strives to spend time with her, but her motives are obvious to my father and myself. My sister has never cared for the lady, and as of late, Miss Bingley has become more tenacious."

Elizabeth arched an eyebrow. "Pray, do not find me impertinent if I inquire as to whom Miss Bingley hopes to impress?"

He shifted in his seat. "I believe she would be ecstatic to marry myself or my father, but I believe I am her preference."

"Do you have a theory why?"

"Her ultimate desire is Pemberley, so her intent lies with the prey who will satisfy her desire the longest. If my father was forced to marry her, he would see her relegated to the dower house upon his death," he leaned forward a hair, "if not sooner."

Did he just make a joke? She grinned and relaxed against the back of her chair. "You will have to pardon my intrusive questions. Your sister piqued my curiosity by her description of the lady."

"My father has sworn I shall not be entrapped by her. Should she manage some scheme, he would wed her in my place. I believe his plan would be to set her up in a small house in town."

Elizabeth lifted her eyebrows and laughed. "Since I do not know the lady, I cannot say with certainty, but I would imagine she would be displeased by such a turn of events."

"Her brother, who is in charge of her affairs, has been told by my father of our stance. He does not find fault with our feelings. Until his death a few months ago, his own father complained often of her spending."

She stiffened when he mentioned why she had not yet made the acquaintance of Miss Bingley. "Before we departed town, I had heard the family was in mourning, but I had not realised it was for their father. How tragic!" Her family was all too aware of what the loss of a father could bring. At least Miss Bingley had a brother to care for her needs.

"His death was a shock. He appeared the picture of health until he took ill with a sudden fit."

"I am grieved for their loss," she said plainly. "I feel as though I have been no better than the gossips in London. I beg you not to think I engage in the tittle-tattle present in most of the London drawing rooms."

He relaxed while he regarded her with a slight tilt to his head. "My aunt and my cousin would not have accepted you so readily if you did."

"Fitzwilliam," called his father. He and Thomas had been in a discussion regarding their investments while she chatted with the son. "I believe I would care to refresh myself before dinner. Shall we go in search of our rooms?"

Her mouth opened to protest, but her husband interrupted before she could speak. "Elizabeth may be as fond of teasing as you, George, but I shall not allow you to make light of her household management. She has been rather anxious over your arrival."

Her face heated when all three gentlemen turned their gazes upon her. Mr. Darcy's eyebrows lifted. Why did her husband mention her worry over their arrival? What would they think of her now?

Her husband gave a smile. "As if you have ever been required to search out your rooms."

"I apologise for any unease I caused," said Mr. Darcy.

She rose and pulled the nearby bell. "Not at all. I appreciate a witty remark as much as anyone, even at my expense."

A footman responded promptly, and the Darcys were off to their rooms while Elizabeth was left alone with her husband.

He gave his legs a quick tap of his hands. "I believe I shall ready myself for dinner also. Thank you for all of your hard work and preparation for this visit."

"I am pleased to do it. I only hope the Darcys will find me as amiable as I find them."

"You should have no fear of that matter. They would not have brought Georgiana or encouraged you to befriend her if they thought you anything less than a true lady." He gave his cuffs each a tug, a habit he employed when uncomfortable. He often tugged his cuffs while alone with her.

"I shall see you at dinner." Without a further word, he awkwardly kissed her on the cheek and disappeared through the door. At least with company, he would not dine within his rooms. Since their marriage, his manner remained polite and friendly, but after eating alone in the dining room for several weeks, she had begun to take her meals within her chambers.

Fortunately, Worthstone's library was well-stocked. Her evenings often consisted of reading until she could no longer hold her eyes open. If she sat for hours in her favourite chair behind the desk in her study, she would begin to resemble her father.

Elizabeth extinguished all of the candles save one and donned her dressing gown for a quick jaunt down the corridor to Georgiana's room.

Dinner had been a grand success with Elizabeth and Miss Darcy both performing on the pianoforte after the men returned from the dining room and their brandy. While they made their way to their bedchambers, Elizabeth took the opportunity to ask if Georgiana would like to talk once they were readied for bed. Without sisters, the girl had never had such an experience, so she accepted eagerly.

With a candle in her hand, Elizabeth peeked both ways to ensure the corridor was empty before she crept two doors down. Miss Darcy's maid answered with a brush in her hand and allowed Elizabeth to enter.

Georgiana beamed with pleasure at her entrance. "All that remains is for her to brush and plait my hair."

"Would you mind if I plaited your hair? My sisters and I used to brush and arrange one another's hair often."

"Did you?" asked Georgiana with wide eyes. "I have always wished for a sister."

The maid handed over the brush, curtseyed, and departed. Elizabeth stepped behind Georgiana and ran the bristles through her long, dark golden-brown tresses. "Well, I do not believe one can have too many sisters, so as long as you do not object, you may consider me your sister."

The young girl pivoted on her seat. "Would you truly treat me as one of your sisters?"

She gave a matter-of-fact nod. "Yes, I would. In fact, you remind me a bit of Jane."

Georgiana faced the mirror while Elizabeth began brushing once more, avoiding the paper rolls for her fringe.

"Is she younger or older?"

"Jane is one year older. She is kind and exceedingly beautiful. My mother is prodigiously proud of her eldest daughter's good looks."

"Tell me more of what it is like having a sister?"

"Well, it depends upon the sister. You have heard my description of Jane. She is my confidante, my dearest friend. There is nothing I cannot share with her."

Georgiana furrowed her brows. "You cannot claim that of your other sisters?"

A laugh escaped Elizabeth's lips while she shook her head vehemently. "Heavens, no! Mary is very studious, but she limits her studies to religion and morals. Should I venture to confide in her, she would spout moral platitudes and scripture. Lydia is bold as brass and is incapable of keeping a confidence. She would not even feel one morsel of remorse for her lack of discretion."

"So you have three sisters?"

"I have four." Elizabeth held up her hand, her fingers further indicating the number. "I described Lydia, who is the youngest, before Kitty because although Kitty is a year older, she rarely thinks for herself. Her every move and whim follow Lydia's direction. Should Lydia one day decide she will marry no man but one in a red coat, Kitty would swear the same in the following breath." A giggle erupted from Georgiana's mouth, prompting a smile from Elizabeth.

"You have not mentioned your parents. What are they like?"

Elizabeth set down the brush when she separated the hair and began to wind the swaths of hair around one another. "My mother is hardly sensible. She complains of her nerves and calls for her salts." Georgiana gaped with her jaw slightly lax. "My mother's main objective is to marry her daughters well so she will not be forced to support us when my father dies." Elizabeth tied off the plait and caught her friend's eye in the mirror. "Do I shock you?"

"I have never heard someone speak of a parent in such a manner."

"I love my mother, but she has done little to earn my respect. Jane and I were out at fifteen, and the last thing either of us wished at that young age was to be wed. My mother had just begun to force Mary to attend social gatherings when I became betrothed to the duke who convinced my father to intercede. Mary will have another year before she is forced out into society."

Her young friend furrowed her eyebrows as she pivoted on her seat. "Do you have reason to believe Mary does not wish to be out?"

"Mary has shown little interest in balls and parties. Those inclinations could alter between now and then, but I do not foresee such a drastic change in her personality."

A knock drew Elizabeth to the door where a maid awaited her with chocolate and biscuits. She motioned to the bed, and the servant placed the tray upon the foot, curtsied, and departed, closing the door behind her.

"Biscuits and chocolate?" asked Georgiana with a high-pitched tone. "Did you do this often with your sisters?"

"I would sneak down to the kitchen and steal a few biscuits, but we did not have chocolate. It was considered an extravagance—even to my mother."

Georgiana climbed upon the bed, broke off a piece of one of the biscuits, and popped it into her mouth. "So, is it much different living at Worthstone?"

Elizabeth laughed and took a seat on the other side of the mattress. "Very much so! It is a grander estate than Longbourn, so while I learned to run a home, I had to adjust to something more than my education encompassed."

"What is your favourite part?"

Elizabeth took a sip of her chocolate. "Of living at Worthstone or being married?"

The youngest Darcy peered up at the ceiling, and then back at her companion. "Both!"

"I believe the best part of being married is planning and purchasing my own gowns. My mother's tastes are not at all suited to me. I do not miss her say."

A giggle erupted from Georgiana's mouth, and then halted. "You are serious?"

"Oh yes, my mother always felt my tastes too plain. She likes lace—lots of lace. Remind me, and I shall show you the gown she insisted upon for the wedding. I have it set to the side, so I can remove most of the trim."

"Do you think it will then suit?"

She crinkled her nose. "I do not know. I might cut it up and make something else out of it. A gown for one of the tenant children, perhaps."

Georgiana swallowed her bite with a gulp. "You would do that to your wedding gown?"

"If it is unbecoming once I have removed the trim, then I see no point in keeping it. I have even caught my maid, Lalande, eyeing it with distaste from time to time."

A genuine smile adorned Georgiana's face. "You have not told me your favourite part of Worthstone yet."

Elizabeth stretched out her legs and set her cup upon her thigh. "I love the grounds, particularly the grove of silver birch trees down by the lake. I take walks every morning and sometimes in the afternoon if I am afforded the opportunity."

"Do you ride?" asked Georgiana eagerly.

"No, Jane learnt from my uncle during one of his visits from town, but I never did."

The girl leaned forward abruptly and clapped her hands. "Then Fitzwilliam and I should teach you!"

Elizabeth's hand paused in mid-air with her cup. "Georgiana, I do not know. Your brother may not want to take the time. You should not volunteer him for a hopeless cause."

"He will not mind! And you are surely no helpless cause. Fitzwilliam is ever so kind, and he loves to ride. When he is not busy tending to estate business with father, we often take the horses around Pemberley."

"I would never presume . . ."

Georgiana grasped her hand, squeezing it steadily. "You will not have to worry about asking him, because I shall. I know he will not mind." The young girl rose to her knees and leaned forward. "Would you? If Fitzwilliam agrees."

"I suppose." Her response was slower and drawn, but Georgiana did not seem to notice.

"Wonderful! I shall ask him first thing on the morrow. Uncle Thomas should have a horse that would suit. He always has more than one horse I can ride in the stable."

She levelled what she hoped was her best stern look at Georgiana. "If your brother does not agree, you must not pester him about it."

The girl waved her concern away with a smile. "He will agree. I am certain of it."

They spent the remainder of the evening chatting of girlish pursuits and accomplishments. Despite Georgiana's young age, she was compassionate and kind, much like Jane, and a joy to have in company.

She remained within the youngest Darcy's room visiting until they began to fall asleep. Neither was aware of the fact until Elizabeth woke in the wee hours of the morning and removed to her own room—much as she did when she and Jane stayed up talking into the night.

More than anything, Elizabeth hoped the discussion of horses would be forgotten before they ventured downstairs for breakfast, but when she entered the small breakfast room, Georgiana held her hands poised in a prayer position at her chin while she watched her brother with wide eyes. The topic of conversation was obvious.

Fitzwilliam paused in buttering his muffin, bowed his head at Elizabeth, and lifted his eyebrows. "Do you truly desire to ride?"

"I have never had the opportunity to try. I should like to make an attempt, but I also do not wish to impose."

He studied her while she took her seat and began to help herself to the food laid out on the table. Did it seem odd for her to try? His steady gaze rendered her a bit uneasy.

"I shall ask Thomas if he has a suitable horse. If he does, then perhaps, if the weather is agreeable, Georgiana and I can give you a lesson. If you determine you want to continue, we shall. Is that acceptable?"

"Of course. Thank you for your willingness to teach me."

Fitzwilliam smiled, placing his napkin beside his plate. "I shall go speak to the stable master. He may have some advice about which mounts are more suitable. Once I have spoken with him, I shall speak to Thomas." He stood and gave a quick bow.

Georgiana stood, ran around the table, and embraced her brother before he could stand. "Thank you, Fitzwilliam."

"It is no bother, Sweetling. I have looked forward to riding while we were here. As long as she wishes to continue, we shall have Lizzy up and galloping all over Worthstone with us within a fortnight."

Georgiana practically glowed while she rushed back to her seat. "I am so excited! You will enjoy riding immensely!"

Elizabeth could not help but feel the girl's enthusiasm. "I am certain I shall. So, what would you like to do while we wait? You indicated you enjoy a morning walk, or we could practise a duet on the pianoforte." Her companion gave a slight start upon the mention of music, and Elizabeth laughed. "The pianoforte it is then. If we have not heard from Fitzwilliam after we have spent some time in the music room, then we shall take a tour of the grounds. Does that suit?"

After completing breakfast, the two practised for an hour on the pianoforte before her husband appeared by the side of the instrument, startling them both.

"Forgive me. I did not mean to interrupt."

Elizabeth put her hands together in her lap. "I am sure we do not mind. Do we, Georgiana?"

The girl wrapped her arm through Elizabeth's. "Of course not."

He waved her to follow as he turned. "I wish to speak to you." He glanced over his shoulder to her companion. "Georgiana, there is no reason why you should not join us."

He gestured towards the library, and they all followed him inside where Fitzwilliam stood by the fireplace. "Fitzwilliam tells me you desire to have riding lessons."

Elizabeth stole a glance at the younger Darcy, whose expression revealed nothing. Thomas would not be angry at the idea of her on horseback, would he? "Georgiana thought I would enjoy the ability to ride around the grounds, but Fitzwilliam wished to ensure you carried no objection, especially in regards to the mount."

"He is most attentive to such matters. George taught him well." Her husband's approval of Fitzwilliam was obvious, but he gave nothing away as to whether he thought well of the idea.

She pressed her palms together. "Do you have an objection?"

Her husband's brow furrowed. "I do not. I merely wanted to ensure it was indeed your desire before I gave my approval. My stable master has made an admirable suggestion in terms of a horse. Once you change into your habit, I shall escort you to meet her." He clasped Fitzwilliam on the shoulder. "Georgiana is already an accomplished rider under her brother's tutelage. I am sure you will be the same."

Georgiana grasped Elizabeth's arm. "Oh yes, we should begin now!"

"I don't think it will be so simple, dearest," said Elizabeth, taking Georgiana's hand. "Let us change, and we shall see whether the horse finds me tolerable before I try to climb atop its back."

Thomas laughed. "Thetis will find you tolerable enough."

She startled and smiled. "Thetis? You named her Thetis? Does she have a foal named Achilles?"

He grinned and nodded. "As a matter of fact, she does."

She gave a quick bark of a laugh. Would that not be asking for a lame mount? "Come, Georgiana. You will not want to wear your nice morning gown to the stables."

Her, Elizabeth Bennet, riding a horse . . . well, Elizabeth Osborne riding a horse. The notion sounded strange, yet Elizabeth stood before the ebony mare while she was saddled. Could she really do this? Thetis appeared mild tempered, but would she be as easy with a rider on her back?

Thetis was a beautiful mare. Her striking dark black coat was accented by a wide white blaze down her face, three white socks, and a coronet band above the last hoof.

She held out her hand, and a soft fuzzy nose sniffed then nuzzled her palm.

"Are you nervous?" asked Fitzwilliam, who had stepped forward to stand beside her.

"Would it be silly to admit that I am? She is so large, and has a mind of her own. I find it difficult to remain undisturbed by our inequality."

He lifted one side of his lips. "Yet, I have no doubt in the superiority of your intelligence over hers. You have a definite quickness of mind that will be of great use while riding."

"How is that?"

"Riding is not just sitting atop a horse and issuing commands for the animal to obey. You must always know your surroundings, and how your mount may react to those obstacles. An oddly misshapen tree stump may give a horse reason to spook. You must anticipate her and be at the ready."

"You make it sound more daunting than I initially believed."

His warm deep laugh made her smile. "I give you my word, it is no more difficult than walking with another person. You must keep your companion in mind much as you do yourself. What barriers may be ahead. How far your company can tolerate to walk." When she turned to face him, his eyes studied her with an intensity with which she was unfamiliar. "I shall remain close by. I promise." Her stomach fluttered while she gripped the crop in her hand.

With a nod, he strode over to Thetis. The groom had announced her ready, but Fitzwilliam checked her girth and her bridle, ensuring everything was as it should be, then instructed the man to lead her to the paddock.

She and Georgiana followed until the mare stood before the mounting block. Elizabeth stepped forward while she listened to her friend's tips for the best way to mount and sit upon the saddle. In the end, climbing atop proved no great difficulty, but when she peered down at Fitzwilliam, she clenched the reins until her fingernails dug into her palms. He was so tall—at least six feet— and she looked down upon him from this vantage point. She would never fall from horseback—ever!

"Lizzy?" He covered her hands with his own, his warmth seeping through the leather. "Horses can sense fear and will take advantage if afforded the opportunity." Her eyes widened, and he gave a slight laugh. "Do not fret. You will do splendidly."

A deep fortifying breath followed by a long exhale helped to settle the butterflies in her stomach as she adjusted herself in the saddle. "I wish I had your confidence."

He grinned while he led her away from the safety of the block. "Then I shall have enough for the both of us."

# Chapter 5

**April 1ˢᵗ 1809**

Elizabeth and Georgiana rode ahead of Fitzwilliam as they proceeded towards the next rise. Elizabeth had told them of the glowing descriptions she had read of the view, and now that she required a place to ride, the location and distance seemed ideal to test her new skill.

Fitzwilliam shifted in his saddle while he kept his eyes on Elizabeth. This was the longest ride she had attempted thus far. Could she cope with the length of time in the saddle?

He had accompanied Elizabeth and his sister daily since he began Elizabeth's lessons, which had progressed from walks and trots around the paddock to a canter in a matter of days. They took their first tour of the park the day prior, and Elizabeth showed no qualms about handling Thetis when necessary. She still required instruction, but nothing time and experience would not overcome.

When they reached the bottom of the peak, Georgiana and Elizabeth waited for him to draw beside them.

"Are you well, Lizzy?"

A laugh bubbled from Elizabeth's throat freely. "I might be sore tonight, but I do not imagine it will be much worse than any other night since I began riding. Do not fret over me. Thetis does not jostle me around as I have seen others mounts do."

He dismounted and checked the girths of both the ladies' horses before he climbed back atop his own. "If she should stumble, give the reins some slack. She will require the excess to prevent herself from falling."

Elizabeth arranged the reins in her hands. "I appreciate your concern, but I shall make it to the top."

A corner of his lips lifted. "I do not doubt your ambition in the endeavour. Pray understand my concern stems from your lack of practice."

Georgiana leaned forward in her saddle to speak across Elizabeth. "Should she do well, Brother, she will gain a vast amount of experience today."

Elizabeth held a hand up. "I still will not venture from the stable block without a more learned rider. I am quite aware of my limited capabilities."

"You are positive you wish to climb the peak?" He held her eyes, searching for any hesitance.

Her eyebrow arched, and she possessed an alluring curve to her lips. "I am certain, sir. I promise to notify you should I find the trip *too* arduous."

He gave a large exhale and gestured before him. "Then let us go forth. This scenic vista awaits us."

They all spurred their horses forward while he glanced over to her gloved hands. They appeared so small and delicate, yet she had proven she could handle Thetis. How ridiculous was he to judge Elizabeth by the appearance of her hands since Georgiana was younger by four years, but could handle a horse nearly as well as he.

"Thank you for taking so much of your time to teach me to ride. I appreciate your effort."

A smile teased his lips while he watched Georgiana guide her horse around a rocky passage ahead of them. "I do not consider the last few days of lessons trying, by any means. I take great enjoyment in riding, and I have taken great pleasure in helping you learn."

She watched Georgiana continue forward. "You do not mind her riding so far ahead?"

His sister's horse moved along at a steady pace while he remained with Elizabeth, who held her horse back. "No, she is an accomplished rider for one so young, and she is not travelling with a fast gait; however, she may regret reaching the top before us when she must wait." Elizabeth's laugh renewed the smile upon his face. The sound was so lively and full of warmth.

"Georgiana mentioned your late nights to my father and me this morning."

Her head whipped around with a slight gasp. "We have only been talking, though I did begin to teach her chess last night."

"Your friendship means a great deal to her. Her excitement at telling us of her sisterly relationship with you was heart-warming. I cannot tell you how much it pleases us that you have taken her under your wing. She has needed a lady in her life for some time. Our aunt tries, but she is not the same as a sister."

Her shoulders relaxed while she resumed scanning the route ahead. "Here I was concerned your father might be upset with me for keeping her up so late."

He laughed and shook his head. "No, nothing of that sort. He will be intrigued that you are teaching her chess. I do not think it ever crossed his mind to make the attempt."

"Well," she said in a slightly higher tone. "You may tell him she did splendidly. I feel certain she will excel if someone takes the time to challenge her."

"Perhaps when we return to Pemberley. In the meantime, she will have more opportunities to practise with you and gain a touch of confidence with the endeavour."

"Confidence is important." With a watchful glance at his sister, she paused. "May I ask you a rather personal question?"

He furrowed his brow. What could she possibly wish to know? "I suppose that depends on the question."

"I understand from my husband that Lady Anne passed when Georgiana was very young. Does she have any memories of her mother?"

He coughed and looked down at his hands, attempting to gain control of himself. The subject of his mother was always difficult. His eyes burned and that blasted lump never failed to appear in his throat.

"Forgive me for being so intrusive. It is only that Georgiana does not mention her mother, and I have been loath to broach the subject. She is such a tender-hearted girl. I do not wish to cause her pain."

Elizabeth was so empathetic, a trait not often found amongst the upper circles. His aunt Lady Catherine came to mind. Empathy was not a trait she was ever taught. Her stern demeanour was legendary.

He blinked rapidly a few times. "No, my mother died when Georgiana was but a babe. I do tell her stories, especially ones from when my mother was expecting her." Those remembrances were particularly difficult, and his throat always choked his words so much he struggled to speak them. Yet one corner of his lips lifted at the memory of Georgiana's bright eyes as he told those tales. "Those are her favourite."

"I can only imagine," she said quietly. "I am not close with my mother, but if it were my father, I believe I would hold a similar attachment to those stories of him."

"Did your father teach you to play chess?"

"As a matter of fact, he did." Her face glowed with pleasure, making his breath catch in his lungs. "I spent many a day in his library, reading books and challenging him at chess."

"Challenging him?"

"You do not have to sound so shocked. I have bested him on several occasions, although he denies those losses with a vehemence not often seen in him."

He grinned. He could only imagine his own father's denial should his sister ever best him at a match. "You must miss him."

"I do," she said. "But he is healthy, and he sends a letter from time to time. Papa is not a faithful correspondent by any means."

She again paused as she took in her surroundings. Finally, she turned back to him. "Would you mind telling me of your mother? I should like to know if your sister favours her in looks or temper."

"With the exception of her dark hair, Georgiana's eyes and complexion are reminiscent of my mother's. She even has her manner." He took a deep breath and gestured ahead to where his sister steered her horse with care. "She has her talent with horses. Lady Anne Fitzwilliam was known within the family for her skill as a rider."

"Was she really?"

"She would join the hunts when it was only the Fitzwilliams and the Darcys." He spoke matter-of-factly.

"As to her character, my mother was a generous and kind person. I have been told by many a tenant's wife of her good works for those who lived at Pemberley. She also did much for the less fortunate of the neighbourhood. She has been missed by more than just her family." His chest remained tight, yet he wished to speak of his mother's memory. He was prodigiously proud of her.

"Your father must have loved her very much. My husband has indicated Mr. Darcy would never think of marrying another."

"He has never said as much to me, but I believe Thomas is correct. She took a large portion of his heart when she departed this earth. He will not be whole until he is with her again."

Elizabeth gave a sniff and dabbed her eyes with the back of her hand once or twice as they continued. While they rode, they continued to speak, yet they left the more personal topics behind them.

Upon reaching their destination at the top, Fitzwilliam did not take in the view around him but observed Elizabeth, who absorbed everything with wide, admiring eyes. "What do you think of it?"

"I believe I have never seen a view equal to this one," she said, her voice breathy and awed. "It is stunning."

"We shall take you to Stanage Edge when you visit Pemberley," said Georgiana. "The view from there is my favourite by far."

Elizabeth glanced between the two of them. "I look forward to it. Is it close enough to ride, or will we need to travel by carriage?"

"Fitzwilliam and I usually take a picnic. He drives us out in a curricle, and we have our luncheon nearby before walking around the peaks."

"How lovely!"

His face warmed with not only Elizabeth's approbation but also a bit of embarrassment at his sister's revelation. He prayed she did not go further and mention how only a few years ago, Georgiana would bring a doll or two, and they would play tea party during their picnics.

"We should have brought a picnic today," said his sister while she looked back at the view.

He could not help but laugh. "With nowhere to tie off the horses?"

"I had not considered that since I can leave Ginger, and she does not move."

"Our horses have been trained to do so, Georgie. Even with that training, it is unwise to leave them untethered for such a long time. Should they spook, we would be returning to Worthstone on foot."

His sister smiled at her new friend. "Elizabeth could manage. She is an accomplished walker."

Elizabeth gave a small jump. "I may be, but it is a long walk—even for me."

"Well, I daresay Uncle Thomas would send a carriage when the horses returned to the stables. We would not be stranded for long."

With a smile, Fitzwilliam gave a nod and a grin. "I am certain you are correct, but I have no desire to test your assumption. We might scare the wits out of our father and Thomas."

After pulling Thetis's head from her attempts to nibble at the grass, Elizabeth tightened up on the reins just as she should. "I arranged for tea to be prepared for when we return. We shall not be deprived. I hope you do not object to having our repast at the temple."

Georgiana's face lit with excitement, and though her hands still clutched the reins, she pressed the insides of her fists together. "Oh, how wonderful! I should take great pleasure in the view of the lake while we rest from the ride. The weather has been delightful. We should enjoy the advantage of the blue sky and sunshine while it remains."

"You have precisely echoed my thoughts on the matter," said Elizabeth. "Nothing gives me greater pleasure than nature, and I try to take advantage of fine weather, for one never knows when Mother Nature may change her mind—she does tend to have a rather capricious disposition."

The glint in her eye, the arch of her eyebrow, and the slight quirk to one side of her lips enchanted him. With a heavy swallow, Fitzwilliam turned his concentration towards guiding his horse back down the incline. Peleus was a sure-footed steed, but he required some time to compose himself.

Elizabeth was bewitching, but it would not do to fall under her spell. She was a married woman—wed to his cousin. Prior to the Darcy's departure from London, he found himself comparing several ladies to whom he had made the acquaintance of at a ball to Elizabeth. Those ladies had fallen short, dreadfully short, which was disturbing. His admiration needed to remain as nothing more than friendship, yet how? How did one keep themselves under such strict regulation?

The dilemma continued to plague his mind as they made their descent from the summit and began to plod along more even ground. His thoughts might have remained on the issue at hand, but the sound of her sweet laugh permeated the fog to bring an unbidden smile to his lips.

"Fitzwilliam!" called Georgiana from beside him.

He started and frowned. "I do not require you to yell in my ear, Georgiana."

"I would not have done so, except we called your name several times and you failed to respond."

A glance behind his sister revealed Elizabeth biting her lip to keep from laughing. "She did indeed attempt to gain your attention, but you did not answer. In the future, dearest, I would recommend touching his arm over shouting while in such close proximity. Lydia has cried out into my ear before, and I can attest that it is a painful experience."

Georgiana cast wary eyes in his direction. "I do apologise, Brother. I had not intended to cause you pain."

He reached over and wrapped a hand around her fist as she held the reins. "I am not angry. After all, I should not have been wool-gathering, and you should have been able to gain my attention without such an extreme measure." With a final squeeze to her fingers, he returned his hand to his own reins. "Was there something you required?"

"Well, Lizzy would like to try trotting again, and I thought we could ride ahead of you while you keep watch."

He looked past Georgiana at Elizabeth. She was doing well, and their return trip would be a crawl if they did not attempt a swifter pace. "The two of you ride ahead. I shall follow."

The ladies both cued their mounts forward. A short time later, Elizabeth exchanged a few words with Georgiana before Thetis began a slow, controlled canter. His sister gave tips for her friend's seat while they rode, so he saw no need to intrude. Georgiana was instructing Elizabeth well enough on her own.

When they reached the stable and dismounted, Elizabeth was aglow with a wide smile. "Did you see me canter?" Her eyes glimmered in the sunlight, and her voice was breathless. God, she was beautiful.

He shook himself mentally and held his reins a little tighter. "I did. You did very well, and you will only improve since the more you ride, the more accomplished you will become."

"So, I shall only improve with constant practice?" She wore an impish grin and lifted an eyebrow.

With a laugh, he shook his head. "I never said constant."

"True, you did not." She glanced over her shoulder to Georgiana, who approached. "We should return to the house and refresh ourselves. I, for one, would like to have tea."

"I would as well," said Georgiana, linking arms with her friend.

Fitzwilliam could do naught but follow until they were separated at the top of the stairs where he was required to forcibly make himself turn towards his chambers. Elizabeth had been laughing at some tale she told Georgiana, and some quality of that bubbling sound was like a siren's song and difficult to resist.

The Grecian-inspired temple at Worthstone was nestled upon a small rise beside the lake. From the windows of the main drawing room, one could appreciate its picturesque placement, and the element of beauty it added to the view.

The folly was nothing more than some columns with a ceiling, open to the elements as well as the cool breeze which made a delightful noise as it filtered through the surrounding trees.

Elizabeth refilled Georgiana's teacup while she admired the lovely scenery. When she first noticed the building during a walk, she had an almost immediate love for its charm.

"I was not aware Thomas ever used the temple," said Georgiana. "However, this is a lovely place for tea. We should stroll by the lake when we are finished."

"Georgiana, you walk around the lake at Pemberley several times a week." Fitzwilliam held an apple, pausing after swallowing a bite. "Besides, Lizzy might not be inclined for the exercise after the long ride earlier."

"I am well. I would enjoy a stroll by the water." She grinned and glanced towards Fitzwilliam. "It will take far more than a long horse ride to curtail my enjoyment of a good ramble."

"As you wish," he responded with a curve of the lips.

"I do wish. The grounds here have been such a comfort to me since my arrival. While in London, there was nowhere I could walk without the escort of a footman and a maid."

Fitzwilliam's brow furrowed, and he stopped before taking another bite of apple. "You should have a trusted footman with you regardless of where you walk."

A laugh escaped before Elizabeth could bite her lip to prevent it. Georgiana directed a puzzled expression at her while Fitzwilliam studied her for a moment.

"Thomas attempted to have a footman follow you."

"He did," she responded, "but I was naughty. I evaded him several times once I was familiar with the grounds."

"You did not!" Her young friend's eyes were wide and her mouth agape.

"I do not recommend you emulating my example, dearest, but I did. I am accustomed to my solitary walks. I use the time to think and puzzle out my problems. I cannot do so with a noisy footman trailing behind me."

Fitzwilliam shook his head but his expression was not angry or upset. "Thomas should still not allow it."

"Oh, Jonathan still follows, but far enough behind that I maintain my privacy. If I happen to think aloud, he is not so close that he hears my babblings."

As Elizabeth took a sip of her tea, Georgiana gasped at the sight of a puppy bounding across the grass near the temple. "He is adorable!" She craned her neck to see around the columns. "I hope he is not here all alone."

Elizabeth caught a glimpse of the small black and white spaniel as it came running back. "Oh, I would wager young Evan is nearby. He does not allow Hazel to run the property unsupervised."

"Who is Evan?" asked Fitzwilliam.

"He is an under-gardener and a nephew of my husband's valet. He could not find work, and his parents could not afford to house and feed him. The duke brought him here and provided him employment and a place to live.

"When we returned from London, the stable manager informed him how Evan was very taken with one of the puppies. Thomas's favourite hunting dog had a litter a few months ago."

"How can an under-gardener afford to keep her fed?"

Elizabeth caught a glimpse of the young pup running by with a stick in her mouth. "I believe his uncle has provided some aid in the endeavour."

"Do you think he would allow me to pet her?" Georgiana was enthralled and so eager.

"Evan is very kind. I am certain he would allow it."

"May I, Brother?" Fitzwilliam nodded, and the young girl rose to rush to the grass in a swirl of her skirts.

Finished with her tea, Elizabeth stood and moved to lean against a column while young Evan introduced Georgiana to his pet. A giggle burst forth when the puppy began licking the richly dressed Miss Darcy, making her chest ache. How she missed those days of being so care free!

A low laugh came from beside her, and she peered up to find Fitzwilliam had joined her. "Father has considered acquiring a small dog for her. She loves to venture out to the stables to play with those he uses for hunting."

"Judging by her response to Hazel, I believe she would take great pleasure in such a gift."

"Hazel?" he asked, with a puzzled expression.

"Evan's pup. That is the name he chose for her."

He turned a soft gaze towards his sister who now held the squirming bundle of fluff as it gave her another big lick on the nose. Fitzwilliam was a wonderful brother. What Elizabeth would have given for such a sibling! Her life at Longbourn would have been so different. Perhaps her mother might not be so silly, and her husband's generosity would not have been required. Her marriage would not have been a necessity. She would have refused the duke. After all, her brother would have inherited the estate after her father's death, guaranteeing them security.

"You seem deep in thought."

She started and smiled. "Forgive me. I was wool-gathering."

"I am not offended. You only appeared so serious that I became concerned something was amiss."

With a shake of her head, she also shook away her useless musings. "No, just idle thoughts. It does no good to dwell on them."

After taking his offered arm, he escorted her down, and they walked beside the lake, keeping Georgiana in sight while Evan showed her the tricks he had taught Hazel.

They maintained a quiet but comfortable attitude while they strolled. Elizabeth, charmed by the golden rays of the sun reflecting off the water and the cheerful sound of the birds in the trees, lost herself in the enchantment of nature and delighted in her happiness at that very moment. Her favourite grove bordered the water nearby, the chalk-coloured trunks that seemed to peel to reveal the reality inside, and brought a peace to her soul. She also had the perfect companion, a luxury she never had.

Her life with her husband was not unacceptable by any means, it was simply lonely and lacked the affection she had dreamt of when she was a young, impressionable girl. Had her youthful wishes been a fool's paradise? Were those relationships even possible?

More than anything, she longed for a child to fill that void but had come to despair that blessed event ever occurring. Her husband never came to her bed, and regardless of the naivety of what was supposed to occur when he did, there was no possibility of conceiving a child as long as he stayed away. If only she could comprehend what he meant when he said, "I cannot."

"Have you enquired of your aunt the places you are to see in Lambton?"

Fitzwilliam's voice again jolted her back to the present. "I received her detailed response a week ago. She provided names of friends and locations that hold special memories or meaning. I am eager to see if the reality is everything I have imagined."

"Our corner of Derbyshire is beautiful and boasts some incomparable views. I daresay you will not be disappointed."

"I have heard nothing but praise of the area from my Aunt Gardiner and my husband. My husband claims it similar to the environs of Worthstone."

"I suppose the regions are similar, but something about home renders the area more beautiful to me." He spoke with such fondness, one could easily discern the love he had for where he lived.

"You were raised in the heart of that country, so one cannot find it surprising you would have a passion for the area. It is your home."

"Your perception does you credit," he said, his eyes crinkling in the corners as his lips curved ever so slightly. "Are you often so astute?"

Her shoulders gave a slight lift. "I enjoy sketching characters, but some individuals make for a simpler study than others."

He grinned widely, stopped, and turned towards her. "Have you sketched my character?"

She blanched and pressed her lips together tightly. This would teach her for speaking so freely. Now she was trapped into answering a question she preferred to keep to herself. "Perhaps I have, but then, perhaps I have not." Would her coy response put off his inquiry or would he press forward?

His eyes narrowed, and he studied her with an intensity that made her want to squirm. "I believe you have and do not wish to tell me."

Her cheeks burned as she began to walk towards Georgiana. She needed her company to deflect Fitzwilliam. A gentle hand to her elbow guided her around to face him.

"You will not offend," he said, leaning slightly closer. Her stomach erupted into a flurry of butterflies, making her gulp. "Pray, I am merely curious of your impression."

What if he became angry? Oh, well! He insisted. She dragged in a deep breath. "When I first made your acquaintance, you hardly spoke and stared in my direction. My husband assured me of your generosity and kind nature, but if I had not his insight, I might have thought you proud and disagreeable. I have since found that you mask your true self behind that stern reserve, keeping strangers at bay."

His demeanour indicated he was not disturbed, and he gave a slight nod for her to continue.

"Since the dinner at Worth House, I have found you amiable, and a kind and generous brother to Georgiana. You are one of the best of men, Fitzwilliam. I am honoured to call you my friend."

Did she overstep? Her eyes searched his, taking in the slightest twitch of his lashes and each nuance of his eyes, in order to gauge his feelings. She had so few true friends. He was becoming increasingly important to her current happiness.

Her letters from Jane had been her lifeline when she first wed her husband, but while she still cherished every word her sister put to paper, Elizabeth had begun to rely on the friendship of Georgiana and Fitzwilliam more. After all, they were present and tangible. She could see them before her eyes, touch them— even if only to lay a hand upon his arm—and speak to them.

"I am pleased you have come to regard me as such," he said warmly. "I have grown to think of you with the utmost respect since our introduction. I hope we can continue to forge a strong friendship. We are now related after all." His lips quirked to one side, and she was amused by his subtle tease at the end of his statement.

"Fitzwilliam! Is she not the most precious little girl!" Georgiana ran towards them, pointing back to Hazel. The puppy trailed after her owner as he departed. Meanwhile, Georgiana's bright eyes glowed from her pink cheeks and she wore the biggest grin Elizabeth had ever seen upon the girl—despite the muddy paw prints on the fine muslin of her gown. Elizabeth pressed her lips together. How many times had she returned home splattered in mud?

Fitzwilliam's expression was inscrutable. "Hazel is an adorable puppy, but I am certain your maid will not be pleased to scrub the mess she has left upon your gown."

With a slight brush to her bodice, Georgiana shrugged. "Brooks will not mind. She dearly loves puppies as well."

Elizabeth laughed and shook her head. "My maid may have some idea how to remove the mud should yours have any difficulty."

Georgiana's hands clasped before her while she glanced back and forth between her brother and Elizabeth. "So, what have you been discussing? You appeared so serious while you walked along the water."

"We were merely discussing Lizzy's trip to Pemberley this summer," said Fitzwilliam. "Her aunt has generously provided a list of places to see as well as friends to meet, and I have vowed to be of aid, to ensure she sees it all."

With her hands still pressed together, Georgiana bounced on her toes. "I wish to help. I cannot wait to show you my home."

Elizabeth looked between the brother and sister. "I anticipate viewing Pemberley through your eyes." Her gaze locked onto Fitzwilliam's and held. Her face became unbearably hot and breathing was a chore, yet she somehow managed to break eye contact and took Georgiana's arm, pulling her ahead of Fitzwilliam. She peeked over her shoulder in his direction as she passed, but his attention was occupied by the sheep on the opposite side of the lake. At least she was the only one who suffered from whatever this was. Fitzwilliam appeared unaffected. The question was how to make it stop?

# Chapter 6

*June 28ᵗʰ 1809*
*Pemberley*
*Derbyshire*

*Dearest Lizzy,*

*I can scarcely believe that in less than a week's time you will be at Pemberley! Fitzwilliam and I have planned outings almost daily to show you all Pemberley has to offer. Do not fret! We have included your aunt's list, and Fitzwilliam has even taken the liberty of messaging your aunt's friends so you might make their acquaintance. We have considered everything, have we not?*

*I could tell you of the happenings here, and what is new, but I shall save that for your arrival. We can have chocolate and biscuits while we chat late into the night as we did at Worthstone. I believe we would have matters to discuss even should I write of what has occupied my time, but it will be ever so much fun this way!*

*Lastly, I know Uncle Thomas has claimed it unnecessary, but I must thank you both again for my little Evie. You should see how she has grown! She is not so little anymore, yet she is still the most adorable bundle of kisses and fur. The trainer who handles my father's dogs has helped me teach her a few tricks, and she is doing so well inside the house. I, however, am not certain the footmen are as pleased with her since they are required to walk her when I cannot. I am eager to show you her accomplishments when you arrive. I am certain Uncle Thomas will be impressed by her progress.*

*Please hurry to Pemberley, Lizzy. We eagerly await your arrival.*

*Yours very affectionately,*

*Georgiana Darcy*

*I hope you do not mind, but Fitzwilliam requested I enclose a letter. He has taken it upon himself to ensure you are well-entertained for the duration of your stay.*

Elizabeth placed Georgiana's letter to one side, beaming in pleasure at her friend's excitement. Her anticipation of their journey had only grown since Georgiana departed Worthstone almost a month prior.

The carriage shifted, and she placed a hand to the seat beside her to steady herself. Her husband watched out of the window but appeared unconcerned, so she turned her attention back to her correspondence.

Fitzwilliam's steady yet bold handwriting stared up at her from the letter, commanding her attention. She traced a finger upon the neat script flowing across the expensive paper. The seal broke easily, and she unfolded the missive.

*June 28th 1809*
*Pemberley*
*Derbyshire*

*My dear friend,*

*Pemberley is ready and awaiting your arrival. I cannot imagine Mrs. Reynolds or Georgiana have missed one detail in preparation for your stay, yet they meet daily to pore over menus and rooms. It is good practice for Georgiana, and I must tell you how I appreciate you beginning her household education while we visited Worthstone. Having her accompany you for your day-to-day meetings with your housekeeper was a splendid idea, and Mrs. Reynolds has commented on how much my sister has learned. My father has been impressed with her new-found knowledge as well.*

*In regards to your aunt's list, Father and I have issued invitations to her friends for a dinner party to be held at Pemberley a week after your arrival. If you are not aware, the Leveson and Sutton families are rather prominent in the area, and Mr. Rowley is the vicar at Lambton.*

*Around mid-July, the Bingleys will pass a week at Pemberley as they journey from their aunt's home in Wales to Scarborough. You will at long last meet the infamous Miss Bingley, though, in all honesty, I do wish she was not a member of the party. Please do not reveal my secret for while my father and sister may guess, you are the only person to whom I have made that egregious confession.*

*If you were not told enough in Georgiana's letter, we anticipate your arrival. It has been many years since we have planned for a month such as this, and I believe even my father is eager for the diversion.*

*With warmest regards,*

*Fitzwilliam Darcy*

"Is that correspondence from Fitzwilliam?"

She tore her eyes away from the closing to her husband's inquisitive look. "It is. He wished to inform me of the plans he had made with my aunt's friends. The Darcys have planned a dinner party so I might make the acquaintance of the Levesons, the Suttons, and Mr. Rowley."

With haste, she folded the missive and held it with Georgiana's. "I hope you do not mind him penning me a letter. We are nothing more than friends."

A corner of his lips lifted as he observed her with a keen eye. "I have no objections at all. I was only unaware of its existence." He placed a marker in the book he had been reading, and rested the volume in his lap. "The friendship you have forged with Fitzwilliam and Georgiana has brought me great delight. I am quite pleased at your willingness to accept my family as your own. I hope you will correspond with both of them often."

Elizabeth furrowed her eyebrows. "How could I do otherwise? Georgiana is lovely and kind. She is intelligent, well-read, and a charming companion. Fitzwilliam, when he chooses, is amiable. He is considerate and thoughtful. I do think him to be one of the best of men, as I am certain is his father. I enjoy their company, and as I have not had the pleasure of seeing my family, I suppose I grasped upon their presence."

She was well aware that her voice had become hard. Her marriage had taken her from all she had known, and when she requested for merely a visit from Jane, her husband always denied her with some excuse: time was never sufficient, he hoped Georgiana would stay during that particular month, they were to spend those weeks at Pemberley. An excuse was never lacking, and she chafed at his restriction.

Normally an independent person, Elizabeth had always had her family when she craved discourse or simply the presence of another. When they had no company at Worthstone, she had only herself. Holding a conversation with oneself rarely answered any of her own questions.

His jaw tightened, and she blanched. He had never lost his temper, yet she had not challenged him so in the past. Cruelty had never been a trait she would have ascribed to him, so she hoped she had no reason for concern. He could be responsible, aloof, haughty, but never cruel.

"You have not been without your family for *so* long, have you?" he said in an even tone.

Regardless of his apparent ire, her courage did not falter. "We were wed in November. It is now July—nearly eight months. You have not gone so long without spending time with your relations, yet you deny me mine. You promised . . ."

"I am well aware of my pledge, Elizabeth, but we have not had sufficient time to plan your sister's stay and have not travelled near Meryton since our return from London."

"Jane has no expectations of grand balls, parties, or stately rooms." Her voice was raised as she sat forward and pressed her case. "She would be well pleased to spend the day with me and would be of no bother to the servants."

With a sigh, he peered out at the passing scenery before returning his attention to her. "Would you object to hosting her for a fortnight during the season? We could break our journey at Stoke, so she could accompany us to London."

A fortnight? She had hosted his family for a fortnight, Georgiana for the month after, and they were to spend a month complete at Pemberley. A fortnight? However brief the visit, she could not refuse the offer. She longed to see her dearest sister.

"That would be agreeable, thank you."

"In the future, Elizabeth, please do not withhold your frustration as you have since we wed. You spoke freely with me when we were first acquainted and while we were betrothed. I would wish for that to continue, no matter the subject."

She nodded and looked down at the letters in her hands.

Her husband tilted his head while he watched her. "Is there something else?"

"Nothing of import." Her voice was light, lighter than her mood had been for some time.

"I would appreciate your honesty. I am your husband. I believe I deserve it."

Her fingers fidgeted with the corner of Georgiana's missive. "Is this to be the nature of our marriage?"

His eyebrows furrowed, and he stiffened. "I do not understand your meaning."

She inhaled a deep fortifying breath and exhaled in an attempt to steel herself. "Is this to be what our marriage is. You have your life, I have mine, and the two only cross for social gatherings."

"It is how most in our sphere live," he said. "Did you believe there would be more?"

"My mother indicated there would be more." Her face was aflame. How could she broach such a subject?

"Aah, I had not considered that she would prepare you so." He shifted in his spot and placed his book beside him on the seat, his hand clenching around the spine until his knuckles turned bright white. "As I said the night of our wedding, I am unable to perform in the manner required. I apologise if our marriage is less than what you expected, but I can do naught about the problem."

Her gaze left the letter in her hands and returned to him. "You do not require an heir?"

"I do, but it is irrelevant since it cannot come to pass. When the time comes, Fitzwilliam will inherit the bulk of my estate, and you will have your settlement and be well-prepared for the future. James will inherit the dukedom and the property that accompanies it and he will be the ruin of the Leeds legacy."

"Then why did you take me for a wife?" Her question was indelicate and impertinent but needed to be asked.

"I had hoped . . ." he said, but shook his head. "I soon found the matter hopeless."

"You asked for my hand when you were not certain you could be a husband?"

He sighed. "No, I knew, but I had hoped . . ."

"You had hopes?" Her heart became heavy and sank into her stomach. She had tied her life to a man who had no intention of even playing the husband and could not provide her with a child. What little happiness she had anticipated in her marriage would be denied her, and her mother—her mother would never cease tormenting her about the lack of an heir. What had she done?

The correspondence she treasured a mere moment ago dropped to the floor of the carriage, and she covered her mouth in an attempt to hold back a sob. Tears welled in her eyes, and one large droplet fell to her skirts creating a large blotch on her gold redingote.

"Should you wish to take a lover, I would not object, but I would beg you be discreet about the matter."

Wait! What? She gasped in a heaving breath that quashed any melancholy remaining within her. "Pardon me, but did you just give me permission to be unfaithful?"

His expression remained flat, similar to that of the inscrutable mask Fitzwilliam often employed. "Yes, I gave you leave to do as you wish. As I said, I would prefer you remain discreet. I would also appreciate a certain discernment in your selection. Should you become with child, I prefer my heir to be more than the by-blow of a footman or a gardener."

An incredulous noise escaped her lips. "How kind of you?" Her voice was laced with sarcasm, but she cared not whether his delicate sensibilities were offended—especially when he had offended hers in such a harsh manner.

"Elizabeth, I am requesting you perform the simple task of being responsible . . ."

"Responsible? You have the audacity of lecturing me on how to be . . .?" Her finger pointed towards his chest while hot tears poured down her face. "When you asked for my hand, you pressed that I could be the means of saving my family upon my father's death. You made me responsible for their wellbeing, and I have taken on all of the obligations of a duchess for you in return. All I asked—nay, hoped, was that I might one day have a child to love." Her finger stabbed at his chest. "You deceived me, sir. By neglecting to tell me of your affliction, you told me an atrocious lie."

He exhaled a measured breath, picked up her letters, and placed them upon the seat beside her. "You could have awaited a man who would love you, but that would not have guaranteed you children. Regardless of who you wed, God may not have chosen to bless you."

"Yet, if my husband loved me, he would not have omitted the information you intentionally withheld."

He leaned against the squabs and gave the bottom of his topcoat a tug. "I made no claim of loving you, Elizabeth. I only said that I thought we could be good friends."

"A friend would not have treated me as you have." She wiped her cheeks with the back of her hand. "You have greatly misjudged my character if you believe I would take a lover," she spat. "I would never dishonour myself or my family—the Bennet family—by inviting such censure."

His shoulders gave a small lift as he gave a brief bark. "George, indeed, had the right of it."

The words were muttered under his breath, but Elizabeth managed to distinguish them. "George? Do you mean Mr. Darcy?"

He closed his eyes. Obviously, he had not intended for her to overhear. "I may have spoken with my cousin after Lord and Lady Vranes's ball."

"And upon a trifling acquaintance, he could discern what you could not. I must give him credit. I love him all the more for it as well."

He reached forward and placed his hand over hers. "I know the words must seem empty, but I do apologise for the misunderstanding."

She turned her glare upon his act of contrition, and he withdrew.

"I do hope one day you will forgive me, yet in the meantime, we must appear as though nothing is amiss. I abhor gossip. I do not want our discord to be the fodder of London drawing rooms."

"You have nothing to concern yourself with on that score. I wish for my humiliation to be made public as much as you wish for your infirmity to be bandied about over brandy and cigars. I shall compose myself accordingly. I shall do my part."

"Your discretion is appreciated, though I do hope you reconsider taking a lover. I would not begrudge you any happiness you might find."

Her fingers clenched upon the fabric of her redingote, wrinkling it. Lalande would be required to spend a considerable amount of time to press the area smooth. "I beg you never to mention such a notion to me again."

His shoulders dropped, and a heavy sigh escaped his lips. "Very well. I had no intention of offending you. Whether you believe me or not, your happiness is of great importance to me."

"If that be so, then you should have left me behind in Meryton. I never aspired to be a duchess and would have been content to remain the daughter of a country squire."

"It was that disposition that made you so appealing." He propped an arm by the window and watched the countryside as it passed. "You did not simper and attempt to gain my favour with flattering nonsense. Instead, you were yourself—you were honest."

"And now you have made me a liar. I shall be forced to play a part while in the company of your family as well as in London society. A perverted twist of irony, is it not? What you appreciated most is what will be lost."

"I do not believe that will be so. You may act as though you care for me in public, but the charade will not extend into our private lives. Your essence will remain unchanged."

Elizabeth reached a shaky hand into her pocket and removed the handkerchief she had forgotten in the midst of their argument. She set the elegant, lace-trimmed, folded square upon her leg and traced her fingers across the embroidery she had used to embellish the piece. The red roses stood out against the pale white of the fabric, but her fingertips continued until she reached her new initials near the corner.

Oh, how a part of her pressed to send the offending article flying from the carriage window, but she could not. After all, how would it appear if the Duchess of Leeds threw a temper tantrum by pitching her handkerchief from their equipage? The thought did draw an unladylike noise from her nose.

"Something amuses you?"

She pressed the fine linen to her face in order to dry the remaining tears from her cheeks. "I considered tossing my handkerchief from the window, but the duchess having a fit of temper might cause talk amongst the servants."

With a laugh, he tilted his head and appraised her. "I was thinking while you were having fantasies of rebellion."

"A dangerous occupation for you, is it not?"

He smirked. "I suppose it is, but I do believe you will like where my mind led me in this instance."

"Then, by all means, astonish me," she said. Her tone dripped with enmity, and her eyebrows lifted. She had no desire to wallow in self-pity or regrets. Those thoughts and feelings were sure to assert themselves from time to time, but it was not in her nature to increase her vexations by dwelling on them.

"If your sister is to spend even a small portion of the season with us, she will require a visit to the dressmaker. Her usual gowns from Meryton will not be sufficient, and since she is taller, loaning her items from your wardrobe will not work. Perhaps, she should spend a month complete."

Her heart leapt. A month with Jane! "She could travel to my aunt and uncle's prior to our arrival. They could escort her to Madame Bonheur's establishment and order her some new gowns."

"Madame Bonheur has an elite clientele," he objected. "She will not agree to an appointment for the wife of a tradesman."

"I could pen Madame a letter explaining that my sister will be staying with us for part of the season and include a list of gowns she will require. I am certain Madame will make an exception in such a case. It is not as if one can discern my uncle's profession by setting eyes on my aunt."

"You make a valid argument, my dear." She lifted an eyebrow, and he gave a shrug. "I hope you will forgive me the endearment. I do think of you as a dear friend, and once you forgive me, I hope we can remain on such intimate terms."

"Intimate terms? I feel I hardly know you, sir. You do not spend a great deal of time in my company, and you do not share your thoughts. We are but two people occupying the same home."

A deep breath helped to quell some of her frustration while she awaited her husband's rebuttal. She had made a concerted effort to calm herself, to at least temporarily subdue her anger and hopelessness, but he had decided to dredge it all back to the surface.

The scenery passing outside of the carriage was beautiful, so Elizabeth turned her attention in that direction as her husband had done on several occasions. On this occasion, his continued observation of her was unnerving. She spoke the truth. He could not be surprised by her assessment of the situation since he was present or not present for the entirety of their marriage. After she did not acknowledge him for nigh on five minutes, he returned to reading his book, prompting a droop of her shoulders. Her equanimity could not tolerate another row with her husband.

"Pardon me, Master Fitzwilliam, but a carriage has been spotted heading towards the house from the main gates. The boy who delivered the message spotted a crest upon the door."

His heart jumped and pounded against his sternum. She was here! "Please send word to Mrs. Reynolds of the Duke and Duchess of Leeds's imminent arrival," said Fitzwilliam to the butler in as calm a fashion as he could. "I am certain she will wish to prepare bathwater and refreshments for our guests."

The butler executed a perfect bow and exited while Fitzwilliam deliberately rose as usual from his father's desk. As he made his way towards the door, a winded Georgiana slid to a halt against the frame. At least his sister could express herself freely.

"Did you hear? They are here!"

He allowed a grin at her excitement and tweaked her nose. "I have heard, Squirt."

With an indignant gasp, she pinched his arm. "I despise it when you call me that."

He laughed and tugged at one of her curls. "Which is part of the fun, dear sister."

"Fitzwilliam," called his father from behind. Brother and sister straightened as the elder Darcy strode forward to meet them. "Did you finish going over the ledgers?"

"I did, Father. Everything appears to be in order. We received a few items in the post today. I shall go over them tomorrow."

Mr. Darcy listened before nodding in agreement. "I think from now on you can run Pemberley without my supervision."

Fitzwilliam's eyes widened. "Father?"

"Should you find you require the help, I shall be here to aid you, but you have proven over the past year that you are more than capable. I do not desire you to learn to manage this estate as I did.

"Despite his long life, my father did not prepare me for the responsibility of an estate as I have prepared you. I made a number of errors before finding my way. My wish when you were born was for you to learn from me, which you have since you graduated Cambridge. Now it is time for you to put your lessons into practice."

He gaped at his father. His heart now raced for a reason besides Elizabeth. What if he failed? "All the same, I should appreciate your wisdom and advice."

"I shall gladly provide either should it be needed. You may also speak to me of your plans. I would be happy to provide you counsel." The elder Darcy placed a hand to his son's shoulder. "I do not wonder if you will make me proud, Fitzwilliam. I know you will be a success. I am already a very proud father."

With a heavy gulp, Fitzwilliam choked back the lump that had risen in his throat. He had not anticipated such a move on his father's part. He was overwhelmed. "I thank you."

Mr. Darcy embraced his son. "We should be in the hall to meet Thomas and Lizzy, lest they believe we have forgotten their arrival."

When they turned, expecting to find Georgiana waiting for them, she was gone, so they ventured to the entrance hall where she stood before Thomas and Elizabeth while they shed their hats and gloves.

He paused where he entered the hall, drinking in the sight of Elizabeth as though he had not laid eyes on her in months. Georgiana's voice broke through his reverie. "I attempted to tell father we would be late, but he was too busy speaking with Fitzwilliam to listen." She bounced on her toes and grasped Elizabeth's hands and pulled her into an embrace. "I am so happy you are here!"

"And we are pleased to be here," said Elizabeth, smiling, "but where is Evie?"

Georgiana waved her hand dismissively. "Oh! Father thought her too full of energy, and I did not want to miss your arrival, so one of the footmen is taking her for a walk."

His father had stepped forward and greeted Thomas while Georgiana spoke to Elizabeth. Fitzwilliam stepped forward a minute later, shaking his cousin's hand before stepping over to Elizabeth.

She smiled softly upon his approach, but as he leaned forward to bow and press a brief kiss to the back of her hand, his attention was arrested by something in her eyes. She smiled and seemed genuinely happy to be at Pemberley, yet a hint of something lingered deeper—something that caused an ache deep in his chest. What could have possibly happened since he fetched Georgiana a month prior?

"I am thrilled to finally set eyes on Pemberley." Her expression became mischievous. She was to tease him, yet her eyes still held that same dullness—grief. That was the emotion he sought, grief! She wore no mourning, so what could it be?

"And what think you of Pemberley?"

"I believe I have never seen its equal for situation and beauty." He searched her countenance, and saw only an earnest opinion freely given.

"I thank you for the compliment."

"Lizzy! Would you care for some refreshment, or would you prefer to refresh yourselves from your journey?"

Elizabeth glanced in his direction, eyes dancing at Georgiana's excitement. With a slight movement of his hand, he gestured towards the drawing room.

A curve of her lip was the only indication she had paid heed to his movement until she took Georgiana's arm. "I do believe I should prefer a cup of tea before I am shown to my room. The trip has made me quite parched."

His father smiled as Georgiana ushered her friend to the drawing room with the men close behind. "Nice work, Son."

"Georgiana has planned the month down to the minutest of details. I only offered Lizzy a small insight in to the correct decision."

Thomas drew alongside them. "My wife is quick to laud her elder sister as the best of creatures with her kind heart and gentle disposition, but Elizabeth is much the same in her own way. The difference between them lies in Miss Bennet's innate ability to only see the good in people. My wife does not have such a blindness to the faults of others." Thomas opened his mouth to continue, but a familiar voice reverberated through the hall.

"Godfather!"

The men all turned at the voice. Fitzwilliam clenched his hands into fists at his sides. Why had Wickham shown himself now? Was he not supposed to be in London? Better there than causing a multitude of problems at Pemberley.

"George," said his father with his arm outstretched. His father never saw the bad in George Wickham. He merely saw the resemblance to the father, an excellent man, who he had considered not only a most trusted steward, but also a friend. "Have you come to stay for a time?"

"Yes, sir." He bowed to the duke. "Though, I was unaware you had visitors. I hope I am still welcome."

"Of course you are. I am certain Mrs. Reynolds can ready your usual rooms before you have need of them this evening. You remember my cousin, the Duke of Leeds."

Wickham dipped his head in a formal fashion in the duke's direction. "Yes, sir. I am pleased to see you, Your Grace."

His cousin nodded his head. "Mr. Wickham." Without further acknowledgment, Thomas joined the ladies in the drawing room, leaving the two of them with Wickham. Thomas had every right to dislike Wickham.

It was Fitzwilliam who had requested Thomas's aid years ago when they were at Cambridge. Wickham had been impersonating Darcy while he gambled and bedded women in a nearby village. Thomas had cleaned up Wickham's mess, namely two girls Wickham had put in the family way, as well as some debts. Fitzwilliam had made Thomas swear not to tell the elder Darcy.

His father rested a hand on Wickham's shoulder. "Come, you must greet Georgiana and meet the new duchess."

His father did not see his eyes close as he followed them into the drawing room. Georgiana was still too young to be in danger from Wickham. Elizabeth, on the other hand, was not.

# Chapter 7

Elizabeth removed her spencer and handed it to the waiting maid. "Thank you," she said before the girl bowed and headed to the servants' passage. Once she was gone, Elizabeth remained standing in the Pemberley's hall, studying the ornately painted ceiling and the various murals adorning the walls. The room's splendour still, even after a fortnight, made her pause to appreciate the view before she continued.

"Good morning, Lizzy."

Mr. Darcy walked down the last two steps where he paused. "Have you just returned from your walk?"

"Yes, sir. The sky is beautiful and a brilliant blue this morning and the day is not yet too warm. I noticed Fitzwilliam riding back towards the stables. He must have partaken in an early ride while the weather was more favourable as well."

"He does enjoy solitary morning gallops across the fields. May I ask where you explored today?"

"Oh, I walked along the river until I found a small footbridge. I crossed there and followed a path that led through a copse of trees to a lovely rose garden. If I have neglected to tell you before, you have a beautiful estate."

He smiled and dipped his chin. "Thank you. I shall have you know that today, you enjoyed one of my wife's favourite walks. I am certain she would be happy to know someone took as much pleasure in it as she did."

"It is indeed a lovely path." She glanced down at the older gown she wore when she walked out. "If you will excuse me, I should refresh myself so I might join Georgiana for breakfast.

"Yes, of course. I am certain she will be down soon."

Elizabeth swiftly climbed the stairs and headed for her chambers, but when she reached the entrance to the family apartments, she jumped back to avoid running headlong into Georgiana.

"Forgive me," said Elizabeth in a gasp. Her hand pressed against her chest while her heartbeat accelerated a bit. "I did not expect you to leave your suite quite yet."

A giggle burst from Georgiana. "And I feared I was late to join you for breakfast."

"No, I have just returned from my walk."

"So, you are to refresh yourself." Georgiana looped her arm through Elizabeth's and began to tug her towards the guest wing. "Then if you do not object, I shall keep you company. I hope you had a nice ramble this morning. The weather certainly appears agreeable."

"It was definitely agreeable. There is still a gentle breeze keeping the air cool. I enjoyed watching the ducks swim and dive for food, and I saw a few deer." As they approached her rooms, raised voices could be heard from inside.

Georgiana frowned at Elizabeth as they stopped and listened for a moment. "If I did not know better, I would swear that is a man's voice."

Unfortunately, they could not hear the subject of the disagreement, but regardless, Elizabeth threw open the door and halted at the sight of Lalande pinned against the wall. The man turned and Georgiana gasped at the sight of George Wickham, who gave an ugly sneer.

"What is the meaning of this?" said Elizabeth in the haughtiest voice she could manage.

Lalande's knee rammed upward with a great deal of force until it hit squarely in between Mr. Wickham's legs. As soon as she withdrew it, Wickham fell into a heap on the floor while he clutched himself and writhed upon the carpet. "You bunter!"

Free to rush towards Elizabeth, the moment Lalande reached Elizabeth's side, she clasped her hands, wringing them desperately. "I returned not five minutes ago from the laundry when I heard a noise in your dressing room. I entered to find this man searching through your jewellery. He is a thief! I swear, Madame. I attempted to pull the bell for aid, but he grabbed me."

"She is lying." Mr. Wickham stumbled to his feet, facing Elizabeth head-on and revealing a series of wide, blood-red scratches marring one of his cheeks. "She invited me here— wanted to lie with me in your bed."

Lalande gasped as did Georgiana. Damn! In the shock of the situation, Elizabeth had forgotten the young girl's presence. The last thing the Darcys would wish was for Georgiana to hear Wickham's vulgar claim.

With a determined step, Elizabeth crossed to the door that separated her chambers from her husband's. She had never had reason to use the entrance before, but today, she most certainly had. Without knocking, she turned the handle, jerked it open, and froze as stiff as a statue. Her jaw worked but no words came from her lips.

"What do you think you are doing, Your Grace?" said Wickham from behind her, his voice oozing and dripping disdain.

Closing her eyes to the scene in front of her, she slammed the door shut before Wickham could see the same picture, and whirled around. "Lalande, pull the bell."

"Oui, Madame." As Lalande moved towards the rope, Mr. Wickham looked back and forth between them, as though he could not decide who to stop first.

Instead of darting for one of them, he yelled, "I took nothing! She is a lying whore!"

Elizabeth winced and glanced at Georgiana who should have been anywhere but witnessing this scene. The problem was

Elizabeth required a witness beyond Lalande. The poor, wide-eyed girl was all she had.

After pulling herself up as tall as her stature would allow, Elizabeth pointed to Wickham's face. "You forget the scratches upon your cheek. Lalande fought you before I entered. You bear the proof of her statements upon your face."

The door to her husband's chambers opened behind her, and Elizabeth struggled to keep from peering behind her. Once they were finished with Wickham, would her husband be furious with her for intruding upon his privacy?

"What is the meaning of this, Wickham?" he said with a rumbling tone. "Why have you invaded my wife's bedchamber?"

"I caught him stealing," said Lalande, her finger aimed in Mr. Wickham's direction. "He carries my Madame's rubies in his pocket."

Mr. Wickham raised his fist while his legs ate up the space between him and Lalande, but before he could swing, a hand grabbed his arm and yanked him back.

"Fitzwilliam!" cried Georgiana.

Fortunately, Fitzwilliam was taller than Wickham, who he tossed back into the nearest chair. "Empty your pockets." Without removing his eyes from Wickham, Fitzwilliam gestured towards the door. "Georgiana, you are to leave at once." Without argument, she hurried from the room. "Well, Wickham? Let us see it. What have you stolen?"

"I need do nothing for you." Spittle sprayed from his lip as he hissed the words loudly. "You cannot tell me what to do."

"But I can," said George Darcy as he strode into the room. "A maid happened to overhear this commotion as she passed and found me immediately. Why is my son telling you to empty your pockets?"

"Godfather! Thank goodness you are here! This bitch claims I have stolen the duchess's rubies when I have done nothing of the sort. She tells lies, yet they believe her over me."

Mr. Darcy crossed his arms over his chest and stepped closer while Elizabeth's heart stuttered frantically against her ribs. "Why are you in the duchess's room?"

"Her maid invited me! That whore invited me! I have nothing!"

"Empty your pockets," said the duke. His voice was cold. Elizabeth had never heard him speak with such disdain. The chill of his command sent an uncontrollable shiver down her spine. "George, while I appreciate that he is your ward, I am not blind to this man's ill nature. I would believe most thieves in Newgate over this worthless young man, and he will not leave this room without producing my wife's jewels."

George Darcy only spared the duke a quick glance. "Very well. George, remove all you carry in your pockets."

Though he remained seated with Fitzwilliam towering over him, Wickham strained from the chair towards the elder Darcy. "I did not steal from the duchess! I swear it! Do you not believe me?"

The duke took a step closer and crossed his arms over his chest so he and Mr. Darcy nearly appeared to be twins. "If you speak the truth, then you have no reason to deny us."

Elizabeth watched the scene with her heart pounding even harder than before. The sensation was a strange one and made her skin seem impossibly tight. She did not doubt Lalande, but what would this mean for Mr. Darcy? He must have trusted Mr. Wickham implicitly to allow him a room in his home.

Mr. Wickham shoved his hand in his pocket but did not remove a thing. "See."

"Turn the pockets inside out, Wickham," said the duke. "Now."

The man sneered and stood with a swagger. Slowly, one at a time, he pulled his trouser pockets until the fine lining showed. Two thuds filled the silence of the room as a set of ruby earrings dropped to the carpet from the first pocket. A louder thump sounded when the matching necklace fell from the second.

"James! Michael!" The two footmen appeared in the door at Mr. Darcy's summons. "Take Wickham to his chambers. As soon as I have spoken to the duke and duchess, I shall join you. Mr. Wickham is to be stripped to be sure he has taken nothing else, as well as his belongings searched. While we do so, I need someone to pack his trunk. He will depart Pemberley immediately."

"Mr. Darcy—"

Mr. Darcy held up his hand and stepped nose to nose with Wickham. "You could be hanged, George."

Wickham's face blanched, and he swallowed as if he might be sick.

"Do not abuse my good will," said Mr. Darcy. "I do this for your father, who would be broken-hearted to witness how you have repaid my generosity. I had heard talk on occasion, but I discounted it as idle rumour. I should have investigated people's claims further. Based on Fitzwilliam's reaction, I now wonder at how much I have missed over the years. I am ashamed at how blind I have apparently been."

As soon as James and Michael dragged Wickham from the room, Lalande scrambled to retrieve the earrings and necklace from the floor.

"What has George done in the past?" Mr. Darcy looked to the duke. "I should know."

"It was me, Father." Fitzwilliam stepped forward with his hands clasped behind his back. "I never had the heart to tell you of Wickham's habits. He gambles and imposes himself on young ladies. I requested Thomas's aid once with Wickham but swore him to secrecy on the matter."

"You should have told me." His eyes moved back and forth between his son and the duke. "I do expect you to tell me all, but now is not the time. I need to see Wickham searched and have him removed from Pemberley."

Her husband shook his head and placed a hand on Mr. Darcy's shoulder. "You would be doing many a favour if you turned him over to the magistrate."

Elizabeth's eyes widened at the duke's words. As Mr. Darcy had said, Mr. Wickham would be hanged.

"I cannot. I held too much respect for his father." The elder Darcy took Elizabeth's hands. "I cannot tell you how appalled I am. I am sorry this happened at Pemberley and hope you understand why I must resolve this in such a manner."

"I do, sir."

He kissed the back of her hand and strode through the door followed by Fitzwilliam, leaving her with the duke and Lalande. Her husband immediately closed the door to the corridor. "Leave us," he said to Lalande. Without a word, she bustled into the dressing room. "How long were you arguing with Wickham?"

"I'd only discovered him threatening Lalande a few minutes before I opened your chamber door."

"We had been in the dressing room. We never heard any argument, or I would have assisted you sooner."

"Forgive me for intruding into your rooms," said Elizabeth with her cheeks on fire. She could not look at him so she stared at the ornate Persian rug on the floor, tracing the lines of the patterns. "I shall not do so again. You have my assurances."

"Pray do not make yourself uneasy. I am not angry. I understand why you entered without knocking, though I hope to keep what you witnessed between us. I do not expect you to understand—as most would not, but I love Colin and have for years. Yes, he is my valet, but he offered to be so after we met and fell in love. It was the best way for us to be together without arousing suspicion."

"This is why our marriage is what it is?"

He exhaled heavily, his posture not as straight and tall as was his wont. "Yes. I have always preferred the company of men to women."

Her mind spun, and she nearly fell over at how dizzy it rendered her. She had never heard of such a thing, but it did not take a great amount of intelligence to realise how people in their world would view the alliance. "How have you kept society from discovering this . . . your affair? Forgive me. I do not know how to discuss this in so casual a manner."

He waved away her unease as he sat in the seat Wickham so recently vacated. "Before our marriage, I visited brothels, but instead of partaking of their services, I paid the women to spread rumours of my patronage. The instances were rare but enough to keep any scrutiny at bay."

"And your valet has a bedchamber attached to your dressing room at Worthstone and Worth House, just as Lalande has hers attached to mine. No one has reason to suspect a thing. Quite convenient." She could not help the sarcasm. "Please do not tell me more." Now that her fear of his anger had abated, she shook and needed to clench her fists to suppress it.

"You are angry."

"What an astute observation, husband. At least now I know the entire story behind our sham of a marriage. It explains why I have your permission to take a lover—after all, you have one of your own, do you not? Why deny it? I have now seen you kissing him. I have seen the evidence of your affair."

"Elizabeth—"

She held up her hands. "No more. I shall not tell a soul of your relationship with your valet. While I am certain society would be unforgiving, I find I am simply angered by your deception, and I cannot bear to hear more at the moment. Pray, I need to walk. If you could tell Georgiana I have lost my appetite, I shall seek her out when I am more equal to being in the company of others."

Her feet carried her with hurried steps back outside and to the river. She walked briskly along the shore, her ire propelling her forward until she broke into a run, sprinting as though fleeing for her life. The cool air rushed through her nose as she ran farther and farther from Pemberley, finally slowing as she neared the footbridge.

Fitzwilliam stood in the centre, throwing pebbles into the river as it passed beneath the stone arch. He must have heard her approaching since his head jerked up from watching the water.

Footsteps drew his reverie from the ripples spreading across the glassy surface of the water to Elizabeth, standing along the bank. Her cheeks held a great deal of colour, her chest heaved as she breathed, her hair was windblown, and she appeared quite wild.

Fitzwilliam's eyebrows drew towards the centre. Could Wickham have caused this much upset? "Are you well?"

"Not really, but pray, do not be offended if I say I cannot speak of it." Her voice was breathless and, despite the inappropriateness of the moment, made his insides flip.

"Wickham did not harm you?"

"No," she shook her head as if he required the emphasis. "I am only disturbed by that which I cannot control. Running allows me to clear my head, albeit briefly."

He straightened and placed the remaining pebbles in his hand upon the ledge. "I find riding helps prodigiously."

"I had not thought of that." She scraped her teeth along her bottom lip as she crossed her arms. "Would Georgiana be upset if I rode without her? I simply do not feel equal to company at the moment."

He held out one arm for her to take while he gestured forward with the other. "Allow me to escort you to the stables. We shall see you on a horse, and I shall personally escort you around Pemberley. If Georgiana is upset, I shall explain. She rides at times to gain perspective and peace of mind. She would understand."

"Thank you," she said as they crossed the remainder of the bridge.

His hand covered hers where it sat upon his forearm. "Do not thank me for what I am happy to do."

She rested her head near his shoulder, and he stiffened as an urge to bestow a kiss to the top of her head pressed upon him. He swallowed hard and kept his eyes on the path in front of them. No, no, no. He could *not* fall in love with Thomas's wife. He needed to be mindful of his place as well as hers.

The grooms did not blink twice when he entered and ordered two horses. Georgiana had mentioned since Elizabeth's arrival how much she had improved, so he specified a horse for her that required a slightly higher level of skill to ride. If she wanted to chase away her problems, a sedate mount would not do at all.

When he turned, he noticed she wore a morning gown. "I did not think for you to change into your habit."

"I do not wish to return to the house," she begged while shaking her head violently. "Pray, let us just ride."

As soon as the groom returned with the horse saddled and ready, he helped her mount the large black mare. "Ride in the grass until I have a horse. I took a chance and ordered Kelpie for you. She is more spirited than the horses you are accustomed to, but I think she will suit your mood more than the mares you have ridden thus far."

"Water horse?"

He patted Kelpie's neck with a smile. "She escaped when she was younger. We found her up to her knees in the river, so she was renamed."

Elizabeth adjusted the reins and sat taller in the saddle. "I like it," she said before she walked the mare over to the small clearing he had indicated.

The horse he requested came not long after, so he joined Elizabeth and pointed in the direction of the river. Without speaking, they rode along a pathway until they reached a field that followed the water's edge. Elizabeth's horse cantered forward as soon as she cleared the trees, breaking into a gallop moments later. Indeed, she had improved greatly to be able to sit a gallop side-saddle as she was.

He followed behind until she eventually stopped at the beginning of a rocky slope where he pulled beside her, his chest tightening when she turned to him, her eyes red-rimmed and her cheeks damp with tears.

"Lizzy?" His fingers trailed along the edge of her jaw as his thumb brushed a droplet away.

"Do not ask, for I cannot speak of it."

Everything in him screamed to drag her into his arms, to stop her tears, and make some witty comment that might induce her to smile. That twinkle he adored in her eyes was absent, their vibrancy dulled. Moreover, she did not carry herself in quite the same manner.

Her hand wrapped around his and removed it from her face. She gave it a squeeze. "I shall regain my equanimity. I am not formed for melancholy. I simply require time."

He had intended to comfort her, but instead, she reassured him. How he wanted to make her tell him. "Is Thomas aware?" His cousin would certainly repair or handle whatever had disheartened his wife so.

Her eyes darted back to her reins as she released his hand. "He is." She surveyed their surroundings. "Where do we go from here?"

"The peak has a wonderful view of the estate, or if you would prefer to continue on as before, we can ride that way." He pointed to an opening among the trees. "It is a large path formed by the deer on the estate. More fields lie beyond those trees."

She dipped her head in the direction of the trail, urging her horse forward. "Do I need to worry of tiring her too much?"

"We shall walk until we reach the next clearing. She will have the rest she requires."

They spent the remainder of the morning galloping through the fields, which gradually sloped upward until they found themselves close to the top of Stanage Edge. He indicated another path, and Elizabeth followed it until they stood upon the top, the wind blowing her hair around her face and destroying her abigail's careful construction. How had he missed that she lacked a bonnet as well?

"It is beautiful," she breathed. She closed her eyes and lifted her face towards the sun for a minute before she was required to still Kelpie, who shifted restlessly from foot to foot. The horse had definitely been enjoying her run and was now hesitant to stop.

As she took in the view, she paused on Pemberley in the distance. "Do we have to return? Can we not just ride that way,"—she pointed north with a shaky finger— "never stopping until we find the perfect place? I do not require much. A small cottage would suit me well."

She turned and gave a smile that did not reach her eyes. "Do not feel you must answer. I know we cannot. It is simply nice to dream once in a while, is it not?"

The circles under her eyes and pale complexion made him grit his teeth. What could have made her this sad and mournful? Surely not Wickham? Regardless, this was not her typical disposition. His heart clenched and split in two. "It is," he said softly.

She did not say another word but steered her horse with care down the rocky path. Their return to Pemberley passed at a slower, more sedate pace since the horses had been worked hard on their outbound ride. Elizabeth remained quiet, only stopping once to watch a herd of deer grazing along the bank of the river.

Once their horses were safely in the hands of the grooms, Fitzwilliam followed Elizabeth to the house but remained in the hall as she climbed the stairs to refresh herself from the morning out of doors. When had her happiness become more important than his responsibilities or even his own needs? He had just spent several hours riding when he should have been meeting with the steward, and he would do the same as often as he could if it meant basking in the glow of her attention.

"Fitzwilliam?"

He started at his father's voice, his eyes having a difficult time leaving Elizabeth as she turned in the direction of the guest wing. "I am certain you wish to reprimand me for never telling you of Wickham."

"After speaking with Thomas, I believe I understand. I hope in the future, you will trust me with any matter, regardless of how you believe I shall respond."

"Of course."

His father took in his attire. "You rode again?"

Fitzwilliam's eyes returned to the top of the stairs. Elizabeth could no longer be seen. She had continued on to her rooms. God help him, he was in love with her. When had it happened? When had he fallen? He could not pin it to a particular moment. His heart had been lost before he had even realised. "Lizzy wished to ride, so I had Kelpie saddled for her and accompanied her in the event she required help."

"She rode Kelpie? I am surprised you did not give her a less spirited horse. Kelpie is not as wild as some, but she still requires a firm hand."

He could not help but allow the slight lift of his lips. "She handled her excellently."

His father pressed a hand to the back of his shoulder. "She is married, Son."

"As I am well aware, Father." He held his father's eye without wavering. "As I am well aware."

# Chapter 8

*July 31ˢᵗ 1809*
*Longbourn*
*Hertfordshire*

*My dear Lizzy,*

*What a wonderful time you had at Pemberley! The Darcys sound so affable and agreeable. I do hope one day to have the opportunity to make their acquaintance, but until then, I shall enjoy reading of them through your letters. You describe people so well. I am certain your assessments cannot be far from the truth.*

*I spoke with Papa about visiting you during the Season. He agreed, though he had little choice once Mama eavesdropped upon my request. I know this is months away, but I anticipate seeing you with my own eyes. I have missed your humour as well as your faithful companionship at Longbourn. Charlotte calls often, yet she is not you and never could be.*

*My father is attempting to educate dear Mary beyond theology. He has hired a master in the hopes of improving her playing, though he holds little hope for an improvement in her singing. His latest idea is for them to read and discuss Julius Caesar. He has dropped her from a high ledge into Pandora's Box by taking her from sermons to politics, murder, and revenge. I do hope she will not be too traumatised.*

*I hope your return to Worthstone was an easy journey. I confess I shall miss your descriptions of Mr. Bingley and his sisters. Poor Mr. Fitzwilliam Darcy! Forced to fend off the advances of Miss Bingley while not offending the brother. The situation sounds unpleasant, to say the least. Her comments about you, dear sister, were uncharitable, though I cannot believe she meant those statements the way they sounded. I do commend your husband and Mr. Fitzwilliam Darcy for defending you.*

*I must go. Lady Lucas and Charlotte have called. Netherfield has new tenants once again, and Mama is beside herself to know who they are. Perhaps Lady Lucas has some news.*

*Yours very affectionately,*

*Jane*

Elizabeth folded the letter and sighed, placing it upon the corner of her escritoire. She had already met with Mrs. Hamilton and arranged for her bedchamber to have new wallcoverings, replacing the faded ones with a floral, blue and white chintz fabric. New draperies were to be made and the furniture recovered all in the dark blue of the fabric along with new bedding.

The effect would be elegant, if a little dark. Dark colours were not typically her favourite, yet she had favoured them more in recent weeks. Perhaps her mood had something to do with her choice?

Without much thought, she rose and went to her room, finding Lalande and requesting her riding habit. She dressed and strode to the stable, pausing when she entered.

"Your Grace?" said a groom, who was passing with a horse.

"I want to ride. Pray prepare a mount for me, but not Thetis. I rode a more challenging horse at Pemberley. If you could find one for me here, I would be grateful."

He held up a finger. "I shall return."

Elizabeth whipped the crop against some grass outside the stable while she waited. Eventually, someone returned, only he was not the groom, he was the stablemaster. "Your Grace. I apologise for not greeting you. I was unaware you intended to ride today."

"Yes, it was a last-minute decision. I hope it is not a problem?"

"Of course not. My groom tells me you do not wish to ride Thetis?"

She exhaled and adjusted her gloves. "I rode a more spirited mare at Pemberley. I simply desire more than Thetis can provide."

He nodded and smiled. "I know just the horse."

When he appeared from the back of the stable, he led a mare so round she waddled. "I hope Daffodil will suit, ma'am."

Her shoulders dropped along with her hands to her sides. "No, she will not, but do not trouble yourself. I shall simply return to the house."

The stablemaster said something or another, no doubt in an attempt to placate her, but she did not bother to turn and continued until she reached the house. She marched directly to the duke's study and knocked loudly. She certainly would not open a door of his without knocking again.

He called her to enter, and she stepped through, coming to an abrupt halt when she stood in front of his desk. "I require a horse to ride."

His forehead crinkled as he sat back in his seat. "I have provided Thetis for your use."

"And I appreciate it. I do like Thetis, but I do not wish for a sedate wander around the grounds. I became accustomed to riding a more spirited mare at Pemberley and only wish the same opportunity to challenge myself here."

"Did you tell my stablemaster?" he asked with his brows drawn together in the middle. "I am certain he has a suitable mount."

Her hands shifted to her hips. "I did, and he produced a mare so round, I would be surprised if she does not carry a foal."

"Daffodil?" he said, his voice high-pitched.

"Yes, that is her name."

He gave a low laugh and pushed himself from the desk in order to stand. "Come. I shall give him permission for you to choose your mount. I did not foresee him limiting you based on my initial suggestion. Georgiana and Fitzwilliam spoke of how well you rode at Pemberley, so I see no reason why you cannot have your choice of horse."

In under a half-hour, she galloped along the fields of Worthstone with a groom following close behind. Thus far, the ride had worked wonders for her mood, but she missed Fitzwilliam. Since they had no expectations of Georgiana being forced to maintain their pace, he often accompanied her on rides after the day they visited Stanage Edge. Georgiana was an accomplished rider, though she had never cared for riding with great speed. For Elizabeth, the speed made her flesh tingle, and her head clear of the troubles weighing her down. She felt more alive than at any other time. By introducing her to this, Fitzwilliam had, in a sense, freed her.

She rode until she reached the summit of the peak she had ridden with Fitzwilliam and Georgiana. The view proved to be truly spectacular, the ridge stretching out before her.

The dark, dapple-grey mare beneath her shifted on her feet, so she tightened her grip on the reins. The horse possessed a flowing, even stride that would keep Elizabeth's rear from being terribly sore on the morrow. Thankfully, at her request, her husband had made the perfect recommendation. The stablemaster had opened his mouth as if he might protest, but wisely, never uttered a word. Instead, he fetched the horse.

After she returned her mount to the stable, she happened upon her husband in the hall as she entered the house. "What do you think of the mare?"

"I enjoyed her very much. Thank you."

The duke nodded. "Your birthday is next week. I confess I was unsure of what to give you, but if you truly like her, she is yours. Her name is Llamrei."

"The mare owned by King Arthur?"

"According to Welsh legend, yes. You can give her a new name if you wish."

"No," said Elizabeth. "The name suits her." She took a step towards the stairs before she stopped and peered back at him. "Thank you for interceding with the stablemaster as well as for the horse. I am certain I shall enjoy her immensely."

"Good. I do desire your happiness."

"I know." The words came out as almost a whisper before she turned and continued to trudge up the stairs. Her husband was not a terrible man by any means. He was kind to his tenants and to her, though they didn't spend a prodigious amount of time in one another's company. Yet, he definitely held a selfish streak she had not known existed prior to recent events. Their marriage and his expectations of her certainly illustrated he considered few beyond himself.

Tears welled in her eyes as she thought of Fitzwilliam, who cared for his sister's needs before his own, and at times, even her own concerns, even though they were no more than friends. She had indeed missed him during her ride, his quiet presence that bolstered her when she required the support. God help her, but she loved him. She loved a man who was not her husband. Her heart squeezed painfully in her chest. Her situation had been hopeless before, and now, it was doubly so.

Lalande helped her refresh herself and don a clean gown, though only Lalande knew why, since it would be unlikely she would spend any time outside of her chambers.

Her husband spent the day in his study with his steward before retiring to his bedchamber and requesting a tray. Elizabeth requested a tray of her own, and after she ate, she read until her eyes could barely stay open. She blew out the candle and was lost to her dreams.

Fitzwilliam dropped into a chair by the window when he finally retired to his rooms. The day had been dreadfully long. He had been needed on one end of the estate, only to return home to discover he needed to ride back out to the same tenant's farm. He was weary to the bone.

He laid his head back and let his eyes flutter closed, imagining Elizabeth standing before him. She caressed his face and pressed her soft lips to his forehead, soothing his aching heart. He missed her dreadfully, though he needed to cease these useless fantasies. She was a married woman—not just married, but his cousin's wife. His father would be horrified to know the object of his affections.

"Sir?"

His eyes popped open and his head jerked upright. "Yes?"

"Forgive me for startling you, sir." Bishop, his valet, stood before him with his dressing gown draped over his arm. "I have water for you to wash."

He rose with the speed of a man of sixty rather than five and twenty. "Thank you."

Once he was readied for bed, he climbed between the covers and stared at the canopy above him. "What am I to do? She cannot be mine, yet I cannot imagine my heart belonging to

129

another." He scrubbed his eyes with the heels of his hands. "I am hopeless."

He rolled to his side and closed his eyes. Elizabeth lay before him, her doe eyes soft and full of love for him, her hair spread in long curls across the pristine white pillow. His lips met hers, and he was lost.

"Sir! Sir! You must wake up!"

Fitzwilliam bolted upright, his entire body shaking and on edge, his breathing laboured. "Yes? What is it, Bishop?"

"Fire in one of the tenant houses."

The last tendrils of sleep retreated, and he took a deep breath, trying to relieve the lingering effects of his dream. "Where? Which house?"

"The Bradleys. The boy who came did not indicate how bad. Only that you should come immediately." He held out a pair of breeches that Fitzwilliam began to slip onto his legs. "I believe your father has been awakened as well. I know he handed over control to you, but with his experience—"

"My father's experience makes him invaluable in this circumstance. He may have given me control of the estate, but he and I still discuss the business together. I value his opinion. He should be present regardless."

"Yes, sir."

Bishop had him dressed in a lawn shirt and breeches with a greatcoat in a matter of minutes, and when he exited through the front door, his horse stood ready. He stomped his front feet and shifted from side to side, no doubt agitated by the early hour as well as the unease in the air. "What of my father?"

"Beggin' your pardon, sir, but he left nigh on twenty minutes ago."

Fitzwilliam did not respond but dug his heels into the horse's flank, propelling the stallion forward into the dark. The waning crescent moon did little to illuminate the paths he travelled to reach the Bradley's farm, yet he did not slow. He had ridden these routes through the forest enough to ensure no low-hanging branches would impede his pace, and he could not tarry. The Bradley's farm, while not terribly far, was not close to the great house. Their cottage could be gone before he arrived if the blaze was too severe.

A haunting glow filtered through the trees before he reached the clearing. "Blast!" He pulled his horse back as he neared and swung from the saddle. One of the nearby tenants grabbed his mount's reins and led it away as Fitzwilliam strode closer to the house, assessing the situation. The other tenants manned a line of buckets from an offshoot of the nearby river to douse the blaze, but it had little if any effect on the flames pouring from the door and through two or three holes in the roof. The fire only grew and spread and would engulf the tiny cottage before long.

He waved his arms in big motions. "Get away from the house! It is too severe!"

One of the men turned. "But, sir," he said, "your father went inside to find one of the children!"

"He what?" Fitzwilliam's eyes hurt from how wide he held them combined with the heat and the smoke that was inescapable, and they stung like the dickens. Why would his father take such an enormous risk? He ran both hands through his hair while he stared at the fire. He gave a yell, rushed to the line, and grabbed the first pail of water, tossing it onto the flames. "Hurry, man! We need to go faster!"

A loud crack sounded, ripping a gaping hole in the night. If Fitzwilliam had not known better, he would have thought someone felled a great tree, but it was evident in a matter of seconds the only thing felled was what was left of the cottage. Fitzwilliam cried out and lunged towards the remains of the door, but several pairs of arms wrapped around him, pulling him back.

As the roof collapsed, everything around him slowed to an eerie unnatural rhythm. People screamed in strange, low sounds, while the roof of the small cottage began to sink into the centre of the structure.

"No!" The voice was his, yet it did not come from him. His arms reached forward as he pulled with everything he had to reach that door. He needed to get to his father! He had to help him! "Let me go!"

With a reddish halo surrounding him, the outline of his father appeared in the now cavernous door as the rest of the structure caved. Fitzwilliam pulled with all his might to rip himself from those holding him back, but not one released him— they drew him back with more force than he could muster.

One or two of his tenants rushed forward, but every last one of them disappeared in the wave of smoke and debris that billowed when the wreckage fell.

"No!"

The hands released him, and he flew at the last place he saw his father. People stood and stared, illuminated by the intensity of the fire still ravaging the debris. Buckets sat forgotten in people's hands. Why would no one move?

"Here!" he cried pointing to where the door once was. "We need water here. We have to find my father!"

In but a moment, he was passed a bucket that he poured over the wood. As they put out flames, they removed charred remnants until they reached his father's lifeless body and pulled him from the rubble.

"Leave it!" He held up his hands to someone who attempted to step closer to the scalding rubble. "'Tis a lost cause! I want no one else harmed."

When they set his father in the grass, he held a bundle of blankets in a tight grip. One of the men withdrew the burden, and as it was unwrapped, a wail burst from the depths.

"Harry!" A woman rushed forward and grasped the screaming and coughing child. "Thank God!" She kissed every inch of the child's forehead while Fitzwilliam inhaled deeply and steeled himself to look at his father.

Fitzwilliam squeezed his eyes closed as he lowered his head, only opening them when his father would be in front of him. His first sight was the charred, angry flesh of his father's back. His inhale this time was not to bolster himself, but to keep from being violently sick at the sight before him.

"Sir, we should put these blankets down before we move him. Would not do to get more dirt in the burns. Might fester."

Through the haze of noise around him, he nodded and helped spread the blanket on the ground. Carefully, he wrapped his arms around his father's hips, trying to touch the remnants of his clothing rather than exposed skin, to shift him onto the makeshift bed. A low moan and cry startled him when they set his father down.

"Father?" He crawled in front of him and leaned closer to his beloved face, marred badly by more burns.

"Fitz?"

"Shh, let us get you back to the house. We shall send for the physician. You will be well in no time." His hand reached out to touch his father's face, but paused. He would hurt him if he laid but a finger on him.

"No." His father coughed, wracking his broken body in the worst way. "The burns—too severe." His voice rasped instead of the normal low tone Fitzwilliam had held dear since a small boy.

The palm of his father's hand lay in front of him, surprisingly uninjured, and Fitzwilliam placed his palm on top, the sole comfort he could provide without causing considerable pain.

"You will be well. I promise."

His father's head gave almost an imperceptible shake as he hissed. "Tell Georgiana—love her."

"Father, no."

"Love—you."

"We need you. Georgiana needs you. You cannot." His eyes burned as a sudden dampness trailed down his face.

His father's fingers wrapped around his hand. "Take care . . ."

"Take care?"

His father swallowed and winced with a laboured whimper. No doubt the action pained him greatly. "Take care—Elizabeth. Thomas—" A shuddering breath jerked his father's body, and he was still.

"No!" He grasped his father's burned cheeks, ignoring the angry sores. "Father, wake up!"

"'Tis for the best, sir."

His body went rigid as he looked up. One of the Bradley's neighbours knelt to his father's other side. "Forgive me, but his injuries. He was in terrible pain. Knew a man burnt in a mine fire once—terrible thing, burn scars. Small ones aren't much of a bother, but when they're large, like these, they're a plague on the man who bears them." The man's eyes held Fitzwilliam's without letting go. "'Tis a blessing, this is. May not seem like it now, but it is."

The man wrapped the free end of the blanket around his father, covering him and preserving his dignity. Fitzwilliam lifted his head away from what he would be forced to face later and absorbed his mind in what was occurring in the present. Neighbours and servants all stood in a group. Some watched the blaze as it finished consuming the home while others watched him.

A few men remained stationed near the opposite side of the house with buckets of water at the ready. Nothing could be done for the structure now, but they could not allow the blaze to spread. Fortunately, the autumn had not been a dry one thus far. A solid rain had fallen but two days ago. The fire was unlikely to spread.

"Sir?"

When he turned, several of the footmen stood to his side.

"We came to help when we heard of the fire," said the one in the middle.

"One of the tenants has offered a cart, sir," piped up a voice from the back.

"We thought it would be a good idea to take your father's body to the house." The one in the middle glanced down to the blanket while he spoke. "It does no good to keep it here, and there is little we can do now. Harold offered to sit with the body and lead your father's horse to the stables for you too."

Fitzwilliam swayed for a moment before he blinked and shook himself mentally and nodded. "Thank you." He wiped his cheeks and rose. One of his father's last acts was to give him control of Pemberley. George Darcy had the confidence in his son to run the estate, though Fitzwilliam maintained he desired his father's counsel. Now, he was on his own whether he desired it or not. On his own to care for his tenants and servants, on his own to care for Pemberley, and on his own to raise Georgiana.

The sun had slowly broken over the peaks by the time the fire became small enough to extinguish. They poured buckets of water into the ruins until the last of the glowing coals had blackened, tossed their buckets in a heap, and headed home for some much-needed rest.

Fitzwilliam rode slowly. He was in no way ready to face what awaited him at Pemberley. How would he tell Georgiana that she would never see their father again? Then, there was the matter of his father's body. He could never allow his young sister to see the body—he could never let her say goodbye. With her tender heart, she would have nightmares for months.

The grooms all gave slight bows when they took his horse or passed him in the stable. They expressed their sadness and grief at his father's death. With a numbness he had never known, he shook each of their hands and thanked them before he walked to the house, taking the door through the kitchen so he could address the staff.

"Oh! Mr. Darcy!" Mrs. Reynolds hurried forward, her eyes red and swollen and a handkerchief clutched in her hands. "I am so sorry." She pressed a hand to her chest. "Your father has been taken to his rooms. His valet, though I told him to wait, has insisted on cleaning the body and dressing him in his finest suit.

"Miss Georgiana is still in her rooms. I have instructed her maid to take her time preparing her. As yet, she knows nothing of the fire or your father."

When he peered behind Mrs. Reynolds, maids, footmen, the butler, and those who worked in the kitchen all stood watching. A few had been crying. He took a breath, but when he went to speak, he could not utter a sound. His mouth moved, yet there was nothing.

"Sir," began Cook, who glanced around her before she looked back at him. "We all cared for Mr. Darcy and are greatly saddened by his death. Pray, accept our condolences."

"Thank you." He gripped and released his hands by his sides as he choked out the words. "I should tell my sister. If you will excuse me."

He wound through the staff, shaking hands with many of them before he took the servants' staircase to the family wing. He was covered in soot and filthy, but his sister needed to hear this from him—not discover by chance when she ventured to the dining room or the music room.

When he reached her door, his hand lifted but paused before he knocked. Her maid answered and allowed him inside with her lips pressed into a fine line. Georgiana pivoted on her heel, her eyes lighting when she saw him. "Why, Fitzwilliam, have you been playing in the fireplaces?" She giggled at her own joke until she truly took stock of his face.

She paled and her hands clutched at her stomach. "Fitzwilliam? What, pray tell, has happened?"

# Chapter 9

The carriage drew in front of Pemberley's grand entrance, and the duke alighted before the step could be placed, helping Elizabeth to alight as soon as his feet were both on solid ground. Without pause, they strode through the entrance, hesitating only briefly at the sight of the hatchment hanging upon the door. The duke's lips pressed tight and his bearing stiffened.

The horrid letter came by express rider as they had finished breakfast in their chambers. Her husband had hastened to Elizabeth's room, not bothering to knock before he entered, to demand her dressed and ready to travel immediately. Never had she seen the duke in such a state! Of course, once she knew the reason, she hastened to join him for the short journey to Pemberley. Their servants were to pack and follow them as soon as they were able. Their swift arrival was more important than waiting on their belongings.

Mrs. Reynolds bustled in to greet them while maids took their coats and hats. "Thank goodness!" She shook her head and wrung her hands. "I am so relieved you are here, Your Grace."

"I wish to see my cousin." The duke's voice remained firm, yet not harsh.

Tears pooled in the housekeeper's eyes. "His valet has washed him and clothed him in his finest suit, but pray be warned, sir. 'Tis not a sight anyone should see. The poor man was burned horribly, but at least the child he pulled from the fire was spared, and dear Mr. Darcy did not die in vain."

Her husband closed his eyes and took a deep, shaky breath. "I should like to see him all the same."

The butler stepped forward and gave a slight bow. "Pray, follow me, Your Grace."

As the duke departed, Elizabeth approached Mrs. Reynolds. "I know you are adept at running this house on your own, but should you require my aid, do not hesitate to ask."

"The seamstress in Lambton will come tomorrow," said Mrs. Reynolds, ticking off one item on her fingers, "to measure the young miss for mourning clothes. We have black crepe put away from when Mrs. Darcy passed." After pointing to a second finger, she stopped to dab her eyes with a handkerchief. "If the duke can be of aid in planning the service, then we shall be grateful."

Elizabeth's forehead crinkled and her insides roiled. "What of Fitzwilliam? He might have some desire to plan his father's funeral." She rarely referred to Fitzwilliam as such to the servants, but Mrs. Reynolds had been present to her addressing him so informally before. At the moment, it prevented confusion.

"Oh, ma'am. He has been in a wretched state since this morning. The poor boy came home just covered head to toe in soot. He attempted to address the staff, but he could not manage to utter one word. The words simply would not come to him. Instead, he went directly to Miss Darcy's room and spoke to her. The poor dear went into hysterics. He tried to calm her, but she was simply inconsolable. Fortunately, her maid had the foresight to prepare a draught with laudanum. The young miss has been sleeping ever since."

"What happened to Fitzwilliam?" She could not imagine losing a father. The three of them were also terribly close—closer than many families.

"He allowed his valet to draw him a bath, and he changed into clean clothing. He then disappeared into the library. He has not allowed one person to enter and has not eaten since dinner last night. I do not know if he can manage this.

"The footmen who helped at the fire told me how the young master held his father's hand so carefully while he begged him to live. Forgive me for saying, but I saw the master's body when it was brought in. His death was a blessing. He had to be in excruciating pain."

Elizabeth's hands clutched her stomach while her own vision blurred with tears. This morning, when she learnt of the express, she found it difficult to believe Mr. Darcy was dead. Now, even with Mrs. Reynolds standing before her speaking of it, she still had trouble crediting that he was truly gone. A mere fortnight ago, they all sat in the music room while she and Georgiana played duets and entertained the gentlemen. They had been such a merry party.

Her hands covered her face while she breathed away the urge to cry. She had to remain strong enough for Georgiana and Fitzwilliam. When she composed herself, she grasped the housekeeper's hands. "You said Fitzwilliam is in the library?"

"Yes, ma'am."

Elizabeth drew herself as tall as she could. "Very well, I shall speak to him."

"I believe he has locked the door, ma'am. I could give you my key, but he might not appreciate the intrusion."

"Never you mind. I shall see to it. In the meantime, we shall need to have refreshments at the ready. Nothing too grand and nothing that will spoil quickly. Tonight's dinner should not be much. I do not think many will have an appetite."

"I had the same thought, ma'am. I shall talk to Cook."

As soon as Mrs. Reynolds disappeared into the servants' corridor, Elizabeth proceeded in the direction of the library. She dismissed the footman standing outside the door and glanced in both directions before she pulled a hairpin from her curls and bent it just so. Jacob Lucas had taught her how to pick a lock when she was nine. She hoped she still remembered the particulars.

Three tries failed before the lock gave way with a satisfying click. She carefully lifted the latch and let herself inside, taking care to be as silent as possible.

Fitzwilliam stood in front of the fireplace, staring at the portrait of his father over the mantel. His bearing was hardly the normal proud, tall stature to which she was accustomed. Instead, he swayed in his spot as he raked his fingers through his curls.

Elizabeth silently closed and locked the door behind her. She trod as quietly as she could across the carpet until she stood a mere few steps from him. "Fitzwilliam," she said softly.

When his head turned, his red eyes and almost wild look tore at her heart. His hair stuck out at all angles, no doubt from running his fingers through it numerous times.

"Lizzy." His voice came out in a rush of air. He took two long steps until he stood before her and collapsed against her, drawing her into his arms and sobbing into the crook of her neck. "He is gone. He is gone," he repeated over and over.

Once the shock passed, she wrapped her arms around his shoulders, cradling the back of his head in her hand. "Shh, I know. I am so sorry. I am so, so sorry."

His legs gave way and pulled her to the floor with him since she did not have the strength to hold them both standing. As he continued to cry, she rocked him back and forth. She kissed his hair and his forehead while she murmured and told him all would be well. When he stilled, she paused, realizing his even breaths meant he had fallen asleep.

Elizabeth examined her surroundings and managed to reach a couple of cushions from a nearby chair that she used to prop her back against the stone edge of the unlit fireplace. Her position with Fitzwilliam was not proper, to say the least, but she did not care. She loved him, and he needed her. She would not abandon him there to sleep on the floor alone.

As he slept, his head slowly slid down until it rested upon her breast, his exhales warming the flesh below while his arms remained tightly wrapped around her body. His legs stretched across the floor between hers, pressing her gown to the carpet below. He had to have been exhausted.

She relaxed into the cushions behind her and continued to comb her fingers through his hair while she held him in her embrace and allowed him to sleep. How long had it been since he had really slept? Had someone awakened him during the night due to the fire? Given the time of the message, it was likely.

The clock on the mantel ticked above them and chimed, but she did not keep track how many and how often while the two of them lay there. Eventually, a key rattled in a lock, startling her, but when the door opened, it was only her husband. His eyes met hers, he glanced at Fitzwilliam embraced to her chest, and nodded before he departed.

Her stomach had jumped within her when she saw him but relaxed when he turned and walked away. Why was she surprised? He had offered for her to take a lover if she wished. He had even confessed his original plan for his cousin to seduce her. Why would he care if she comforted the son?

"The young master has fallen asleep on the sofa," said the duke, his voice muffled by the door. "Presently, Her Grace reads a book while she ensures he remains well. You need not fret, Mrs. Reynolds. My wife will see to him for now. I believe we should give Fitzwilliam some privacy and time."

Elizabeth exhaled heavily, relieved that it had been him to enter and not a footman or a maid. If discovered, their position would certainly invite gossip of the worst kind. The key clicked in the lock, ensuring they were blessedly alone for the time being.

He nuzzled into the warmth below him and lifted his head to bury it into the crook of her neck, caressing his lips against that spot where her pulse fluttered against the skin. "I love you," he whispered.

"I love you too."

Those wide doe eyes that had fascinated him from the beginning caught his when he lifted his head. Instead of withdrawing as he should, he found himself drawn closer and closer until their lips met.

What began as a gentle exchange soon turned into more as he opened his mouth and coaxed her lips to follow his lead. She was a little clumsy at first, but he groaned when his tongue dipped in and tasted hers. This was even better than he had ever imagined. Her lips were soft and sweet and clung to his so passionately.

His fingers dug into her sides, anchoring himself, and his need only became greater. He moaned and dragged her atop his lap, pressing her as flush as possible to his body. "Lizzy," he breathed as his lips moved back to her neck.

"Fitzwilliam, we must stop."

He let her voice sink into his brain and ripped himself away, pulling himself against the sofa and standing. "Forgive me. I forgot myself."

That dullness that had slowly disappeared from her eyes during her visit to Pemberley was once again visible to those who looked close enough. The edges of her eyelids were red-rimmed and well . . . sad.

"I believe we both forgot ourselves—though not our true selves. Both of us expressed ourselves honestly for the first time. Do not feel regret for that." She took his hand and slowly rose to her feet. "You should know my husband told Mrs. Reynolds you slept on the sofa while I kept watch."

"He knows?" Why had Thomas not pulled him off and demanded satisfaction? He had his head on his wife's breast for heaven's sake!

"I believe he borrowed Mrs. Reynolds's chatelaine to ensure you were well."

"I must apologise to him," he said as he closed his eyes and covered his face with his hands. "God help me. What would my father say?"

She surprised him by grabbing his wrists and pulling his hands away. "You owe your cousin no apology, for he will not care. Our marriage is of a peculiar nature. While it may sound odd, I daresay he would be pleased that you took comfort from me."

His chin hitched back a bit. "You make no sense."

"I shall explain when we do not have other matters to address. Mrs. Reynolds expressed the need for my husband to message the vicar for your father's service. Should you wish to handle matters, you may want to make that desire known. There is also the matter of your sister. She will need you when she awakens."

He blinked away the sting of tears. "I cannot do this."

"You can and you will, Fitzwilliam." Her hands wrapped around his forearms. "The people of this estate need you, your sister needs you, and we need you to be well. Your father would not want you to despair. He trusted you with your sister as well as Pemberley."

"He wanted me to have time to make decisions while he ensured I did not fail." He needed his father still. He could not do this on his own!

Elizabeth shifted closer and cradled his face in her hands. "No, he had confidence in you but knew you required time to have confidence in yourself. Do not doubt yourself. He had faith in you."

"She is correct."

His head shot back from her hands, and he clenched his fists at his sides. "Forgive me, Thomas. I had not meant—"

"Stop, Fitzwilliam. My wife and I have no romantic attachment. She is free to do as she likes as long as she is discreet."

His eyes lifted to Thomas's and then darted to Elizabeth's. They could not be serious!

"But that is not important at this moment. I simply do not want you to flog yourself when you have done nothing to deserve it." His cousin pressed both hands upon his shoulders as Elizabeth shifted back. "Your father had every faith in you. He and I discussed how well you would do when this time came. When his father died, George had no experience running Pemberley on his own. He wanted precisely what Elizabeth said: for you to gain confidence in yourself before he died. Only God had other ideas."

How could he not believe his godfather? His eyes lifted to the portrait of his father over the mantel then searched the face before him.

"Should you not believe me, I know your father left a letter for you with his important papers. He also left one for Georgiana. I daresay those should be of great comfort during this time. Elizabeth and I shall remain at Pemberley for as long as you have need of us. After, I hope you will come with us to Worthstone for a while. It might do you good to be away. The harvest will be done."

"What of your own harvest?"

"My steward is more than capable. If he has need of me, I am not even a day's carriage ride away. After all, what is fifty miles of good road?"

"Thank you." He took one last long look at the portrait and gulped down that lump he could not seem to be rid of. "I should find those documents and letters. Have you notified the vicar at Kympton?"

Thomas shook his head and cleared his throat. "I have spent the afternoon with George. It may sound nonsensical, but I had a great many things I needed to say. He excelled at listening to them all." He coughed again and tugged at his cravat as though it choked him. "I confess I am glad Mrs. Reynolds warned me. I hope you do not let Georgiana say goodbye in person. She should not see her father in that state."

He shook his head. "No, I fear it would do more harm than good."

"I agree."

"Should *she* not be allowed to decide?" Elizabeth stood so straight she could have had a board strapped to her back. "She is not a small child."

"Lizzy, even you should not see," said Fitzwilliam softly. "My father was terribly burned—even his face."

She glanced back and forth between them before she walked through the door and towards the stairs. What was she doing? He made to catch her, but Thomas grabbed his arm as he followed. "Let her. She will see. My wife is no weakling. She can manage better than most of her sex."

They had not needed to rush since a footman kept her from entering. Upon Fitzwilliam's word, the man allowed her into the master's bedchamber with him and Thomas trailing behind. She marched inside and straight up to the bed, gasping and covering her mouth as soon as her eyes set upon the form on the coverlet.

A sob rent from her throat and Fitzwilliam grabbed her when she turned and held her to his chest. "Do you agree with us?"

Her head bobbed up and down under his chin. "Forgive me. I am but a silly girl."

"You love Georgiana and Fitzwilliam," said her husband. "Your compassion does you credit. Pray do not think yourself silly for wanting what is best for them."

"How much of him is so badly burned?" Her eyes searched Fitzwilliam's, and he could not lie. He also needed to speak of it. He needed to say it to someone.

"The entirety of his back and the backs of his legs," he said. "He held the boy in a blanket in his arms, protecting him from the blaze, which kept his chest from burning. I believe he had the unblemished side of his face against the blanket."

"He saved the boy, Elizabeth." Thomas clasped his hands behind his back. "George would have that be the most important consideration."

A knock came from the door, and Elizabeth backed from his arms.

"Yes!"

"I beg your pardon, sir, but Miss Darcy is awake."

Elizabeth placed a hand on both of their forearms. "I shall go to her. I told Mrs. Reynolds not to have a large dinner for this evening. I feared none of us would have much of an appetite."

"I agree." Fitzwilliam still had that dry knot in his throat that he could not seem to swallow or purge. He doubted he could eat much without casting his accounts.

"We shall also have callers and those who come to the funeral. I instructed that refreshments be ready for when callers arrive."

"Thank you," he said. "You will help keep Georgiana from this room?"

Elizabeth's eyes darted back to his father. "Yes. Your father would not want her to remember him this way. Perhaps we shall call on the family whose child he saved. That might also be a way to reconcile her feelings. She can also visit the headstone once he is buried."

"I want him interred in the church at Kympton with my mother."

Her hand squeezed his arm. "I am certain he would like that."

She hurried out, leaving him with her husband—his cousin and godfather. What did Thomas think of him? Despite Elizabeth's reassurances, Thomas could not be so indifferent towards his wife, could he?

"In regards to the incident in the library, you are truly not angry with me?"

One side of Thomas's lips curved. "No, I am not. Now, let us go find that letter and your father's paperwork. Have you messaged everyone in the family—Lord and Lady Matlock and Lady Catherine?"

Fitzwilliam started towards the study. "I sent an express to my uncle when I penned one to you. I have not sent any notice to my aunt as of yet."

"Thank goodness," said Thomas. "We shall need to do so this evening, then we shall have to be prepared. Once she knows, she will spare no time in arriving and demanding her own way. You will have to stand your ground against her. She is a formidable woman, but do not give her manipulations any credence."

"My father always expected her to demand I wed Anne."

"I expect the same. Do not be surprised if she drags that sickly child here as well to carry her point. I also would not put it past her to demand Georgiana live with her."

He stopped in his tracks while his body went rigid. "She will not take Georgiana. My sister remains with me."

"Good. You will need to maintain that strength of determination with her. Do not worry. I shall be with you. We shall not let her have her way."

# Chapter 10

*August 11*<sup>*th*</sup> *1809*
*Doves House*
*London*

*My dear friend,*

*As I write this, word circles London of Mr. George Darcy's tragic demise. My husband has penned a letter to the son expressing our condolences, yet as I am sure you and your husband are providing whatever aid the Darcys require. Pray ensure they know we are pleased to be of aid in whatever manner they require. Mr. Darcy was such a fine gentleman. His loss will be keenly felt by all who knew him.*

*I was delighted to receive your letter a few days ago, though by the date, the delivery was quite delayed. I am certain Miss Geddes will be happy to paint your portrait. I have dispatched a letter to her in Salisbury to ascertain whether she can travel to Worthstone for the work, or whether she would prefer to paint in London when you are here next. Since she is still rather young, I am unsure of her father's decision. I shall certainly be bursting to tell you as soon as I receive her next correspondence.*

*Please stay well, dear friend. Your last missive felt more melancholy than I would expect for one with your lively disposition. I am sure you grieve for your friends, yet such gloom is unlike you. Perhaps one of the Bard's comedies might lift your spirits?*

*Yours,*

*Lady Laura Vranes*

Elizabeth sighed and folded the letter. She would need to pay better heed on her next correspondence to Laura. While she adored the countess's open nature, which was so unlike most of the *ton*, she had no wish for her friend to suspect anything amiss. She could certainly never explain the true reason for her melancholy, which extended beyond Mr. Darcy's death.

*August 13<sup>th</sup> 1809*
*Longbourn*
*Hertfordshire*

*My dearest Lizzy,*

*I could not help but cry at the contents of your latest letter. Poor Mr. Darcy! He was too good to run into that burning house and save that child! Thank heavens he saved the dear boy, yet the price he paid was so severe. My heart simply breaks for Mr. Darcy and Miss Darcy. I hope his son and daughter can find peace in that their father did indeed provide the family with an invaluable service. He was a tremendous blessing to them in their time of need.*

*As you requested, I have tasked Papa with penning you a letter. Do remember he has always been a dilatory correspondent, though two months without a letter is poor—even for him. He is well, though has hidden more than his wont in his library due to Mama's overactive nerves.*

*Forgive me for such a short letter, but Mama has been beside herself with preparations for tonight's assembly. The new occupant of Netherfield, a Mr. Price, is to bring his brother this evening. Mama was put out to discover Mr. Price married and has decided his brother must be a bachelor of good fortune and connections. Nothing has been said to indicate he is so, yet she has decreed it, so it must be. Wish me well. She is determined I shall be the most beautiful at the assembly. After all, he must be in want of a wife! I believe she has already called for her salts three times this morning.*

*Affectionately yours,*

*Jane*

"Oh, Mama," she said on an exhale.

"Trouble from home?"

She glanced up from folding her letter. Fitzwilliam stood a short distance away. This bench near the river had been her refuge since their arrival at Pemberley, and as she had nearly every day, she walked downstream until the footbridge where she crossed. The bench had such a lovely view of the river, the bridge, and the great house off in the distance. The sound of the water as it passed along its banks soothed her as little else did these days.

"No, Jane writes of the assembly. My mother's dearest wish is for her daughters to be well-married, of course. A new gentleman arrived in the neighbourhood, and Mama was in a state, you see."

One side of his lips curved. "So she is not unlike the matchmaking mamas of the *ton*?"

"No," she said with a sigh. "I believe she is just as tenacious." She shifted to one side of the seat. "Would you care to sit with me?"

He took the place beside her and angled to face her. He removed his hat and set it between them. "We have been so busy since your arrival."

"We have. Georgiana fares better, I believe. She is with her governess this morning."

"You have taken wonderful care of her. I cannot express my gratitude enough."

She shook her head while she ran her finger along the edge of her letter. It was so difficult to hold his eye. "You need not thank me. She is a dear, sweet girl. I am happy to be her confidante."

His eyebrows furrowed, and he cleared his throat. "That first day in the library. Would you tell me what you and Thomas meant? About your marriage?"

A lingering exhale trickled from her lips. She had known this would come, but though she had done nothing wrong, the conversation would not be a simple one. "'Tis not an easy tale."

"I am at your leisure."

She tucked her correspondence in her reticule. "I suppose I should start with how I met your cousin, for I do not know how to explain it any other way."

At the dip of Fitzwilliam's chin, she took a deep breath. "I first met your cousin when he came to the great house at Stoke. He had travelled to Hertfordshire to assess the property and implement any changes required to its upkeep. At my mother's insistence, my father called on him, and he called on us in return.

"My mother was beside herself to have a duke in the neighbourhood, and not just a duke, but a bachelor at that. She pushed Jane to make herself agreeable, but much to Mama's vexation, your cousin singled me out instead. He called several times during his stay, and we discussed books, plays, and even politics. After approximately a month, he requested to take a turn in the gardens with me. While we walked, he offered me his hand in marriage."

Fitzwilliam's eyes never left her, making her stomach flutter, and her knees quiver—despite the topic of their discourse.

"I told him I was honoured by his proposal, but I did not love him. He spoke to my father and departed for London."

"You were forced by your father?"

"No," she said with a slight shake of her head. "We discussed the duke's offer—the settlement he intended to bestow upon not only me, but also upon my sisters. Papa, however, informed me he would stand by my decision. The problem was my mother discovered the duke's proposal—quite by accident, you see. She heard me speaking of it with my sister Jane."

His eyes closed, and he breathed out evenly.

"After, I never had a moment's peace. I went to my father and told him I would accept the duke's offer, but only if my sisters could marry the men of their choosing. I did not want them forced by Mama.

"I thought it would be as any other marriage, yet on my wedding night, the duke came to my bedchamber, he kissed my cheek, he embraced me, and wished me goodnight."

Fitzwilliam's shoulders pulled back as his forehead crinkled. "You mean he did not . . .?"

"No, he did not. I did not understand that would be the constant of our marriage until our carriage ride to Pemberley in early July when I finally gathered enough courage to ask him. He merely explained he could not, which I did not understand."

"But why take a wife?"

"Why indeed?" Elizabeth watched her fingers while she passed one thumbnail over the end of the other, making a sound. "He intended and still does intend for me to carry an heir."

"But how if he cannot?" Fitzwilliam leaned toward her.

"He confessed that as well. He requested your father seduce me. Your father refused."

Fitzwilliam shot from the bench and gave an incredulous bark before turning. "I am not surprised he refused, though I am astounded by Thomas's audacity to make the request. What has he intended since my father would not accede to his wishes?"

"He has offered that I might take a lover, yet requested I be discreet and choose well. I am not to bed a footman or a stable boy." She could not help the venom that crept into her tone. "I believe you to be his new object—if you were not before."

He clasped his hands behind his back and stared at the grass beneath his feet. "Has that been your object? Have you intended to have me fall in love with you? Manipulate me to father your child?"

She should have been furious, but considering the betrayal he must feel at his cousin's plan, she could not blame him for asking. "No. When I realised I was falling in love with you, I assumed I only risked my own heart by not distancing myself. I had no idea your feelings ran along the same vein until you kissed me in the library." She relived those few moments of bliss at every free and solitary moment. How she wished they could be together, but how could she commit Fitzwilliam to a hopeless relationship? He would require his own heir one day. He deserved to have his own family. "I do want a child, but I shall not seduce you. I fear if we gave in, it would make our situation all the more hopeless.

"I know Thomas's nephew is dissolute and owes a substantial fortune."

"Yes, and creditors have extended him further funds as a result of his inheritance. Your uncle intends to leave the bulk of his estate to you. The only part which will pass to James is those properties associated with the dukedom and the title. Your cousin refuses to see what he has worked so hard to build and maintain lost at the gaming tables."

His arms swung forward and clapped in front of him while he began to pace. "How did I not see this in Thomas? He has always been like a close uncle."

"I believe your father was one of the few who knew my husband's secrets."

Fitzwilliam halted mid-stride and pivoted to face her. "Please do not call him your husband. Call him Thomas or the duke, though I do not understand why you would show him such deference. He has done little to earn your respect."

"He is in a difficult situation few would understand."

"Do you?" he asked, his voice raised.

"No, but his preferred lifestyle would bring him ridicule, scorn, not to mention death. He has done well to hide it from society for as long as he has."

"My God," he said on an exhale. "You cannot be in earnest."

"Without knocking, I entered his room when Georgiana and I caught Wickham stealing. I witnessed him and his valet in an embrace. He has confirmed it. I ensured Georgiana and Wickham did not see."

He ran his hand along his mouth. "You can never tell anyone but me of this knowledge. Do you understand?"

"I have only told you. I am only revealing the full truth to you. I also believe your father would desire you to know. He would not want you to underestimate Thomas or his scheming."

"My father mentioned Thomas *and* you before he died. If you had not told me of my cousin's machinations, I would have thought my father meant something drastically different."

She lifted her head and squinted into the sun to see him. "What did your father say?"

"To 'take care.' Then he said your name and Thomas's name."

Elizabeth stood and walked to the bank of the river. "He was pleased to find you in my arms the day of our arrival."

He pulled a leather box from his coat pocket and held it before him. "Thomas mentioned your birthday was a few days ago. Georgiana should have at least had a special dinner for you on the day, but she has planned one for this evening. I wished to give you this now."

She stared at the box with her heart screaming to snatch it like a gooseberry tart—her favourite. "I should not."

"I asked Thomas. He does not mind."

With hesitant fingers, she took the gift, which if she had to judge by the case, was jewellery. She unfastened the latch and lifted the lid, gasping at the flat cut, deep red stone surrounded by pearls and accented on the outer row by smaller deep red stones.

"'Tis beautiful. They are garnets, are they not?"

"Yes, I noticed it this summer while shopping for Georgiana's birthday. I cannot explain why I purchased it for you then. I knew I could not give it to you, but I thought of you. You have such beautiful skin. I believed the colour would be striking against your throat."

When she lifted the pendant, it hung on a simple gold chain, simple enough that she could wear it for every day if she wished. She arranged the chain back in the box and placed it on the bench while she unfastened her own necklace. They could not be together, but she could wear his gift—she *would* wear his gift.

She pulled the new necklace and went to clasp it around her neck.

"Allow me to help you." His warm fingers were a shock as they brushed the sensitive skin on the back of her neck, peppering little pebbles of gooseflesh down her spine. What she would not give to feel his lips caress her shoulder—but she would never ask it of him. They tread on shaky ground as it was.

"Thank you," she said, blinking rapidly as she turned to face him. "I adore it. I shall wear it every day."

His hands gripped and released. "I am glad." He looked into the trees before his eyes met hers again. "You have not ridden since your return."

"Georgiana has not felt equal to riding. Even if you were not busy, I thought our rides may no longer be a good idea."

He stepped closer and trailed a finger along the top of her hand. "I have missed our outings. While we should not, would you ride with me on the morrow? I may not be able to court you as I would like, but I would be loath to lose our one guilty pleasure."

"Yes, I shall ride with you."

"Sir!"

Fitzwilliam stepped back quickly and slipped his arms behind his back. "Yes?"

The footman slowed from his run as he approached. "Sir, Lady Catherine de Bourgh has arrived. She has ordered Miss Darcy's trunks packed and loaded atop her carriage. As I left, His Grace had intervened, but Mrs. Reynolds insisted you be notified."

"Thank you, James." He glanced back at Elizabeth and held out his arm. "We should return quickly. I hope Georgiana remains with her governess in her sitting room, but if she does not, then she will be overwrought. My aunt has a way of discomposing my sister in the worst possible way."

Elizabeth hurried, needing to take two to three steps to equal his one long stride so they would arrive at the house before Lady Catherine did too much damage. When they entered the hall, a woman bedecked in a gown dripping in lace that would make Elizabeth's mother envious stood imperiously tall before the duke, one arm outstretched and the other with her cane pressed firmly to the ground. "You have no authority over Georgiana! I demand you produce her immediately!"

"I, however, do have authority over my sister." Fitzwilliam's voice filled the large room, and his tone brooked no argument, though from what Elizabeth had heard of Lady Catherine, the woman would still make the attempt.

"Fitzwilliam! I am not accustomed to waiting, yet I have been here nigh on a half hour before you greet me. Shameful!" She sniffed and placed her free hand atop her cane so both rested upon the silver handle. "I have come for your sister. She will require a woman's guidance and a lady's example, which she will find at Rosings with myself and Anne."

"She requires her brother at this time," said her husband through his teeth.

Fitzwilliam stepped forward so he was slightly in front of the duke. "If Georgiana has need of a lady's example, she has the Duchess of Leeds nearby. She has no need to live at Rosings."

"The Duchess of Leeds!" Her exclamation echoed off the walls and made a servant about to step through the entrance, hurry back from whence he came. "I have heard of that upstart your cousin wed, or I should call her a harlot! You would expose Georgiana to the worst sort imaginable!"

"You speak of my wife when you know naught of her." The duke drew Elizabeth from behind Fitzwilliam, though she resisted. She had no desire to meet Lady Catherine, much less be brought to her notice. "Elizabeth's intelligence and *compassion* do her credit. You would do well to learn from her example. After all, compassion and empathy have never been traits at which you excelled."

The woman puffed up like a bird and spluttered. "I am celebrated for my compassion!" Elizabeth pressed her lips together to keep from laughing. She had to agree with her husband. The lady likely showed little empathy for anyone but herself.

Fitzwilliam crossed his arms over his chest. "Have you any other object in coming other than retrieving Georgiana?"

"I am certain you require my counsel now that your father is gone. Pemberley will require a strong hand. I can help you. We also need to finalise your betrothal to Anne."

"I am not marrying Anne." His words were calm and measured.

"You will!" She pounded her cane against the floor. "The two of you have been formed for each other. It was the dearest wish of your mother."

"It was not her wish at all." The duke laughed derisively and shook his head. "I thought you might attempt to manipulate Fitzwilliam with the memory of his mother. You forget, Lady Catherine, that I knew Anne Darcy. I know the wishes she held for his marriage. Your spoilt, selfish daughter was never a consideration. By the way, where is Anne? Have you left her in the carriage to overheat?"

Lady Catherine pursed her lips. "Where is Georgiana?" Her voice again boomed through the Great Hall. "She will be brought to me now—or have you dumped her in some godforsaken seminary?"

"My father stipulated Carlisle and myself as Georgiana's guardians, Lady Catherine. You cannot remove her from Pemberley." Fitzwilliam stepped forward so he towered over his aunt and stared her down. "If you do, I shall see you arrested for kidnapping."

Spittle gurgled as she sucked air through her teeth. "How dare you! I shall speak to Carlisle. He will be made to see sense. Georgiana should be removed from such unsavoury influences. I assure you I shall carry my point!"

Elizabeth backed slowly away in the hopes of going unnoticed while she watched the exchange. When she could peer through the front door, two silhouettes could be discerned through the shadow from the huge coach just outside.

"I would not count on that," said Fitzwilliam. "Lady Matlock and the duchess are friends. My aunt thinks very highly of Her Grace, and I know Carlisle is of the same opinion. I doubt your arguments shall persuade either of them to see the matter differently."

His aunt sniffed and pulled back her shoulders. "Anne and I will require our usual rooms for the night."

Fitzwilliam's gaze flitted to the duke's before he turned his attention back to Lady Catherine. Fitzwilliam held out an arm towards the door. "I shall be happy to direct your driver to the inn in Lambton. I hear it is comfortable, and you will be well taken care of."

"An inn? I have a bedchamber here, and I intend to use it!"

When Elizabeth glanced up the stairs, a movement from behind a column drew her eye, and she started up the staircase, hoping her departure would go unnoticed and unmentioned.

"You forget, aunt. This is my home, and I will not have you upsetting Georgiana. This week has been more than she should have had to endure at so young an age. I will not subject her to your vitriol and ridiculous applications. You will render her overwrought. Until you can treat my family with the respect they are due and abide by my wishes, you will not be welcome at Pemberley."

"I have never been treated thus! And in my sister's home!" Another loud rap reverberated off the walls. Someone should take that ridiculous walking stick from her! "And where is that upstart going? She has not taken her leave of me!"

"As she did not request an introduction, she has no reason to speak to you," said the duke.

At Thomas's statement, Elizabeth glanced behind her. Lady Catherine had puffed up larger than Mr. Goulding's prize rooster. "Request an introduction! *I* would be the one to notice *her*."

The duke's low laugh made Elizabeth's insides clench. She had never heard it so cold.

"You forget, *Lady* Catherine, that Her Grace, the Duchess of Leeds, outranks you. Your husband was a baronet, was he not?"

Elizabeth had slowed when the woman mentioned her leaving, but now, continued to tiptoe up the stairs carefully, eyes still glued to the spectacle behind her. Lady Catherine faced the duke, gaping, her complexion the colour of puce. Elizabeth turned to the steps in front of her, hastened to the top, and grabbed Georgiana's arm, dragging her down the corridor. "You should be in your rooms."

"I heard my aunt. Will I be made to live at Rosings?" The poor girl shook from head to toe, and her eyes were about to burst from their sockets.

"No, your brother and your cousins will never allow it. There are too many peers of rank to challenge her claim—not that she carries any claim whatsoever. Your brother does not want you upset, nor does he want your aunt to see you. I would not put it past her to attempt to physically remove you. He can better protect you if you remain locked within your bedchamber."

"You will notify me when she is gone?" Georgiana's wide eyes tugged at Elizabeth's heart. The dear was truly terrified of her aunt, who seemed a great deal of bluster and wind rather than actual action.

"Yes, of course. Have you completed your studies for the day?"

"Yes, we finished just before you found me."

Elizabeth squeezed the girl's hand. "Then read a book until one of us comes for you."

The door clicked and the key turned in the lock after Elizabeth closed it behind her. The noise from the hall had diminished, yet she still peered around the corner before she continued down the stairs.

Voices came from outside, but instead of venturing to the portico, she shifted so she could see through the door. Two footmen stood on either side of Lady Catherine while she protested vehemently at being stuffed back into her coach. The duke held her walking stick. Had she finally attempted to bludgeon someone with it?

Once the coach pulled away, the men returned inside, Fitzwilliam striding with more purpose than her husband. "What occurred to make you leave?" His voice had not lost its hard edge from the encounter with his aunt, but Elizabeth ignored it. His tone was not aimed at her.

"Georgiana hid behind a column at the top of the stairs. I hastened her back to her rooms and bid her to engage the lock. She is petrified of her aunt and being made to live at Rosings."

Fitzwilliam closed his eyes and scrubbed his face before lifting it to her. "I should speak to her. Thank you for your help." He nodded to Elizabeth and shook the duke's hand. "Both of you. I am uncertain if I could have dealt with my aunt on my own."

"You could have," said Elizabeth, holding his eye. "You care too much for your sister to allow Lady Catherine's destructive influence in her life. Do not doubt your ability to protect her."

He nodded once more. "Thank you."

Her husband placed a hand to Fitzwilliam's shoulder. "Do not thank us for something we are happy to do. Your father was a brother to me much as Carlisle is a brother to you. I would do anything to be of aid to his children."

Elizabeth bit her tongue. He would be of aid to George Darcy's children, yet it did not stop him from having his own intentions. He might not be pushing as Lady Catherine was, yet why did he not consider that his deceptions could be just as damaging?

# Chapter 11

*September 1ˢᵗ 1809*
*Worthstone*
*Derbyshire*
*Dearest Jane,*

*Though we intended to remain at Pemberley until the end of the harvest, important business called Mr. Darcy to London. My husband accompanied him in the event his assistance was required while Georgiana returned to Worthstone with me. While we would have been content to remain at Pemberley, we preferred not to chance another encounter with Lady Catherine without my husband or Mr. Darcy present. I have no legal claim to Georgiana, and the poor dear would be overrun in Lady Catherine's charge. The woman has the softness and tact of an elephant, like the one I saw at the Royal Menagerie.*

*I was pleased to receive your last letter, though I must shake my head at Mama. I am certain her nerves were in a right state after discovering the brother was married as well. A giggle unlike what I had not uttered in years escaped me upon reading your description of my mother's antics, though I felt your embarrassment at her behaviour just as acutely. Unfortunately, I fear she will never be what we wish in that respect. We can only hope time and her daughters' marriages might temper her enthusiasm for a single man of good fortune.*

*We have but a few short months until the duke and I return to London for the Season. I anticipate having you join us for the balls and dinners. A respite from Mama is surely what you require after these trying weeks, though we shall not participate much until the height of the Season because my husband wishes to have a longer mourning period out of deference for his cousin. If he did not have to return for Parliament in January, we would probably remain at Worthstone instead of partaking of the Season.*

*Please hug Papa for me. I shall write to Mama at my next opportunity and post the letters together, so she will not feel left out.*

*Yours most truly,*

*Lizzy*

Elizabeth set down her pen and sanded the paper, peering out the window while she gave the sand a moment to work its magic.

A light rain fell and a lingering fog made for a dreary day, the resulting chill making it necessary to light fires to warm the house as well as ward off the damp in the air. The sombre chords of the pianoforte in the music room almost pounded through the nooks and crannies of the house, creating an even gloomier atmosphere. She had hoped to persuade Georgiana to play less mournful music but had no success in the endeavour thus far.

Fitzwilliam confessed before his departure that his father had arranged for Georgiana to attend school that autumn near London where she would enjoy the benefits of masters and friendships with other girls her own age. Mourning put a swift end to that endeavour. School would now wait for a year, though that did not upset Georgiana or Elizabeth too much. Instead, they both took great delight in the time they would have together.

She poured the sand from her letter, folded it, and sealed it. After she penned the direction, she set it to the corner of her escritoire before she gazed once more out of the window.

A shadow appeared in the distant fog, making her blink and look again. Two minutes later, a carriage emerged from the soup and continued steadily toward the house. The equipage resembled the one her husband and Fitzwilliam had taken to London. Could they have returned so soon? They were not expected for another week.

Elizabeth practically ran headlong into the housekeeper as she hurried from the room.

"You have seen the carriage, Your Grace?"

"I have, but do you think it the duke? Could he have returned so swiftly?"

"None would make calls in this weather, ma'am. I have ordered fires lit in his room as well as a guest room for Mr. Darcy. Bathwater is being warmed, and Mrs. Bunting has some fish as well as potatoes she has added to the menu for dinner."

"Very good," said Elizabeth clasping her hands in front of her. She had no reason to fret. Worthstone's housekeeper was adept at running the large home on her own. She usually had all sorted before she met with Elizabeth every morning. In some instances, she appreciated the initiative more than in others.

"Is that a carriage?"

She whipped around to Georgiana, who poked her head through the door to the music room. "Yes, we believe your brother and cousin have returned early."

A rare smile—these days anyway—burst across the girl's face. "Fitzwilliam!"

The butler strode forward to the door, opening it as the carriage drew in front of the house. In a flurry of activity, the duke and Fitzwilliam entered, shedding greatcoats and hats as soon as they stepped across the threshold.

"Fitzwilliam!" Georgiana swept forward and embraced her brother while Elizabeth curtseyed to the men, clenching her hands to prevent herself from rushing into Fitzwilliam's arms as well.

"I am glad to see you too, Sweetling." He held his sister for a few moments, his eyes closed, obviously savouring the moment. "My business took less time than anticipated, and we hurried back to Derbyshire as swiftly as we could."

His eyes met Elizabeth's over Georgiana's head and held until she coughed and diverted her attention to the duke. "Fires have been lit in your rooms and bathwater is being readied. I am certain both of you would care to warm yourselves after travelling on a day with such a chill in the air. Dinner is to be served in an hour."

"Wonderful," said her husband. "I am famished, but I shall wait until dinner. I am certain whatever you have planned with Mrs. Bunting is worth the wait." Georgiana withdrew from her brother and embraced her cousin.

Elizabeth worked to smile while everything in her pulled her towards Fitzwilliam. Why was this so difficult? Why did she love a man she could not have? Why did her heart persist in this useless infatuation? "Pray refresh yourselves. It would not do for either of you to take ill."

Fitzwilliam paused while he watched her for a moment, but she held a hand towards the stairs. "It is good to have you at Worthstone."

He smiled softly. "'Tis good to be here."

After one last tug to his topcoat, Fitzwilliam dismissed his valet and made his way to the library. The entire ride from London, he had anticipated seeing Elizabeth more than anything. Of course, he had looked forward to seeing his sister again, yet his heart had yearned for what he desired most.

He entered the library and locked the door behind him. Elizabeth stood at the window across the room, staring into the fog, which had grown thicker since his arrival. She no longer wore her day gown, but her complexion glowed in the pale grey gown that stood out in stark relief to the darkness outside.

With careful steps, he approached her from behind. "Lizzy," he said in a low tone, making her whip around to face him.

"You startled me."

"I wanted to surprise you." His lips tugged upwards. His fingers inched forward eager to barely graze hers. "I have missed you so much."

"I have longed for you as well," she said on an exhale.

At her confession, he took her hand, entwining his fingers with hers. "You wanted to embrace me much as Georgiana did when we arrived, did you not? You had this look in your eyes. It took all I had not to pull you into my arms."

"I did. We must curb this, yet I do not know how." Her fingers rubbed at the pendant around her neck—his pendant. Why did that make him want to hold her closer? He wanted to carry her away where he never had to share her with anyone, much less his cousin.

"I feel the same. I have no desire to stay away from you, yet 'tis what is right." His free hand rested upon her cheek, his thumb caressing her temple. He pressed his forehead to hers and sighed. "We are two lost souls—lost to each other."

She bestowed a kiss to his palm. "We did well to stay away from each other at Pemberley."

"Except for our rides," he said. "This was much simpler when I thought you felt naught for me but friendship. I should never have kissed you. Told you how I felt."

Tears welled along her lower eyelashes, making him physically hurt. He never wanted her to feel such sadness. He desired nothing more than to see her happy and smiling all of the time. "I could say the same, but I have not felt so alone since your confession. I know it is selfish—"

He shook his head while his forehead remained touching hers. "No, I believe I understand, but my cousin was selfish in his marrying you."

A pathetic smile crossed her lips. "If I had not married him, I would never have met you. We would have led quite disparate lives."

He almost could not breathe at the idea of never knowing her. Since his father's death, Elizabeth and his sister were the only people who made him *feel*. When he was not in their company, he was numb. The sensation was not one he enjoyed.

No matter how much his heart screamed to kiss her, he removed his hand from her face and stepped back, attempting to ignore the pain that stabbed him in the chest at the separation. "I should go before someone discovers the door is locked."

"Fitzwilliam?" She stepped forward and held his one hand with both of hers.

"We should not. We need to try to ignore this, no matter how difficult. Do you not think?"

"I do, but I never fathomed how unbearable that would be until now. The longer I know you, the further I fall and the more desperate I become. 'Tis so strange. I lived for eighteen years without you, but I now cannot imagine my life without you, though I know I must."

His eyes blinked furiously to eliminate the sting her words caused. She had the same thoughts and feelings he did; however, they should not—they could not. "I shall always be your friend. You will never truly be without me."

He brought her hands to his lips before he tore himself away, slipping out after he had checked to ensure no one lingered in the corridor. He had been alone with Elizabeth before, but he had never locked the door. Instead, it had always been wide open. He did not want any questions or rumours filtering through her household staff.

After knocking on the door of Thomas's study, his cousin bid him enter. "I must thank you again for accompanying me. I would never have completed the business with my father's solicitor so swiftly without you."

Thomas rose and pointed to the decanters of brandy and port on a nearby table. "Would you care for a glass?"

"Yes, brandy, thank you."

He took a sip of the fine brandy Thomas handed him. "I need to return to Pemberley on the morrow."

His cousin's eyebrows drew to the centre with his frown. "I wish you would stay for at least a week or two. You and Georgiana can rest before you journey home."

Fitzwilliam nodded and sat in the chair in front of Thomas's desk. "I would not mind, but I should return. Georgiana and I need to face Pemberley on our own eventually. We cannot flee our reality forever." He could not really say why he needed to leave Worthstone—especially now that he knew the entire truth.

"You have hardly avoided your present situation."

"No," he said crossing an ankle over his knee, "and I admit that being with Lizzy has helped Georgiana immensely."

Thomas walked around his desk and patted Fitzwilliam on the shoulder. "Think about it tonight. You might feel differently in the morning."

If only Thomas knew how he really felt! He would be happy to stay and be with Elizabeth forever, but would his heart survive it?

"Come, I am sure the ladies await us in the drawing room by now."

When they joined Elizabeth and Georgiana, Thomas poured a glass of wine and handed it to Elizabeth. "I assume nothing of import occurred while I was gone?"

She took a sip and arched that darned eyebrow that made Fitzwilliam want to kiss that smug look from her face. "No, your steward never required my aid, and I saw nothing of note when I walked the grounds."

"That is a relief," said Thomas with a smile and a lift of his glass.

"I beg your pardon." The housekeeper stood in the doorway. "Dinner is served."

"Thank you," said Elizabeth as she stood. When she reached her feet, she was a bit unsteady before gaining her footing.

Thomas offered Georgiana his arm, so Fitzwilliam approached Elizabeth. "Shall we?"

Her small hand fit perfectly into the crook of his arm. He ignored the fact he could feel her touch so acutely through his fine lawn shirt and his topcoat. It practically felt as though nothing stood between the gentle way her fingers rested upon his sleeve, but he could not continue to dwell on that. He saw her to her chair before he took his own.

Once the first course was served, Thomas smiled. "I was just telling Georgiana how I hoped the two of you would remain with us longer."

His sister paused with her utensils over her plate. "I would dearly love to visit more with Lizzy."

Elizabeth took a drink from her glass and set it on the table. "I would dearly love more time with you, dearest, but how long you remain is the decision of your brother."

Thomas perked up and looked between all of them. "I have a wonderful idea. We should spend Christmas together. If you do not plan on venturing to London, Elizabeth and I would be pleased to join you at Pemberley. We should be a merry party."

"Oh, yes!" Georgiana turned to him. "Can we? It would be so nice to have someone since Papa shall not be there."

Fitzwilliam nodded and glanced back to Elizabeth who took another swallow of wine. "Christmas at Pemberley sounds lovely," she said. She brought the glass back to her lips and his hands stilled over his plate. No sooner had she set the glass on the table than Thomas motioned to the butler to fill it.

For the remainder of the meal, Georgiana and Thomas carried the conversation with only occasional bursts of input from him and Elizabeth. By the time they stood so the ladies could withdraw, Fitzwilliam could have repeated very little of what was discussed. He had spent too much time watching Elizabeth drink wine as though she were drinking tea at a party.

When she stepped towards the door, she swayed, so with a hand to her elbow, he steadied her. "You must be exhausted, Lizzy."

She pressed her palm to her forehead and frowned. "I suppose I am. Pray forgive me, Georgiana, but I believe I should retire."

"Oh! I should be pleased to walk you to your chambers. I believe I should prefer to retire early as well." She kissed Fitzwilliam on the cheek. "Good night, Brother."

The smile he forced tightened his face. "Good night."

He and Thomas escorted the ladies into the hall and watched them ascend the stairs. Elizabeth did not take the steps with her usual vigour but held the railing until she reached the top. Her other arm was wrapped through Georgiana's.

"Her abigail will set her to rights. The last few weeks have been difficult upon us all."

When Fitzwilliam turned, Thomas held out his arm towards his study. "Do not allow the ladies' early evening ruin ours. Come, let us have brandy." As he passed, Thomas slapped him on the back. "Have you ever heard of the Irish custom of honouring the dead? They drink and tell tales of their loved one. I have some wonderful stories of your father I should tell you."

Fitzwilliam took the same chair he occupied earlier as Thomas poured them both a generous drink and handed one to him. "Have I ever told you the story of when your father stole your grandfather's horse?"

He swallowed the sip in his mouth and regarded his cousin with lifted eyebrows. "No, I have never heard that one."

"I was twelve and your father eleven, and I dared him to ride my uncle's, your grandfather's, horse. Your father was an excellent horseman—even at that age—yet the horse I challenged him to ride was a spirited stallion named Hades. This horse could only be ridden by your grandfather. He would not accept a groom and had injured several who had attempted to work him in your grandfather's stead."

"What happened?"

He chuckled and sat behind his desk, relaxing into his chair. "The horse let your father take him as far as the footbridge before he bucked him off. Your father hit his head and did not wake until the day after." Thomas smiled and shook his head. "Your grandfather whipped me, and when he was done, my father did the same. I could not walk without remembering what I had done for a week."

Fitzwilliam took another drink from his brandy. "Father was fortunate he was not killed."

"He was. Very."

His cousin smiled wider. "Oh! What of when your father attempted to kiss your mother at her coming out?"

"He did?"

And so the evening passed. Thomas recounted story after story of Fitzwilliam's father while they enjoyed his fine brandy. Fitzwilliam had heard some stories from their time at Cambridge from his father, yet it seemed Thomas had dozens of them, and he continued to regale him of them until the clock suddenly struck midnight.

Thomas threw back the remnants in his glass. "I have enjoyed tonight. Thank you."

After sitting forward, Fitzwilliam set his empty glass on the desk and stood, but his head spun when he got to his feet. He found it necessary to prop himself with the strong surface of the desk to gain his balance.

Had he really had so much to drink? He furrowed his brow while he tried to remember how many glasses he had imbibed. For the life of him, he could only think of one instance of Thomas pouring him more brandy. Thomas had partaken of significantly more but seemed no worse for wear.

"That brandy has a kick to it, does it not," said Thomas, putting an arm around him. "Let me help you."

Fitzwilliam attempted to follow the route they took, but Thomas helped him up the servants' stairs and through several corridors he did not know until he stopped before a door. "Here we are. Can you manage on your own? Your valet has surely retired for the evening."

"I shall be well."

With a swift turn of the latch, Thomas ushered him inside. "Good night," said his cousin softly before the door clicked shut. The fireplace provided precious little illumination, so he blinked his eyes in a futile attempt to adjust to the lack of light.

He shed his topcoat and waistcoat, tossing them over a chair. He attempted to work at the knot of his cravat but simply pulling at the fabric made him rock on his feet and need to steady himself using the back of the sofa.

"Blast," he said as his free hand continued to work on that damned knot. He finally liberated himself from his neckcloth and easily stripped his remaining clothing, crawling into the welcoming bed awaiting him.

He stared up at the dark canopy before he rolled to his side. Just like every night, Elizabeth awaited him, her curls spread across the pillow, her expression serene. Her large doe eyes opened and met his, and just like every night that preceded this one, he leaned in to claim her lips.

# Chapter 12

Elizabeth took a deep breath while she relaxed into the warmth of the coverlet. The scullery maid must have tiptoed in quite early to replenish the fire because she had never been so delightfully ensconced in warmth upon awakening.

Her eyes never opened while she burrowed back into the source of her comfort only to meet with human flesh that groaned deeply and pulled her tighter against him. Those same eyes she had yet to open nearly popped from their sockets. She shifted her hand down to the strong and slightly hairy arm that wrapped around her waist, the palm flattened against her stomach. Her heart beat out of her chest, and she bit her lip.

Oh, why had she drunk as she had? What a stupid thing to do! She never overindulged, yet last night, she struggled to walk to her bedchamber without falling into a heap on the expensive carpets and apologized profusely to Georgiana because she was simply too tired to talk over chocolate and biscuits in her rooms.

When she entered her dressing room, Lalande awaited her and aided her in preparing for bed. As she closed her eyes and struggled to recall any image of what occurred next, all that sprang to mind involved a movement in her bed. She had opened her eyes to Fitzwilliam lying next to her. At the time, it seemed a lovely dream, so when he kissed her, she indulged in the one way she could hold him close—in her dreams.

"Lizzy," he said, slurring her name as his hand shifted and his fingers entwined with hers.

She covered her mouth with her other palm. It was certainly not a dream! The sight of her nightshift tossed haphazardly in the window seat made her stiffen, and she peered down, coming to the realization that she wore naught but a sheet—as well as naught between her and Fitzwilliam.

As carefully as possible, she removed her hand from his and turned to face him, a tear landing against her nose when she set eyes upon his dear face. He still slumbered, his features more relaxed than she had ever seen him, even when he slept in her arms the day after his father's death.

Her palm rested against his cheek, and she cherished the ability to caress the light spattering of stubble that graced his face. He was always cleanly shaven. She had never before seen him thus. Her thumb traced along his eyebrow and down the length of his nose. He was so beautiful with his sculptured features and dark chestnut locks that currently shot out in all directions.

She pressed a kiss to his forehead, then the tip of his nose, and finally a gentle peck on the lips. His head jerked back, and his eyes popped open. His chest heaved a few times before he glanced around the room and back to her. "How did I get here?"

"I know not. I awoke to find you curled against my back." His eyes closed, and he groaned while he relaxed back into the pillow. "Forgive my brusque awakening. You startled me."

She smiled and rested her hand over his heart. "I am certain no more than you startled me. I awoke, thinking the maid had replenished the fire. I was rather taken aback when you pulled me closer and mumbled my name."

His hand covered hers on his chest while his eyes searched hers. "How much do you remember of last night?"

She blew out a breath and winced at the memory. "I believe I have pieced together the relevant details. After you left me in the library, I drank two large glasses of brandy. I remember wanting to numb that ache my chest. I did not want to hurt and miss you as I have as of late. You escorted me to dinner where I continued to drink wine. The butler refilled my glass, but I am unaware of how many times."

"I believe three times." The fingers of his free hand brushed a curl from her face. "When Thomas motioned to him, I thought to stop him, but I hesitated because of Georgiana. I did not want to arouse her suspicions of anything amiss between the three of us."

She nodded and turned her hand to hold his. "Your sister and I walked upstairs together. She escorted me to my door but wished to talk as we have in the past. I told her I was too fatigued. Lalande helped me prepare for bed, and I do not remember anything else until I opened my eyes to find you thus. I confess I thought you a wonderful dream."

"I thought the same when I found you in my bed last night." He rubbed the heel of one hand against his eye. "I fear Thomas took advantage of both of us. Once he had you sufficiently indisposed, he insisted we drink brandy and tell stories of my father. I believe he filled my glass on several occasions when it was not yet empty, and I was not looking. After hours of imbibing and sharing tales, I was surely well in my cups—as much as you were in the dining room, if not worse. Thomas helped me to my bedchamber—your bedchamber, I should say. He led me here, opened the door, and ensured it was closed after I stumbled inside."

He bit his lip and squeezed her hand. "I remember merely bits and pieces after. Forgive me for hurting you."

Her fingers covered his mouth. "My mother told me there would be some pain. You did nothing I did not expect. Feeling so close to you was worth every bit of the discomfort, which was fleeting." She leaned in and pressed a kiss to his lips. "You were so careful and gentle with me. I felt loved and cherished. I could not ask for more."

He returned her kiss, brushing his lips ever so gently against hers before deepening their connection. She shifted into his arms, craving his body closer to hers, but a door opening startled them apart. Elizabeth pulled the covers to her chest and quickly sat up to find her husband standing in the doorway adjoining their rooms.

"Good morning," he said, in entirely too cheerful a manner.

Fitzwilliam sat up beside her and propped an arm on his knee. "You are certainly happy this morning. I suppose you are content that you have your dearest wish."

He sighed and stepped further into the room, tinkering with a book on her escritoire along the way. "I shall be well pleased not to witness your incessant moping. You will have no need of such drama since the two of you are together."

"You made that choice for us," said Elizabeth, her tone hard. "I shall not thank you for that."

The duke crossed his arms over his chest, and after moving Fitzwilliam's lawn shirt aside, leaned against the back of a chair. "I may have, but 'tis done and done for the best. Now, I have told Georgiana that both of you are feeling unwell this morning and are not equal to company. With your *exhaustion* last night at dinner, Elizabeth, she had no problems believing you had taken ill." He dropped his chin and levelled a no-nonsense look at Fitzwilliam. "I simply told her *you* were fatigued from the schedule you have maintained since your father died. I did not want her to worry excessively over you."

"How kind of you," said Fitzwilliam dryly. "But to what end? What do you hope to accomplish?" He glanced at the clock on the mantelpiece. "'Tis not terribly late. We could still join her for breakfast."

"I thought to give you a day to yourselves." Thomas's gaze stayed on Fitzwilliam. "From your time at Cambridge with Wickham, I know your valet is trustworthy. He is aware of your current location and shall sleep in your chambers tonight at the instruction of my valet. We do not wish your bed to be too pristine.

L.L. Diamond

"Elizabeth, you should know Lalande discovered the two of you early this morning. It was she who kept the scullery maid from entering, claiming I was in residence and replenished the fire herself. The servants probably believe you remain in your chambers due to an amorous night with me." He giggled, an odd sound from him, and shook his head. "I give her credit for her ingenuity, which serves our purposes well.

"I ordered breakfast to be brought to your sitting room. Lalande shall knock when it is delivered. I am certain you do not appreciate my interference, but when Elizabeth over imbibed on wine last night, I saw an opportunity for the two of you to be happy—even if you deny yourselves the company of each other after today and make yourselves miserable hereafter."

Elizabeth glanced over at Fitzwilliam before levelling a stern glare at her husband. "Thomas, get out."

Her husband did not so much as flinch. He simply laughed once more. "As you wish, my dear." After an over-exaggerated bow, he departed to his rooms, leaving them to each other.

She pulled the coverlet to keep herself covered as she rose, leaving the sheet to cover Fitzwilliam. "He does have gall. I shall give him credit for that." She bit her thumbnail while she paced in front of the fire. "He wants an heir but simply because we spend a day sequestered together does not mean his desire shall be granted. Some couples are never blessed, though they are intimate for years. I tell you, he is too overconfident in his assumptions. Lalande and your valet might be circumspect, but to tell them goes beyond the pale."

Fitzwilliam rose from the bed, and she halted in her place. He wore not a stitch of clothing and had not covered with the sheet. "My valet will not say a word, and frankly, all I ever do is consider what might happen—how everything could go wrong, how to please others. I am tired of worry. I am tired of wanting

179

with all that is in me what I cannot have." He brushed his fingers through his unruly curls. "Am I upset with Thomas for making decisions he had no right to make? Yes, wholeheartedly. Yet, at this moment, I cannot bring myself to muster the righteous indignation I know I should feel. I only want to be with you, whether we have one day together or five. I want to be selfish for once in my life. I do not want to consider what others might think."

He reached out and grabbed the corner of the quilt she held near her shoulder, pulling the coverlet away from her and dropping it to the floor. His eyes roved over her exposed flesh, making her gasp and her skin pebble with his intense gaze. "You are stunning. My dreams never did justice to the reality."

Her heart pounded so hard, it split and oozed everything she had attempted to hold inside for these last few months. When he pulled her into his arms, she did not resist but wrapped her arms around him as his lips claimed hers. His tongue dipped inside, and she swallowed his groan as he lifted her into his arms.

He set her on the mattress and continued to kiss her until her head spun and she could hardly breathe. When his lips finally left hers, they trailed down her neck and chest until he pressed a kiss to her navel. He looked up, his vivid blue eyes capturing hers. "I love you, Lizzy. Let me show you how much."

His fingers trailed along her stomach and her sides while he continued to kiss her belly, her breasts, her neck. She pressed her hands to his shoulders to savour their strength and anchor herself so she did not drown in the heat and fluttering he incited so easily.

"What of tomorrow?" Her voice sounded so strange to her own ears, low and husky with a catch while he lightly nipped at the side of her breast.

"No," he said as he cupped the same breast. His thumb and finger toyed with her nipple, making her clench her thighs together tightly. How could he have complete control over her body with so little effort? "No talk of what occurs when we leave this room."

He wrapped his lips around the tip, sucking lightly and grazing his teeth along it. She closed her eyes and clenched the bedsheet below her, tendrils of warmth travelling to every inch of her. "'Tis inevitable," she moaned.

"Yes, but live for the now. Live for us until we are forced to face reality."

His lips claimed hers and prevented her from speaking, not that she had any desire for him to stop what he was doing. Her heart, her body, and her soul all screamed for him to continue, to do whatever he wished as long as he made her continue to feel like this.

One hand slipped between her legs, and she greedily widened them to allow him access. He stroked, and she whimpered into his mouth as one of her hands released the sheets long enough to attach itself to his side. She would not lay here with him like this and not touch him. She had held herself back so many times in the past. How could she do so when this might be her one chance to partake of those urges?

He paid homage to each of her breasts as he had earlier before kissing down the mid-line of her stomach. A finger slipped inside and pressed upward, making her lift her hips from the mattress as she gasped.

What followed proved to be something her mother never mentioned when she discussed marital relations! His tongue traced between her folds before he began sucking a spot that made her writhe and squirm at the overwhelming pleasure. One of her hands grasped her own hair as her back arched from the bed and the fingers of her other hand threaded into his locks.

When she looked down, his eyes bore into hers as his mouth and tongue continued to work at that place—that place that made her squirm and her eyes roll back in her head. Breaths burst from her lips unevenly while she practically sobbed. "I cannot bear it."

His only response was to suck harder, making her cry out as everything disappeared but the throbbing he caused between her legs that transformed into almost a burn, spreading through her body and paralysing her limbs until she collapsed into the mattress.

"Fitzwilliam," she said in a whisper as he appeared above her. Her palm cradled his cheek as he sank inside, filling her and soothing the lingering ache. She inhaled sharply at the slight sting that accompanied the intrusion.

"Are you well?"

"Yes, pray do not stop."

He wrapped her legs around his hips and began to move within her. With a deep groan, he kissed her lips. "I love you so much."

"I love you too." Tears rolled past her temples and into her hair as their eyes held. How by joining their bodies did it feel as though their hearts connected as well? Dear Lord, but how could she return to her everyday life when this time was over?

"Stop thinking." His hand wrapped around her hip and grasped her rear to pull her closer with his next thrust. "Just feel how much I love you."

The depth struck some place he had yet to touch. She moaned and flexed her fingers so they dug into the skin of his buttocks, pulling him back. "Again."

His lips claimed hers and refused to let go until he swallowed her cries when she reached her release. Then, he buried his face into her neck as he called out his own fulfilment, collapsing on top of her.

When he started to lift himself away, she tightened her arms and legs around him. "No. I must let go soon enough. I want nothing more than to be as close to you as possible until then."

"Am I not too heavy?"

"No." She shook her head as more tears fell from her eyes. "You are perfect."

Elizabeth yawned and sank back into Fitzwilliam's arms while they watched the sun rise over the peaks in the distance. The duke's lies bought them two days of relative seclusion within her rooms, and the dawn brought their final moments before Fitzwilliam needed to dress and slip from her bedchamber like a thief in the night—or in this case, the dawn.

Ripping her eyes from the view, she lifted her face into his neck and brushed her lips against the sensitive flesh near his ear. "I do not want you to go." They had talked, read favourite verses to each other, and made love. They had wasted little time as they only separated when necessary and only when one of them ventured to the dressing room for some reason or another.

His arms clutched her tighter. "I have no desire to let you go. Yet, no matter how I wish it, we cannot change what is. Georgiana will fret if I do not emerge from my chambers today." He pressed a kiss to her hair. "We will depart for Pemberley on the morrow."

She sat up and straddled his lap, wrapping her arms around his shoulders. "I have an artist coming to Worthstone to paint my portrait next week. Perhaps Georgiana could stay? She could keep me company while I have to suffer the endless torture of sitting perfectly still."

"You know I can deny you naught which I have the ability provide." His eyes watched his fingers as they toyed with the necklace he had given her for her birthday. Unless she needed to wear jewels from the duke's family, she always wore Fitzwilliam's. It bound them, even though they could not be together in truth. It was a part of him that was always with her.

"Thank you." She sounded oddly winded. She leaned in to kiss him, letting him deepen the kiss as his fingers dug mercilessly into her hips. "Fitzwilliam?"

"Hmm?"

"Love me. Just one more time." Her voice cracked, and she blinked back tears. She could not bear this. He might not be leaving forever, but she might never be with him like this again.

His hand lifted and cradled her cheek. "I thought you were sore."

She pressed her forehead to his. "I am, yet a slight discomfort shall not deter me from losing myself in your embrace. I want to be with you."

His lips brushed against her top, and then bottom lip before he claimed her mouth, slipping his hand beneath the coverlet and caressing her until she moaned loudly. Before long, all that surrounded them disappeared as he slipped back home and guided her atop him while the sun continued to rise above the horizon.

An hour later, Elizabeth sat before her dressing table while Lalande piled her hair atop her head in a mass of curls. She wore her dove grey gown out of deference for Fitzwilliam and Georgiana, but in some fashion, it suited her mood. Fitzwilliam would not come to her tonight since he planned on departing early the next morning, so she mourned their separation. As she continued to remind herself, they could not continue their affair indefinitely. After all, he required an heir just like her husband. He needed to find a wife, though a small selfish voice deep inside prayed he would not do so soon.

She let her eyes fall closed and sighed. He had been so gentle with her until their last time together when he became what she could only describe as desperate as he took her. After she found her release, he had picked her up and moved her to the bed where he held her so tightly and thrust harder than before, panting as though he had run for miles when he finally collapsed on top of her.

"*Je suis finis*," said Lalande in her thick French accent. "Does Madame require more this morning?"

"No, thank you." Elizabeth stood, turned, and took the girl's hands. "I must also thank you for your discretion. I know how all of this may seem—"

"Madame." Lalande put up a hand, palm toward Elizabeth. "You owe me no explanations. My duty is to care for you and protect your secrets." Her head tilted as she looked at Elizabeth with a peculiar expression. "Forgive me for being forward, but while the servants are unaware, I had already recognised your relationship with your husband was not of a romantic nature."

Elizabeth's eyes surely widened too far. "May I ask how?"

"When I first came to England, I worked for a gentleman who married for other considerations than those of the heart. That gentleman wed a pretty woman for her fortune and connections, though I suspect your husband had other motives as he has no need of money and is a duke who truly has little need for further connections."

"And I had neither if I am honest."

Lalande allowed a small smile. "My former employer was not careful about his mistress and his habits away from his wife. Not long after they wed, the wife of that gentleman took men to her bed as she wished. She did not care for them and indulged herself out of loneliness. I have seen how miserable a marriage such as yours can be. My last mistress was very young when she wed, much like you, and spent her years as a wife crying and alone more than she was happy. You hide your feelings well, but you love Mr. Darcy. If he brings you happiness, then I am pleased to help you."

Elizabeth clasped her hands in front of her. "Is that how my husband found you? Did he know this gentleman?"

Her maid nodded. "*Oui*, Madame. After the wife died in childbirth, the husband recommended me to the duke, who searched for your lady's maid." She picked up the hairpins on the table and put them away in their box. "My former mistress led a pitiful existence. Whether society says it is right or it is wrong, I do not wish such a joyless life for anyone." Once she replaced the box in the drawer, she stood facing Elizabeth. "Will Mr. Darcy be coming to you tonight? I can arrange matters with his valet."

"We have not discussed it."

Lalande picked up Elizabeth's dressing gown. "I shall take care of it for you. Talk below stairs says he departs in the morning. We can sneak him back to his rooms before the maids are about."

"If you cannot, know I appreciate your effort." Elizabeth started to turn towards the door, but a sudden thought made her to pivot around on her heel. "My sheets. There was blood on them."

"I removed them while you bathed, Madame. They are soaking in your bathwater. In a moment, I shall scrub what remains of the stain and hang them over the bath. When the maids wash laundry next, I shall put them directly into the washtub myself."

Elizabeth likely gaped at Lalande while she spoke. She always had the solution for any situation, though she likely learnt her methods from her last mistress.

"I should not doubt you. Feel free to chastise me should I do so again."

Her maid laughed and wagged a finger back and forth. "No, Madame. I am not infallible. I would prefer you ask than to assume I remember."

Elizabeth smiled and stepped back towards the door. "I shall keep that in mind."

"Have a lovely day, Madame."

"Thank you." As Elizabeth walked the corridors to breakfast, how odd and almost foreign her own home appeared after being isolated in her rooms for two days. Had she changed so much in that small period of time or was some other explanation to blame?

When she entered the dining room, Georgiana bounded forward. "Lizzy! I am so glad you are well."

"I am very well, Sweetling. Now, what shall we do today?" Her eyes found Fitzwilliam's across the room, and she lifted her eyebrow. "I have been cooped up for far too long."

"Yet you are no longer ill. Fitzwilliam has rested in his chambers for the past two days, and he appears much improved. Does he not? He has worked so hard since Papa died. I am certain he needed the respite."

"I did indeed." His low, smooth voice caressed her without so much as a finger being laid upon her flesh.

Elizabeth squeezed Georgiana's hands. "I am pleased he could take that time at Worthstone. The duke and I are available to the both of you should you ever require it. Do not ever doubt us."

"You are too good to us." The girl almost bounced to face her brother. "Is she not?"

"She is indeed, Sweetling. She has requested you remain for a time. Would you like to stay or would you prefer to return to Pemberley with me?"

A footman pulled a chair for Elizabeth to sit beside Georgiana, who had hurried back to her seat. "You may do as you wish," said Elizabeth as she took a piece of toast. "I shall not be offended if your desire is to return home. I promise."

"I believe I should like to stay." She glanced back and forth between Elizabeth and Fitzwilliam. "Then you can return me to Pemberley and stay a few days before you travel back to Worthstone."

Fitzwilliam's eyes burned into hers. "As long as Thomas approves, I believe it a sound plan. Do you object, Lizzy?"

How did he make her body roar to life with only a look? "Of course not. You know I adore Pemberley." Her cheeks had to be glowing, they were so warm. While Georgiana might not notice, Elizabeth would need to be more careful in company. No one could suspect hers and Fitzwilliam's attachment, or her reputation would suffer. Society already questioned her suitability as the duke's wife. She could not afford to invite further scrutiny. All who derided her would crow of how correct their claims proved to be. She could not allow that to happen.

# Chapter 13

*September 20<sup>th</sup> 1809*
*Worthstone*
*Derbyshire*

*Dearest Laura,*

*I thank you for sending Miss Geddes to us! I knew from our meeting with her that she is a delightful young lady and extremely talented, but to see her create a portrait from a blank canvas is astounding. She is very worthy of your patronage, and in time, I hope the rest of the world takes note and appreciates her skill as well. She has amazing potential. The sketches and portrait she brought with her are reminiscent of those portraits we viewed by Thomas Lawrence, so it would be a shame if she did not receive similar recognition. I do realise that equal standing in the art community is unlikely since she is not a man, yet I can still hope.*

*I do have a confession to make, my dear friend. At the time Miss Geddes visited, Miss Darcy was at Worthstone so instead of painting my portrait, I asked her to paint Miss Darcy's as a gift for her brother. I must say Miss Geddes rendered a remarkable likeness to her subject and even included Miss Darcy's young spaniel Evie in the portrait.*

*Do not be cross for I have arranged for Miss Geddes to paint my portrait during the upcoming Season. Mr. Darcy had recently commented of the need to have Miss Darcy's likeness taken, and my husband agreed the painting would be an excellent way to lift the spirits of both brother and sister after such a trying time. His birthday is also at the end of this month. Hopefully, this will be a grand surprise. Miss Darcy is vastly excited at the prospect, and I must confess His Grace and I are as well. I must again express my gratitude at making the surprise possible.*

*In regards to the upcoming Season, I do anticipate being in your company again. Since we have been invited to pass Christmastide at Pemberley, we plan on returning to London after the new year. I am certain you will have an exhibition in mind to visit when we arrive, so send a note when you have decided. I shall be at your disposal.*

*Yours sincerely,*

*Lizzy*

Georgiana grasped Elizabeth's hand as they crossed the stone bridge over the River Derwent. "Look! We are nearly home."

The duke smiled as he peeked out the window. "Was your stay at Worthstone so tedious, my dear?"

"Oh no! On the contrary!"

After rolling her eyes, Elizabeth squeezed her hand. "Pay him no mind. He is teasing you. While he might not be so openly excited, he exhibits his own form of happiness at arriving home, I assure you."

The carriage rolled to a stop before the entrance, and once the step was set, the door opened, allowing her husband to alight. He handed out Elizabeth and Georgiana while Fitzwilliam stepped from the door.

"Brother!" Georgiana ran up the steps and flung herself into her brother's waiting arms. "I have missed you."

Elizabeth's feelings were always the same when setting eyes on Fitzwilliam after a separation. Her every muscle was strung impossibly tight to prevent herself from launching into his arms just as Georgiana had only a moment before. Instead, she held herself stiffly even as she approached him. After he released

Georgiana, he shook his cousin's hand before he bowed over hers and kissed it, though not the lingering kiss she would have preferred were they alone. He held out a hand to usher them inside and into the library where tea and refreshments were served moments after their arrival. From previous visits, Elizabeth was aware of Fitzwilliam's fondness for the room. She did not find it surprising he chose to entertain them in comfortable surroundings over a drawing room.

While they drank their tea, Elizabeth did not speak much unless it was to Georgiana or her husband. The urge to hold Fitzwilliam proved too great for her to retain her equanimity. Instead, she assiduously avoided him, staring into her cup of tea or concentrating on Georgiana as a distraction—they were poor substitutes. Her eyes desired nothing more than to rest upon Fitzwilliam and study every beloved curl of his hair and every nuance of his dear expression.

An hour later, Mrs. Reynolds escorted her and the duke to their chambers to rest until dinner, and Elizabeth all but collapsed in relief when the door closed behind her. How did people wear masks every day of their lives? The concentration and attention required were exhausting.

"Are you well, Madame?"

"Yes, simply out of sorts. 'Tis difficult not exposing my feelings."

Lalande finished turning down the covers on the bed while Elizabeth sat and removed her boots. "You have missed him. Your unease in company is understandable."

A strange sound from the wall made them turn and stare at Fitzwilliam, who emerged from a door concealed within the panelling. "I beg your pardon."

Elizabeth stood and froze in place. Lalande merely curtseyed with a crooked smile and bustled through the dressing room door.

"What has made you so shy of me?" His voice hummed low while he closed the door behind him. "I have never seen you so quiet."

Releasing the strain of holding herself in such regulation, she rushed into his arms. "I have missed you so. I wanted nothing more than to run to you as Georgiana did, yet I could not."

His lips pressed against her temple. "I am quite relieved then. I worried you no longer cared."

"No!" She shook her head and drew back. "I care too much."

He kissed her hard, his tongue plundering as he pulled her tight against him. Her fingers worked at the knot in his cravat before she attacked the buttons on his topcoat and waistcoat. While she frenziedly worked at his clothes, he unfastened the back of her gown enough to expose her breasts.

Once she liberated him of his coats and cravat, he wrapped her legs around his waist and walked them to the bed, lying her flat on her back. Her skirts were swiftly rucked to her waist as he dropped to his knees.

She had not expected him to come to her at Pemberley. As far as she had known, their affair had ended when he departed Worthstone, so she relished the ability to touch him when he finally moved over her. She slipped her hands under his shirt, caressing the solid plane of his abdomen, before she reached for his fall and unfastened it.

Her eyes rolled back towards the headboard when he joined with her. She gasped and clenched her fingers into his sides. Before, their joining had always stung due to her inexperience, but today, nothing kept her from appreciating every sensation of their coupling. He nearly withdrew his entire length before thrusting harder, making her gasp and clutch the mattress with one hand to brace herself.

"Am I hurting you?"

"God, no." She had ached for him since he left Worthstone. While their every encounter held a place in her heart, the way he had expressed himself on their last morning was one of her most cherished memories. His impatience to be inside of her again, and his desperation did not offend her. On the contrary, his passion matched her sentiments exactly.

She lifted her hips to meet his pace, each thrust bringing a vocalization from her when he touched that spot deep inside that made her burn even hotter. Meanwhile, he kissed her as though he needed her to survive.

He released her lips, lifted, and shifted her leg over his shoulder, their eyes never leaving the other's. Lord, how could he go deeper than before? It was all she could do not to close her eyes as that coiling inside began to build to unbearable heights. Her hands grasped his hips and her nails dug into his skin. That delicious heat slowly spread until it engulfed her completely and she cried out, tears leaking from her eyes.

A roar from him signalled his completion, and he carefully removed her leg before he collapsed on top of her. She smoothed his hair back from his face when he propped himself on his elbows, though he dropped his head to nibble at her earlobe. "I could not wait until tonight," he said against her neck.

A giggle burst from her while she looked down to their dishevelled clothing. "I may have noticed. Are you still wearing your boots?"

"Yes, I am." His chest shook from laughter. He lifted once more, letting his eyes rove over her face. "You are well? I was a bit rough."

Her head shook while her fingers traced his cheek. "You were as desperate to be with me as I was to be with you. Do not apologise." She bit her lip and peered quickly towards the door. "Do you think someone heard me? I was rather loud."

"No servant has reason to be in the main corridor, and at this time of day, only the valets should be in the servants' corridors, but yours connects through the dressing room. I daresay the only person who may have heard is Thomas in the adjoining room." He gestured with his head towards the door. "Mrs. Reynolds did seem puzzled when I requested her to change you to these rooms. Thomas has occupied the same guest room since I was a child. I would have preferred more privacy, but I could not give you this room without suspicion unless I gave Thomas the adjoining bedchamber."

"I understand. I assume you preferred this bedchamber due to the passage?"

"Yes, there are hidden passages and stairways between certain rooms. Some are not even known to Mrs. Reynolds." He kissed her lips more than once. "We have two hours before dinner. How long do you need to prepare?"

"If Lalande readies a bath, an hour."

"May I stay until then?"

She grasped the edge of his lawn shirt and drew it over his head. "I would be sad if you did not." His request fulfilled her every wish. How could she deny him when it was all she desired as well?

After dinner, the ladies departed to the withdrawing room while Fitzwilliam and Thomas adjourned to the study. Fitzwilliam poured his cousin a drink and had no sooner sat in his chair than Thomas grinned. "I do hope you and Elizabeth had a satisfactory reunion."

Fitzwilliam sputtered and choked. "Must you be so crass?" he asked when he regained his breath.

His cousin sniffed disdainfully. "I am by no means crass. I simply see no reason to prevaricate. Your relationship with Elizabeth pleases me. She deserves to find happiness as I find mine."

His free hand clenched, and the fingers of the opposite whitened against the crystal. "Happiness? You call loving someone you cannot be with happiness? Your past heart episodes allow for you to keep your valet—I believe Colin is his name—close without suspicion. After all, he would be required immediately if you became severely ill as you did before. I cannot uproot myself and reside at Worthstone without inciting talk."

Thomas tilted his glass a little to the side with his head. "That is true, though you are welcome to visit at your leisure. Our houses have always been close. No reason exists that you and Elizabeth cannot have a long relationship and spend time together often." He took a sip of his brandy and tugged at the waist of his topcoat. "For example, I could allow Elizabeth, accompanied by her maid, a holiday in the Lakes next summer. You could always have business in London or even that dreadful estate your father inherited in Ireland as far as Georgiana or others are concerned."

Fitzwilliam took a sizeable gulp of his brandy and bared his teeth when he swallowed. His cousin's officiousness was off-putting. "We shall see what the summer holds. Autumn is barely upon us, and you are already considering next year."

"Nevertheless, think on it. Speak of it with Elizabeth."

At a knock on the door, they both started.

"Come," called Fitzwilliam. When Elizabeth entered, the gentlemen stood.

"I know I interrupt your brandy, but Georgiana and I have planned a birthday surprise for you, Fitzwilliam. Will you join us in the music room?"

Thomas's lips were slightly upturned on the ends. Fitzwilliam furrowed his eyebrows. Did his cousin know what they had planned?

He followed Elizabeth, having a difficult time tearing his eyes from the curve of her neck and that spot just below her ear. He adored the noise she made in the back of her throat when he gently suckled there. He cleared his throat and redirected his attention to his feet, taking a deep breath to keep himself under regulation lest he embarrass himself before his young sister.

They entered the music room, and he came to an abrupt halt at the sight before him. Elizabeth indicated a portrait was to be painted of her, but that was . . . "Georgiana?"

"Is it not wonderful? Lizzy had planned to have her own portrait made, but at the last minute, requested the artist paint me in her stead. Miss Geddes was ever so kind and even suggested including Evie." She glanced quickly at Elizabeth. "Do you like it?"

He stepped closer and studied the work, the serene expression on his sister's face, the way Evie appeared as if she might jump from Georgiana's arms at any moment, and the gentle detailing of her gown and hair. "I think it is wonderful. We shall have to think of a place to display it."

"Perhaps in the gallery upstairs next to that of you and your parents," said Thomas.

Fitzwilliam's hands gripped at his sides before he shook himself and took Elizabeth's, kissing her cheek. "'Tis a brilliant gift. Thank you." He hugged Georgiana. "You appear so grown up. Father would be very proud." Lastly, he nodded to Thomas. "Thank you."

His cousin held up his free hand. "Though I would love to take credit, the idea was Elizabeth's."

Before he could thank her, Elizabeth held her hands towards his sister. "Georgiana also has several pieces she wishes to play for you. We have also practised a duet for tonight, so pray, sit and let Georgiana begin."

The first strains of a sonata filled the room while Fitzwilliam continued to stare at the portrait, dumbfounded. His amazement was such, he found it difficult to look elsewhere, but he did eventually tear his attention away from the painting to Georgiana. Elizabeth sat by his sister's side, poised to turn the pages, glowing and joyful. As the music continued, Fitzwilliam lost himself while he watched the two ladies who owned his heart perform. With Thomas out of his line of sight, he managed to briefly forget Elizabeth was wed to another and not his wife; however, his fantasy came to a swift halt when Thomas clapped at the end of their performance, startling him from his reverie.

His chest heavy, he joined Thomas's applause. He hated wishing his cousin away so easily, but he could not help desiring Elizabeth was his, could he? However wrong his love for her, he could not walk away. Yes, it was selfish, but he would not only break his heart if he ended the affair, he would also break Elizabeth's. Could he still be considered selfish if he considered her feelings as well?

Elizabeth paced her bedchamber while Lalande gathered her evening gown and jewels. Fitzwilliam's wide eyes and expression when he saw Georgiana's portrait had been all that she had hoped. The evening had been lovely.

Now she awaited him to step through that passage, yet he had not come. Surely a man did not take as long to ready for the night as a woman? She paced before the fireplace. "Why has he not come?"

"Let me hang Madame's gowns, and I shall check."

She wrung her hands while she continued her back and forth. "Thank you." Nearly twenty minutes passed while she continued to wear a faded line in the carpet, only she had taken to biting her thumbnail rather than wringing her hands.

A soft knock made her stop, and the door cracked. "Your Grace, if you will come." Lalande stood in the slightly opened door.

Without question, she hurried into the corridor where Fitzwilliam's valet stood, a candle in his grasp and his eyes on the floor. The small flame did not do much to illuminate their path as he led them through the walls of the house, but it did allow them to find their way. They turned once and travelled up a set of stairs and back down before he slid open a door at the end of the passage. "Ma'am."

She stepped through into a dark room where a fire burned merrily in the grate. At first glance, the bedchamber appeared empty, but when she took another step, she shivered at a cool breeze and turned. That was when she saw him, standing in an open balcony door, his arms awkwardly clasped behind his back.

As she approached, she stepped to his back and slid her arms around his chest, hugging him from behind. "What troubles you?"

"Vain wishes and circumstances I cannot change."

Her stomach clenched at his words as well as his tone. "My marriage?"

A heaving sigh moved his chest. He released his hands and covered her arms with his. "When Georgiana played, I found it surprisingly easy to pretend you were my wife and we enjoyed a perfect evening at home. Thomas was not in my line of vision to ruin the dream. Reality intruded painfully when Georgiana completed her performance."

Her heart squeezed so, and she bestowed a kiss to the middle of his back. "I do not know how to give you up, but I will if I must.

I love you too much to prevent you from finding your own future."

He turned in her arms and leaned so his forehead pressed to hers. "I should. I should let you go, but I cannot. I cannot rip my own still-beating heart from my chest. You are my undoing. I cannot imagine my life without you."

Her hands cradled his cheeks. "By law, I may be his, but my heart and my body belong to you. I am yours and only yours."

His lips cradled hers for a moment. "I miss you so when we are apart."

She shuddered and blinked back the sting of tears. "I long for you more than I ever thought possible, but somehow, arranging Georgiana's portrait for your gift helped."

He lifted her into his arms and sat on the bed with her straddling him. One of his fingers caressed a place under her ear. "As you walked to the music room, I stared at this spot."

"You did?" Her fingers stroked the lines of his chest through his dressing gown.

"You make this noise when I kiss you here," he continued. "I thought about how much I would love to mark you." His breath came out ragged while he blinked rapidly.

Mark her? He would think her terribly naïve. "How do you mean?"

"By suckling until it bruises." His fingers clenched her hips as his hardness began to press insistently between her legs, making her shift closer.

"Why do you not?" She sounded all hoarse and breathy. Why did such an idea appeal to her?

His hand found her neck again, fingering that spot as she began to tremble. "What would Georgiana say? What would anyone who saw you think?"

Her fingers parted his dressing gown, pushing the silk from his shoulders. "No one will know it was you." She bestowed a kiss to the hollow of his throat. "I am not a maiden who must withstand the scrutiny of her parents or those at a ball. You can mark me as much as you wish, though I would beg you not render me incapable of leaving my room." She let one side of her lips quirk upwards.

He grasped her hips and pressed her down harder on his erection, causing her to moan. She untied her own dressing gown and tossed it to the side so she wore not a stitch of clothing. His lips found her shoulder, and she pressed her cheek to his. "Where do you want to mark first?"

His nose nuzzled under her ear before he latched on to the sensitive flesh and making the ache between her legs only grow in intensity. She lightly scratched her fingernails over his chest and nipples making him groan and pull harder at her neck.

She may not be his, but she would give him everything in her power that he could possess. Given their situation, it was the least she could do.

Four days later, Elizabeth sat across from her husband as they began their return to Worthstone. With every hoof strike, they drew farther and farther from the part of her soul that remained at Pemberley while she did no more than clutch her reticule tightly in her grasp.

The night prior, Fitzwilliam had given her a stack of letters she now carried in that small bag. When she missed him, she was to read one of his love letters. She left a similar bundle with him to pass those moments when their separation became unbearable.

Thomas laughed and drew her attention. "You created quite a stir below stairs with that mark under your ear," he said, his grin never flagging.

She startled and lifted her eyebrows. "I beg your pardon?"

"Your maid did an admirable job of placing that tiny curl over the bruise, yet one of the footmen noticed it while serving you dinner the first evening you bore it. The butler and footmen were surprised a man of my advanced years had such passions." He continued to laugh, his shoulders shaking. "Colin found the gossip excessively diverting."

"I am glad he found it so amusing. I suppose it gives him leave to do the same to you, although in society, I suppose that would make me a wanton."

Thomas's laughter died, and he clasped his hands in his lap. "I find that term distasteful, to say the least. Men can find fulfilment with women as they wish, yet women are to suppress their own desires. I hope Fitzwilliam does not expect such behaviour from you. If he does, I shall set him straight."

A bark of amusement rang through the carriage. "That would be an awkward conversation, do you not think? My husband instructing my lover that he should satisfy me."

"Only if he believes that antiquated nonsense, though I cannot imagine George ever teaching him to be so cold."

Elizabeth concentrated wholeheartedly at adjusting her gloves while she was certain her glare could have scorched her spencer. "You need not worry on my account. I would also appreciate your lack of attention when it comes to my intimate encounters with Fitzwilliam. Your interference would not be taken well."

"He is a kind lover, then?"

She huffed and brought her eyes to his. "Is Colin?" A slight flare of his nostrils was his only reaction to her challenge.

"Exceedingly."

"And I am exceedingly uncomfortable with this conversation, yet if you must know, I have no complaints. He is attentive. Does that satisfy you?" She looked out of the window at the passing countryside.

"I only wish for your happiness."

Her head snapped back. "You continue to say such ridiculous things. If you had truly wished me content, you would have left me where you found me—with my family in Hertfordshire."

"You would have never met Fitzwilliam."

"Maybe, maybe not, but I prefer to believe he would have found me at the proper time, and we would have married without defying the conventions of society and God to be together." She laced her fingers to push her gloves back between her fingers. "Are we done?"

"Yes," he said, nodding. "Forgive me. My interference was kindly meant."

She did not respond.

# Chapter 14

*December 14<sup>th</sup> 1809*
*Pemberley*
*Derbyshire*

*Dearest Lizzy,*

*Thank you for your letter informing me of Thomas's latest episode. Since you were not witness to his last, I am certain it was frightening. Georgiana and I are both heartbroken you will not be at Pemberley for the Christmastide, yet it is with a heavy heart that we decline your invitation to Worthstone.*

*Mr. Bingley and his sisters will break their journey to London at Pemberley before Christmas, and I have invited them to pass the season with us as I expected you to travel here. Though I would prefer to rescind the Bingleys' invitation, it is too late to do so now.*

*Please convey our wishes to Thomas for a happy Christmas season. Of course, we do not exclude you in those wishes. We hope you have a blessed holiday season as well.*

*Georgiana and I intend to travel to London next month. I wish to give Georgiana some time with the masters, though I shall not venture out much to balls and dinners. As you are aware, I am not comfortable in those settings, so I am content that mourning Father will prevent my attendance. If Thomas is well enough to make the journey for the start of Parliament, pray send a note. We should dearly love to have you for dinner.*

*God Bless You,*

*Fitzwilliam Darcy*

Elizabeth folded the missive and placed it back into her reticule. She read and re-read Fitzwilliam's letters often, though that specific one did not particularly speak to her soul. They had discussed the need to keep posted correspondence formal in the event the letter was read by the wrong person or misdirected, which despite his calling her Lizzy, explained his tone. Still, it was January— nearly four months since she had laid eyes upon him—nearly four months of poring over each and every missive in that reticule until they nearly fell apart from the use.

Would he still love her when they were finally reunited? Had he decided she was not worth his effort and decided to adhere to the duties expected of him—specifically marrying and producing an heir?

"How are you feeling?" Thomas remained pale though the physician had indicated he was well enough to travel.

She dropped her head back against the plush velvet squabs and exhaled. "This infernal rocking is not helping."

"We shall arrive soon." He watched her for a moment. "You must be eager to see Fitzwilliam."

"I am nervous."

His eyebrows drew down in the middle with a frown. "I do not understand why."

Though she still had bouts of anger at Thomas for his officiousness, she could not remain angry at him forever. Instead, during his illness, she helped his valet care for him and often read to him while he convalesced. Despite their circumstances, they had become closer friends than they had been when they wed.

"He has had four months to decide I am not worth his time. What if he decides to wed another? After all, he cannot marry me."

Her husband reached forward and took her hand. "Elizabeth, one thing you should know about the Darcy men is that we do not fall in love at random. Despite being an Osborne, I inherited the steadfast Darcy heart from my mother. We love one person and only that person until we die." He patted her knuckles in an almost grandfatherly manner. "Do not fret. I shall speak to him."

"And say what? Pray, do not marry. Remain my wife's lover? What a ludicrous proposition." She winced and covered her mouth with her free hand while she took a keen interest in what lay outside the window. Unfortunately, the quick passage of houses and storefronts did little to help the incessant churning of her stomach.

His hand squeezed hers and was joined by the opposite. "Elizabeth, look at me."

Reluctantly, she pulled her gaze from the window and met his eyes.

"I am still weak," he said, "and I lose my breath easily now. After past episodes, I was myself again by this time."

She lowered her hand from her mouth to her chest. "It has only been a month."

"Colin agrees that I am not regaining my health as I did on prior occasions. I shall not live forever, and I feel the end will come sooner than later. I do hope to see the babe born before I die, yet that is in God's hands."

Though she could eventually be with Fitzwilliam if Thomas died, she did not wish for Thomas's death. Despite her feelings toward him and his scheming, she did care for him. She would be a horrible person to wish him dead. "We do not even know that I am with child."

Thomas smiled and leaned back into his seat. "The midwife felt certain of it, and you have changed if you have not noticed. Your face is a little rounder, and your figure is as well. I assure you Fitzwilliam will notice." He glanced out of the window for a moment, likely seeing if he recognised their surroundings. He took a deep breath. "I intend to return you to Worthstone when we are certain. I do not want to take any chances with you or the babe."

Her hands clenched, and she withheld the urge to snap at him. "I could be here for days if what the midwife says is accurate. This was a long journey for such a short visit."

He swayed some with the movement of the carriage. The journey had not only been arduous on her. "I had no desire to deny you or your sister. If the babe quickens in a few days, you may remain a fortnight. That will provide you some opportunity to spend time with your sister and to see Lady Vranes. I know you have missed her society also."

Elizabeth nodded. "I have. I should also have a few gowns made."

"Of course," he said with a hoarse laugh. "A woman always longs for a new gown."

"Or one that fits appropriately." She crossed her arms over her chest. "Most of my gowns are cut along my figure and do not have the excess of fabric required to accommodate a growing child. They are also tight in the bosom."

His eyes darted to her breasts and back to her face. "So soon?"

She rolled her eyes at his higher-pitched tone. Since she became aware of his relationship with his valet, his aversion to the feminine figure had become more noticeable. Even now, he almost seemed to recoil at the notion of her burgeoning breasts. "Yes, so soon. The midwife indicated the occurrence was not unusual."

"Then send a note to Madame Bonheur as soon as we arrive. I do not wish for your discomfort."

"Thank you." She smiled and glanced through the window to see the large façade of Worth House quickly approaching. "At last, we are here." She took a deep breath and released it. "I shall not have to sleep in an inn tonight."

L.L. Diamond

"I cannot find fault with your sentiment. I also prefer the comfort of my own bed." When the door opened, he stepped out and handed her down, offering his arm to enter the house. "I confess I thought to surprise you."

She glanced back at him. What did that mean? How did he hope to surprise her? Before she could ask, the door opened and Elizabeth whipped around to smile at the butler. "Good afternoon, Mr. Hughes. How are you?"

"Very well, Your Grace."

When her eyes shifted to the opulent hall, she started and covered her mouth with her hands. Jane stood primly in the middle, bouncing on her toes. "Lizzy?"

"Jane!" Elizabeth threw herself forward and into the embrace of her sister while they both wept. She drew back enough to kiss Jane's cheek and cradle her face in her palms while her dearest sister wiped the tears flowing freely down Elizabeth's cheeks. "I knew you would come, but I thought tomorrow."

Jane shook her head while she used her fingers to wipe her own tears. "Your husband sent Uncle a note, requesting I arrive this morning, and before I forget, Aunt desires word of your plans so she knows when to call."

Elizabeth pulled her fine linen handkerchief from her reticule and dabbed her sister's face. "I require a few new gowns, so we shall be required to travel to Cheapside for fabric. We could meet my aunt, and she could accompany us to Madame Bonheur's."

Thomas stepped closer, and Jane curtseyed. "Your Grace."

He kissed her hand. "Brother or Thomas, if it makes you more comfortable. Family does not call me by my title—well, unless you are my nephew James, who is undeserving of the connection." With a fatherly pat to Jane's hand, he glanced up the stairs. "If you will excuse me, I am fatigued from our trip and require rest. I am certain you do not desire my presence for your reunion. You, no doubt, have topics to discuss where you would prefer my absence." He bowed. "I hope you enjoy your stay with us."

"Thank you for having me . . . Brother."

No sooner had Thomas disappeared at the top of the staircase than her sister grasped her hands. "Is he well? He appears wan."

"The physician approved his travelling for the start of Parliament, but Thomas has simply never regained his colour after his last illness."

Jane held out Elizabeth's arms and perused her gown with a smile. "You are looking well."

"And so are you," said Elizabeth. "I know Aunt took you to Madame Bonheur's, but I hope you will not mind accompanying me."

"I would be happy to keep you company."

Elizabeth released one of Jane's hands and pulled her towards the stairs while her entire being sang in contentment. Jane was here. They would have time together at last. "Are you settled? Do you require anything?"

Her beloved sister shook her head while she followed. "No, your servants have been most attentive."

As soon as they were closed behind the doors of Elizabeth's sitting room, Elizabeth released Jane to remove her gloves, setting them on a small table inside the door. She turned and took in the wall coverings, which were bedecked in colourful wildflowers.

When she faced Jane once more, she exhaled and clasped her hands in front of her. "We extended this invitation for the Season, yet I shall likely return to Worthstone before long. Forgive me for not telling you sooner, but I am uncertain of how long I shall remain in town."

L.L. Diamond

"You are with child." Jane's tone was so even and matter-of-fact.

"How?"

Jane giggled and cupped Elizabeth's cheeks in her palms. "Really, Lizzy? Have you looked in the mirror lately? Your figure is curvier and your face has become rounder." Jane's thumbs softly caressed her cheeks. "I remember well when Mama carried Lydia. You greatly resemble her at the moment."

Elizabeth lifted that eyebrow she favoured. "I should scold you for that remark, Jane Bennet." How dare Jane compare her to Mama!

"Mama has always been a handsome woman. You should not be insulted."

"I am not truly." Elizabeth sighed and sat upon the cheerful robin's egg blue sofa. "Not that I relish the idea of being compared to her in any way." If Jane had compared them in terms of personality, then Elizabeth would have much more cause for insult.

"She will be positively beside herself when she learns she is to be a grandmother."

Elizabeth groaned and sank farther into the cushions. "Could we not delay telling her for a time? Perchance until after the birth? The child's fifth birthday would suit well."

"Lizzy!" laughed Jane.

"Can you not hear her? 'Bless me! The grandmother of a future duke! I shall go distracted. Hill! Fetch me my salts!' Besides, I could never tolerate her when I was ill. Could you imagine during childbirth? I am terrified enough as it is."

Jane slid beside her and wrapped an arm around her shoulders. "But look at what comes from it. Will it not be worth the pain and effort?"

"You say that, yet you will not endure it," said Elizabeth with a smile. She shifted her eyes to where her thumb rubbed across the palm of her hand several times, making flesh pucker and shift. Her eyes burned and she blinked. Fitzwilliam's child would be more than worth the effort. A living part of him she did not have to hide or be without. If only he could have such a token of her. She cleared her throat. "Yes, I do believe this babe will be worth every last bit of discomfort."

"Lizzy?"

She blinked some more and sat up. "Forgive me. I seem to weep with little provocation these days."

"You must be exhausted from travelling in your condition," said Jane, squeezing the arm around Elizabeth's shoulders. "Perhaps you should sleep until dinner."

"I should." Elizabeth shook her head and leaned further into Jane. "Yet I do not want to give up one moment with you."

Jane held out a hand to help her stand. "Come, show me which door leads to your dressing room. I shall brush your hair and sit with you until you fall asleep. Would you like that?"

"Very much." Jane was a dear sister. She could not ask for a better one. Only Georgiana came close with her innocent, sweet disposition.

Once Lalande helped her from her gown and Elizabeth donned her nightgown, Jane brushed her hair while they chatted of the goings-on in Meryton: who was now betrothed to whom, new babies, and other changes around the quaint town. When she laid down, Jane pulled the curtains, tucked her into bed, and laid down beside her. "What determines when you return to Derbyshire?"

"My husband desires my swift return upon the quickening. He fears the consequences of exposure to the foul air of London for too long if I am truly with child."

"When do you expect the babe to move?"

Her palm pressed against the slight swell. "Any day. My husband has promised me a fortnight with you regardless. If his nephew had not amassed such a staggering debt, he might give me more time."

"He fears for the future of his tenants and his home. It is understandable and laudable. After all, our father has no such control over Longbourn's future. This child could guarantee prosperity to the dukedom and his other properties for another generation, and by extension, the families that rely on it."

"I do understand his position. His nephew's creditors continue to extend him more and more due to the promise of James's inheritance. This babe will not be welcome news to those men or his nephew, yet I do not believe us to be in any danger." She added the last at Jane's wide eyes. She would not want her dearest sister to worry unnecessarily. "James is a drunkard, a seducer, and a gambler. He also has little to do with Thomas."

Elizabeth yawned and snuggled further into the covers. "Tell me more of my sisters. I hope they are becoming less silly and more accomplished."

After a slight laugh, Jane folded the pillow, propping her chest upon it. "Very well." And so, she began. At least until Elizabeth's eyes fluttered closed and she lost her awareness of her surroundings and the sweet voice of Jane.

"I am so pleased to have happened upon you," said Lady Matlock, who sat opposite Elizabeth in Madame Bonheur's comfortable parlour. A full tea set sat on a table before them. "I hope to have a small dinner soon. Now, I simply must set the date, so I can send you an invitation."

The fusee bracket clock chimed on the wall behind her, and the countess startled. "Oh my! Is that the time? I should be going.

This has been ever so much fun. It has been a pleasure meeting you, Mrs. Gardiner." She nodded to Elizabeth's aunt, then Jane. "Miss Bennet."

Elizabeth made to stand but Lady Matlock pressed a hand to her shoulder. "Pray do not worry." She kissed Elizabeth's cheek. "I remember those early days well. Save your feet, for they will swell to the size of gammons soon enough."

Once the countess swished through the door in a wave of primrose silk, Elizabeth's aunt lifted her eyebrows while she placed her teacup on the table. "She should not make assumptions. You never so much as indicated your suspicions in front of her."

On the other hand, Elizabeth had informed her aunt, seeking advice while they travelled across London. Her aunt helped her select a variety of fabrics, which included some for baby clothes, before venturing to Madame Bonheur's to select patterns for her own gowns.

They were the last customers of the day, so Madame had encouraged them to finish their tea before departing.

"Lady Matlock is more practised amongst others, yet she is quite open with me. I am unsure why." Elizabeth set her own cup beside her aunt's and Jane's and stood. "Have we any further business here or nearby? I am ready to go home."

"You do look tired, dearest," said Jane, who stood and wrapped her arm through Elizabeth's.

"You give the loveliest compliments."

She and her aunt laughed while Jane gasped. "You do enjoy vexing me."

Elizabeth laughed a little harder and met her aunt's glance out of the corner of her eye. "You sound like Mama."

Jane pinched Elizabeth's arm. "You must take that back."

"Take back the truth," she said. "What a novel idea." Elizabeth tugged Jane to the door while her aunt followed.

After they loaded into the carriage, Elizabeth rested back into the plush squabs and caught her aunt's attention. "I understand if you cannot, but I would appreciate your attendance at my lying-in."

"I would love to be there for you. I shall speak to Edward, though I should tell you that I have my own suspicions." Elizabeth sat up straighter while Jane pressed her hands together. "I believe I am a month from the quickening, but if I am indeed with child, I could not travel so close to my own confinement."

Elizabeth shook her head, though her eyes burned. She did not want to be alone for the birth—should there be one, but to be near tears? "And I would not expect it of you. Travelling to London is difficult enough. I do not anticipate the return to Derbyshire one bit. The sickness has waned, but I am increasingly achy in my hips."

"The rocking of a carriage is also no friend," said her aunt. "I remember the journey to Hertfordshire when your grandmother died. I was two months from my lying in, and I did not forgive Edward until the soreness dissipated. It was a miserable carriage ride only to console your mother and receive callers."

"Oh, Aunt!" Jane reached across and took her aunt's hands. "Maybe I can come to London and help with the children. You will require someone when your time draws near, not to mention afterwards."

"Your aid would be gratefully received, my dear. Lizzy came three years ago when Isaac was born. I do not know what I would have done without her."

The carriage stopped in front of Worth House, and they alighted once the door was opened and the step placed. Upon entering the hall, a whirl of golden-brown curls rushed from the drawing room and hurtled into Elizabeth's arms. "Lizzy! I am so glad you have finally come!"

"Georgiana!" Elizabeth laughed and drew the girl back by her shoulders. "What a wonderful surprise. I did not expect you this evening."

"Thomas invited Fitzwilliam and me for dinner. Did you not know?"

Elizabeth handed off her pelisse to a waiting maid. "No, my husband has kept a number of secrets from me, it seems." She turned as Thomas and Fitzwilliam emerged from the drawing room. "What of the menu?" She fought to keep her eyes on her husband and not stare longingly at Fitzwilliam. They had not been together in so long.

"I am certain Mrs. Grigg did a laudable job." He put a hand to Fitzwilliam's shoulder. "Fitzwilliam Darcy, Georgiana Darcy," he said, gesturing to them both. "Allow me to introduce Elizabeth's aunt, Mrs. Gardiner, and her sister, Miss Jane Bennet." They curtseyed while the gentlemen bowed.

"Are you the aunt from Derbyshire?" asked Fitzwilliam.

Aunt Gardiner smiled and dipped her chin. "I am. I must thank you for helping Lizzy when she visited Pemberley. She wrote to me of meeting my friends and seeing my favourite places. I was overjoyed she could have the tour I would have wished for her."

"Georgiana and I enjoyed the excursions; I assure you."

Her aunt's smile dimmed, and she clasped her hands before her. "Allow me to say how sorry I was to hear of your father. He was an excellent man."

"Thank you," Fitzwilliam nodded and blinked rapidly. He would wear dark colours and the black armband for a year, but it would take longer for his father's death not to smart.

Her aunt turned and kissed Elizabeth's cheek. "I am afraid I must be going. My children will be missing me, and my husband should soon be home." She curtseyed to Thomas and the Darcys. "It was a pleasure to make your acquaintance."

After they returned the farewell, Aunt Gardiner hurried back to the carriage, which waited at the kerb to return her to Gracechurch street.

"Come," said Elizabeth to Georgiana. "You must tell me all you have learnt from these London masters. Remember that I never had the luxury. I am envious indeed."

"I provided a piano master last season." Thomas's dry tone did not escape her notice.

"Yes, but only briefly, and dear Georgiana also has a cello master."

"And drawing," said Georgiana. "Though I am not very accomplished at drawing."

Elizabeth's eyes caught Fitzwilliam's, and she passed in front of him with an extra bit of sway to her hips. "Your brother will need to find employment of his own if he hires too many masters."

His warm laugh from behind filled that hole that had been ever-present since she departed Pemberley. The problem was it would reappear as soon as he departed at the end of the evening.

Georgiana giggled and pressed her elbow into Elizabeth's side. "You do enjoy teasing my brother."

Elizabeth nudged her back. "And you. I have teased you often enough. I do confess your brother enjoys such a stern façade, that I take great pleasure in making him smile."

A light laugh came from Jane. "My sister has always been thus." She glanced down to her gown. "Should we not change for dinner?"

"We should," said Elizabeth.

Everyone paused just inside the door to the drawing room, and Thomas glanced at the clock. "We have enough time before the meal is served if you would be more comfortable, though we are a small family party. It is hardly necessary."

"I believe I would prefer it." Jane looked to Elizabeth. "Would you mind terribly?"

"No, as I would care to refresh myself." She turned to their company. "Pray, excuse us for a moment. We shall return soon."

Elizabeth and Jane curtseyed and hurried upstairs where Lalande made quick work of cleaning up Elizabeth and readying her for dinner. Upon her return to the drawing room, she strode straight to the couch to sit beside Georgiana. "Now tell me what you have learnt." To which, the girl had no difficulty in recounting the lessons she had partaken of since coming to London.

Almost ten minutes later, Jane arrived at the same time Mrs. Grigg entered to announce dinner was served. While they dined, Georgiana regaled them with tales of Evie and her bravery with the swans at the Serpentine. They further discussed her studies and what she currently practised on the pianoforte.

The main object for Elizabeth was to avoid Fitzwilliam as much as possible. She could not discount Jane's knowledge of her disposition. If she paid Fitzwilliam too much attention, Jane would recognise more than they should reveal. However, the exercise in restraint was not an easy one. By the end of dinner, her skin almost strangled her while she fought to keep control over her emotions.

As usual, the men departed for Thomas's study for brandy while the ladies adjourned to the withdrawing room. Jane sat near Georgiana, but not accustomed to the grandeur of a duke's home, folded her hands in her lap. "My sister tells me you are very accomplished at the pianoforte. I hope you will play for us."

Georgiana peered at Elizabeth, who nodded. "'Tis only Jane. She will think it lovely no matter your mistakes. She claims Mary plays her ponderous etudes well."

"Lizzy!"

"You do."

"Your Grace?"

When Elizabeth turned, Mr. Hughes stood in the door. "I beg your pardon for interrupting, but the duke wishes you to join him in his study."

"Does he request your presence for brandy often?" asked Jane, her voice a mite high.

"No, tonight is the first time he has sent for me. I cannot credit the request, actually." She stood and smoothed her gown. "I should see what he needs. Do not let Georgiana become shy. As you saw earlier, she is not so reserved once she is comfortable—a trait both Darcys share, by the way."

"You have my word."

"Miss Bennet has been very kind." Georgiana spoke primly with her fingers fidgeting in the folds of her skirt. "I am certain we shall get along well."

Elizabeth passed through the corridor to her husband's study and knocked.

"Yes," he said loudly.

She stepped inside her husband's refuge, which was lined with shelves of books and possessed a large portrait of his mother over the fireplace. Finally, she gave herself free rein to look unreservedly at Fitzwilliam, drinking him in as if she had not laid eyes on him in years. He looked fit and well. She could not ask for more. "You sent for me?"

Thomas stood with a smile. "I thought you and Fitzwilliam would like a moment or two alone. I have noticed you take more care to be circumspect with Jane than with Georgiana."

Her eyes held fast to Fitzwilliam's. He was not offended, was he? "Jane would more readily recognise my feelings. I must be more careful—especially now. I trust my sister not to speak of it, yet I do fear her censure. I cannot bear to have her think poorly of me." Her hands clenched and wrung at one another. "I hope you were not offended."

"No." Fitzwilliam stepped closer and flexed and released his hand as though he itched to touch her too. "I suspected your reasoning. Do not make yourself uneasy."

"You have ten minutes," said Thomas. "I believe if you take too much time away from Jane and Georgiana they may ask too many questions." Thomas walked towards a door that connected to the library. "I shall knock softly before I return."

When the door closed behind him, she rushed into Fitzwilliam's arms. He held her close and kissed her hair twice before drawing back, cradling her face in his hands. "You are with child."

"How does everyone know by simply looking at me? Jane, my aunt, Lady Matlock, and now you have all guessed." She put her hands over the small swell that was still concealed by her gown. "The babe has not even quickened, so I cannot be sure. The midwife believes it is so."

His fingers caressed her cheeks and her neck until his palms rested on her shoulders. "At Pemberley, then?"

"Yes, I had my courses between your visit to Worthstone and ours to Pemberley. Do I truly appear so very different? My aunt and yours are not as surprising since they are familiar with the condition, but Jane recognised it from when Mama carried Lydia."

"Have they said how they knew?"

She nodded and sighed. "My face is fuller."

He nodded while his fingers trailed another line down her cheek. "Your breasts are also larger."

He pressed a kiss to the top of each globe, making her smile and roll her eyes. "You noticed what Thomas did not."

That low chuckle she adored rumbled from his chest before he kissed her lips softly. "He has little interest in them whereas I am quite fond of them." He drew her to the sofa where he sat and pulled her gown taut across her stomach. "You are also rounder here." His forehead pressed just above the slight bulge before he kissed it. A shuddering breath came from him. "I knew this could happen. I also knew it would be painful to watch you bear a child I could never claim. Yet, a part of me is satisfied you will have a part of me and my heart inside of you. Is that nonsensical?"

"No, I have wished I could provide you with some irreplaceable part of myself."

His eyes were shiny when he looked up. "You have, when you gave me your body. 'Tis a gift I shall never forget."

"But you cannot carry it with you."

"Perhaps a lock of your hair? I shall not attempt to cut one myself. I do not want to risk your abigail's wrath, but if she could—"

"Of course."

He drew her onto his lap and wrapped her in his arms—those arms where she belonged, where her soul calmed. He kissed her long and softly, his tongue languidly touching hers as their lips melded together.

"How I want you to love me," she said in that breathy voice that always appeared after they kissed.

"I would not want to harm you or the babe."

His hand covered their child, and she leaned her head against his shoulder. "You could never harm us."

"There is also little time for me to love you as you deserve." His hand slipped under her skirts to where their babe rested inside her. He leaned down and kissed near her navel. "Be kind to your Mama. I love her just as much as I love you."

"Thomas will make me depart London once the babe quickens." She fought the tears that burned her eyes, making her voice crack.

"I am loath to part from you, but I agree with him." He removed his hand from her skirts and placed his palm back on their babe while his thumb caressed it through her gown. "There is too much disease here. I also would not want you harmed by James when he discovers your condition."

Her hand covered his as her stomach clenched. Could she truly be in danger? "Do you think it likely?"

"He owes more than he can repay on his current income. He may become desperate. After the issue with his heart, Thomas has revised his will out of concern over the possibility, replacing my father who was his executor. That duty now falls to me, which makes me guardian of any children upon Thomas's death."

She sighed and shook her head. "I do not want to think of James in that manner. If I consider the situation too much, I would never cease fearing for myself and this child."

"Do not fret. No matter the circumstances, know I shall do everything in my power to protect the both of you."

She kissed his temple. "I know. He is fortunate to have both you and Thomas looking after his well-being."

The light knock came from the door, and Elizabeth kissed Fitzwilliam once more before she dragged herself from his lap. She had no desire to remove herself, yet she was not comfortable in such an intimate position in front of Thomas since he was by law and the church her husband; however, she did retain hold of Fitzwilliam's hand.

Thomas entered a moment later and smiled. "I trust you had a good visit. Did Fitzwilliam tell you of my visit to my solicitors?"

"Of your will?"

"Yes. I believe James too much of a drunkard to attempt to harm you or the child, but I am taking no chances."

Fitzwilliam brushed his lips against the hand he held. "You should return before your sister and mine seek you out."

After one last caress of her fingers down his dear face, she fought every urge in her body to remain and let propriety and society be damned and walked through the door. Her heart bled with every step that took her further from her beloved.

# Chapter 15

Elizabeth held her skirts out of the dirt as she alighted the carriage and entered the large building belonging to the British Institution. Before leaving London last Season, she had accompanied Lady Vranes to an exhibition at the Royal Academy, though Laura had indicated on several occasions how much she preferred the winter exhibition at the British Institution since they carried more contemporary art rather than the old masters the Pall Mall location featured in the summer.

"I am pleased you could join me today," said Lady Vranes, who walked beside her. "I enjoy your society much more than others, and you always have such interesting reasons for liking a painting when I do not. I am only sorry your sister could not join you."

"My aunt was unwell this morning and sent a note requesting Jane's aid. My sister is too good to say no."

Lady Vranes regarded Elizabeth with her head tilted a fraction. "The two of you are not so dissimilar then. You would do the same, would you not?"

"I would, though Jane is much more gracious about it."

When they entered the first room, Elizabeth surveyed the myriad of paintings hanging on the wall. The works littered every surface and contained such varied subjects: everything from portraits, to histories, to landscapes, to still life all on display for a viewer's perusal.

She followed her friend to the first painting, a landscape by a man named Turner. Elizabeth studied the sweeping brush strokes and the play of light and colours on the canvas before her. The sky glowed with the rising sun. She was tracing the edge of one of the clouds when a gentle fluttering in her belly made her stop and place her palm against the swell. She held her breath as she stood stock still waiting. Would it happen again? Her heartbeat echoed frantically in her ears. Was that really what she thought it was?

"Lizzy? Are you well?"

She turned to Lady Vranes who watched her instead of the work in front of them. "Yes, I believe the child moved. I felt a slight flutter—really a trifle of a thing."

Her friend smiled and looped her arm through Elizabeth's. "That does explain your inattention. I asked what you thought of the painting, and you merely stared at your hand."

"Forgive me."

"No need for that. I am certain I would be much the same if it were me. We have never been blessed, but I shall say that if you want him to move again, maybe you should not bestow all of your attention on the possibility. What is that American proverb I once heard? A watched pot never boils?"

Elizabeth let one side of her lips curve. "I like that." She turned her eyes back to the painting and allowed the scene of fishermen attending their catch on the shore while several large ships loomed in the background settle in her mind. As she had first noted, the setting sun certainly captured the eye—particularly the colours and the way the sunlight seemed to diffuse through the clouds.

She pointed to one of the larger vessels. "That is a warship, is it not? I have only seen illustrations before."

"I believe so. I believe the other is a prison hulk."

Elizabeth laughed and looked at her friend. "Laura, how would you recognise a prison hulk?"

With a roll of her eyes and an elbow to Elizabeth's ribs, Lady Vranes huffed. "Because we sailed from London when we travelled to France before the upheaval. During our departure from the harbour, my husband told me of the different ships. His brother was in the navy, and my husband took an active interest in the vessels for that reason."

"You must have been quite young."

"I was seventeen and newly married. We travelled to Paris and then Italy."

How fortunate to have the ability to see those foreign places! "How long did your journey take?"

"We were gone a year complete."

A sigh came from Elizabeth's lips as she turned back to the painting. "I would dearly love to travel. Maybe someday."

"His Grace certainly has the means," said Laura before she peered at Elizabeth's mid-section. "Though I doubt you will be having any grand adventures for the rest of this year."

She glanced down at her palm still resting on her belly. "No, I shall return to Worthstone where I shall remain until my confinement. Perhaps we shall return next season. I suspect our plans will depend on my husband's health and whether we wish to travel with a babe." She would miss Lady Vranes and a few of the diversions of London, yet she would prefer to remain in the country with her child.

Elizabeth pointed to the painting. "Do you think he refers to the war?"

"Very likely," said Lady Vranes. "I do like how he captures the light and how it disperses in the mist."

"I do too."

With a tug on her arm, her friend pulled her to the next painting. "Come, I must decide what I wish to purchase."

"Do you have a place to display it?" asked Elizabeth with a ridiculously girlish giggle. Every wall in Lady Vranes's home bore the paintings the family had collected for generations.

Lady Vranes cocked her head over her shoulder. "Do I require one?"

The two dissolved into laughter while they shifted through those around them who stared at their happiness. Why could people not enjoy themselves? Such a ludicrous notion.

When they stopped in front of the next painting, that flutter returned for another brief moment. She bit her lip to prevent a gasp. He was truly there, inside her—a joined part of Fitzwilliam and her.

Elizabeth reminded herself to focus on Lady Vranes's comments on the work in front of them. She might as well enjoy as much of London as she could. After today, she had a fortnight before she would be force-marched from London to the isolation of Worthstone. While home held a certain appeal, the lack of company rendered her melancholy. How long would she be on her own? And how would she bear it?

Elizabeth stood by the side of the dance floor while her husband spoke to some lord or another behind her. He never enjoyed watching the gowns and the people on the floor turn and step the pattern of each and every set while Elizabeth found a certain enjoyment in the graceful lines and movement. With a lack of partners in Meryton, she was occasionally forced to sit out a dance so all the ladies could have an opportunity to enjoy a set. During those times, she had learnt to appreciate the show as well.

Jane's hand gripped hers a little tighter. They had only arrived moments ago, so the poor dear was beside herself at the thought of a ball as grand as this one. The hosts, another lord and lady of some title she had no interest in remembering, held this ball annually to celebrate the commencement of parliament, which was why her husband had been so set on attending.

"Good evening."

She and Jane startled and turned at Fitzwilliam's deep voice from behind her. He stood tall dressed in a fashionable yet understated black suit with his black armband prominently displayed.

"Mr. Darcy," she said, curtseying and gripping her free hand into a tight fist. "I hope you are well."

"I am, thank you." He held out a hand next to him. "I hope you remember my cousin, Viscount Carlisle."

Elizabeth dipped her head in greeting. "Yes, sir. How are you, my lord?"

"I am very well." Carlisle allowed his lips to curve slightly as he bowed. "Pray, would you introduce me to your companion?"

"She is my sister, Miss Jane Bennet." Elizabeth leaned a bit closer to her sister. "Jane, this is Viscount Carlisle. You met his mother, Lady Matlock, at Madame Bonheur's."

Jane curtseyed and wore her usual placid smile. "I am pleased to meet you, my lord."

The viscount looked to the dance floor where the most recent set now disbanded. "Miss Bennet, are you perchance free to stand up with me?"

Her sister's eyes gave a slight flare, she licked her lips, and nodded. "I am."

"Would you do me the honour?" Jane placed her hand atop Carlisle's, and he led her to the line as the next dance formed.

"He surprised her," said Elizabeth. "Did you tell him to ask her?"

"No." Fitzwilliam stepped forward to stand beside her while they watched the dancers join the line. "He spotted your sister upon entering the ballroom and requested me arrange an introduction. I would have done the duty myself only he became impatient."

She could not help her grin. "My mother always says, 'Jane could not be so beautiful for nothing.'" That low laugh from near her shoulder again filled that familiar aching hole.

"Carlisle dances but rarely," said Fitzwilliam, leaning a bit closer, "and I have never seen him so eager to meet a lady."

She exhaled audibly, watching Jane blush as she curtseyed to Carlisle's bow. "I must counsel her to keep this to herself, or Mama will begin predicting their marriage within a se'nnight."

"How are you?" Though they were in company, his voice had changed to a softer, more intimate tone. With the music and so many people dancing, the likelihood someone would notice was slim.

"I am well. The child has quickened. I depart for Worthstone in ten days."

He inhaled in one long, even sound. "You will miss your sister greatly. I know you planned to spend a great deal of time with her this Season." He was correct. She would miss Jane terribly. She had waited so long to spend that time with her beloved sister only to be made to separate from her once more.

"I shall miss many of the diversions of London. Do you intend to remain much longer?" How she wished he could return with her!

"Another month. Lady Cathcrine has decreed we shall spend Easter at Rosings this year. Georgiana and I shall travel to Kent, then back to London for a fortnight before we return home to Pemberley. I do not look forward to the time at my aunt's. I would have remained in Derbyshire had I not felt I was cheating Georgiana of the masters here. I confess I am greatly anticipating our return home."

How tedious this was to carry such a neutral conversation. She did hope he understood her hint that she would miss him.

"Fitzwilliam!" Her husband emerged from the group where he had spent the last twenty minutes. "Did you come alone? You rarely attend a social function without Carlisle in tow."

Fitzwilliam smiled though it was still not as joyful as before his father's passing. "I believe he drags me along, cousin."

Thomas shook Fitzwilliam's hand. "Too true I believe." He held out his arm for Elizabeth, which she took lest it appear she was angry with him. She might have lost a great deal of respect for him due to his scheming, and yes, she also held resentment at his officiousness, yet he was still her husband. They were also in a crowded room full of those who would latch onto any discord and promote it for their own selfish reasons. "So, where is Carlisle?"

"Dancing with Jane," said Elizabeth, pointedly looking at Jane when she responded. Her sister's cheeks still held a healthy pink hue while she demurely watched Carlisle out of the corner of her eye.

Thomas's eyebrows lifted high. "Carlisle is wearing a ridiculously lost expression, and they have only just met. Perhaps I should raise her fortune?"

"I would prefer he care more for her than her fortune." Elizabeth's lips pressed into a tight line as her eyes met Fitzwilliam's. "Happiness in marriage is not simply a matter of chance. A couple should be in love."

"I do not believe you should have a problem there. He appears half-way in love already." Thomas chuckled and returned his attention to Fitzwilliam. "I hope you will join us for dinner soon. Elizabeth wishes to return to Worthstone, and as you know, I can deny her nothing. I am certain she would dearly love to visit with Georgiana before she departs."

Not exactly the truth, but again, too many people milled about.

"Georgiana will be eager to spend an evening with both of you. I shall look forward to your invitation."

Fitzwilliam disappeared not long after, presumably to check on the colonel, whom they had left in the card rooms. Meanwhile, Carlisle returned Jane and fetched her punch when she was not dancing. He even requested the supper dance upon the conclusion of their first set together, though he also stood up with Elizabeth.

After supper, Elizabeth begged fatigue, so they departed for Worth House. As soon as Elizabeth entered her bedchamber, she nearly fainted at the sight of Fitzwilliam sitting on her bed.

"What are you . . .? How?"

"Before supper, Thomas put me in his carriage, claiming I had overindulged on spirits. Worth House is significantly closer than Darcy House, or so the driver said when he helped me inside. I was shown to a bedchamber and shortly after, your maid brought me through the servants' passages here."

"This is too risky," said Elizabeth, covering her face with her hands. "I cannot deny that I want you here—more than anything—yet what of our situation. What of Georgiana?"

"Your maid will wake me before the servants are about so I can remove to my bedchamber. Tomorrow, I shall depart as any other guest." He stood and pulled her into his arms. It was so difficult not to sink into him—not to breathe in the scent of his cedar-tinged cologne combined with that unique part that was only him. "I have missed you so. I only want to hold you in my arms for what time we have. I am more likely to be caught sneaking back now than in the middle of the night."

"I suppose." Her arms wrapped around his waist. "I have missed you dreadfully, yet I worry for our exposure. My sister would not understand."

"Do you expect her?"

"No, she knows I begged to depart due to exhaustion. Carlisle danced a second time with her. Does she have reason to hope?"

"He has never danced a second at a ball with the same lady. I would expect him to call." He rubbed his hands down her sides and grasped her hips. "Turn around. I am your abigail tonight."

She laughed while she turned in place. "You are a rather handsome abigail. I have never seen one so tall or wearing trousers." He had shed his topcoat, his waistcoat, and his cravat before her entrance. His dishabille only made him appear manlier.

Her gown loosened, and she helped him remove it, laying it across a chair with her stays following suit. He brushed her hair once it was free from the pins and ran his fingers through her long curls. "Your hair is lovely. Pray do not cut it."

"Lalande trims the ends when they require it, but I do not want it too short. My sister Mary keeps hers just below her shoulders, and it looks very pretty when styled. I simply prefer mine longer."

When they finally climbed into bed, he drew the chemise over her head and tossed it on the floor. "I know you are tired. I only want to see you and hold you close." He had shed what remained of his own clothes before he laid down.

He trailed his fingers along her breasts before resting his palm on the swell that was his child. "You have changed so much."

"We have discussed that my breasts are larger. I have needed to order new gowns. I do not believe I mentioned that they ache too."

"Your nipples are darker."

"Are they?" She rolled to her back and looked down, trying to discern if there was truly a change.

He kissed one and reached up to press his lips to hers. "Yes, but it is slight." His fingers began to trail soft circles over the babe while he moved down and touched his lips just above her navel. "I love you, little one. I should not be here as often as I would like, yet never doubt my feelings for you or your mother."

Tears welled in her eyes and stung mercilessly. He rested his head against her abdomen while his eyes held hers and her fingers trailed up and down his back. "What does it feel like when he moves?"

"A very light flutter—like a butterfly's wings. I almost did not recognise it for what it was when it finally happened."

"My mother found herself ill early on with Georgiana."

"I felt poorly. I was sick a few times, but nothing too arduous. The journey here did not help one bit. However, now that the sickness has waned, my stamina is better, and I am also hungrier than I was. The midwife also said I would have a greater appetite for marital relations." Her face burnt during the confession.

He drew up on his elbows. "And do you?"

She concentrated on where her fingernail scratched the bedsheet instead of looking at him as she nodded. "I have missed you so dreadfully. I suppose I also desire that connection."

Fitzwilliam crawled over her, lifting her face so they were eye to eye. "You no longer fear my constancy?"

A warm tear landed upon her cheek which she swiftly wiped away. "I fear you abandoning me due to our hopeless situation. None of this is easy—especially for you."

He touched his forehead to hers and his chest heaved. "I do find this arduous, yet you have it no easier. My affection for you is not so trifling or inconstant, though I confess seeing you carry our child is more painful than I could have imagined. I want so much to drag you away, so I can be with you both—so he will know I am really his father."

She reached to kiss him, to convey every bit of her heart with every movement of her lips. "I love you. You are this child's father. You always will be, regardless of what society believes."

He carefully covered her and deepened the kiss while one of his hands cupped her breast.

"Careful. They hurt."

She ached for him more than she ever had in the past. This one night would likely have to carry her through to her confinement since she had no idea when they would see one another again. Her hands dug into his shoulders as that same hand abandoned her breast and slid between her legs. Her fingernails dug small crescents into his skin, and she moaned.

"You are so warm."

"I need you so much." She reached down to guide him toward her core. "I need you to love me."

When he slipped home, they both groaned and started rocking with one another, their gazes locked and holding steady. How was this so much more fulfilling than before? Was it merely the effect of the babe or had missing him made her more sensitive to his touch, his smell, his mere presence? Another warm tear landed upon her cheek, this one trickling down her temple and into her hair. Fitzwilliam brushed his lips along that damp trail and pressed his forehead to hers.

"I shall always love you, Lizzy. Do not ever doubt me. I shall love you until I die."

*February 27th 1810*
*Worth House*
*London*

*My dearest Fitzwilliam,*

*I must depart London in the morning, yet how I wish to stay and have more time with you! The past month has passed far too swiftly and too little time was spent in your embrace to satisfy me. I do not know, however, if all of the time in the world would appease me. We can stand in the same room, and I want naught but to be in your arms. 'Tis useless to deny. I can control my feelings no more than I can control the movements of our babe in my womb.*

*I am indebted to Lalande, Colin, and Thomas for arranging our night together, which must keep me contented until we can see one another again.*

*Do not doubt that a part of my heart remains with you. You claimed it from nearly the first moment of our acquaintance, capturing me with those crystal blue eyes and your caring soul. In the past year, I have learnt every emotion you feel is with your entire being and is conveyed through your expressive eyes. Though you do your best to mask your emotions, your love for me and our child shines from them when you look at us. I know you too well. I see what you try to hide from the rest of the world. I see you.*

*If you and Georgiana can journey to Worthstone for the summer, you would be most welcome. My dear aunt is with child herself and is unable to travel for my lying-in, my sister will be home (unless your cousin claims her first). Thomas was kind enough to offer for Jane to journey and remain at Worthstone with me for a time, but she receives your cousin's attentions with pleasure. I do not wish to remove her when she may find her heart's desire is indeed Carlisle. I cannot deny her what I would want with all my heart if I had the same opportunity.*

*I will not invite my mother—no matter how much she cajoles me to do otherwise.*

*I know it will be difficult, but I ache for you to be near. I do understand if it is more than you can bear.*

*With all my love,*

*Lizzy*

# Chapter 16

*March 28<sup>th</sup> 1810*
*Gracechurch Street*
*London*

*My dear Lizzy,*

*How much has occurred since you departed nearly a month ago! As you know from my last letter, I remained in London with my uncle and aunt, who wrote to father and requested my continued presence. You must help me believe all that has happened, for I still have difficulty crediting what has occurred for myself.*

*Before I returned to Gracechurch Street, Viscount Carlisle called upon me several times as did one other gentleman who I met at the same ball. I did not confess to you at the time, but for some reason, I felt unfaithful to the viscount by allowing the other gentleman to call. I am not certain why I felt as I did on such a trifling acquaintance, yet I did.*

*The other gentleman ceased his calls once I removed to Aunt and Uncle's home—thank goodness! Perhaps he felt Gracechurch street below him, though Viscount Carlisle did not. He has continued to call, Lizzy!*

*He is everything a gentleman should be. He is handsome and kind, and I enjoy his conversation. He is livelier than me, but I do not mind. He brings roses when he comes, he takes me on walks in the park, and he has planned excursions with aunt and uncle. We shall attend the theatre this evening.*

*I must thank you for inviting me, even if for just a few weeks. For had not you and your obliging husband allowed it, Viscount Carlisle would not have expressed his intention to court me last night after dinner. I can scarce believe it! I asked Aunt to pinch me after he departed. Lizzy, I am so happy!*

Elizabeth wiped the tears from her face as she folded the missive. All she had ever hoped was Jane and her sisters marry for love, so why was she weeping like a babe when she should be celebrating her sister's happiness?

*April 14<sup>th</sup> 1810*
*Longbourn*
*Hertfordshire*

*Dear Lizzy,*

*Have you heard the news of our dear Jane? Oh, I am beside myself with such flutterings and nerves I do not know what to do. I have insisted upon travelling to London to help Jane ensnare this viscount who is courting her, but your father adamantly refuses to allow it. He will not give me the carriage or even the funds to travel by post! You must write to him and tell him how much Jane needs my aid. Your aunt is a lovely woman, yet she will not push Jane along as I shall. You must see that! I know he will listen to you.*

*While we are indebted to your aunt and uncle for allowing Jane to remain, I am appalled at your departure from London—and without your husband! Jane indicated in her latest correspondence how you abandoned him while he remained for the House of Lords. He is such an important man, so you must have displeased him in some fashion. He requires an heir, Lizzy. You cannot become with child when you live separately. Oh, what am I to do with you? I am certain you have disgraced us somehow, and Jane's suitor will abandon her. You ungrateful child!*

*Now, you must return to London post haste! I care not for your excuses. Do as I say, child. I know what is best for all of you. Besides, now that Jane looks to be so advantageously wed, you must invite Mary and introduce her to rich men as well. She certainly will not attract a duke, but a gentleman would do quite well.*

*Your mother,*

*Francine Bennet*

Elizabeth groaned and covered her eyes with her hand. "Oh, Mama. The last thing I shall do is pen a letter to Papa. You would ruin everything." She pressed her palm to her bulging abdomen. "I know I am a coward for not telling her, but I do not want her present when you are born. She would make us both miserable."

A hand or a foot pressed into the side of her stomach, and she gently pushed against that spot. The tiny limb moved and hit back hard at her palm, making her smile. "No, Mama. We are content to remain exactly where we are."

She tossed the letter into the fire.

*May 10ᵗʰ 1810*
*Gracechurch Street*
*London*

*Dearest Lizzy,*

*I do not have the time for a long missive, but I wished to pen a note as soon as possible. Nicholas has proposed! I love him, and oh my, but I am engaged to him! I dread him meeting Mama, but he has assured me of his constancy regardless of how silly she behaves. Yes, I am being uncharitable, yet I know you will understand. Forgive me for the brevity of this letter!*

*Yours very affectionately,*

*Jane*

She wiped her damp cheeks—this time with her handkerchief. Thanks to her, Jane had a fortune which would ease her way into society, which was something Elizabeth had not possessed. Jane would also have Elizabeth's position as a duchess to help her along. Jane also had love. Elizabeth should want to dance a jig, yet she touched the back of her hand and checked the tone of her skin to ensure it had not turned a despicable shade of green. How terrible of a sister she was!

Her hand covered the spot where her child kicked within her. She had a piece of Fitzwilliam. She needed to learn to be content with what she had and not what she wanted and could not possess.

"Your Grace?"

When she looked up from her letter, Mrs. Hamilton stood in the doorway. "Yes, is something amiss?"

"A messenger arrived a few moments ago with this." She held a letter in front of her as she walked forward. "I have paid him. He is currently having luncheon with the staff while his horse rests. He indicated he was to remain in the event you had a response."

Fitzwilliam's even hand covered the outside, and she hurried to break the seal.

*May 12*$^{th}$ *1810*
*Worth House*
*London*

Why was a letter in Fitzwilliam's hand addressed from Worth House?

*Dear Lizzy,*

*A week ago, I received a letter from Thomas's valet, requesting my immediate presence in London. I have never known the man to exaggerate so I set out as swiftly as possible. Unfortunately, with the lack of a full moon, we had no light to journey through the night but travelled as long as we had sufficient light, setting off as soon as the first rays of the sun peeked over the horizon.*

*Without beating about the bush, Thomas had another attack or episode as you called it last year. He lives but is weak—exceedingly weak. I have never seen him so ill. The physician has bled him, though we do not know if it will help his current condition, which is grave indeed.*

*Despite the physician's recommendation, Thomas is insistent he wishes to return to Worthstone. He is weary for home and desires to be close when the child is born. We travel at first light on the morrow so we should not be far behind this message.*

*Pray, have Thomas's rooms prepared and notify the local physician. I do not intend on rushing the trip, but I cannot guarantee Thomas will weather the journey well.*

*Yours,*

*Fitzwilliam Darcy*

"Ready His Grace's apartments and prepare Mr. Darcy's usual rooms. We shall need to adjust the menus for the next week as well as plan the duke's meals."

Mrs. Hamilton placed a hand to her chest. "He has had another episode?"

"Yes, and Mr. Darcy writes to let us know of their immediate return. His Grace has travelled against the advice of his physician, so we must notify Mr. Barrow. He will need to come as soon as the duke arrives."

"This one was worse than in the past?"

"Yes, Mr. Darcy claims it is his worst yet."

The woman shook her head. "I shall set the maids to work and set Mrs. Bunting to making broth and food the duke will require."

"Thank you."

"Ma'am?"

Elizabeth glanced back up.

"Are you well?"

"I am. Why do you ask?"

"I am probably being overcautious, but I saw you crying when I entered. I know you have been lonely since your return, but I understand why the master would have you in the country in your condition. Too much pestilence in the city, even during the winter. If only Miss Darcy could visit. She always lifts your spirits."

She gave a small lift to her lips, though she would have preferred sagging into the chair. "Miss Darcy is a dear, sweet girl. Perhaps once my husband is settled, Mr. Darcy will send for her."

"The Darcys are both great friends of yours and my master's. I daresay they will lift your spirits right up." The woman smiled, curtseyed, and bustled off while Elizabeth turned the missive in her hands.

How poor was Thomas's condition? Though she did not love her husband, she did hold a certain affection for him—not love, but a friendship of sorts. On the occasions where they spoke or when they were in company, their relationship was quite amiable.

Well, she could do naught but wait for the time being. She would soon know all.

The next evening, Elizabeth reclined on her bed, propped on a multitude of pillows to be comfortable. She did not expect the babe for another month, yet her back ached fiercely and her feet were swollen to the size of one of the work horse's hooves.

Despite the book in front of her, her eyes had just started to flutter closed when a horse whinnied from outside and the tell-tale racket of an approaching carriage carried through the open window.

"Thomas and Fitzwilliam," she said as she shifted her way to the edge of the mattress, pulled on her dressing gown and slippers, and pushed herself up to stand. The babe made walking difficult as well, so she waddled down the corridor, pressing a palm to her lower back while she moved.

She held the railing while she took the stairs with haste. When she reached the bottom step, her foot somehow missed the solid surface and sent her to the floor in a heap.

"Lizzy!"

"Elizabeth!" The voice was weak, though forceful.

Bewildered at the sudden change of height, she glanced up to Fitzwilliam, Thomas, and Thomas's valet, who stood before her, their eyes wide. Fitzwilliam and Colin each held Thomas by an arm, helping him to walk without being carried. The duke's horrid complexion appeared a mottled grey rather than a healthy pinkish hue.

She placed her hands on the floor and rolled to all fours so she could hoist herself up. "I am well. My rear end will likely be bruised, but I am well."

When she reached for the stair railing, Fitzwilliam stood before her with his hands out for her to take. As he helped her to stand, he wore a tremendous scowl. "You should not take those stairs with such haste. What if harm came to you or the child?"

With a huff, she planted her feet and stood. "I heard the carriage. I did not think I moved so very fast." She frowned at him and crossed her arms over her chest. "I have descended those stairs daily since my return to Worthstone. I have not fallen until tonight. I am simply fat and ungainly."

He took Thomas's arm and wound it back over his shoulders as Mrs. Hamilton and Mr. Gibbs, the butler, hurried into the hall.

"Forgive us, Your Grace. We did not expect you so late."

"I wanted to sleep in my own bed tonight, so I insisted we continue."

Fitzwilliam's eyes met hers, and she held out her arm to the stairs. "We should get His Grace into bed and comfortable. He has had a long journey. Mrs. Hamilton," she said, pointing to one of her fingers. "Pray heat some water for Mr. Darcy and His Grace and send tea to the duke's bedchamber. I daresay he will desire refreshment, and if this is similar to the last, the physician will limit his brandy and port."

"Mrs. Bunting has broth prepared."

"Good, send some up. He has likely not eaten as he ought during the journey."

The men neared the top of the stairs as Elizabeth turned to follow them. "We shall need to send word to Mr. Barrow first thing on the morrow."

"Yes, ma'am."

Elizabeth's hand returned to her lower back as she started back towards the family wing. She had no sooner made it half-way than Fitzwilliam appeared. "I am capable of climbing the stairs."

"Forgive me if I wish to ensure your safety. We have enough to fret about with Thomas."

He walked the remainder of the way at her side, an arm poised behind her as though she might collapse at any moment. She wanted to slap that hand down and chastise him but could not without giving some hint of their intimacy to someone who might overhear.

Fitzwilliam knocked before entering Thomas's bedchamber, and Colin answered without delay. "He is comfortable for now."

"I ordered tea and broth to be brought to his sitting room. Water should be delivered soon."

"Good. I am certain some nourishment would do him good, and he has always detested the dust of travelling."

She waddled over to her husband's bedside and took his hand. "Thomas, do you require anything?"

"A new heart," he said with a breathy laugh. His hand reached out and rested on her now sizeable stomach. "He has grown considerably."

Elizabeth shifted his hand to where the babe pressed against her side. "What if he is a she?"

The child rolled and Thomas's eyes softened. He cleared his throat. "She will inherit all but the dukedom. If this is a boy, all is saved. James will not ruin everything I have worked to build. I needed to try, you understand." Their eyes met. His were too shiny. "You refer to him as a 'he' as well, do you not?"

"I do, but I never considered why. I do not know what he is."

He cleared his throat again as his eyes fluttered. "We shall know soon enough. I survived this journey. Now I simply must live long enough to see him born." His eyes opened and watched his hand. "Regardless of your suspicions, I believe this is my heir—the future Duke of Leeds."

He relaxed his arm back onto the mattress, so Elizabeth tucked the covers around him before she stepped over to

Fitzwilliam. "Will you remain or will you retire? I can have someone show you to your rooms."

"Let Colin take care of me," said the duke weakly. "No one need hover over me as if I might die at any moment. You need your rest, Elizabeth."

Elizabeth huffed and set her hands on her hips. "The two of you arrive after months of my being alone in this house and immediately tell me how to live. I am well and have done admirably thus far." Without another word, she marched through the door to her own apartments and slammed it behind her.

She had been lonely for months, and finally, someone arrived only to issue commands and criticise. If she had known their intentions, they could have remained in London!

Fitzwilliam followed Lalande through the servants' passages. Due to the late hour, no one milled about, yet he had a suspicion Colin was standing guard nearby keeping them from discovery.

They reached a door, and she opened it. "I did not tell Madame you were coming."

He slipped inside and bit his lip to keep from laughing. How many pillows did she have between her and the headboard? She lay propped in an elaborate nest of cushions and had obviously been reading since her book rested on the top of her stomach. She also snored lightly.

He trod carefully to the bed and sat on the side. He brushed a few loose hairs back from her face and sighed. He had been selfish. He and Georgiana had returned to Pemberley in April. Here it was nearly June, and he had not come to see if Elizabeth was well. He had not brought Georgiana to visit. Elizabeth had been cooped up in this house since March, her only company the ladies of the neighbourhood—only most of consequence were still in London, limiting her to the wives of the local country squires and the vicar's wife. Her existence must have been quite solitary.

His heart squeezed and broke open, and he clenched his eyes shut. He would not cry. The knowledge that she carried his child was difficult enough. The more she increased, the more painful it became. He loved their child, yet he could not claim him—he could not give him the Darcy name or Pemberley if it was a boy. This child would always believe Thomas was his father. The torment of that knowledge was why he had stayed away. He had missed Elizabeth dreadfully, but he had thought it easier when he was not in her company. He was wrong.

"Fitzwilliam?" Her musical voice opened his eyes. "I did not know to expect you. I hoped, but . . ."

"Colin and Lalande arranged my passage as usual." He removed the book from her stomach with a smile. He could not let on about how he felt. Elizabeth's lot was not any easier than his. The revelation would only cause great upset. "You appear comfortable."

"This is an improvement. My back has ached a great deal as of late."

"Perhaps I can help by rubbing it for you. Lie on your side."

She rolled and arranged the cushions so she could relax. "My lower back and my feet have been difficult as the babe has grown."

He dug his fingers into the flesh on either side of her backbone and rubbed toward her shoulders. Once he had gone four or five inches, he returned to that starting point again and repeated the process.

"Does this help?"

"Yes. Can you continue until this child decides to be born?"

He smiled and pressed a bit harder. He peered down at her ankles and winced at how swollen they appeared. Elizabeth had always had such dainty feet. Those were hardly petite anymore.

"I can rub your feet too, if you like."

She took his hand and kissed it. "You are too good to me." A long drawn out breath made her chest expand and contract as she relaxed into his fingers. "Have you seen Jane?"

"I attended the ball Lady Matlock gave in her honour. She was radiantly happy. When you are not so sleepy, I shall tell you everything. I promise."

"Good. I did not want to miss it."

"She understood," he said softly while her eyes fluttered. "She even asked if I had seen you recently."

He massaged her back and feet until she fell soundly asleep. He had even said her name, but she lightly snored, insensible to all that was around her.

For a time, he laid in front of her on his side while he watched her doze, his palm poised on her belly until the babe inside kicked strongly and rolled. He closed his eyes pressed his lips against the hard swell. "I love you, little one."

That fall on the stairs had frightened him as much as when he learnt his father had run into that burning cottage. Thomas even gave him an odd look when he took his arm to wrap around his shoulders. An hour complete was required for him to stop shaking completely. He knew the dangers of the childbed, but the tumble had brought it all rushing to the forefront of his mind.

What if Elizabeth died in childbirth? What if she and the child both died? The possibilities made his jaw clench tightly, his chest heavy, and his stomach roil. Could you lose someone who was never really yours? He could never publicly mourn her for what she was—the wife of his heart.

He shook off his melancholy thoughts and shifted behind her, pressing his chest to her back and wrapping his arm possessively around their child. Then, for the first time in a long while—since his father's death—he prayed.

# Chapter 17

*"Then landing in the moonlight dell,*
*Loud shouted of his weal to tell.*
*The Minstrel heard the far halloo,*
*And joyful from the shore withdrew."*[1]

Elizabeth paused at Thomas's hand to her arm. "What is it?"

"I am tired, and it is difficult to concentrate. Perhaps we can continue later?"

"Of course," she replied, tucking the covers around him. His colour had not improved, and instead of rallying as he had in the past, he had only deteriorated over the past fortnight. "Would you like some tea or broth?"

He shook his head and screwed his lips into a grimace. "No. I can barely tolerate what Colin makes me drink."

"You love him very much."

His eyes opened a little—as much as they had these past few days. "Yes, as much as you love Fitzwilliam. I have had the privilege of Colin's companionship for these past thirty years. I could not imagine spending my life with anyone else, though I do wish we could have been together in truth. Hiding our relationship has been difficult." He coughed and winced as he swallowed. "I would have liked to take him to the theatre, or promenade with him in Hyde Park, hearing his commentary on the ladies present." A wan smile appeared upon his face before it disappeared just as quickly. "One advantage of my passing will be that you and Fitzwilliam can finally be together. You will have no need of knowing my one regret."

The hair on the back of her neck stood on end while she squeezed his hand. "As much as I desire my life joined with Fitzwilliam's, I do not desire your death."

"No, you are too good for that. You are more practical, yet more like Jane than you realise. You also have a keen mind. 'Tis why I chose you."

She ran her fingers over the new book Thomas had brought from London. She had been reading it to him during those times Colin needed to leave Thomas's side. His valet had been a most faithful companion to the duke since their return, but his duties did require him to tend to business below stairs from time to time.

With a deep breath sucked into her lungs, she closed her eyes. "Why do you think Fitzwilliam left? He only spent the one night." She attempted to mask the shuddering exhale. Tears took so little to come these days.

Thomas's eyes flared and his frail hand covered hers this time. "Do not doubt my godson. He loves you with all that he is. Our situation is not easy, and I am certain seeing you carry his child also causes a certain amount of pain and conflict within him. I do not doubt his return. You should not either."

She flinched and rubbed her side.

"Another pain?"

"The midwife claimed they were not true labour pains," she said while attempting to relax. "However, if they are not, I now dread bringing this child into the world."

"You will be splendid." His voice trailed off.

"I shall probably keep you awake with my screaming. Jane has mentioned that Mama screamed for hours with Lydia."

His eyes remained closed as he smiled. "When does Jane wed?"

"Tomorrow."

"'Tis an extremely good match. I am only sorry you will miss the grand event."

She massaged where the pain persisted and pressed herself to stand. "I do not relish being embarrassed by Mama. My father will tell me all in his next letter. I do hope I can hold my head up around Lady Matlock the next time I am in her company."

A broken laugh escaped his lips, but he did not otherwise respond. Elizabeth set Sir Walter Scott's *The Lady of the Lake* on the side table and proceeded towards her bedchamber, but paused at the sound of the servants' door. Colin, holding a tray of broth and tea, kicked the door closed behind him.

"He has only just fallen asleep."

His shoulders dropped. "He needs to have some broth."

"He did not want it."

Colin peered to where Thomas lay. "He might not, but he should still take some nourishment."

She was not going to argue. She cared for Thomas, but Colin loved him and would, no doubt, do all he could to push for a recovery that would never happen. The physician declared a rally unlikely upon Thomas's return home. His continued deterioration simply confirmed the physician's dire prediction. The coming months would not be easy for any of them, particularly Colin. At this moment, she hurt for him. When all was over, she would be able to wed Fitzwilliam, but Colin would lose his nearly life-long companion. No matter how Thomas's illness progressed or improved, someone would lose.

A week later, as she read to Thomas, Colin returned earlier than expected from his meal below stairs. "A visitor has arrived."

"A visitor?" Who would come now? It was common knowledge in the village of Thomas's illness and her condition. Rumour from London claimed James spent most nights in his cups at his club, continuing to lose money he did not possess, so it certainly was not James—not that James ever dared show his face at Worthstone. Thomas would not have received him.

"He has been shown to his rooms, and Mrs. Hamilton is sending up water. As soon as he is refreshed, I shall bring him here."

"Colin," she said as a jolt coursed through her. She could only think of one person who would be brought to Thomas's rooms. "Is it Fitzwilliam?"

"Yes, ma'am."

She smoothed her dressing gown down her front. Lord, she must look affright! She had not left hers and Thomas's chambers for a week. Between napping, and helping care for her husband, she simply did not have the opportunity or see the necessity.

Colin stepped over to the bed, sat down, and took Thomas's hand. He had drifted off again now that she was not reading. He seemed to sleep more and more. He complained of pain at times, and his hands and feet were swelling. Colin still persuaded him to take nourishment, but it was becoming increasingly difficult to coax him into the slightest amounts as his illness progressed.

She sank into the sofa, not wanting to go far. Her feet resembled the gammons Lady Matlock had predicted months ago. Elizabeth walked no further than she needed these days rather than the long jaunts she once enjoyed. Until a fortnight ago, she rambled around the gardens in front of the house, but even that took her breath away these days.

Colin answered the door at the knock, allowing Fitzwilliam inside his cousin's bedchamber. He looked well, dressed in his customary well-tailored suit, his hair in its usual curls atop his head. Dark circles marred the undersides of his striking eyes, but she was likely the sole person to scrutinise him so closely.

He bowed over her hand and kissed it before he moved to the side of the bed, saying Thomas's name to wake him. "How are you?"

"Thank goodness you are finally here," said Thomas in his now croaky voice. "You must pull Elizabeth from this depressing mood she has adopted since your departure. Next time, pray wake her before you leave. I cannot bear that morose expression she has been wearing." He paused every two or three words for breath. Speaking required too much effort these days, which was why he had taken to speaking so rarely.

Her back stiffened and her cheeks burned. How could Thomas speak so to Fitzwilliam?

"Forgive me," said Fitzwilliam, his eyes darting to hers.

"Stop feeling sorry for yourself." Thomas coughed several times. "Soon enough, I shall be gone, and they will be yours—as it should be." Elizabeth bristled. How she wished he would stop speaking of their freedom once he died. The words rankled her every time he spoke them.

Fitzwilliam clenched his hands at his sides, the only hint of his disquiet. "The world will believe him to be your son." His voice attempted to be its usual deep tone, but her ears picked out the subtle lows not usually present.

"And he will never know me, which is likely for the best. I am a rather selfish bastard, do you not think? You will be a much better father than I would ever be."

"Thomas—" began Fitzwilliam before Thomas began shaking his head.

"No, I have always wanted what is best for you, but I betrayed you by using your affection for Elizabeth to my advantage. I hope one day you will forgive me." He gasped in a breath. This was more than he had said in a fortnight. "I did not send for you to watch me die. Go spend time with Elizabeth. She needs you more than I do."

She fiddled with the folds of her dressing gown. Perhaps Fitzwilliam did not want to spend this time with her. What if he did not?

Colin approached and stood behind Fitzwilliam. "Mr. Darcy, I will be sure to tell those below stairs how you have spent the afternoon and evening with your cousin. Lalande can help should I require it, and no one will know where you truly are. I assure you."

Hesitantly, Fitzwilliam rose. Being so dismissed had to be disconcerting, to say the least. Without a word, she walked stiffly through the connecting door to her chambers as he followed, shutting it behind him.

"Are you well?"

She crossed her arms over her chest. "Why did you leave without saying goodbye?"

He scrubbed his face before throwing his arms down to his sides. "Because this is difficult. Because I love you and want to be with you, yet I feel guilty because for that to happen, my cousin has to die. Because while that child will inherit more than I can give him, I cannot give him what is his due as a Darcy. He will not bear the Darcy name."

She rushed forward and took his face in her hands. "Yet, *you* will be there for him throughout his life. You will mould him into who he becomes. *You* will teach him to fish and to ride his first horse, and it will be *you* who he asks for help when he inherits this estate. *You* will be his father in every way that matters. Do you not see that?"

"What if you die?" His voice was so small compared to his usual deep tone.

"Then your duty will be to raise him completely—to ensure he resembles you—the best man I have ever known. You must tell him frequently how much you love him, and how much I shall always love him." Her voice broke during the last, and he took her in his arms, holding her as close as he could.

"I would never let him forget you. What else would you ask of me?"

She drew back enough to look in his eyes. "Help me bear this child."

"Pardon?" His tone grew higher and his eyes wider. "I believe the midwife might become suspicious."

"No," she said, shaking her head. "When the midwife visited a few days ago, she indicated the babe had lowered. He is ready to be born, but I have yet to begin labouring."

"The midwife said mid-June, did she not?"

"He is not too early. That is but two weeks away." Her fingers toyed with his cravat while she spoke. "She told me walking helps, but I can only walk a short distance before my feet ache unbearably. They are too swollen." Elizabeth scraped her teeth along her bottom lip as she peered up at him. "The midwife also said it was a shame my husband was so ill since marital relations are known to cause childbirth."

"You want me to love you?" His tone was higher if possible.

She stepped back and crossed her arms over her chest. Was her current state truly so distasteful? "I realise this must be a rather unattractive offer, but—"

He yanked her back into his embrace and kissed her forehead. "You are still as beautiful as the first time I laid eyes upon you. You carry my child. How could I think you anything but lovely?" His lips met hers with a gentle touch.

"I am not lovely." She looked down towards her breasts and removed her hands to hold them at her sides. "I am too big. Naught about me is small. Instead, it is swollen and clumsy and fat."

He drew her with him until he sat on the bed. Carefully, he untied her dressing gown and opened it, letting the fabric flow over her shoulders to the floor. He untied the ribbon at the top of her nightgown and gathered it over her head so she stood bare before him.

His fingers traced along the tops of her breasts and around, down to her belly where his palm pressed against a small bulge to one side. After a merciless jab from the hand, foot, or elbow, the baby shifted and pushed back. Fitzwilliam kissed the bump. "There you are, little one." After another jab, his hand rubbed where the baby pressed. "He is so strong." His voice held this breathy quality that bespoke of his awe.

He peppered a trail of pecks around to her navel, bestowing one last just above where a dark line now traced down her abdomen. "We must find a way that will be comfortable for you. I do not want to cause you pain."

The buttons on his topcoat and waistcoat gave easily as he stripped them off and let them join her clothes on the floor. "Blast. My boots," he said in a mutter. He shifted Elizabeth to the side. "I shall return directly."

"What are you about?" She laughed while he hurried to the door and walked through to Thomas's room, closing the door behind him to preserve her modesty. She hurried over and cracked it, listening from behind.

"Sir?" said Colin.

"I am attempting to convince Lizzy to take a nap," followed Fitzwilliam, "but she will only lie down if I sit with her. I need my boots removed, if you would help me." How red were her cheeks at this moment?

"Yes, sir."

Fitzwilliam soon strode back into the room, dropping his boots the moment he closed the door behind him. He smiled at the sight of Elizabeth waddling back to recline in her nest of pillows. His shirt and breeches joined the rest of their clothes before he climbed back atop the bed. He sat beside her, his hand in its favourite spot upon her stomach. "Your skin is so soft and your belly so hard." He shook his head while he continued to rub the taut skin. "I fear I lack the experience for this. Perhaps if you lie on your side?"

Elizabeth watched him while she moved. Once she lay on her side with her knees bent, he crawled behind her and pressed himself to her back, wrapping his arm around to touch and caress her. When she finally writhed and moaned in his arms, he rose onto an arm so he could kiss her lips while he slid home.

It felt so good to be connected to him again, and her breathing hitched when he groaned and dropped his forehead against her temple. She clutched at his hips with one arm while she attempted to move with him, though with her current size, shifting was more difficult than in the past. Their releases came quickly. After, Fitzwilliam tucked the coverlet around them and held her until she slept.

Lalande knocked when their dinner arrived in her sitting room. Once they ate their fill, they made love again, and he read to her until she slept once more.

When he snuggled against her, he buried his face into her hair and held her as close as he could, which suited her well. The babe would come soon, and though she did not want it, he would be forced from her. She could imagine the furore and scandal her insistence he remain would cause. Her mother would never forgive her for disgracing the family. On second thought, maybe her mother would stop writing and pestering if she did?

Moans permeated the darkness as his dreams receded and reality intruded. He drifted off for a moment or two until the sound began again. "Lizzy?" As his eyes opened, the flesh under his palm hardened impossibly, making him blink and rise to his elbow. "Lizzy?" He glanced down to where his hand rested upon her abdomen.

"I believe it has begun." She panted out the words while she gripped the pillow with white knuckles. She rested on her side, her legs tangled in the covers.

"How long have you been labouring?"

"For several hours, I believe. What is the time?"

He opened a panel of the bed curtains and rummaged through his clothes until he found his pocket watch. The sun was streaming through the gaps in the closed draperies, so it was at least four. He popped open the cover and managed to hold the watch in a bit of the sunlight sneaking inside the room. "Four-thirty."

"Three and a half hours. I remember the tall clock in the hall striking one."

"You should have awakened me. The midwife should have been called." He ran his fingers through his hair and pulled on his breeches.

"Fitzwilliam, wait. Not yet."

"What do you mean 'not yet'?"

"I mean my mother laboured for two days with Jane and for twenty-six hours with me. She never allows us to forget her misery. I only began having pains a few hours ago. The midwife would be here for an entire day if we send for her now."

Was she insane? "That is why she is paid handsomely."

Elizabeth struggled to sit and pointed to their clothes. "Please hand me my nightgown. The midwife claimed I should walk."

As he handed her the shift, he pinched the bridge of his nose with the other hand. "I do not believe this a good idea."

"Well," said Elizabeth in an entirely too cheerful a voice, "you cannot exactly run below stairs and send for the midwife. It would cause talk. You would need to wake Lalande, and she is employed by me. I will order her to wait."

Once she wore her gown, she held out her hands for him to help her stand, then looped her arm through his. "I cannot have you accompany me down the halls, so we can walk around my bedchamber, sitting room, and dressing room."

"I cannot believe I am allowing you to do this." He really could not credit his acceding to her wishes. He must be mad to go along with her hare-brained idea. He should go tell Colin, but would he go against his mistress's decision? Thomas's condition was too fragile to worry him.

"Fitzwilliam, when the midwife comes, you cannot be here. The closest you can remain is in Thomas's chamber with him. Forgive me if I wish to keep you with me for as long as possible." She bent over and clutched her stomach.

He breathed to ward off dizziness while he held her hands as she panted. Her tight grip gave some indication that, regardless of her claims, her pain was not a trifling pinch. After nearly a minute, she stood and rubbed her stomach.

"What is that room?" he asked, pointing.

"The nursery." She tugged him in that direction, opened the door, and led him inside. "Mrs. Hamilton keeps insisting I shall have a wet nurse, though I have told her I have no need, which is why the cradle is still in here. I would prefer it in my bedchamber."

"I can move it for you."

She allowed her hand to slip from his arm so he could lift the heavy wooden cot. He carried it through to her room, placing it not too far from the fireplace. When he returned, she was bent over the larger cot while she swayed back and forth. She moaned almost as if she were singing.

"Your pains are coming too close together, Elizabeth."

"Do not call me that." She spoke through clenched teeth. Whether from her discomfort or from her anger, he did not know.

"Why ever not? 'Tis your name." He dug his fingers into the small of her back, massaging and eliciting another groan for his efforts.

"Thomas calls me Elizabeth. I never minded before except he is the only person who regularly does. I have never wished for you to call me anything but Lizzy. Oh!"

"What is it?"

She lifted the hem of her nightgown to reveal a puddle slowly growing on the floor at her feet. "We need to wake Lalande."

He helped her into the dressing room where Lalande now stood dressed and prepared for her day. She glanced between them "Madame?"

Fitzwilliam relaxed a great deal simply at the maid's presence. "We need to send for the midwife."

"No!" Elizabeth pointed at Lalande. "I am not ready to call that woman yet."

He closed his eyes and bit back a growl. Becoming impatient or intemperate would do him no favours, but why did she insist on being so recalcitrant? "The pains are coming fairly close together and your waters have broken. Let Lalande send for the midwife."

"We have plenty of time." She bent at the waist and clutched her stomach once more. "Oooh!"

Lalande lifted her eyebrows while she bit her lip. Her hands were tied. No matter how irrational Elizabeth behaved, her maid could not gainsay her. "Madame, Mr. Darcy is correct."

Elizabeth's breaths came out in pants, and her grip was not far from crushing a bone or two in his hand. "I do not want him to go. If the midwife comes, he must leave."

"If she does not come, Mr. Darcy or I must deliver the babe. I have only witnessed two births. What if the child is turned the wrong way? I would not know what to do."

"I have only delivered sheep and horses," said Fitzwilliam, praying she would finally relent.

A high giggle came from Elizabeth as she closed her eyes and rubbed her stomach. "Not exactly the same."

"No," he said firmly. "'Tis not."

She took a few deep breaths. "I feel so strange."

Lalande cocked her head and looked at him with raised eyebrows. "What do you mean?"

Fitzwilliam wrapped an arm around her. "Let us get you back to bed."

He propped her up much as he had Thomas nearly a month ago, but Elizabeth doubled over again. This time, she collapsed to her knees and she rocked back and forth on all fours right where she had once stood in the dressing room.

His chest heavy, Fitzwilliam pulled her nightgown over her rear and clenched his teeth. "I can see the babe's head, Lizzy." He wanted to yell and insist how he knew this would happen, but this was not the best time. "We need to shift her to her back," he said to Lalande.

Her maid helped him coax Elizabeth to change positions once the pain subsided. When she lay propped in Lalande's lap, he ran his hand through his hair once more. "What if I do something to hurt him? You can be the most wilful and stubborn. . ." He had to stop. No matter how frustrated he was at her hard-headed demands, he would only upset her if he continued.

He rested his hand on her belly, which tightened when the next contraction began. "Push," he said insistently. What else should he do? If he had known Elizabeth would do this, he might have read a physician's book on childbirth, but how could he have foreseen she would take leave of her senses?

"Push, Madame." Lalande reached to a shelf behind her and opened a bottle that she wafted under Elizabeth's nose. "Lavender oil," she said.

Elizabeth bore down, her face screwed up in concentration and pain before she panted when the pain let up. The baby's head had moved dramatically with her effort, the top ready to emerge. With the next, she bore down again, her face contorting and her lips pressing tightly together to keep from crying out. She took a deep breath and pushed again when it was required.

His eyes shifted from her face to where the babe's head not only emerged but gradually rotated to its side, his eyes squeezed closed. He pushed her gown further up, and when the contraction ended, he rubbed the top of Elizabeth's thigh. "Lizzy, look."

Her maid helped her sit up a bit further and Elizabeth let out a sob when she set eyes upon her child. Lalande caught his eye. "You need to free his shoulder."

His stomach flipped, and he held up shaking hands. "How?"

"The midwife inserts her hand at the top and guides it down. The last time I attended a birth, the midwife showed me."

"You should be down here for this." He muttered the words but the slight curve to one side of the maid's lips indicated she had heard him.

He held his breath when Elizabeth bore down and he did as Lalande suggested. In the end, the manoeuvre proved easier than he had anticipated since the babe slipped right out into his hands.

"Put him on Madame." Lalande placed a towel over Elizabeth's nightgown, and he lay the child upon it as the maid began scrubbing it vigorously. After a tense moment or two where Elizabeth's eyes widened, and she rubbed just as furiously as Lalande, the babe began squalling at the top of his lungs.

"The entire household will know soon," said the maid with a huge smile. "Have you noticed, Madame?" She lifted the towel, so they both could see. "You have a son."

Elizabeth started to cry as he collapsed back onto his heels. A son. Everything Thomas wanted, he now had—except for his health. At least he would know his estate was secure before he passed from this life. Fitzwilliam and Elizabeth would ensure the dukedom prospered until this child was old enough to take on the responsibility himself.

A groan came from Elizabeth, and Lalande looked up at him. "The afterbirth needs delivering. If you can move here and support her, I can manage the rest."

Still unsteady, he shifted so Elizabeth reclined against his chest. Lalande bustled around the room, gathering items before she sat at Elizabeth's feet. She used a bit of ribbon to tie the cord and cut him from his mother which prompted him to wail once more.

"Put him to your breast, Madame."

He fumbled to help her untie and pull her shift from her shoulder so she could offer the child her nipple. The babe latched on and began suckling as if he had not eaten in weeks.

Fitzwilliam dropped his forehead against her shoulder. "Pray, do not ever do this to me again."

"What? Bear your child?"

"No," he said with a growl. "Insist I deliver it. This had to be the most terrifying experience of my life."

She winced and tensed before she let out a long breath. "I honestly thought the lying-in would be longer. I did not know he would be in such haste to be born."

"Madame, I have no warm water, but we should at least change you to a fresh nightgown." Mindful of the nursing baby, Lalande helped Elizabeth peel off the shift, sliding it down her legs, so he could move her to the rug rather than have her remain on the damp floor.

Once Lalande had Elizabeth dry and ready, he lifted the two most precious beings in the world into his arms and carried them into the bedchamber, placing Elizabeth delicately on the mattress. She beamed at him while the babe suckled from the other breast. "He is so beautiful."

He sat next to her and covered the top of their son's head with his palm. "He is." His lips caressed her temple. "I should go. The footman stationed in the hallway surely heard him cry. Someone will knock soon, and Lalande needs to request warm water to clean the two of you."

She placed a hand to his face. "You *will* return, will you not?"

Lalande hurried in and knocked on the door connecting Elizabeth's chamber to that of Thomas's. After a moment, Colin answered. He was already dressed and peered around her, his eyes the size of horse chestnuts. "Thomas swore he heard a babe."

"I heard the floor squeak in the servants' passage," she said with haste. "You must let Mr. Darcy inside."

Fitzwilliam kissed Elizabeth's lips quickly as he stood. "When Lalande and Colin feel it is safe, I shall return." Without further instruction, he hurried into Thomas's room while Lalande gathered his remaining clothes and pushed them into Colin's arms.

No sooner had the door closed behind him than a knock vibrated from Elizabeth's bedchamber door. He leaned back against the hard oak and closed his eyes. That had been too close.

"Fitzwilliam?"

He turned his head towards Thomas's croak, straightened, and stepped over to the bedside, sitting in the chair stationed there. "'Tis a boy. They are both well. Elizabeth was positively infuriating. She claimed she would not deliver for hours, which made it necessary for me and Lalande to act the part of midwife."

Thomas coughed instead of laughing. "Elizabeth can be headstrong," he said when he caught his breath.

"The house will be a flurry of activity for some time," said Colin. "I shall order breakfast sent here for you and put it about below stairs that you spent the night sitting by your cousin's bedside. In the meantime, you should dress in your cousin's dressing room and depart through that door." He pointed towards the family corridor. "Your valet can put you to rights before you return. When it is safe to go to the mistress, you can do so easily without arousing suspicion from this bedchamber. As far as the household is concerned, you are spending a great deal of time with your ill cousin."

Two hours passed before he laid eyes upon Elizabeth again. During their separation, the harried midwife, who had rushed over when called, had apparently scolded her for waiting so long that her maid had to deliver the child, not to mention barking strict orders for her to lie in a darkened room and remain abed. If Elizabeth listened to one word, it would be a miracle.

Mrs. Hamilton, scandalized by Elizabeth nursing the babe herself, insisted duchesses did not feed their own children. Elizabeth, however, brooked no opposition to her wishes. Mrs. Hamilton, much to her surprise, was summarily threatened with her immediate release if she did not eject the wet nurse from the manor without delay. When Thomas stood behind Elizabeth's decision, Mrs. Hamilton relented, though not without excessive grumbling, according to Lalande, who was privy to the woman's rantings below stairs. Based on Elizabeth's expression at the news, Mrs. Hamilton would likely not keep her position for long.

"Help me up," said Elizabeth as soon as he entered.

"You must be joking. The midwife indicated you should remain abed."

She rolled her eyes and shifted to the edge while she removed her blankets. "My aunt has never remained abed for weeks on end in a darkened room, and she is as well as anyone."

Her manner made it clear that she intended to ignore him, so he aided her to stand, ensuring the babe was secure in her arms. Regardless of her stability, he kept a supportive arm around them both. "Where are we going?"

"Thomas's bedchamber."

Colin called for them to enter at his knock, and once Elizabeth sat on the edge of the bed, she touched Thomas's hand. When he opened his eyes, they immediately became shiny and filled with tears. "He is big," he breathed.

"Not so very," she said pressing the blankets back from his chubby cheeks. She glanced at Fitzwilliam and back to Thomas. "He needs a name, but we never discussed your wishes."

Colin stepped forward. "Thomas discussed names with me." He nodded at Thomas, who blinked in return. Colin often spoke for Thomas recently, saving his long-time companion the effort. "In our discussions, he planned to request your preferences."

She glanced at Fitzwilliam then back to Thomas. "We discussed Alexander. What do you think?"

Fitzwilliam held his breath while he watched the floor. She remembered their early morning discussion from that last night in London. Elizabeth had hoped for Nathaniel, but he wanted Alexander. She was deferring her preference for his.

"Thomas always intended you to select his forename," said Colin. "He selected the middle names as long as they met with Mr. Darcy's approval."

Fitzwilliam's head lifted, and he furrowed his brows. Why should he have approval? Despite their actual situation, Thomas did not need to defer to him at all.

"With your selection in mind, Thomas's preference for the name is Alexander George Darcy Osborne. Does that suit?" Colin's eyes moved from one to the other while Elizabeth gasped.

How ironic that a child his father would not approve of should bear his name. Fitzwilliam rubbed his forehead while he watched Thomas, who lifted his eyebrows. The name settled him to an extent. While the child would always be an Osborne, the remainder of his name signified who he was in truth. He was a Darcy.

"In honour of your father," croaked Thomas. "This is his grandchild."

"And leaves you the ability to name a subsequent child George in honour of your father should you wish it," said Colin. "He will be called Alexander."

Fitzwilliam nodded and exhaled. He would not reject the gift Elizabeth and Thomas now gave him. "Thank you. I think it a fine name." Why did it seem this situation would never become less complicated? Would a day come where he could simply live with Elizabeth and not be concerned of every possible thing that could go horribly amiss?

---

¹*Sir Walter Scott. The Lady of the Lake.*
https://www.gutenberg.org/files/3011/3011-h/3011-h.htm#link2H_4_0006

# Chapter 18

*July 13th 1810*
*Worthstone*
*Derbyshire*

*Dearest Jane,*

*Please forgive me the delay in penning this letter. The last few days have been a flurry of activity, yet I do not have the time to tell you all.*

*Firstly, you are an aunt! Alexander George Darcy Osborne entered this world in the early hours of July 11th. He is strong and a voracious eater thus far, but such a blessing. He sleeps and eats well and the physician who checked him yesterday is pleased with his condition and his progress since his birth.*

*I do not know how much you know, but not long before Alexander's birth, Thomas summoned Mr. Darcy to Worthstone due to his declining health. Thomas's condition is continuing to deteriorate. Since Alexander's birth, he has refused all food and all liquids and mostly sleeps. Mr. Darcy has informed me of his wish that you and your husband convey his sister to Worthstone so she might say goodbye. With your excellent heart, I know you will do so swiftly. I thank you. I know Thomas would wish to see Georgiana before he passes.*

*I would ask of my family and your health and tell you all of Alexander, but as I shall see you soon enough, I shall save it for our reunion. I anticipate your arrival.*

*Yours affectionately,*

*Lizzy*

At the sound of horses and a carriage approaching, Elizabeth rushed from her chambers and bustled down the stairs until she reached the hall where she skidded to an abrupt halt.

Mrs. Hamilton looked down her nose at Elizabeth and sniffed. Yes, she would need to replace her housekeeper sooner rather than later. Who knew that when she finally challenged the woman, she would turn into one of those snobbish women of the *ton* without the money or a title to support her?

Without being able to leave her rooms much less the house, attending a Mop Fair to interview potential replacements had been impossible. Elizabeth had sent out inquiries, yet that was the only action she could take. At the moment, the household simply could not do without a housekeeper until a replacement was found.

When the butler opened the door, Elizabeth bounced on her toes as her guests were shown in. Georgiana ran forward with her arms outstretched. "Lizzy!"

Elizabeth hugged her tightly while rocking her back and forth. Her heart rejoiced to see Georgiana once more. She did not doubt the girl would be upset at losing her beloved cousin, but it was still wonderful to see her. "I am pleased you came."

"I would not miss seeing Thomas one last time," said Georgiana, her eyes bright. "I also cannot wait to see Alexander. I can hold him, can I not?"

A smile came unbidden to her lips at the girl's enthusiasm. "Of course, you can." Elizabeth looked at Jane and Carlisle as they approached. "I cannot wait for all of you to meet Alexander." Elizabeth embraced Jane, who held her as though she might break before she turned to curtsey to Carlisle.

"Do not dare," he said with a grin. "We are brother and sister now. I would never make my sister curtsey . . . Well, maybe Lydia now that I give it more thought." He kissed her hand then held it with both of his. "I am pleased to see you again. I hope you will call me Nicholas."

"Then I am Lizzy."

He nodded and glanced around the hall. "It has been many years since I was last here." He turned his attention back to her. "Darcy said Leeds wishes to speak to me."

"If you desire time to refresh yourselves, he will understand. We shall have to rouse him, so he will not even know that you waited."

"Where is Darcy?"

"He rode out to deal with a tenant the steward mentioned. While I do not mind tending to estate duties, I cannot ride out at the moment."

"I should hope not," said Jane with her hand to her chest. "You only gave birth a week ago."

Elizabeth rolled her eyes and crossed her arms over her chest. "You have helped Aunt Gardiner after her lying-ins. Has she remained abed for weeks at a time?"

"That is true, but you are more stubborn than my aunt. If you were allowed to step outside, you would go on a three-mile ramble in the woods."

Georgiana gasped and giggled. "Lizzy! Would you really?"

"I have not yet had the urge to go on a three-mile walk, I assure you, but I shall let you know if the whim suddenly strikes. Are we agreed?"

Jane laughed and shook her head. "I shall refresh myself. Nicholas, what do you wish?"

"I believe I shall see Leeds first."

After a hand gesture to Mrs. Hamilton, Elizabeth turned towards the stairs. "Mrs. Hamilton, pray show the ladies to their rooms. I shall take Viscount Carlisle to see His Grace. We shall have refreshments in my sitting room in an hour."

"I hope you are not scandalised," she explained to her relations, "but since I am supposed to remain in my rooms, I shall entertain you in my sitting room, though I intend to come to the dining room for dinner. My rooms are becoming too confining." She ignored the housekeeper, whose lips were once again drawn into a fine line. Had they really disappeared entirely?

"I cannot say I blame you," said Carlisle. "I believe I would feel the same were I to be confined to my room for a length of time."

Mrs. Hamilton led Georgiana and Jane down the guest corridor while Elizabeth led Carlisle to the family wing. When they entered the sitting room, she paused and faced him. "One thing before we enter. Thomas does not speak much these days since it is too taxing for him. From what I gather, since the first episode with his heart, he has discussed many of his wishes with his valet, so do not be surprised if his valet speaks for him. He has been my husband's trusted servant for many years. I believe he required someone in the household who would know his wishes should he die unexpectantly."

Carlisle gave a slight hitch back of his head and pursed his lips for a moment. "What of his steward?"

"I believe he knows what is to occur with the estate." She stepped over and knocked on Thomas's door, waited a few moments, and at Colin's call, entered. "Viscount Carlisle," she said, "this is Mr. Smith, the duke's valet."

Colin bowed and stepped back as they made their way to Thomas's bed. She sat along the side and pressed her hand against Thomas's arm. As he stirred, he moaned. He truly looked horrible, so pale and thin. Even though he was an older gentleman, he had always been handsome. Now his colour grew worse by the day, and he was positively gaunt.

"Forgive me for waking you."

He grimaced and swallowed hard.

"Are you in pain?" How much laudanum was Colin giving him or was he giving him any at all?

"Yes," he managed.

"He has not had any laudanum since this morning. I shall give him some after you depart. He cannot be awakened so easily after he has taken it and wanted to have the use of his mind as much as possible while the Viscount was here."

Thomas blinked and turned his head just barely to the side. He lifted a hand, but Carlisle jumped forward. "Do not use more of your energy than necessary. I am certain, were you able, you would shake my hand and greet me properly. Today, I consider it done so we might discuss why you wished to see me."

"Alexander," said Thomas in broken syllables.

"If you will pardon my impertinence," said Colin from the opposite side of Thomas's bed. "His Grace wishes you to join Mr. Darcy as a second guardian to his heir, much as you are to Miss Darcy. He knows Mr. Darcy will be an exemplary model for the young Master, yet we do not know God's plan for any of us. He respects you and would appreciate your assurance that should it be required, you will be of use to the young Master, and even Her Grace should she need you. At this time in the young Master's life, he needs his mother. That is the most important consideration."

Elizabeth swallowed the lump in her throat and rubbed Thomas's arm as his eyes fluttered, keeping him in the present for the time being.

When Carlisle looked at Thomas, Thomas nodded and took a shuddering breath.

"I am honoured," said Carlisle. "I hope you know I would do so without you asking, and not only because Lizzy is now my sister."

Colin gave a slight bow. "His Grace did believe as much when he took the liberty of adding your name to his latest will, but he never had the opportunity to make the request before he fell ill in London. He merely did not want to surprise you with the responsibility. Particularly if something were to happen to Mr. Darcy."

She closed her eyes and exhaled as she stood, allowing Carlisle to stand closer to the bed. Fitzwilliam held her heart in his. She could not think of him passing without considerable distress. They had not even had their chance to truly be together.

"I would have understood," said Carlisle. "My Uncle Darcy had many of the same reasons. Now, though, you should take your tonic and rest. You should not fatigue yourself. Between Darcy and myself, your son and Lizzy will always be protected. Do not worry."

She turned back just in time to see Thomas mouth "Thank you."

When Carlisle walked toward her, she led him through to the sitting room. "Thank you," she said once the door closed behind them. "I know this must seem odd."

"His valet speaking for him certainly is, yet I do not find his request so very strange. I have known Leeds all my life and given my uncle's will, Leeds would know he could trust me. My marriage to Jane makes me family. If something does befall Darcy, James, as the duke's relation, could legally try to claim your son. He is right to appoint us both."

Alexander's loud cry carried into the room from her bedchamber, and she glanced in that direction. "I am certain he wishes to be fed." When she peered through the door, she waved Lalande over. "Please show Viscount Carlisle to his rooms. 'Tis the blue room in the guest wing.

"I shall see you soon for refreshments," she said to Carlisle. "Thank you for bringing Georgiana."

"We were pleased to be of aid. Jane has greatly desired to see you for some time. I am glad we could come." He took her hand and gave it a gentle squeeze before he followed her maid into the corridor.

Alexander gave another wail, and she smiled. "I am coming." When she stood over his cradle, he waved his little arms while his face screwed into a frown that would make Fitzwilliam proud. "Come, come, little one. 'Tis not so bad."

She sat on the bed in the midst of her pillows and unfastened the top of her gown. Madame Bonheur's brilliant suggestion of a bib-front style made it less time-consuming to feed him during the day. She would have to thank her the next time she required new gowns.

He latched on quickly, and she relaxed while his little gulps and grunts filled the air. Those were the most beautiful sounds. She wiggled her little finger where his tiny fingers held tight as he fed. How could she love someone so much? Her heart was so full, it felt as if it might burst. He was so perfect—each of his fingers and toes, his crystal blue eyes and serious expression that resembled Fitzwilliam's. He also had this one perfect curl on the top of his head that she adored caressing with her finger.

When he was done, she changed his napkin as Lalande entered. "Miss Darcy and Miss Bennet are in your sitting room."

"Thank you," she said, picking him up and cradling him to her. "Would you like to meet your Aunt Jane? And I think we should call Georgiana, Aunt Georgiana. What do you think?"

He puckered his lips and waved his fist in the air.

"I am glad you agree."

When she entered, they both rose while Georgiana clasped her hands. "Oh, he is precious!"

Elizabeth stepped over and passed him carefully to her. "You must support his head." Her hand touched the underside of

273

Georgiana's elbow. "Good. Perhaps you should sit down. You might not be so anxious."

"Well, I have never held a baby this young before."

With a serene smile, Jane sat next to Georgiana and tucked the blankets back from his face. "'Tis not difficult." She touched the curl. "He is beautiful, Lizzy. Your husband, Alexander, Mr. Darcy, and even Georgiana all have the same colour eyes. They are so bright."

"My father and Thomas favoured one another a great deal when they were younger," said Georgiana. "You can see it when you look at their portraits. Thomas's hangs downstairs in the gallery off the ballroom. When you come to Pemberley, I shall show you the one of my father."

After a knock, Elizabeth bade the person to enter. "I finally get to meet the famous Alexander," said Carlisle as he strode inside. "He is barely a week old, and I see has commanded all the ladies' attention. I believe I am jealous."

"Really, Nicholas," said Jane, laughing.

"He has all of you talking of naught but him. Is not that enough?"

"He is worth speaking of, are you not, little one?" asked Georgiana in a crooning voice.

With Alexander settled for the moment, Elizabeth set to work serving tea. "How are my parents?"

"I dare say much the same as when you last saw them." Jane put down her teacup so Georgiana could pass Alexander to her. "Papa received the book you sent him as a gift. If it had not been for my wedding, we would not have seen him until he finished the very last page. Mama declared herself in a fit of nerves over the affair."

Elizabeth sighed while she shook her head. "Oh, Mama."

The door suddenly opened making everyone startle. "Lizzy! Mrs. Hamilton said you left this room. How could you?" He came to a sudden stop. "Forgive me for interrupting. I believe Mrs. Hamilton hoped I could talk some sense into her. She informed me Lizzy was having tea. She did not mention you had arrived."

She stared at Fitzwilliam with an eyebrow raised. He liked to accuse her of being headstrong and impulsive, yet he could claim the same attributes—of all the nerve! "I did myself no harm, and in fact, I feel better than I have since Alexander was born."

"He is so handsome, Brother," said Georgiana, gushing.

"He is, Sweetling. Have you visited Thomas yet?"

"No, not yet."

Fitzwilliam held out his arm. "Let us see if we can rouse him enough."

Once he led her out, Jane laughed while she held Alexander's little hand. "I see I need not worry for you. Mr. Darcy is good enough to ensure you do not overexert yourself."

Elizabeth smiled while part of her rankled at his admonishment. "That he is." How she wanted to slap Fitzwilliam. She would not risk herself or Alexander, so why did he feel the need to scold her like a child?

After dinner, Fitzwilliam returned to his room and sank into one of the chairs with a groan. What a day it had been. He had ridden out to deal with a tenant who had not tended the sheep on his land as he ought. The poor beasts were emaciated and needed to be put down, yet the tenant argued he had cared for the animals diligently. The entire morning was spent dealing with those sheep and evicting the tenant.

Then he came back to realise Elizabeth had left her rooms. When he realised it was likely to meet her sister, he could not blame her, yet she was not even supposed to leave her bed much less go traipsing about the house or go on one of her walks.

All he had to do was look at her to know she was furious. That one eyebrow he loved was high on her forehead, and her lips were not pursed in amusement or giving a half-smile that made him want to drag her to bed. No, instead, her lips pressed tightly together.

The biggest problem was how Carlisle regarded him with an odd look after his blunder. He removed Georgiana in the hopes his cousin would not ask questions as well as to collect himself before he was in company again, but Carlisle's eyes had not ceased to watch him when they were all together.

Dinner proved to be the culmination to an abominable day. He tried to catch Elizabeth's gaze on multiple occasions, but she would not look at him unless he spoke to the entire table, and her eyes never lingered on him. In the past, she was always more circumspect out of the privacy of her rooms but not to this extent.

A knock came from the door, and his head shot up. The sound was not from the servants' corridor, which did not bode well for the remainder of his evening. "Yes?"

When the door opened, Carlisle stepped inside and closed it behind him. "You can tell me to go to hell, but I want to know what is happening in this house. I will not depart until I have answers, so you may as well tell me."

Fitzwilliam furrowed his brow and stood to step over to the liquor on a side table. "Brandy?"

"Yes, I shall take some. I feel as though I shall need it." Carlisle strode over and sat in a chair. "Are you going to tell me or pretend you do not know of what I speak? I do not mind asking Lizzy or even Leeds should it be required."

"Why do you believe things to be out of the ordinary?" He handed his cousin the glass of brandy.

Carlisle took a sip and leaned back in his chair, staring at him. "Are you serious? I was brought into Leeds's room where his valet told me of his wish for me to be a second guardian for Lizzy and his son, which I do gladly. I know how much Jane loves her sister, and if James gained control over that boy, he would remove him from Lizzy's care and his life would be a nightmare."

A wince came to Fitzwilliam's face at the idea of his son in the custody of James. No, that could never happen. "I agree. I am relieved Thomas thought of you."

"His valet asked me, Darcy—not his steward, not his solicitor—his valet. Then you burst into Lizzy's sitting room without knocking. By your expression when you entered, you had no idea we were present. You scolded her as if she were your wife. I know the two of you are good friends and have been for some time, yet your interaction was not one of two mere friends. She is another man's wife, for God's sake."

"I know that," he said in a low voice.

"Are you in love with her?" His tone was not confrontational but asked the question in a blunt fashion. "Jane even mentioned the possibility when we were in our rooms."

"Does it matter if I am?"

He stood up like a shot. "Of course it does. She is about to lose her husband and will be in mourning for a year after. You cannot do anything about your feelings now. You would be a bastard for even speaking to her of your affection with Leeds on his deathbed."

Fitzwilliam barked out a laugh. "I would not be so sure if I were you. My cousin is a master of illusion. He constructed what he wanted others to see, and only allowed certain people to know his true self. Believe me, that circle is exceedingly small. My father knew, but I did not truly know Thomas until after my father's death. Georgiana, hopefully, will never know."

Carlisle put down his brandy and clasped Fitzwilliam by both shoulders. "Then you must tell me. What if some individual knows what you do? They could use it against Alexander and

Lizzy. If you love her, then you should want to protect her and her son."

"By telling you, I increase the risk of exposure," he said through gritted teeth. "No one can know, and Lizzy would never forgive me if Jane cast her off."

"Cast her off?" His cousin backed away and frowned. "I doubt Lizzy has committed any such crime, and even if she had, Jane would never reject her. She would sooner sever her own limb."

Fitzwilliam turned and watched the empty grate as though a fire truly burnt at the coals inside. He took a drink, closed his eyes, and shook his head. Carlisle's hand to his arm pulled him around once more.

"You must tell me. Could this harm Leeds's son?"

"He is my son."

His cousin flinched, likely at the venom in his tone, and stepped back. "What?"

"You heard me. Alexander George Darcy Osborne is my son. Thomas and Lizzy even named him to signify it, not that anyone would readily know. I wanted the name Alexander while Lizzy wanted Nathaniel and Thomas desired to honour my father."

"Good God! Thomas knows?" He rubbed his hand over his mouth then downed the rest of his brandy and held out his glass. "You had best give me more. I have a feeling I shall require it very soon."

Once Carlisle had a full glass, Fitzwilliam told him all from Thomas's original plan to how he used their drunkenness against them to facilitate the start of their relationship. "We did not plan to love each other. One day we simply did. We tried to do what we felt was right, yet once we were together, we found it impossible to be apart. Surely you must understand. You love Jane."

"I do, and I cannot fathom what the two of you have endured—how you must feel to have your son claimed by another." With his elbows propped on his knees, Carlisle ran his hands through his hair and hung his head between his arms. "Leeds had a reputation at the brothels. Did he catch a disease?"

A sarcastic laugh escaped before Fitzwilliam could stop it. "I asked him of that rumour once. He explained how he had the women spread it about that he paid for their services. He never bedded them, but paid them handsomely to speak of what he wished."

"But why?" He continued to look at the floor while he spoke. His hands on the back of his neck.

"To hide what he really was."

Carlisle's head slowly rose, and he gradually shifted to give Fitzwilliam a side-long look. "No," he gasped. He shot up from the chair. "I cannot believe you would not tell me. Leeds claims Alexander as his son, and he is married to Lizzy, so Alexander should never lose his inheritance. He is Leeds's son in the eyes of society. Whether rumours abound about you or not, Leeds's wish is secure. Lizzy's reputation, however, could be in tatters. Eventually, some other scandal would come along and people would forget, but if what I am thinking is true, some people feel that to be contagious, which could affect Alexander—especially if people believe him to be Leeds's son." He scrubbed his face with his hands before he picked up his brandy glass and refilled it. "The valet is his lover." He spoke matter-of-factly.

"Yes," said Fitzwilliam.

"Lizzy knows?"

"She does. On her first visit to Pemberley, Wickham intruded into her rooms to steal her jewellery. When she opened the door connecting her chambers to that of Thomas's for help, she witnessed them in an embrace. She then learnt the true nature of her marriage."

"Who knows?"

"The obvious is you, me, Thomas, his valet, and Lizzy. Her maid and my valet know of our relationship and that I am Alexander's true father but naught of the rest. Our valets and her maid orchestrate what is said below stairs as well as ensure we can spend time together."

Carlisle nodded and took a sip of his brandy, baring his teeth. "You will go to her later?"

"Yes, I have spent every night with her since my arrival. I delivered Alexander if you can believe it."

Carlisle coughed and spluttered and Fitzwilliam stood to slap him on the back. "You must be joking?"

"No, she was recalcitrant as hell and refused to let us send for the midwife. I could not wake Thomas to issue a demand, and Lalande is employed by Lizzy. That stubborn woman insisted it would be hours. She was wrong and gave birth on the floor of her dressing room while I trembled and feared I would faint dead away. I was terrified I would harm him."

His cousin blew out a long breath and shook his head slowly. "I could not watch Jane endure so much pain." He raised his glass for them to toast. "To you and your son. Between the two of us, I swear he will be ready to manage the dukedom when his time comes."

"Thank you," said Fitzwilliam quietly. "Will you tell Jane?"

Carlisle swirled his brandy around the glass. "I promised to never keep secrets from her, and this would be impossible to hide. I must tell her. You have to believe that she loves her sister too much to think ill of her. You have naught to concern yourself with. I hope you know that."

"You had best be correct, or Lizzy will never forgive me."

Carlisle downed the last of his brandy. "The incident today, as well as your constant watching of her at dinner, gave your feelings away. You must be more circumspect in the future. The two of you will have your time, but you must wait a while longer."

He closed his eyes and groaned. "'Tis difficult. Tonight, I knew she was angry. I only wanted to catch her eye for a moment."

"Keep it behind closed doors," said Carlisle setting his glass on the table. "Too much is at stake. While Alexander's inheritance is secure due to Lizzy's marriage, gossip of his true parentage could bring too many questions. Thomas's relationship or relationships cannot become fodder for society."

Fitzwilliam swallowed a gulp of his drink and winced at the heat in his gullet. "I know."

"Jane and I agreed to remain for an indefinite time. We shall help with the funeral since I do not expect Leeds to survive for much longer. After the will is read and the churching, we shall journey to Hertfordshire where I have leased an estate close to Longbourn. If it proves a convenient place to stay to visit her family, I might purchase it. I could not live for any length of time under the same roof as Mrs. Bennet. I would not survive."

"Is she as bad as Lizzy says?"

He returned to his chair with a slight shrug of his shoulders. "I have not heard Lizzy's description, but Lizzy does not see things in the same rosy hue as my wife. I would think her picture an accurate one."

"Are you aware the great house at Stoke is part of Thomas's estate?" asked Fitzwilliam. "You need not purchase this estate if you merely required a place live for short periods. I am certain Lizzy would be happy to host you."

"That was how they met. Jane told me, but I had forgotten." Carlisle slapped his hands against his thighs and stood. "I should be going." He grinned and clapped Fitzwilliam on the shoulder. "Jane is waiting for me." After two steps, he stopped and turned around. "By the way, I thought you would wish to know that Wickham is to be hanged."

"What?" He had not given one thought to Wickham since the wastrel attempted to steal Elizabeth's jewels.

"He was caught with a necklace belonging to the wife of a baronet. I am unsure of the circumstances. I merely thought you would wish to know."

"Yes, thank you," said Fitzwilliam softly. He had ceased to care for Wickham a long time ago, yet he had been a considerable part of Fitzwilliam's childhood. "Good night," he said as Carlisle held up a hand and departed.

A second later, a knock sounded from his dressing room. "You can come in, Bishop." When his valet entered, Fitzwilliam downed the last of his own brandy. "How much did you overhear?"

"Nothing that I did not already suspect. I hope you know I would never betray your trust or that of the duke and duchess."

The last thing Fitzwilliam wanted was for another person to be privy to their secrets, but after all this time, he would have been amazed had Bishop not had some idea. "I do, and I thank you for your loyalty." He studied Bishop for a moment. His man stepped back and clenched his hands at his sides.

"What is it, sir?"

"I need to see the duchess."

"Her Grace's maid says her mistress wishes to be alone for the evening."

"I need to speak to her." Fitzwilliam stood and shifted to stand face to face with his valet. "Can you ensure no one sees me if I go myself?"

Bishop watched the floor for a moment before he looked back up. "I can, but we must make haste. Lalande sought me out after

Her Grace retired. It would not do to meet her maid in the corridor."

"Then, pray, lead the way."

# Chapter 19

Elizabeth traced Alexander's tiny knuckles with her index finger while he firmly gripped her thumb. He nursed as though he were starved, taking long draws and gulping the milk down greedily. If he kept eating so, he would grow entirely too swiftly for her liking. As he was, he was the perfect size to cuddle to her breast while she smelled his sweet hair and kissed his little curls.

The door to the servants' corridor opened, but she had no need to look to see who it was. Lalande had said good night when she departed an hour ago. "I intended to be alone this evening."

"I did understand the message," said Fitzwilliam. The bed creaked, but the mattress had not dipped. Since he had not sat on the bed, she could only assume he leaned against the beam to the canopy. "I thought we should talk instead of going to bed with this disagreement between us."

"You burst into my sitting room—without knocking, I might add—and scolded me as if I were an errant child."

He took a noisy breath. Why did he do that? Was he the one striving for patience? "You are not supposed to leave your bed, much less your rooms," he said evenly, "and you ventured downstairs. Did you think I would not be upset?"

"As I have said before, my aunt does not lie in a dark room for weeks on end, and she does not suffer any ill-effects. Tenants have children and are up and working again as soon as they feel capable. I am not a weakling, Fitzwilliam."

"I did not say you were, but you do not need to harm yourself by doing more than you ought."

She closed her eyes and tamped down that rush of anger that made her skin taut. Would her flesh split open if she let the words she withheld free? "Perhaps my father spoiled me, but I have always had a say in my life. I could have refused Thomas's proposal had I wished. Since my marriage, I have had precious little control over what happens to me. Thomas married me with an objective in mind. Despite our reluctance to surrender to our feelings, he decided for both of us that fateful night. After the quickening, I would have been content in London for another month or two, yet the two of you felt Alexander and me to be safer here so hence I travelled, spending months in this house with only myself for company. I tried to content myself by visiting tenants and reading letters from my family and those Thomas sent from you, but that time was isolated and lonely." If only he could understand exactly how much she longed for anyone even if only to discuss naught but a poem or a book!

Alexander had drifted to sleep, so she removed him from her breast and adjusted her gown. Once she had him on her shoulder so she could pat his back, she finally allowed her eyes to set upon Fitzwilliam.

"I truly had not planned on you delivering Alexander, but I suppose I wanted to have a say in what happened to me for once—to not be relegated over to the care of a virtual stranger before it was necessary. Since our son's birth, I have had Mrs. Hamilton following behind me, arguing my every choice, and attempting to force her beliefs on me. Now you threaten to reveal what must remain hidden with your carelessness."

Alexander began to squirm, having been awakened by the movement, and she lowered him to eat from her other breast. "Jane came and spoke to me just after Lalande retired. She asked if you are in love with me. I have told you before and meant every word. I cannot have my sister think ill of me, Fitzwilliam." She swallowed the lump in her throat and blinked madly to keep from crying. "This is not a mere trifle of a thing, and your behaviour during dinner did not remedy the situation but made matters worse. You had to know I was trying to avoid you, yet you continued your attempts to catch my eye."

He sighed and ran his hand through his hair. "Carlisle knows."

A lead weight dropped to her stomach, and she closed her eyes tightly, fighting sudden nausea.

"His suspicions were first aroused by Colin speaking for Thomas. A valet speaking for his master's wishes is not a common practice. I admit my behaviour also gave him reason to believe circumstances were not as they first appeared."

"And you simply confirmed his suspicions. You will be here to raise Alexander while Thomas will die. Is that not enough?"

"You know it is," he said, sitting near her knees. "I promise to be more circumspect. I always have in the past. As for Carlisle, Thomas charged him, as he did me, with protecting you and Alexander. Carlisle asked so he knew how best to do so. He will not betray us."

She wiped a warm, damp tear that had fallen to her cheek. "But he will tell Jane."

"Jane loves you dearly and will love you still. You will see." His lovely deep voice held an urgent note she longed to heed. "I love you too. You have to know that. I only want what is best for you and Alexander. My mother died of a fever a week after giving birth to Georgiana. I cannot help but feel overprotective of you both. I cannot lose you, Elizabeth. I cannot lose either of you."

With a sigh, she pressed her palm to his cheek. She had to make him understand. "I shall not overexert myself. I promise you. But you must allow me to do as I see fit. I swear to you Alexander will not come to harm." He had to realise that she would never put their son in jeopardy.

"You would protect him with your life as would I." His hand covered hers upon his cheek. "You are such an active sort of lady. My only desire is your continued health."

"I do know that."

L.L. Diamond

His thumb rubbed the top of her hand. "Am I forgiven for being such an overbearing dolt?"

A single large laugh burst from her at his description. "I suppose, though if my relationship with Jane changes, I reserve the ability to be angry with you again."

He leaned forward and touched his forehead to hers. "I shall remember. I did not know how I would sleep apart from you tonight. I do not care for being the recipient of your ire. All I desired was to come hold the two of you. I needed to ensure all was well."

"Just because I am angry does not mean we cannot resolve matters. 'Tis the same if you are upset."

He glanced down and smiled at Alexander, who had once again fallen asleep. His head had dropped to the side and his mouth was open, milk dribbling from his lip. "Our little glutton," he said softly. "Here, let me change his napkin for you."

"You?" Did he know how? Men did not usually trouble themselves with such a distasteful task.

He carefully lifted their son from her arms and patted his back while he carried him to a table Lalande had set up for the very purpose. "I have changed him before. In those first days, I let you sleep a little longer before he fed."

"I always assumed it was Lalande."

She watched her two favourite men with a settled air, resting back into the pillows while she smiled at the sight of Fitzwilliam handling the small child with such tender care. Once Alexander was cleaned, Fitzwilliam sat in the middle of the bed with Alexander cradled in one arm and held out his other so Elizabeth could cuddle to his side. "I promise to try and be more understanding."

"I shall also."

He frowned and picked up a letter she had left on the bed when she began feeding Alexander. "What is this? The handwriting resembles that of Mrs. Reynolds."

"I requested her aid in finding a new housekeeper. Mrs. Hamilton has always been overbearing, but I refuse to overlook her insubordination as of late. Thankfully, Mrs. Reynolds suggested a suitable replacement. I sent my response to be posted with Lalande before dinner. Tomorrow, I shall release Mrs. Hamilton."

"Are you certain? She has run this house for a long time."

"Yes, and she has done an admirable job, but I refuse to fight to have my orders followed. With Thomas near death and Alexander's birth, her insistence for me to adhere to what she believes I should do is unwelcome and misplaced."

"Do you desire me to be present?"

"I should hope it unnecessary, but given her recent temper, I would appreciate you there. Jane will also join us. I do not want the confrontation to be solely you and me." Lord, her eyes were so heavy, and they fluttered while an enormous yawn made her pause.

"Go to sleep, dearest. Alexander will wake you soon enough. We can talk more later."

Early the next morning, Fitzwilliam, Jane, and Elizabeth gathered in the master's study. Elizabeth rubbed her stomach, which clenched as though someone gripped it tighter and tighter in their fist as this moment approached. "You told her to come?"

"I did," said Fitzwilliam. "She was scolding a maid for something or other. She indicated she would attend us when she finished."

Jane crossed her arms over her chest with an uncharacteristic glower. "Does that not seem high-handed? Rather than dismissing the maid and telling her she would speak to her later, she makes the mistress wait. Even my mother would not accept such treatment."

After swallowing hard, Elizabeth clenched her hands so tight, her fingernails dug into her palms. "No, but Mrs. Hill would give the maid some tedious or onerous occupation to keep her busy while she spoke with Mama."

At a knock on the door, Elizabeth took her place behind the desk with Fitzwilliam slightly behind her to her right, and Jane in a similar position to her left. "Come!"

Mrs. Hamilton entered as though she owned the estate rather than worked there and stopped to stand within the open door. "You requested to see me, Your Grace."

"Please close the door," said Elizabeth while desperately trying to maintain a tempered tone.

The housekeeper pushed the door closed behind her and stepped before the desk. "Ma'am."

Elizabeth clasped her hands behind her back, so Mrs. Hamilton would not see them tremble. "Mrs. Hamilton, you have been an asset to Worthstone and His Grace for many years. However, since my arrival, you have attempted to make it clear you run this house. You leave me the inconsequential chores, attempting to limit my authority."

"I only do what is best for His Grace, ma'am."

Elizabeth's hiked her eyebrow up on her forehead. "And His Grace trusts me to run his home and raise his heir as I see fit—not as you see fit. Your services are no longer required by this household. You will pack your belongings and remove to the inn in the village until you can arrange transportation and employment elsewhere."

"You do not have that power," the woman hissed. "Only His Grace can release me."

"On the contrary," said Fitzwilliam. "The housekeeper is answerable to the mistress of the estate who can replace her at her whim. His Grace, were he able, would support Her Grace's decision. As it stands, until his heir is of age to take possession of Worthstone, Her Grace will be in charge of the duke's holdings with myself and Viscount Carlisle to aid her should she require it. His Grace has shown a great deal of trust and confidence in her abilities and intelligence."

Elizabeth cleared her throat and placed both hands on Thomas's desk. "I have arranged for you to stay at the inn for a week, and I am providing this," she lifted a pouch with a small allotment of funds from the desk, "for you until you have found your next position. Good day."

Fitzwilliam opened the door and waved in the footman who stood in the hall. "Please see Mrs. Hamilton to her quarters. A cart awaits at the servants' entrance to convey her, as well as her belongings, to the inn in the village." He held open the door for Mrs. Hamilton. Elizabeth awaited a storm of tirades, but instead, the woman clenched her hands and her jaw before marching out the door.

A gush of air came from Jane as soon as she was gone. "I thought she might start yelling for a moment."

Elizabeth laughed and dropped into the chair. "I know, and I worried you might faint if she did."

"I am not so weak with nerves like Mama." Jane's tone was curt, yet her amusement broke through.

Fitzwilliam placed his hand on Elizabeth's shoulder with a gentle pressure. "I need to ride out and ensure Abbot has vacated the farm. His neighbour knew of someone who wished for the tenancy. I shall stop at that home and ascertain if he has word."

"Thank you," said Elizabeth, leaning her head against the back of the seat. "I think Jane and I shall return to my sitting room—that is if she would care to join me."

"I did promise Georgiana a walk through the gardens when she finished with her governess, but she should still be another hour or two."

When Elizabeth stood, she looped her arm through Jane's. "That is just as well. I shall likely desire a nap after Alexander feeds again." They all departed the study with Fitzwilliam heading through the door in the direction of the stables while she and Jane took the stairs to her rooms.

"Would you care for tea?" asked Elizabeth when they reached her sitting room.

"No, not yet." Once they settled into their seats, Jane stared, fixated at the skirt of her gown, toying with the folds. "Nicholas told me of your relationship with your husband as well as Mr. Darcy last night. Though he attempted to justify why you did not tell me, I do wish *you* had confided in me."

Elizabeth crossed her arms, hugging herself. "How should I have approached that, Jane—particularly before your own marriage? The conversation would have hardly been appropriate."

Jane sighed and shrugged. "I know you are correct, yet I did ask you last night. You told me naught. I suppose I am hurt you never trusted me."

"I trust you as much as Fitzwilliam." Elizabeth shifted over to sit beside her sister and take her hands. How could she make her understand? "I honestly did not know how to face you. I did not plan to fall in love with Fitzwilliam, but it happened. I already loved him when I learnt that my marriage was hopeless, which rendered me resentful and despondent. What Thomas expected of me made me feel worthless—that he was so willing to give me away to someone else. I might not have loved him, but I did respect him. Learning his initial motive for marrying me was devastating. Even when I understood why he felt he had no other option, I attempted to hold fast to the values I was taught. One night of drinking more wine with dinner than I ought, and Thomas had the perfect opportunity to implement his scheme, ignoring that Fitzwilliam and I otherwise refused to act on our feelings."

Elizabeth released Jane's hands and paced. "Once that barrier was broached, Fitzwilliam and I did not fight ourselves or our consciences any longer. He has stayed away at times because the situation has been difficult to bear, yet he always returns. He has been all that is good, and despite the immorality of our situation, he has been all that is right in my world. Without Fitzwilliam, I would not have Alexander, and my life would have been desolate. People might think me wanton or scandalous, yet I could never regret Fitzwilliam or my son."

"I would not ask that of you." Jane stood and hugged her tightly before releasing her just enough to catch her eye. "I confess I do not understand the relationship between your husband and his valet."

"Do not call him my husband," said Elizabeth softly.

"That is what he is in the eyes of the law and the church."

Elizabeth shook her head and took Jane's hands once more. "Yet, he never behaved as my husband. After we married, I called Thomas my husband until the night he deceived us. Since then, I cannot refer to him by that title though I will do so in company because it is expected. I care for him, and I suppose I am his friend, yet I lost a tremendous amount of respect for him. As far as I am concerned, he made a choice that he had no right to make. I have forgiven him, but that is all I can muster." Jane might not understand, but Elizabeth could not lie to her. Her dearest sister now knew all. She only hoped Jane would still accept her as unreservedly as before.

Jane drew her back to sit on the sofa. "Nicholas did not mention that the duke had tricked you."

"That evening, I was upset after speaking to Fitzwilliam. We had confessed we loved each other, but agreed we could not act upon our feelings. I drank some brandy in the library before dinner then several glasses of wine with the meal, which I hardly touched."

After Elizabeth finished the tale, her sister shook her head and pressed her hand to her chest. "I want to say he made an honest mistake, but I cannot—especially when I know you and Fitzwilliam are together with his sanction."

Elizabeth choked back a sob. "I could not bear it if you thought ill of me. As much as I love Fitzwilliam and Alexander, I never wanted you to know this part of my life." She covered her face with her hands until they were pulled away.

"I confess I cannot imagine how difficult your situation must be, but I could never think ill of you. That precious child was born out of love, and I shall protect him as fiercely as I would my own. I give you my word." Jane pulled her handkerchief out of her pocket and wiped Elizabeth's cheeks.

"I want you and Nicholas to be Alexander's godparents."

Jane's eyes searched hers. "What of Darcy and what of Thomas?"

"Fitzwilliam will for all intents and purposes be Alexander's father in feeling and appearances. When I looked in on Thomas earlier, he was still asleep. His breathing is worsening as is the cough."

"The poor man," said Jane, shaking her head.

"Colin said they had never discussed godparents and considered my choices appropriate."

"Nicholas and I would be honoured." Jane hugged Elizabeth and pulled her to sit beside her on the sofa. "Now, about that tea. I think we should have a cup before that adorable boy of yours wakes. While you take your nap, I would be pleased to watch over him if Georgiana is not ready for our walk. He is such a dear."

She wiped the tears from her cheeks with her handkerchief. "I am so fortunate to have him. A part of me worried he might not live. That God would punish me somehow."

"You cannot think that way. I know people believe such things, but I do not." Jane kissed Elizabeth's hand. "Once you are out of mourning, you can be with Fitzwilliam, and what is amiss will be the way it was supposed to be all along."

"He has not asked me yet, Jane."

Jane put an arm around Elizabeth. "But he will. I know he will."

*July 20ᵗʰ 1810*
*Worthstone*
*Derbyshire*

*Dear Papa,*

*In the early hours of the morning, my husband finally succumbed to his illness. When he began to cough, I was summoned along with his cousin and nearest relation Mr. Darcy. Unfortunately, he coughed so violently for one so weak that he could not catch his breath. His life had become a pitiful and painful existence I know he did not relish. All who knew him will mourn his loss; however, his death, while sad, was a release for him. I take comfort in that he is no longer suffering.*

*Due to the warm weather, his funeral will occur soon. His family already journeyed hither, so we see no reason to delay.*

*While I am certain you and Mama are eager to meet your grandson, I am unsure of what will occur after the funeral. Jane and Carlisle have offered for me to stay with them at Netherfield, yet I also have the great house at Stoke so I have no need to impose on them so early in their marriage.*

*Alexander continues to grow and thrive, and I have managed to escape the confines of my chambers on numerous occasions. I would adore a walk in the gardens! Maybe tomorrow morning I might manage a short stroll.*

*I shall send you another missive when I know my plans.*

*Yours,*

*Lizzy*

# Chapter 20

Elizabeth led Fitzwilliam, Nicholas, and Jane into the library and closed the door behind them. Thomas's solicitor had just read his will, and though they knew most of his last wishes, one item had been a surprise, to say the least! Not even she had known all of Thomas's intentions—not that she had ever completely known his mind.

"He left him an estate," said Nicholas almost as if he needed to say it to believe it.

"I think it was lovely." Jane glanced between them all as she sat on the sofa. "I know society and the law forbids their relationship, but such a bequest indicates how strongly he felt for his valet."

Elizabeth sat beside her and took her sister's hand. Regardless of the shock, she was not angry. "It does indeed. Colin took excellent care of him. I do not begrudge him this gift. 'Tis a small estate as I recall, earning only one or two thousand per annum and is only for his lifetime. With his lifestyle, he will not beget an heir, so according to the terms, the property will revert back to the Leeds estate upon his death."

After Fitzwilliam gave the men a small glass of brandy and the ladies sherry, he sat in one of the large wingback chairs and crossed his ankle over his opposite knee. "I agree with Lizzy. I have spoken some to Colin over the last few weeks. He thought Thomas might give him a few thousand pounds so he might live out his life in comfort. This was beyond even his expectations." He took a sip of his brandy. "Despite the size of the property, a competent steward is in place. I daresay Colin likely learnt some of managing an estate over the past few decades. The steward will be there to help."

"I suppose you are correct," said Nicholas. "I must admit that I am surprised we have heard naught from James."

Fitzwilliam swirled his brandy in his glass. "He is in Brighton. I have wondered if word has reached him."

With a swift turn of her head, Elizabeth gave an incredulous laugh. "And how have you come by that information?"

"Simple." He held up his glass as if toasting. "After the quickening, Thomas and I hired an investigator to watch James and report on his general whereabouts as well as any plans to travel. The man has been quite thorough and has even taken employment as a groomsman from Thomas's wayward nephew in order to gain information more readily. James has been at the Royal Pavilion in Brighton with Prinny for the past fortnight."

A snicker came from Nicholas. "He must be attempting to win a few pounds to pay his debts."

Elizabeth closed her eyes and shook her head. James would bring his own ruin. Thank goodness, he had not seemed concerned about Alexander and shown his face at Worthstone. "More than a few pounds are required to pay off the tens of thousands James owes. I do not care where he goes so long as he stays far away." A murmured agreement came from Jane before she took a sip of her drink.

"He will not come near you at Pemberley." Fitzwilliam chuckled and finished off his glass.

She started and turned to him, her neck becoming rigid. "I beg your pardon?" Pemberley? Who said anything of Pemberley?"

He set down his glass and rested his hands on the arms of the chair. "Well, with you spending your mourning period at Pemberley, I shall be present to protect you and Alexander. Once we are married, he would be a fool to attempt harming you."

"Once we are married?" Elizabeth's eyebrows had not remained idle but had risen incrementally with each bit that Fitzwilliam revealed.

"Yes, when we are married."

Elizabeth stood and walked closer to the fireplace before she whirled around. "Forgive me, but I thought a proposal preceded a betrothal, and for the life of me, I cannot remember receiving one."

"Perhaps we should leave the two of you to talk." Jane leaned forward as if to stand.

Elizabeth threw out a hand in Jane's direction. "No, you and Nicholas may remain. I have naught to hide at this point. After all, Fitzwilliam has told you all."

"We have discussed this," said Fitzwilliam in a frustratingly even tone. "It has always been understood that we would marry."

"So, because we have had a relationship and I have borne your son, I do not deserve to be courted or receive a formal proposal? Does the fact that you have shared my bed make me less worthy than a maiden or someone you might have met in a more traditional manner?"

"Of course not!"

Though she found no humour in the situation, she gave a laugh. "Thomas may not have been much of a husband, yet even he made an attempt at courting me. His proposal sounded more a business arrangement, but in the end, I suppose it was. I was simply the ideal broodmare in his view." She covered her eyes with her hands for a moment before she crossed her arms over her chest with a huff. "And who determined I was to live at Pemberley during my mourning, because I have yet to hear of it?"

Fitzwilliam gaped at her as though she had suddenly sprouted antlers. "Why would you not? 'Tis as safe as anywhere."

She shrugged her arms up to her sides and dropped them heavily. "We have done all we can to prevent talk, and you expect me to pass a year at Pemberley." She closed her eyes while she tamped down the tirade that threatened to explode from her chest. "You have spoken of your intention to place Georgiana in school this autumn. Is it to be just the two of us at Pemberley?"

He stood and stepped towards her. "Lizzy," he said in that voice that begged her patience. Why did that tone only increase her ire?

"If only the two of us live in that house, you know what people will say—what rumours will abound. Do you know how long it has been since I have seen my family?" She leaned forward and put her hands on her hips. "Well, do you?" He opened his mouth to speak, but she pointed to Jane while she attempted to control the shaking of her entire body. "With the exception of my aunt, my uncle, and Jane, I have not spent time with my family in nearly two years. Instead, I have passed that time being controlled by a man who I thought I could trust, yet I could not. Did you think I would appreciate you planning my life for me without my say? Did you think I would enjoy being informed that I am to marry you?"

He peered over to Nicholas, who picked a piece of fluff from his breeches while his lips were pressed tightly together. His cousin did not look at him.

"My brother knows better than to put his oar in." She ignored the untouched glass of sherry she had set on a side table and poured herself a small measure of brandy. "I love you, Fitzwilliam, yet you can be the most infuriating man. You might run Pemberley and make decisions for Georgiana, but you do not control me." She downed the brandy and grimaced at the bite.

"Elizabeth," he said as he stood and stepped toward her. "You are overreacting."

Jane gasped, and Nicholas groaned and covered his face. She could not have agreed more, though she merely lifted her eyebrows once again.

"I am overreacting? Apparently, I must protect my own reputation since you do not give a care. If I remained under your roof for a year, I would be considered your mistress, but then I suppose by some definition, I already am, so why would you think I should behave any differently?"

"Elizabeth—"

"What would happen if I live at Pemberley? Would we have a similar arrangement to here where you sneak into my chambers every evening? Where Lalande wakes you early enough to creep back to your rooms? What if I were to become with child again before my mourning is complete?"

She pressed her hands together in almost a praying gesture, meanwhile praying for enough patience to keep from completely humiliating him. "I do not want the world claiming me to be some wanton whore. I do not want people speaking of me in such terms to Alexander one day either. I shall not go to Pemberley. I have no fixed plans, but believe me, I shall make some, and soon."

Lord, but she needed to get away! She had already said too much, and if she kept at her rant, she would simply keep repeating the same arguments. Before Fitzwilliam could say a word, she pivoted on her heel and departed the library, slamming the door behind her.

The three of them flinched at the loud bang of the door.

"She is correct," said Carlisle as he placed his glass on the table. "She cannot live with you at Pemberley for a year without Georgiana there, and before you insist on keeping Georgiana from school another year, remember this was your father's plan. She must go to school.

"Jane and I shall talk to Elizabeth. She will not behave in a foolhardy fashion, I assure you."

He dropped back into his chair and groaned. "I only want to protect them, to spend time with my son."

"But you can," said Jane who stood and put a hand on his shoulder, lightly squeezing. "I hoped to convince her to come to Hertfordshire. Whether she stays at Netherfield with us or at Stoke, we can ensure she is safe. She can also spend time with Mama, Papa, and my sisters."

Fitzwilliam dropped his head and closed his eyes. He could not spend a year without Elizabeth. He had already spent too much time missing her. Was he truly going to have to endure this for another year?

Jane lowered beside the chair to better catch his eye. "You can visit us as well. I believe she will insist on living at Stoke, so you can stay with us and call on her—court her and ask Papa's permission. You might not live with her, but she will not keep Alexander from you. You will see him as much as possible. She knows you love her just as you know she loves you. Treat her as a lady of free will, with a sound mind of her own, and she will accept you happily when the time comes."

He gripped his hands at his sides. "I have always treated her thus."

"Today, you assumed a great deal," said Jane. "The duke's demands of her, as well as her love for you, have influenced her—have changed her. She is not the same impressionable girl who accepted a duke's hand two years ago. You must allow her to have her say and not command her. Even before, she would have chafed, but now if you do not take care, you will push her away."

Carlisle moved to stand beside Jane and took her hand as she stood. "My wife not only knows Lizzy, but she is wise. You would do well to take her advice."

That sinking in his chest echoed that Jane was correct. Elizabeth had married Thomas to help her family and more specifically her sisters, yet Thomas had used her. He had his own intentions and, when she did not comply, he forced matters to have his way. She may not have shown it to him, but at times, she must have felt rather helpless over her own fate.

"I shall speak to her."

"I would leave her be," said Jane. "If I am not mistaken, she has probably fled to the gardens. Allow her to walk off her frustrations. She will come to you before long."

He rubbed his hand back and forth on his forehead. "She mentioned before her demand to have a say in what happens to her, but my only desire is to be with her and Alexander. I confess I did not consider the ramifications. The propriety of her visit was never something we needed to consider in the past."

Jane smiled softly and clasped her other hand over where hers joined with her husband's. "You are close to having everything you have wanted for so long. I know you do not rejoice in your cousin's death, yet his passing has provided a way for you to eventually join your life with my sister's. I have no doubts it will happen, but you must have patience. You still have a year to wait."

He turned to look out the window, catching a glimpse of her black mourning gown as it disappeared behind a tall hedge. Lord, he despised black on her. The colour did not do her justice as much as certain shades of red or even green.

A deep breath shoved away that niggling unease in his gut that pressed him to chase her down. She could be such a stubborn and wilful woman—such a contrast to Georgiana and his mother. He loved her independence, yet he always failed to consider her perspective.

She appeared at the end of the hedgerow and walked towards the front door of the house. He clasped his hands behind his back and stood rigid to restrain himself from meeting her there. He needed to heed Jane's counsel on this. As well as he knew Elizabeth, Jane's knowledge of her sister was far superior and more worth his consideration.

Carlisle clapped him on the back. "We will convince her to come to Hertfordshire. Settle Georgiana in school then follow us there. You will be welcome at Netherfield anytime."

"Why do you believe she will insist on living at Stoke?" He would prefer her stay at Netherfield with her sister. He and Carlisle would ensure her safety by employing people to remain at Stoke with her, but James and any other man seeking the fortune at her disposal would be less likely to approach her while she was under his cousin's protection.

"She told Jane some nonsense about giving us our privacy. Netherfield is not Pemberley or even Worthstone, but 'tis large enough to afford us more than enough solitude. Do not fret like a woman, we have not given up hope she will live with us."

He continued to stare at the gardens as the door opened and closed behind him. Why did he allow his heart to overrule his head? Elizabeth was correct and thought of the repercussions he overlooked in his determination to be with her and their son. Why could she not understand how much he despised their separation?

That evening, she took dinner in her rooms and retired without resolving a thing between them. When he climbed into the strange bed in his chamber, he immediately jumped out and drank a large brandy. Perhaps drinking himself to sleep would work since he would not find sleep any other way.

Elizabeth lifted her hand and knocked upon the study door— not that she knew why she did. Since Thomas's death, it was as much her domain as it was Fitzwilliam's, yet she had never entered one of Thomas's rooms without knocking, especially after Pemberley.

"Yes," he called.

She entered and closed the door behind her. When Fitzwilliam looked up from the ledger, his eyes flared for a moment. Dark circles shadowed the undersides of his eyes. She lived in a slightly exhausted state from waking during the night with Alexander, so it took her a short time to find sleep, but she had slept last night. Had he?

"I spoke to Jane after our disagreement, and we spoke again this morning. She has insisted Alexander and I pass our mourning at Netherfield, and I have accepted. Pray understand how much I would dearly love to see my family. At Netherfield, I shall be close enough to do so without my mother pressing me towards a place at Bedlam. You must know why I cannot stay at Pemberley. I do love your home. You also have to know how much I love you, but I cannot think only of myself. I need to consider Alexander as well as our future."

"I understand," he said, quickly before she could continue. "I behaved abominably yesterday. I love you too, but I cannot bear us being apart. I had not considered Georgiana's schooling or that you would desire to return to your home. You have begged me to think of you as a rational woman, and I did naught to please a woman worthy of being pleased. You had every right to be angry with me."

She sniffed as a tear splashed upon her cheek. "I know you do not intend us harm. I should not have become so intemperate."

He stood and rounded the desk to take her in his arms. "I deserved your ire."

"You are not usually so impulsive."

"No," he said softly. "You bring that fault out in me. I have said before that you are my undoing." He brushed his lips against hers, and her body truly relaxed for the first time since their disagreement the day before.

"Do not blame me for your failings." She lifted her one eyebrow while lifting only one side of her lips. Thankfully, he laughed in response.

"I understand Mrs. Hamilton's replacement is doing very well."

"She is excellent. I could not be more pleased."

"I must confess to being relieved when Mrs. Hamilton departed the inn without incident. A small part of me worried she would return to commit some mischief. Under the new management, however, the house will be in capable hands." He stepped back and lifted the ledger he had been studying. "The books are in order. I have spoken to the steward who will message both of us should he have an issue. All that remains is for you to decide when you will depart."

"The Vicar at Worthstone comes tomorrow to christen Alexander and will perform the churching ceremony here in the chapel. I would prefer to depart on Monday. I can have myself and Alexander packed and ready. We shall have a week to travel should we need to take extra days for Alexander."

"Then I shall plan to depart Monday as well. Georgiana and I shall journey to Pemberley so Georgiana can pack for school."

Elizabeth touched the precise folds of his cravat, swallowing the lump in her throat. That lump had to be the size of one of those rocks on the peaks. "You will come to Hertfordshire, will you not?"

"I will. You know I will. You could not keep me away."

She blinked back the sting from tears. "I should go. I need to return to Alexander."

"May I come to you tonight? I only want to hold you. I confess to sleeping dreadfully without you."

"Yes, Alexander will be pleased to see his papa."

He drew her back into his arms and pressed a kiss to her forehead. "I promise I shall make you happy."

"I have no doubt of it."

After one last chaste kiss, she departed and returned to her rooms and their son. She did not anticipate the coming months—the time they would need to spend apart as well as his meeting her mother. Regardless of his love for her, Mrs. Francine Bennet was a trial to anyone. How would she bear it if her mother's uncouth behaviour altered his feelings for her? Yes, she was being nonsensical, but that worry would be ever-present until he met Francine Bennet and still proposed marriage.

As planned, two carriages rolled away from Worthstone on an intemperate Monday in August. When they reached the main road, the carriage with the Darcy crest headed north-east towards Pemberley while the other headed southeast in the direction of Hertfordshire, leaving Worthstone, with its perfectly manicured gardens and polished grandeur, behind them for home—at least the homes Fitzwilliam and Elizabeth had always known.

# Chapter 21

*September 11<sup>th</sup> 1810*
*Netherfield*
*Hertfordshire*

*My dearest Fitzwilliam,*

*I have thanked Nicholas more times than I can count for enclosing these letters in his own, allowing us to communicate. I confess I still find addressing him as Nicholas strange, but I suppose if I had a brother born a Bennet, I would not address him as Bennet, but by his given name. I may still stumble over the familiarity, but I am becoming accustomed to it.*

*I have also enclosed a letter of business, but news of myself and Alexander seemed odd to mix with information of homes, leases, and tenants.*

*I am certain first and foremost you wish to know of Alexander. I cannot wait for you to see him! How he has grown in the past month! He is more aware of me, as well as who holds him. He smiles and coos—particularly after he first wakes in the morning. He has charmed the entire staff at Netherfield, though for some reason, he does not like Mama (I confess I cannot entirely blame him). She has insisted on holding him on several occasions, and he has screamed unlike anything I have ever heard. If I had not known better, I would have thought my mother pinched him. Since he is her only grandson—and of course a boy—she insists during every visit that he has never cried while she has held him, yet every time, he wails in her arms. She then insists he will become accustomed to her. Jane and I do not hold the same optimism.*

*The families of the neighbourhood have called to welcome me back to Meryton, and I have taken great pleasure in learning the news of each and every person. My dear friend Charlotte calls regularly, and I have enjoyed her society greatly.*

*I have also hired a nursemaid for Alexander. Millie is the niece of Mrs. Nichols, the Netherfield housekeeper, and has been known to me most of my life. She is five and thirty and worked for a family in Watford before her return a month ago. The children she cared for are now grown and the family no longer in need of her services. She had been with that family for twelve years. They were sorry to see her depart.*

*Millie sits with him while he naps during the day and cares for him if I am busy helping Jane or receiving callers. She also sees to him when he wakes during the night and notifies me if he needs to eat. He still wakes twice, which is a vast improvement over the three to four after he was born. I know I do not gain much sleep, but I do feel significantly more rested.*

*I am eager to hear more recent news of you. How does Georgiana fare? I envy her the ability to attend school. I hope you are concluding your business in London swiftly. Summer is never nice in town and disease is always a problem. I find myself eager to hear the wheels of your carriage approach. I long to hear your voice and let it soothe the ache of your absence.*

*Do not keep me waiting, my love.*

*Lizzy*

*September 17<sup>th</sup> 1810*
*Darcy House*
*London*

*Dear Lizzy,*

*In response to your letter of business, I have found a tenant for the great house at Stoke. Since you presently live at Netherfield, I agree leasing it for a year is a good plan to raise funds towards a piano master for Miss Bennet. I am sorry to hear the master Mr. Bennet employed was so unreliable. From your descriptions of your sister, I am certain she will learn a great deal and also appreciate the experience. The benefit to your own ears will no doubt be considerable as well.*

*I have met with your solicitors and all appears to be in order. Thomas did well to save a substantial fortune, so do remember you need not raise money to gift your sister with a piano master, though I do understand your hesitancy to take funds without replacing them. Until Alexander's majority, the estate is yours as well as Alexander's and is meant to support you both. Pray remember you are entitled to spend as you please. I have seen your books from Worthstone and from Worth House as well as the bills for your past purchases. You are not a spendthrift. You will not harm Alexander's future. I assure you.*

*As to your invitation to Netherfield, I appreciate the sentiment, but unfortunately, business and Lady Matlock keep me in London. My aunt wished to return for the little Season and has insisted I attend a small ball as well as a dinner she is holding. You know my sentiments on such diversions, but my aunt has refused to accept my decline of her summons. I fear I am forced to remain in London at present.*

*I am expected to meet Mr. Bingley shortly at White's, so I must close. Forgive me the brevity of this missive.*

*God Bless You,*

*Fitzwilliam Darcy*

*Since writing the above, I have found an interested party for Stoke. My friend Bingley has apparently been searching for an estate to lease. He has accepted our terms, and I have sent a note to the solicitors to draw up the contracts. Bingley hopes to take possession before Michaelmas. FD*

Elizabeth let her hand holding the letter drop to her lap. What was this? She had penned him a billet-doux *and* a letter of business. Was he not capable of doing the same?

She stared at the correspondence with a frown. The tone was so formal and stiff. Not at all the Fitzwilliam she loved.

"Lizzy, is anything amiss?"

With a quick jerk of her head, she looked at Jane. Mary, who often came to Netherfield to escape their mother, sat beside her, holding a sleeping Alexander. "I am not sure. I believe I require some time alone." She stood and paused in front of Mary. "When you tire of holding him, call for Millie. She can bring him to my rooms."

Mary rose and bent toward Elizabeth to hand over the child. "I hope you do not mind, but I want to practise the pianoforte before I return to Longbourn. The Broadwood here is so much nicer than ours, and I want to work on what the master taught me a few days ago."

"I do not mind," said Elizabeth. As soon as Alexander was in her arms, she itched to bury her nose in his downy hair and kiss his tiny nose. Holding him close proved to be of great comfort while Fitzwilliam was away.

Once Mary bustled from the room, Jane stood and stepped close. "What is it? You restrained it well, but I could see your excitement when Nicholas handed you that letter. Now you appear nearly in tears. What did it contain?"

"Oh, Jane!"

Her sister moved to the door and closed it before returning. "Was it from Fitzwilliam?" He had invited Jane to call him thus before they departed Worthstone, and though she was as uneasy calling him Fitzwilliam as Elizabeth was with Nicholas, they had both given in to using their given names.

"Yes, but 'tis not what I expected. He writes so formally I do not know what to think. What if his feelings have changed?" She held out the horrid note. "You read it."

Jane unfolded the paper and read over Fitzwilliam's words while she bit her thumbnail. "You penned him two notes, did you not?" She flipped the paper over to determine if it might have more on the reverse.

"Yes, I did have a letter containing my thought of leasing Stoke, but I also included one where I told him how much I missed him and longed to see him. How I wanted him to come. He has only responded to the business correspondence."

"Perhaps he did not have time, and the second letter follows?"

Elizabeth huffed and touched her forehead to Alexander's. "That would not be like him. He can be rather fastidious about this sort of thing." How many times had she watched him pen notes and work on estate business while he was at Worthstone? Instead of using the master's study, he used the sitting room while the household thought he consulted with Thomas. Thomas was too ill to truly be of help.

"Come," said Jane, waving Elizabeth to follow.

"Where are we going?"

"I believe the best person to ask why Fitzwilliam is behaving in such a way is Nicholas."

Elizabeth halted in mid-step and backed away. Nicholas? Why did all of her personal business need to be discussed between both Jane and her husband? "No, I am humiliated enough that both of you know the entirety of our relationship. I cannot ask my brother for romantic advice." She all but hissed the last. "Would you wish to ask Fitzwilliam?"

Jane shrugged though her face pinked. "Why not? Besides you and Georgiana, Nicholas knows Fitzwilliam best. They are like brothers. I am certain if I had a problem with Nicholas, Fitzwilliam would have the answer."

She shook her head and gave a laugh deeply rooted in how tense she was. "Nicholas does not need to know my intimate problems, just like if they existed, I would not need to know his."

Jane made a noise similar to a growl and propped her hands on her hips. "What if I required advice on marital relations or dealing with a husband's mood? Would you not help me?"

"Yes, of course I would, but that is different."

"Not if I need advice on marital relations." Jane nearly sing-songed the phrase.

"To be honest, I would answer, yet I hope you speak openly enough with Nicholas that he might put you at ease and my advice would not be required." The conversation would be awkward, but not nearly as horrible as Mama's talk the night before Elizabeth married.

Jane crossed her arms over her chest. "After Mama's speech about my wedding night, I am afraid we had to speak of it. I was too terrified otherwise. That night was mortifying, but our marriage is stronger for it."

"Thank goodness," said Elizabeth. "I do understand. I trembled while I waited for Thomas, then he hugged me and departed, and I did not know what to do."

"You were not scared with Fitzwilliam?"

She looked down at the carpet while she thought back. "No, I was not. Perhaps it was the brandy and wine, but we simply acted. The next morning, I understood how much Mama had exaggerated."

"But she and Papa have a different sort of marriage. Perhaps her wedding night was like that for her?"

Elizabeth shuddered and crinkled her nose. "I have no desire to give much thought to Mama and Papa's marriage bed."

Jane laughed and wrapped her arm around Elizabeth's shoulders. "I confess I also do not wish to think about it." She used her arm to press Elizabeth forward. "Now if you do not come with me, I shall bring Nicholas to you."

Elizabeth groaned and hung her head. "You will not disregard my ridiculous fretting, will you?"

"No, I shall not."

After a knock on Nicholas's study door, they entered, and Elizabeth sat directly in one of the chairs while Jane walked around his desk and proffered the correspondence from Fitzwilliam. "Do you know of any reason why your cousin would respond to Elizabeth with only a letter of business?"

He read over the paper and looked up with his eyebrows drawn towards the middle. "You sent him one of business and the other was more, was it not?" He waved his hand around to keep from explaining.

"Exactly," said Elizabeth. "But he only responded with the one."

Nicholas stared at the letter for a moment before he leaned his head back on the chair and laughed. "Darcy, you dullard."

"What is it?" asked Jane who leaned upon his desk.

"Correct me if I speak too freely, or if I am mistaken." He levelled Elizabeth with a steady gaze. "Was he more circumspect that last night at Worthstone? In front of only us, he held your hand but he sat slightly apart from you—further than I would sit from Jane."

"Yes, but we had argued the day before."

"Has he reacted similarly when you have argued in the past?"

"Uh, no." Her cheeks pinked. "I suppose he did not behave as . . . as he had in the past." Jane giggled and Elizabeth glared at her. "I would thank you not to find humour at my expense, my dear." Alexander squirmed and she rocked him back and forth. "I do not understand."

"The morning we departed Worthstone," said Nicholas, "he made a comment. I thought naught of it at the time, but I believe that with this letter, he is attempting to prove a point."

A point? Why would he choose to do this when they were apart? "And what point would that be?" she asked.

He folded the letter and began tapping it on the desk. "That he respects you and your intelligence."

Jane rolled her eyes. "He could do that and still write her a billet-doux."

"He could, but during their disagreement, Elizabeth commented that she was, for all intents and purposes, his mistress. I can guarantee my fastidious cousin was horrified by the notion of her referring to herself thus. His father would not have approved as you well know." He regarded Elizabeth with steady eyes. "I would wager Fitzwilliam, despite his love for you, holds a certain amount of guilt. You have almost ten months until he can court you. In the meantime, do not be surprised if he is more proper than he has ever been in your presence—at least since you began your relationship."

Jane took the letter and turned it over in her fingers. "How sweet."

This time, Elizabeth rolled her eyes and scoffed. "I do not want to pretend the past year did not happen." Lord, this—Fitzwilliam—exhausted her. "I simply want to move forward."

"Since your relationship must . . ." Nicholas waved his hand again. ". . . not pass certain boundaries until your wedding is near, his scheme is not a bad idea. Allow him to court you as if the two of you just met, without the intimacy and stress of your past getting in the way. You complained of his assuming you would marry. He will not do so again. If he knows how to court, he will behave in that fashion as much as possible. I do not know if that makes sense."

"I suppose it does," she said softly. "We once again become friends rather than lovers until we can become lovers again." She sighed and traced her finger down Alexander's nose. "That does not mean he cannot send me a letter better than that one."

Nicholas laughed and took the missive from Jane to hand back to Elizabeth. "If my mother is haranguing him into dinner parties and balls, she is attempting to matchmake. She will not let him depart London easily."

A lump rose in Elizabeth's throat, making her swallow hard. "Your mother is parading ladies in front of him for however long he remains in London?"

"He loves you, Lizzy." When she looked up, Nicholas levelled a steady gaze. "I have never seen him behave as he does when he is with you. He is more open and free. In his heart, you are his wife. He has said as much to me. You have naught to fear. Have faith in him. Those women failed to turn his eye before he knew you. They will not gain his attention now. The moment you are free from mourning, he will propose. You can rely on him."

She nuzzled her nose in Alexander's hair and breathed. Fitzwilliam loved her. He loved their son. He would return. He had to return. "Perhaps I am overtired. I shall return to my rooms until dinner."

Elizabeth stood and left Nicholas and Jane to themselves. When she was finally in the privacy of her rooms, she placed Alexander in his cradle and watched him sleep for a moment. Once she was assured he would not immediately wake at not being in someone's arms, she laid down on the bed and cried herself to sleep.

"Blast!" Fitzwilliam set down his pen, propped his elbows on his desk, and rested his forehead in his hands. Why could he come up with the words he wanted when he was at the solicitor's or at his aunt's, but when he tried to write to Elizabeth of his feelings, the attempts reminded him of bad poetry—the kind that would starve a deep, healthy love entirely away.

He penned that letter of business to Elizabeth, but he had not responded to her other correspondence. The letter had been aught that he had needed to hear. He had not the words to tell her of his frustration at Lady Matlock's matchmaking.

While he missed Elizabeth and Alexander dreadfully, he had found it easier, for the time being, to be away. He could not reveal what he should not when he was in London, and he did not have the stress of pretending he and Elizabeth were no more than friends.

He sighed and stared at the blot of ink on the paper in front of him. Eventually, he would give in and travel to Hertfordshire, but for now, he would let as much time pass as he could stand. Perhaps it would be easier for the both of them.

A knock at the front door rattled through the house. Footsteps passed the door to his study and the voice of his aunt filtered through the gaps at the door. Swiftly, he covered the letter he was attempting to write and stood when the butler opened the door.

"Lady Matlock, sir. I apologise, but she insisted."

"What is this?" His aunt pushed past the butler and held up the note he had sent that very morning.

He drew his eyebrows toward the centre with a frown. "Have you not read it?"

"I have, and I am quite put out. When I learnt you would be in London, I organized this ball to help you find a wife, and you refuse to come."

He exhaled and prayed for patience. "I am well aware of your reasons, Aunt, yet I never requested your aid."

"Well, apparently you have need of it. Nicholas is married and settled, and you require an heir."

Fitzwilliam drew himself up as tall as he could. "None of those ladies you paraded in front of me at that ridiculous dinner interest me. None of the ladies you have invited to this ball will interest me either. I hold a *tendre* for a particular lady. When she is able to wed, I shall request the honour of her hand and only her hand. I shall marry no other. Your attempts are futile, and I beg you to cease this hideous mission you have adopted."

His aunt's eyes were now wider, and she bent a bit closer. "Who is this lady?" Her voice had adopted a higher pitch. Blast! He had set a dog after a bone.

"I shall tell you at the proper time. Until then, that is between myself and the lady."

Lady Matlock's expression became pinched. "This is an excuse. You will present yourself at my house. Now that Richard has returned, he will be present as well. Perhaps one of these ladies will do for him."

Good grief! None of them would consider Richard!

"You may apply to Nicholas if you wish to know the truth of the matter since he knows all the particulars, though he will not tell you the name of the lady either."

His aunt pressed her lips together. "Very well, I *will* ask Nicholas. However, if you truly have a lady in mind, I can aid in your courtship."

A weary laugh escaped before he could stop it. Elizabeth liked Lady Matlock, but he could only imagine her reaction to his aunt's interference. "No, you cannot. Please let well enough alone."

His aunt gripped her hands into fists at her sides. "I am seriously displeased, Fitzwilliam."

"I apologise." Why did she suddenly remind him of Lady Catherine? With Nicholas married, Lady Matlock seemed to become ripe with a fever for all of them to wed. Who she thought she could convince to marry Richard did make him curious. Perhaps she hoped he might settle and become respectable? One thing was certain, that would need to be one unalterable settlement, else he would squander the lady's fortune in a fortnight.

With a huff, she marched from the house. As soon as the carriage could be heard departing, he dropped into his seat. He needed to find a place to hide!

"Sir?"

He looked up to the butler poking his head through the door. "Pardon me for interrupting, but a courier arrived a short time ago with a letter. I thought it better to wait until Lady Matlock departed." Mr. Briggs entered the remainder of the way and held out an envelope.

"Thank you."

Upon the door closing, Fitzwilliam noted Carlisle's handwriting and immediately broke the seal. Was Elizabeth well?

What of Alexander? His fingers fumbled when he opened the piece of paper only to find two sentences written in a single line.

*Darcy, you addlepate! Send Lizzy a letter of love, not business!*

He sank into his chair and blew out a noisy exhale. If Carlisle sent this message, Elizabeth must have been upset. Oh well! He had tried, but he had also promised to treat Elizabeth with more respect, which was why he wrote the letter of business first. He drew out a sheet of clean paper. Whether this one resembled horrid poetry or not, it had to be sent.

# Chapter 22

*October 18<sup>th</sup> 1810*
*Darcy House*
*London*

*Dearest Lizzy,*

*I hope you are enjoying this time with your sister and the rest of your family. I am pleased to know of Bingley's safe arrival at Stoke, though perhaps not so much of poor Miss Bennet's dilemma from your mother to pursue him. It is good of you and Lady Carlisle to stand up for her as you do. She has no need to hurry to the altar should she not desire it, and should she never wed, she has a place in your home and I know Carlisle's too for the rest of her life. It is only right you protect her as you ought.*

*As for Miss Bingley and Mrs. Hurst, I advise you to use the excuse of mourning whenever they visit. You are well aware of the nature of both ladies. They will seek you and Jane out for the purpose of advancing themselves within the* ton *rather than some notion of kindness. If you can avoid them, it would be best to do so while you can.*

*Georgiana does well with school. She misses me and has expressed her wish to see you and Alexander soon. Perhaps Carlisle and Jane might bring you to London during the Christmastide. You begin your half-mourning in February, so you could order suitable gowns and spend time with Georgiana also.*

*Lastly, I love you, and I miss you. I am uncertain if being away is less painful, yet I firmly believe I could not be near without wishing to be closer than is proper. I shall do this as I should have from the beginning. You are my heart. I shall prove that to you.*

*Yours,*

*Fitzwilliam*

Elizabeth sighed and leaned her head against the side of the window seat. Early in her stay at Netherfield, she had found one window tucked to the back in a small alcove of books where she could hide and read. Some days, she sat while Alexander slept against her chest. At times, Lalande would close and lock the door so Elizabeth could nurse him. Mrs. Nichols and Millie also knew of her preference for the spot and knew where to find her should Alexander require her.

At the moment, Miss Bingley's strident tones could be heard through the walls from the drawing room where Jane had requested tea when the callers arrived. Lord, Elizabeth detested Miss Bingley and Mrs. Hurst! The former simpered and fawned the last time they had happened upon each other during a call while the latter merely smiled and allowed her sister to do all of the talking.

Under different circumstances, Elizabeth would laugh off the ridiculous woman, however, Miss Bingley never failed to mention Fitzwilliam in the most familiar of terms. "Mr. Darcy is such a great friend." "Mr. Darcy arranged Stoke for us." "Mr. Darcy is the best of brothers." "We shall soon return to London to be in Mr. Darcy's company once more."

"Mr. Darcy uses a solid gold chamber pot," said Elizabeth softly in her best Miss Bingley impression.

"She would like to believe that."

Elizabeth's head whipped around to Nicholas standing behind her, laughing. "Forgive me," she said, "I suppose I am intemperate today."

He shook his head and stepped closer. "She grates on my nerves as well, and I do not have your excuse." He pointed to the letter in her hand. "Is that his most recent?"

"No, this is from a fortnight ago. When he mentioned us travelling to London for the Christmastide." A part of her desired nothing more than to rush to him, but she was ill-equipped to face those who would whisper behind their hands and stare while she shopped for her half-mourning attire.

"Have you changed your mind about making the journey?"

She shook her head while she stared at the letter. "Madame Bonheur is sending one of her seamstresses to us, and my aunt has sent me some lovely fabric my uncle brought home. I miss dearest Georgiana, but I do not want to travel to London."

Lord, she longed for Fitzwilliam, and she did want to see Georgiana. She simply had no desire be forced to contend with London society. Lady Vranes and Lady Matlock, however, were the exceptions—even in the face of Lady Matlock's scheming to marry off her Fitzwilliam.

"Well, sister," said Nicholas, holding out his hand to help her up. "I have come to inform you that you have a surprise in the hall."

"I do?" Her stomach fluttered. Could Fitzwilliam have finally come? She hopped up and hurried to the hall, pausing when she entered. "Miss Geddes?"

The girl curtseyed and smiled. "Your Grace." She stepped forward and held out a letter. "Lady Vranes sent me along with this note."

Elizabeth took the missive and unfolded it.

*October 25th 1810*
*Vranes House*
*London*

*Dearest Lizzy,*

322

*Yes, I have sent Miss Geddes to you once again. I send her to you so you might finally have your portrait made, and she is under strict instructions to paint only you this time. I do not mind your gift to Mr. Darcy, and I am pleased you did so since the Darcys needed a bit of happiness during that trying time. Miss Geddes is extremely proud of the work. I have seen her sketches and studies, and I know she painted a beautiful portrait. This time, however, I want you and your son immortalised for a place of honour at Worthstone.*

*I know you are in mourning, but I hope you will wear colour for the portrait. While black might be the tradition, other colours complement you more.*

*I shall miss your company greatly this season, but I do understand your reluctance to journey to town. I shall anticipate your eventual return or your acceptance to visit us in Bedfordshire. Your son is welcome as well. I would never expect you to leave him, particularly at such a tender age.*

*Yours sincerely,*

*Laura*

Elizabeth lightly laughed while she folded the letter. "What colour do you suggest?"

Miss Geddes smiled and tilted her head. "Perhaps a shade more suitable to half-mourning—lavender or plum rather than grey. If you are more comfortable in black, I do not object."

"If the portrait is to hang at Worthstone, 'tis my preference to remain in mourning attire. I would not want anyone to assume I had so little respect for the duke to mourn him less than was his due. Perhaps you could paint a smaller piece—a miniature, for me? You could copy the larger work, if possible, but paint my gown a different colour?"

The girl smiled and nodded. "I could certainly do so, ma'am."

Nicholas wore a wide grin when Elizabeth turned to him. "I shall speak to Mrs. Nicholls about a room for Miss Geddes," he said. "The Bingley sisters have been here nearly fifteen minutes. If we wait for them to depart so Jane might do so, Miss Geddes will be standing in the hall until dinner."

Her brother only disappeared for a moment before Mrs. Nicholls bustled in and gestured them to follow her upstairs. She settled Miss Geddes in a guest room, insisting the sitting room would give the artist the necessary space to set up and paint. "Footmen will clear a space for you this afternoon. Pray let us know what you will require for Her Grace to pose."

After agreeing to begin the following morning, Elizabeth excused herself to feed Alexander since he would certainly be waking soon. When she entered his room, he pushed his head from the cot and smiled the moment his eyes set upon her.

"You are such a sweet boy," she said softly when she lifted him. "Are you ready to have your portrait painted, young man?" He smiled and buried his face in her chest. "I think you would prefer to eat at this moment."

As he always did, he latched on without difficulty, swallowing in large gulps when her milk came. "The weather is much nicer since the fog lifted. Would you like to go outside?" He paused suckling while the corners of his lips turned upwards and his eyes shone. He was such a happy child. His break to smile did not last long since he soon became more serious about finishing his meal.

Lalande brought her two shawls and a spencer once he finished eating. After Elizabeth donned her spencer, one shawl was wrapped around Alexander to keep him warm and to support him in an almost sling tied to her body. The weather was not too cold today. He should be well in the shawl as well as the extra she would wrap around herself.

She held the other shawl and her bonnet as she walked downstairs, nearly turning immediately back up at Miss Bingley's cloying voice in the hall.

"Your Grace, I was beginning to think you had departed the neighbourhood. I must say we have not seen you in a fortnight at least. You should have come to the assembly last week." Mrs. Hurst followed Miss Bingley into a tirade of titters. "I daresay the fashion of Hertfordshire was not to be missed."

Lord, help her. She needed to keep a neutral expression, but the woman made her spine rigid, particularly the sarcasm Miss Bingley used to deride anyone the so-called lady felt beneath her. "I am in mourning. I keep to small family parties and the dinners my sister hosts. I really have no desire to attend more at this time."

Miss Bingley's beady eyes lit when she noticed Alexander strapped to Elizabeth's side. "Is this the young duke?"

Elizabeth barely suppressed a cringe. Her son might be a duke at his tender age, but she disliked people referring to him with his title. He was a mere babe and she did not want him given such deference at an early age. It would not do well for him to think himself too highly else he become like James or even like Miss Bingley. "Yes, this is my son." She put on her bonnet. "I am taking him out to the garden for a walk. Pray excuse us."

"Well!" Miss Bingley placed a hand to her chest. "I have never heard such a thing. Do you not have a nursemaid to do such a tedious chore? A woman of your standing should, though you may not have been informed." A gasp burst from Jane, but Elizabeth did not look at her. Her body shook in a way that threatened to explode.

"I do have a nursemaid," said Elizabeth, holding Alexander a little closer. "However, I enjoy spending time with my son. He does not interfere with my duties, and I want him to know I care for him. I have precious little respect for women who only have their children brought to them once a day for a few moments simply to lay eyes upon them. Those are not parents. Their child is nothing more than a thing to parade before company."

"Hear, hear!" Nicholas strolled into the hall. Had he heard her from his study? "My mother certainly never relegated us over to the nursemaid for constant care. She spent a great deal of her time with us. She even taught us our letters and how to write our names."

Mrs. Hurst's eyes darted between Nicholas and Elizabeth while she clutched her reticule. "Caroline, perhaps we should take our leave."

After rolling her eyes, Miss Bingley scoffed. "I suppose we should return to that wretched little hovel Charles saw fit to take. Why, the drawing rooms are ridiculously small. I can hardly receive callers without stuffing the room as one would a pheasant."

"On that point, you and my mother agree," said Elizabeth. "Since I am fond of small parties, I did not mind the size of the drawing rooms when I lived there."

"*You* lived at the great house at Stoke?" Caroline's voice rose and the pitch turned higher while she spoke.

"Why, yes." Elizabeth lifted her one eyebrow, pushing down that simmer that was threatening more and more to boil over. "The duke and I resided at Stoke briefly after our marriage. Since the estate is a part of the Osborne holdings, I could have spent my mourning there, but my sister and her husband were good enough to offer a room at Netherfield so I would not be lonely."

"You own Stoke?" asked Miss Bingley while Mrs. Hurst turned a sudden pasty colour.

"Yes, Miss Bingley, I do."

Nicholas began coughing furiously before he bowed. "Pray excuse me. I shall check on your carriage, Mrs. Hurst, Miss Bingley."

Elizabeth curtseyed. "Miss Bingley, Mrs. Hurst."

Jane's lips were pressed together as Elizabeth passed, but she said not a word. Her dearest sister would never be angry with her—especially in light of Miss Bingley's appallingly rude behaviour. The problem was when that pretentious woman baited her, Elizabeth simply could not sit idly by and allow the insult to her family or the neighbourhood.

One of the footmen stood near the house, keeping watch on her and Alexander while she walked through the gardens. While she studied a rose that had the temerity to bloom at the wrong time of year, footsteps made her look up.

"You should not have lost your temper with Miss Bingley."

"She is rude and ill-tempered. I said nothing she did not deserve." Elizabeth sniffed the rose. Its perfume was not as fragrant as those that bloomed in the summer, yet a hint of that odour lingered.

"You would have dearly loved what she said after you departed."

Elizabeth looked at her sister and shook her head. "Would I?"

"She said 'it was shameful that James lost his inheritance to a child who lacked the proper breeding and would suffer for his upbringing.'"

"Oh, I hope I see that woman when I am next in town."

Jane gave her that look—the one that never failed to make Elizabeth feel the size of an ant. "Nicholas said much the same. Do not forget the disappointment she will feel when your mourning is over and certain events come to pass."

"Just desserts," said Elizabeth. "I shall not feel pity for her. Fitzwilliam would never accept such a petty woman as his wife."

"No more than Nicholas would. I understand she boasts a fortune of twenty-thousand, yet she is five and twenty and unwed."

"Then perhaps she should wed James. He is in desperate need of funds."

"Lizzy! Would you truly wish such a fate on any lady?"

Elizabeth gave a bark of laughter. "On her? I do believe I would." She walked further out towards a copse of trees. "I am thankful my mourning provides me an excuse not to associate with the likes of those women."

"And if they talk when they return to London?"

"I hope they do." Elizabeth closed her eyes and lifted her face towards the sky, allowing the breeze to caress her face. "Laura, Lady Vranes, will cut them for me. I am certain Lady Matlock would as well." After one glance at Jane, she turned and sighed. "She insulted my son, Jane. She may not have said it to my face, but she did say so. I am tired, I am lonely, and I am impatient to be done with this infernal year of mourning. I do not have the tolerance for her balderdash. She had best steer clear of me."

"Her brother is certainly amiable," said Jane who took Elizabeth's arm.

"He has no spine. He is, as Shakespeare says, 'led by the nose as asses are.'"

Jane giggled and tugged at Elizabeth's elbow. "Come, join me for tea. You can warm yourself and Alexander by the fire. Mary is here to practise and you know she will wish to hold her nephew."

"Is Mama with her?"

"No, Papa refused her the carriage. Mary walked."

Elizabeth smiled and let Jane lead her towards the house. "Mama surely loved that. I can hear her. 'Walk three miles! You will not be fit to be seen!'"

"You had best prepare yourself. They come to Netherfield Sunday after church and will stay for dinner."

"Nicholas must truly love you."

"Lizzy!"

"Well, he must. When Fitzwilliam endures Mama and still wants to marry me, I shall know he loves me and cannot live without me."

"Lizzy," said Jane in a low tone. "You know Fitzwilliam loves you."

One side of Elizabeth's lips curved. "Yes, but Mama could kill even the stoutest love."

"Lizzy!"

*November 23rd 1810*
*Netherfield*
*Hertfordshire*

*Dearest Laura,*

*Miss Geddes has just departed, and I must thank you again for sending her to us. The number of sketches she made before even laying a brush to canvas astounds me. She has painted a beautiful portrait of Alexander and me that will hang in Worthstone for generations to come, though I hope you will forgive me for wearing black. It seemed appropriate since anyone who knows Alexander's age will know I was in mourning at the time. I do not wish people to think I did not give my husband his due.*

*Your latest letter made me laugh harder than I have in some time. I must thank you for the days of enjoyment I received from your description of Miss Bingley. I have managed to avoid her since that day, thanks to Alexander and Miss Geddes, but I know I must face her eventually. She is insufferable, though my sister is too good and begs my patience with her. I do not know why since she has also insulted Jane on several occasions. I disagree with your assertion that Miss Bingley plans her barbs. Instead, I believe her insults are the impulse of the moment, yet they are still horrendously rude.*

*The months drag by, though I hope the upcoming holiday season will hurry a bit of the time along so I might do more as I please. While I do not mind the solitude from Miss Bingley, I do miss certain diversions—such as visiting art exhibitions with you, dear friend.*

*Alexander grows swiftly. He holds himself up when I carry him and he can laugh. I adore every new nuance to his personality, though I mourn the disappearance of his newborn features. While I wish time to hasten for one reason, I cannot bear it passing with such speed that I lose this precious time with him as a babe.*

"Lizzy!"

Elizabeth groaned and sanded the paper in front of her. "Yes, Mama!"

Her mother bustled into the doorway and frowned. "There you are. You should be in the drawing room. The Bingleys have called."

"Again?" If only they would call on the Lucases or the Gouldings. They seemed to be here incessantly.

"What does it matter if they have called before? You should greet them."

"I have met them, Mama. I have no desire to greet them today."

Her mother clucked and crossed her arms over her chest. "Mr. Bingley has five thousand a year! I have great hopes he might take a liking to Mary since your father will not let me introduce him to Kitty. If only Lydia were out! I could have them wed by Easter!"

Elizabeth closed her eyes and took a deep breath, exhaling slowly. "Mama, Lydia is not yet fifteen. She has no business at an assembly much less courting. None of my sisters will be goaded into marriage as I was. Do you hear me?" She glared in an attempt to calm her mother.

"As if marriage to the duke harmed you! Look at the property and homes you have! Your son—my grandson is the Duke of Leeds! How well that sounds." The last was said as though she only just realised that point. "I did you a great favour by pressing you into marrying the duke."

Her mother clasped her hands in front of her. "Where is Alexander? You should wake him and bring him down. They should see my grandson—my grandson the duke!" The last words gained in volume and pitch. She knew that tone anywhere. Her mother would push and push until she gained what she desired, to use Alexander to curry those horrid women's favour.

"No, Miss Bingley belittled Alexander the last she saw him. He might be a babe, but I do not want her near my son." Not to mention Alexander, who smiled much more than he cried, still wailed whenever in his grandmother's presence.

"Mrs. Bennet." Mr. Bennet entered without pause and took his wife by the elbow. "Lizzy is in mourning, and it is more than proper for her to avoid company while remaining at Netherfield. Go help Jane entertain her guests and try not to embarrass her."

"Embarrass her? I would never!"

Once he had all but shoved her mother from the room, Mr. Bennet sat in a nearby chair and relaxed. "How are you today, my Lizzy?"

"I am well enough. I was taking care of my correspondence while the Bingleys were here."

He grimaced and sighed. "Why your mother is so desperate to gain the approbation of those ladies is beyond me. They are the most disagreeable sort, and the brother is as beetle-headed as they come. He smiles and is altogether too happy. I doubt he has ever put his foot down with that sister of his."

"As you put down your foot with my sisters before the duke insisted."

He laughed and straightened some, tugging at the front of his topcoat. "Once I insisted on them not coming out until seventeen and weathered the storm, life returned to normal. I had no need to exert myself any further."

Elizabeth set down her pen and crossed her arms over her chest. "If Thomas had not insisted, Kitty would be out and Lydia would be out next year. They have become brash and uncontrolled. You must exert yourself with them now before they expose themselves to censure or some rake ruins them. I would be pleased to send Lydia to school. Perhaps I might find one that will help with her spoilt and wilful disposition."

"And your husband's fortune saves us again," he said, sarcasm lacing his tone.

"Do not call him that." Elizabeth spoke through her teeth.

"What? Your husband? You were married before God and this family. He could be little else."

Elizabeth rose and cleared her throat. "Thomas was a great many things, but he was no husband. Pray excuse me, this conversation has left me desirous of solitude."

Her father furrowed his brow but merely watched her while she departed. When the door closed behind her, she sagged against it and dropped her head. She needed to better control her temper.

# Chapter 23

Fitzwilliam slowed his horse at the first glimpse of Meryton. How many times had Elizabeth described in vivid detail the town as well as Longbourn? He passed several small cottages before he noticed the sign for Mr. Phillips, Elizabeth's uncle and the local solicitor. She had certainly mentioned him and his wife on numerous occasions.

The assembly rooms stood on the opposite side of the street. After he passed the inn, the road forked, and he followed the pathway to the left, bringing him through a small forest.

When he emerged from the trees, the road curved again and Netherfield stood proudly in the distance, its sand-coloured limestone gleaming in the afternoon sun. He pressed his horse forward into a gallop. Blood rushed through his veins, roaring in his ears, and his heart threatened to burst from his chest. He would see Elizabeth! After nearly four months, he would finally lay eyes on her and their son.

A groom hastened forward as Fitzwilliam approached the house, taking the horse so he could climb the front steps. The door opened and Carlisle emerged with a huge grin. "You finally gave in."

"I must return to fetch Georgiana from school in a week. I plan to bring her here if you do not object."

"You and Georgiana are always welcome to visit. I have told you for weeks to come. Did you think I would change my mind once you journeyed as you have? That would be uncharitable."

Fitzwilliam laughed and clenched his hands. Everything in him wanted to shove his cousin out of his way and burst inside yelling Elizabeth's name. "You could."

Carlisle grabbed him by the shoulder and tugged him through the entrance. "Miss Bennet comes often to play the pianoforte. I am certain she and Georgiana will do well in each

334

other's company; however, I must warn you that the Bingleys call frequently, particularly Miss Bingley and Mrs. Hurst."

A wince came without thought to Fitzwilliam. "Perhaps we can keep my presence a well-guarded secret."

"Hah! Good luck! Once you have met Mrs. Bennet, she will have your name and income thrown around three counties before she considers her task complete." Carlisle did not stop but let the butler close the door behind him upon their entrance to the hall. The house was not as grand as Pemberley or Matlock, but it was in good repair and well-furnished. "Lizzy is walking with Alexander. She has taken to waking early and strolling the gardens after she feeds him, but she enjoys taking him out every afternoon if the weather permits."

"She is guarded?"

"A footman follows regardless of whether Alexander accompanies her. When she brings Alexander, she rarely strays past the gardens. He truly seems to enjoy the fresh air."

"Did you tell her I am coming?" A part of him hoped they had not. He wanted to see the expression on her face.

"No, Jane thought you would prefer to surprise her." Carlisle wore a grin while he led Fitzwilliam through to a comfortable drawing room.

Jane stood and hurried forward to hug him. "Lizzy is in the rose garden. At least she set out in that direction when I left her not five minutes ago. You should find her for me and convince her to return for tea." Her head tilted to the side a hair, one side of her lips curving a bit more than the other. Elizabeth always said her mother was the worst at matchmaking before Thomas proposed. Jane also seemed to enjoy the practice.

With a slap on the back, Carlisle pressed him towards a door that led to the back gardens. "Follow the centre path out until it splits and go right. You will find her."

Fitzwilliam shook his cousin's hand. "Thank you."

He strode along the path and turned where Carlisle had indicated, taking him between two tall hedgerows. When he reached the end, a round garden of roses lay mostly dormant for the winter. Elizabeth stood in the centre walkway, staring at something in the distance.

She pointed and spoke in soft tones, holding Alexander securely to her side. She wrapped her free hand around their son's back while she continued to talk. After bestowing a kiss to the babe's temple, she cuddled him a little closer.

Fitzwilliam cleared his throat. "Lizzy," he said gently. He wanted to surprise her, not scare her out of her wits.

She gasped and turned abruptly. "Fitzwilliam!" As fast as she could move without jostling Alexander, she hastened around the roses while he strode to meet her. When she finally stood directly in front of him, she lurched forward but drew herself back before she stepped into his arms.

He glanced over her shoulder to where a footman stood at the edge of the garden.

She shook her head with shiny eyes. "I cannot believe you are here."

He lifted a shoulder. His hand reached only slightly before falling back to his side. The urge to touch her was overwhelming. "I could not stay away another day. I shall need to return to London to fetch Georgiana for the holidays, but I plan on bringing her here."

Again, he reached out his hand. Once she placed her small gloved one in his palm, he bowed properly over it, kissing her knuckles longer than he truly should have. "Your Grace," he said. "'Tis wonderful to be in your company again."

"Are we to be *so* proper?" Her eyes rolled slightly while she smiled. "I love that you want to do this, but pray, let us start as we

336

L.L. Diamond

were before, friends. I call you Fitzwilliam, you call me Lizzy, and we converse in the same manner we always have."

He laughed and took a deep breath to shove down that part of him that wanted to kiss her and pull her closer. That battle would wage until he made her his, and he had best control this yearning for as long as possible. "Of course." He let Alexander's fingers wrap around one of his larger ones as he had when the babe was first born. "He certainly has grown." Alexander was no longer a tiny baby but had grown somewhat taller. His hair still had the one curl that coiled upon the top of his head.

"Indeed, he has. He can support his own head and even roll from his stomach to his back. He adores smiling—particularly right after he wakes. Do you not, Alexander?" Their son gave a large toothless grin while he attempted to yank Fitzwilliam's finger into his mouth. "He also enjoys sucking on his hands or the fingers of anyone holding him."

She drew the boy from the shawl she had tied around her waist. "I am certain you wish to hold him."

Fitzwilliam nearly trembled out of his boots when he took his son. He had not held him in months and never outside like this. What if he dropped him?

Even after he had him in his arms, she kept a hand to the baby's back. "Bring him to your shoulder. He enjoys looking around."

Alexander's wide blue eyes examined him before he smiled again and rubbed his face against Fitzwilliam's shoulder. When Alexander straightened, his tiny hand found Fitzwilliam's cheek. Fitzwilliam covered his son's hand and turned his head to kiss the palm as he would Elizabeth. "I have missed you, my little man." How full his heart was at that moment! All he had longed for was so physically close. If only he could embrace Elizabeth as well.

"I have missed you too," he said, catching Elizabeth's gaze. "You do not know how many times I almost ordered my horse saddled so I might ride here to spend an evening. The problem lay in leaving. If I came, I could not walk away so soon. I know I shall find it nearly impossible to depart after Christmas."

She shook her head and pressed her palm to her stomach. "I would prefer not to speak of it now. That day will come soon enough. I would prefer to live in the present."

"Do you ever think of the past?" He clenched his teeth and attempted to steel himself. As much as she had affirmed he still held her affection, he did not want her to regret how they had begun.

"I prefer to remember the past as it gives me pleasure. Only a very small portion of our acquaintance is not remembered with fond memories."

Alexander had relaxed against him, filling his chest with hope that they could eventually be father and son. Though rearing one's own child was not exactly a popular occupation among the *ton*, Fitzwilliam had always spent a prodigious amount of time with his parents. They had not conformed to the usual practices, and he would never understand how most neglected their own flesh and blood. He wanted to witness as much of Alexander's youth as possible. He would miss so much in this year apart.

"I hope you will forgive me," said Elizabeth, her eyes suddenly twinkling.

His eyebrows drew down with his frown. "I see nothing for which you should be forgiven."

Her happy laugh mingled with the breeze, rustling the fallen leaves the gardeners had thus far not cleaned. "You will when my family comes for dinner this evening. My mother has been pushing Mary towards Mr. Bingley. When she learns you are more than twice Mr. Bingley's worth, she will forget Mr. Bingley exists in a trice."

"Poor Bingley," he laughed.

She held out her arm along the path, and they began to walk. "Mary has improved in many ways. She is no longer so pious. My father insisted on introducing her to literature beyond Fordyce, and with the aid of the master who comes twice a month, her playing has become more than tolerable."

"What of her singing?"

"Alas, I am unsure if much can help her voice. Jane and I have delicately suggested she not sing when performing."

He smiled and kissed his son's temple. "And has she heeded your advice?"

"Surprisingly, yes, she has. She has even taken to playing some lighter melodies and not the ponderous pieces she once favoured."

"Progress, indeed," he said. "How is your mother with Alexander?"

"Poor, I am afraid. She does not understand why he cries, but she will not temper her volume. He startles whenever she is near. She sent most of us out to a tenant until we were weaned, so she has very little experience with a child so small. She is scandalized that I have not done the same with Alexander."

He rubbed the babe's back while he studied him for a moment. Mrs. Bennet's laments towards Elizabeth's care of their son were unfounded. He was robust and rosy. Fitzwilliam much preferred Elizabeth caring for him as she did and envied her ability to do so. "Ignore your mother. He is a splendid child—hearty and happy. I would not have you raise him any other way."

"Thank you," she said softly. Her hand found its way into the crook of his arm. "I confess I cannot leave him over to Millie for too long. I go to church on Sundays, and she keeps watch over him while he naps or if I take the time to greet callers, though I have begged Jane to excuse me most days since it is often Miss Bingley and Mrs. Hurst."

"Mourning is the perfect excuse."

"The few times I have been in those ladies' company, I was in the drawing room when they were announced. I could not very well flee, even though it was my most fervent desire."

He grinned and stamped down that frustrating impulse to kiss her. "How long do you remain outside with him?" Alexander had been well-wrapped in several shawls, but his little hand was beginning to feel cold.

"I was about to return to the house when you came." She reached up and touched Alexander's fingers. "Is he chilled?"

"I do not have him as well swaddled as you did."

She untied the shawl draped around her waist. "Lalande knew of this method of making a sling for him. I have preferred it since I feel it keeps him warmer."

She put her hand back in the crook of his elbow as they ascended the steps. When they entered the hall, Elizabeth tucked the shawls around Alexander. "We can sit in front of the fire to help warm him."

"Mr. Darcy!"

The three of them started at the exclamation, but he stiffened into a human tree. Why was Miss Bingley at Netherfield today of all days? He turned and bowed formally. "Miss Bingley, Mrs. Hurst, I hope you and your family are well?"

"We are well, thank you. Charles was meeting with the steward at Stoke when we departed."

Fitzwilliam furrowed his brow. "I hope there is naught amiss."

Miss Bingley waved his comment away, briefly glancing to Carlisle when he entered the hall. "Oh, he meets with the steward once a week to learn more about running an estate. I told him he should learn from you as you would know more than a mere steward, but he does not listen."

"I learn a great deal from my steward," said Fitzwilliam, ensuring no censure entered his voice. "He has more experience than I and a vast amount of knowledge from which to learn. He is an invaluable asset to Pemberley."

"But you would only employ the best of people at *Pemberley*." Miss Bingley adopted the cloying tone that sent an unpleasant vibration up his spine. Jane, who stood behind Miss Bingley and her sister, cleared her throat demurely, which was certainly an attempt to cease the conversation and move them into a drawing room.

"Are you insinuating the duke did not give similar consideration to those who care for his properties?" Elizabeth's one eyebrow was lifted and her tone was pinched. He could not blame her. From what she had indicated in her letters, Miss Bingley continually insulted her. Why the woman insisted on killing herself socially astounded him.

Miss Bingley paused and paled only a fraction while Mrs. Hurst cast glances between Jane and her as she stepped beside her sister. Her eyes then flitted to Carlisle, him, and Elizabeth before her wide gaze turned to her own sister. "I am certain Caroline did not mean to imply the duke was lackadaisical in his management by any means."

"I would think not," said Jane. "My brother was exceedingly attentive to those who relied on him for their well-being, and his estates prospered under his excellent management."

Carlisle clasped his arms behind his back and nodded. "They did indeed."

Miss Bingley's face turned a slight crimson and her lips pressed together while her sister and Jane spoke of her ill-conceived words. She recovered quickly, however, and smiled calculatingly. "I had no idea you were so fond of children, Mr. Darcy. I have always been told they should remain in the care of a nursemaid."

He did his best to disguise a deep inhale. How did this woman never learn? "My parents certainly never left me in the sole care of my nursemaids or my governess. My aunt never relegated my cousin to the sole care of others. I am at a loss as to where you come by your information, Miss Bingley. My cousin knew of the duchess's plans to care for their son, and he supported her. He married her because he thought enough of her character to know that she would go to great lengths to care for her child."

"I have mentioned that my mother cared for us before," said Carlisle. "Truly, Miss Bingley, I believe you must learn that not everyone has the same habits or beliefs."

"Well, I—"

"I do not wish to hear it, Miss Bingley," said Carlisle. "Since your arrival in the neighbourhood, you have called, several times a week, and proceeded to deride the people of Meryton and insult my wife in her own home, as well as our sister and nephew. My wife is too charitable to ban you from this house, but I do not share her qualms on the matter. Pray, depart Netherfield without delay. I will give the butler direction that you are not to be admitted to this house again."

Mrs. Hurst stepped forward, her eyes darting between Carlisle and her sister, whose mouth gaped like a perch. "My Lord, I am certain my sister did not—"

"Your sister should be more aware of her snide remarks and her backhanded compliments. She must also learn from her mistakes. Do you not agree, Darcy?"

He stiffened and adjusted Alexander so he held him more securely. He hated offending Bingley, yet Elizabeth should not need to hide in what was essentially her own home for the time being. "I do. I would have implemented the same long ago had I not enjoyed the friendship of Miss Bingley's brother."

Miss Bingley blanched and clenched her hands into fists at her sides. "I am the model of a perfect lady."

"No, you are certainly not," said Fitzwilliam. "You insult anyone you feel below you, and in this case, those who are far above you in rank and behaviour. You have insulted a duchess and a viscountess as well as my aunt, a countess."

"They are both from Longbourn," said Miss Bingley with a sputter. "Their mother is vulgar, and they hardly have the fortune a duke or a viscount should aspire to wed!"

"And you are a tradesman's daughter." Carlisle's jaw pulsed, and his eyes narrowed. "You should consider your own background before you deride that of others. In the case of the duchess, I am certain the Duke of Leeds saw what I did in my wife—beauty, intelligence, and *kindness*—a trait you sorely lack."

Fitzwilliam became distracted when the butler entered and dipped his chin in Carlisle's direction. Had his cousin realised the direction of the conversation and planned the Bingleys' ejection before he even entered?

"Your carriage is prepared and awaits you." Carlisle lifted his arm towards the door. "Pray give my regards to your brother." He whispered to Jane who looped her arm through Elizabeth's and led her into the drawing room.

At Carlisle's hand to his shoulder, Fitzwilliam startled from watching Miss Bingley's strained expression. Carlisle pressed him to follow Elizabeth while he tilted his head in that direction. Fitzwilliam allowed himself to be led into the drawing room and the door closed behind him.

"Nicholas," said Jane. "I understand a set down was necessary, but do you really think shunning her is the best idea?

What if chastisement alone was enough to change her ways? I would hate to think her friendless."

Elizabeth sat on the couch and leaned against the arm. "She is already friendless. Most of the ladies she claims as confidantes only associate with her for gossip. Her own popularity is an illusion she enjoys but will soon find a figment of the past since many ladies have tired of her. London next Season will be a different place for Caroline Bingley."

"My mother has never been amused by her," said Carlisle, who now poked at the fire.

"Lady Vranes has not either," said Elizabeth. "Miss Bingley, and by extension, her brother were excluded from the guest list for the Vranes's ball for the past two years. That will not change. I would not be surprised if Laura gives Miss Bingley the cut direct this Season. Miss Geddes was present for some of Miss Bingley's behaviour and mentioned it to Lady Vranes upon her return to London."

Fitzwilliam sat near Elizabeth, but not so close as to be inappropriate. "Lady Vranes does hold significant power within the more intellectual circle of the peerage. If she publicly cuts Miss Bingley, they will assume it is with good reason. They will follow suit."

"Enough of Miss Bingley," said Elizabeth. "The short time I have spent in her company has made me desirous of never speaking of her again. Fitzwilliam has come, and I am anticipating Georgiana's visit. I do not want to dampen my own spirits by giving attention to someone who does not deserve it."

Fitzwilliam nuzzled Alexander who had begun to fuss. "Well said."

Elizabeth peered across the room to the clock and held out her hands. "He is due to be fed." Once she had the baby settled in her arms, he buried his face against her chest while she kissed his crown. "I shall see you at dinner."

L.L. Diamond

He nodded and watched the sway of her gown when she departed. The past months had been interminable, but being in the same house would not be easy. He was not accustomed to keeping his distance, yet the sacrifice was required. She had been right when she had scolded him after the reading of Thomas's will. She could not fall with child while in mourning. Of course, he would marry her immediately, but he understood that she had no desire to incite talk.

A clap to his shoulder startled him from his reverie. "A great deal of time has passed already. You have a mere seven months. You will make it."

"I have wanted to be here more than anything. I know we must start over in some sense, yet being with her but not really being with her is difficult."

Jane smiled and reached over from her chair to take his hand. "You must know she feels the same. Patience has never been Lizzy's strongest trait. Do not forget how she pushed the midwife's boundaries after Alexander's birth."

"I have not." He stood and quickly kissed the back of Jane's hand. "Thank you for the invitation to spend Christmas with you and my insufferable cousin."

"You are welcome to stay as long as you want," said Carlisle from behind him.

"I would dearly love to be with them every day, yet keeping my distance from Elizabeth when she is so close is an arduous occupation. After the holiday season, I shall return Georgiana to school and travel to Pemberley for a time. I plan on re-decorating the mistress's apartments. I shall return for Easter unless you have need of me before."

"I thought Lady Catherine would demand you journey to Rosings for Easter."

"She has insisted in her letters, but I have informed her of my plans to pass the holiday with you. I also informed her once again that I would not wed Anne."

"When did you do that?" said Carlisle with a horribly mischievous smile.

"Before I departed London."

"I look forward to the letter she pens in return."

Fitzwilliam could not help the tug to one side of his lips. "It is good one of us does."

# Chapter 24

"Madame," said Lalande, standing in the door to Elizabeth's dressing room. "You wished to be notified when Miss Darcy arrived."

Elizabeth peered down to Alexander, who had fallen asleep on her breast, his usual milk dribbling from his lip. "Thank you."

After her maid departed, Elizabeth put her gown to rights and set her son to her shoulder, rubbing his back while she scooted from the bed. She then placed him in the cot in the adjoining room where Millie awaited him. "Please let me know when he wakes." Millie nodded while she further tucked the blanket around him.

Elizabeth arrived in the drawing room to the familiar greeting of Georgiana calling her name and rushing to embrace her. Thank goodness school had not changed her! Elizabeth would have missed these greetings had Georgiana ceased to bestow them.

She squeezed Georgiana to her. "I have missed you too, Sweetling. Are you enjoying school?"

When Georgiana drew back, her nose was crinkled and her lips pursed. "I enjoy the piano lessons I receive from the master, but I do not know why I need to take drawing. I am terribly inept at it."

"Have you made any friends?"

"I enjoy the company of two girls. Several asked me loads of questions when I first arrived, mostly about you and Brother, before they decided whether I was worth the association."

Elizabeth rolled her eyes. "Did you pass muster?"

"Apparently, though they behave much like Miss Bingley. I am kind, yet I do not seek their company."

"Good girl," said Carlisle. "You have naught to concern yourself with here. Miss Bingley is no longer welcome, so our only callers are Jane's family and her friends from the neighbourhood."

"You cut Miss Bingley." Georgiana turned abruptly to her cousin with her jaw lax. "What of Mr. Bingley?"

"He came to call the following day," said Fitzwilliam. "Carlisle and I sat him down in the study and told him of what his sister had said to Lizzy and Jane."

"He made excuses." Carlisle laughed as he sat by Jane and took her hand. "Caroline had been indulged as a child, she was trying to impress Darcy, but in the end, we explained her behaviour would soon see her cut from most of the drawing rooms of London."

"I do not think he believed us." Fitzwilliam sat on the sofa and gestured to a chair near the fire. "Come warm yourself, Georgiana. You complained so of the cold in the carriage."

"Yes, we do not want you to become ill." Elizabeth saw her seated before she took the place near Fitzwilliam. How she wanted to sit closer, but he had been so careful in his behaviour since his arrival. He never strayed beyond what was proper— except for occasionally lingering over her hand while he kissed her knuckles or leaning a hair too close to speak to her privately. Those instances were typically in the sole company of Carlisle and Jane. They would not dare speak of it, so there was no cause to worry. They also could sympathise with how difficult remaining apart had been, and how they must not go beyond certain boundaries during Elizabeth's mourning. The hardest part had been the evenings. Neither had strayed to the other's bedchambers—even to talk between themselves.

Fitzwilliam usually accompanied her when she walked with Alexander, which made sense when one viewed it with propriety in mind. A footman typically followed along, and she had

Alexander. There was naught they could do with a small child and a footman in tow.

"I am curious to hear more about your school," said Jane, bringing Elizabeth back to the conversation at hand. "Elizabeth and I never had the opportunity. We would love to know more of what you do."

She stole a glance at Fitzwilliam, only to find his eyes on her. Georgiana must have begun speaking, but later, Elizabeth could not have repeated any of it. She was too absorbed with him.

Elizabeth awoke the morning of Christmas Eve, having hardly slept the entirety of the evening before. Since Georgiana's arrival three days ago, they had not heard from her family with the exception of Mary, who still walked to Netherfield for the quiet and the Broadwood Grand. Today, however, the Bennets would invade Netherfield for dinner and return on the morrow after church. The entire prospect was enough to make Elizabeth nauseous.

The weather for the past few days had been rainy and cold, so Elizabeth had not ventured out on her own, much less taken Alexander outside. Instead, Georgiana had dearly loved playing with her little cousin on the floor of the drawing room.

He would lie on his stomach while she talked to him and made him smile. Fitzwilliam would often sprawl out on the floor with him as well, which made Elizabeth's heart swell. She loved her two men with her entire being.

"Lizzy?"

Elizabeth glanced from her needlework to Georgiana, who had been playing with Alexander on the floor. "Yes, Sweetling."

"What are your plans when your mourning is over? I shall have a break near that time. Perhaps you could come to Pemberley? We could ride and have ever so much fun."

"I do believe it a wonderful idea," said Fitzwilliam, who picked up Alexander. Fitzwilliam rolled over to his back and held their son above him, lowering him and lifting him back.

"You might be careful." Elizabeth cringed when he lowered Alexander to his face once more. As he lifted him, their son lost a portion of his luncheon, which hit Fitzwilliam square on the nose. Georgiana laughed while Elizabeth pursed her lips together and held her amusement inside.

He passed Alexander to Georgiana and took out his handkerchief to wipe his face. "You fed him over an hour ago. I did not believe him still capable."

Georgiana returned Alexander to the blanket on the floor. "What do you think? Would you like to visit Pemberley again?"

"I certainly would, but we shall have to see what happens during the summer." She peeked at Fitzwilliam, who watched her steadily. "I do hope to spend more time at Pemberley."

"And we would enjoy having you," said Fitzwilliam with a gaze that could melt ice.

At Georgiana's gasp, they both jumped. "Lizzy, look!" Georgiana pointed to Alexander, who had pulled himself up to his hands and knees with a tremendous toothless grin.

Fitzwilliam smiled and lifted his eyebrows. "I have yet to see him do that."

"It is the first time he has done so." Elizabeth set her embroidery in her lap while Fitzwilliam put his head on the floor and talked to their son.

"You are so strong," he said while Alexander rocked back and forth with a giggle. "He will be crawling soon if he continues."

Elizabeth sighed. "And then he will be walking and talking. I look forward to it and dread it all at the same time. One day, he will not want me to cuddle him anymore."

"You have some time yet." Fitzwilliam smiled while he picked up Alexander, this time holding him at his shoulder. "Perhaps you might marry and have more children after your mourning. You would be overrun if you cuddled them all."

She could not help but gape at him. What a thing to say in front of Georgiana? What if she asked questions?

"Your Grace?" She turned her head to the butler. "The Bennets' carriage has arrived."

Elizabeth stood and smoothed her gown. "Notify Viscount Carlisle and my sister. I shall receive my family here once they are inside."

The butler nodded and hurried off as Fitzwilliam stepped beside her. "Do not be nervous."

"Why should Lizzy be nervous?" Georgiana's eyebrows were drawn together in the middle while she glanced between the two of them.

"Only that her family can be rather boisterous compared to us," he said.

"They cannot be so bad." Georgiana shrugged and pulled herself up from the floor. "Mary is not inappropriate."

Before Georgiana could say more, the sound of her mother and Lydia filtered in from the hall. The butler showed them into the drawing room, and Mrs. Bennet, as was her wont, headed straight for Alexander. "There is my grandson!" Alexander started, and his little hand clutched Fitzwilliam's cravat tightly in his tiny fist. "And you must be Mr. Darcy."

Elizabeth closed her eyes and counted to five. "Mama, may I present Mr. Fitzwilliam Darcy and his sister, Miss Georgiana Darcy. They are the duke's cousins."

While Georgiana curtseyed and Fitzwilliam bowed, her mother reached for Alexander who shrank back further into Fitzwilliam's embrace. The moment she touched him, he wailed as though someone poked him with a needle.

"Why does he not care for me?"

"He does not like anyone," said Lydia, dropping down indecorously into one of the chairs. "He is the crossest baby I have ever known."

Mary stepped forward and took Alexander from Fitzwilliam, lightly bouncing him until he ceased his crying and stared at her. "He rarely cries. He is usually a rather content baby."

Lydia scoffed. "If he likes you, then he is beetle-headed."

Jane, who had only just walked in, stopped in her tracks. "Lydia!" she shouted in tandem with Elizabeth, who had to restrain herself from slapping her youngest sister.

"What? Who would want to be around boring Mary?"

"I do not find Mary boring," said Georgiana. "We have spent several mornings together playing the pianoforte and talking. She is lovely."

Lydia's eyes swiftly roved over Georgiana's gown, and she sprang to her feet. "Where did you buy your gown? Do you like soldiers? I do so love an officer in a red coat!" Lydia inherited her mother's penchant for analysing a woman's wardrobe with a glance as well as a preference for officers. Mrs. Bennet had mentioned many times how heartbroken she was in her youth at the departure of Colonel Millar's regiment.

Georgiana, however, levelled Lydia her fiercest Darcy glare. "I have no interest in any gentleman. I am not yet out." Her honesty brought a slight curve to Fitzwilliam's lips, but Lydia rolled her eyes and flounced back to her chair.

"Lord, but you are just as dull as Mary."

"Papa!" said Elizabeth with her arms stiff at her sides.

Her father closed his eyes and exhaled noisily. "Lydia, if you cannot improve the silence in the room, pray do not speak." He sat in a chair by the fire and looked expectantly around the room.

Elizabeth stepped around Fitzwilliam to see her father better. "Is that all you can say?"

Mama sat upon the nearest sofa with her chin held high. "What should he say, Lizzy? Lydia has always been such a good-humoured girl. She should not be restrained at her young age."

"She should behave with decorum and manners," said Elizabeth. "This is not simply a family party. We do have guests."

"Lizzy?" said Mary. "We should bring Alexander to Millie to be cleaned up."

Elizabeth nodded and kissed Alexander's forehead. "Yes, thank you for your aid."

After Mary and Georgiana departed, Fitzwilliam stepped forward. "I should refresh myself." He held his soiled handkerchief in his hand. "Pray, excuse me."

Mama huffed. "Well, two prouder people I have never met."

Jane's jaw had dropped long ago, but she blinked a few times as though she were waking up. "I beg your pardon, Mama?"

"He hardly spoke a word, and the few instances Miss Darcy spoke, she meant to insult my Lydia."

"Lydia said my son was stupid and Mary boring. Georgiana was defending her friend and her cousin. You have also been unbearably rude to both Mr. Darcy and his sister." Elizabeth turned to her father. "I married the duke to improve my sisters' fortunes and marriageability, yet you allow Lydia to behave thus? Kitty has not spoken yet, but between my mother and Lydia, I am certain she cannot find the time to utter one word."

"You behave so high and mighty since you became a duchess." Mrs. Bennet sniffed and straightened her skirts. "You think yourself above us."

Elizabeth crossed her arms over her chest. "The duke increased my sisters' fortunes and insisted on their not coming out due to their immature behaviour. Jane's manner was never an issue, but my younger sisters were. Mary needed to cease her study of sermons, and even at a young age, Lydia showed she spoke whatever thought entered her feeble mind. While Mary is much improved, my father has not done as he ought and kept you from further spoiling Lydia."

She glanced over to Kitty, who stood with her hands primly clasped in front of her. "Do you wish to be just like Lydia, or do you think for yourself? I have offered to send you to school, but Papa insists it is not necessary."

"What need does she have for school?" Mama's voice sputtered and shrieked through the room. "I have taught her all she needs to know, just as I have Jane and Lydia."

"You instructed me on how to run a small estate, Mama," said Jane. "I have had to learn from Mrs. Nichols more of what a larger estate entails. When we journey to my husband's estate in Staffordshire, I shall be required to learn of that estate, and I learnt a great deal of how to entertain in London from Lady Matlock. She began teaching me when my husband and I became betrothed. Lizzy is correct that my sisters should have more than the knowledge gleaned from Longbourn."

"Did you not see Mr. Darcy's expression?" Elizabeth pointed towards the door, which Nicholas had closed before he took his place by Jane's side. "He is a man of consequence, yet he would never consider Lydia because of her behaviour. She is brash and rude, and when she comes out, she will shame us all."

"What need do I have of Mr. Darcy? I have a daughter who is a duchess and a daughter who will be a countess."

"Yet, my cousin's income is greater than the Matlock earldom," said Nicholas. "Do not discount him due to a lack of title. His grandfather was the second son of the Earl of

354

Holderness, who inherited Pemberley, a profitable and grand estate in its own right. They are well-known for their management of their holdings and wealth. Darcy's aunt married the Duke of Leeds, which is how he was related to Lizzy's husband. He does not have a title, but he does not desire one. I truly believe he would refuse should one ever be offered."

"Then why are you not pressing Mary in his direction?" Elizabeth's mother stood and began to bustle for the door when Jane stepped in front of her.

"No, Mama. Mary has no interest in him, and he has no interest in her. I beg of you to heed my husband's and Lizzy's advice. They want what is best for this family, and the scene when you arrived was awful."

Mrs. Bennet sat rigid and sniffed. "Then perhaps I should close my mouth and not say another word."

"If only that were possible," muttered Mr. Bennet.

Nicholas stepped forward and pointed to Lydia. "You will behave and be respectful as long as you are in my home, or you will not be welcomed back until you can. Do you understand?"

Lydia rolled her eyes and sank into an unladylike position. "Yes."

He turned to Mrs. Bennet. "Your daughter paid a price for your family to have a better life. She has lived in higher society and knows of what she speaks. You would do well to heed her counsel. Her offer to send Kitty to school is generous. With Lizzy paying for Kitty's schooling, I would be willing to send Lydia. Between my cousin and myself, I am certain we could find an appropriate place. She cannot remain unchecked and indulged as she has been. No man of standing would have her."

Lydia crossed her arms over her chest. "I want an officer. School will not help me find one."

"No man, officer or not, wants a silly wife," said Mr. Bennet. "You will be respectful today, or *I* will send you to Longbourn. That includes you, Mrs. Bennet."

"What?" said Mrs. Bennet in a shriek. "What have I done?"

"I could explain, but I doubt you would give my chastisement the thought it deserves." He stood and stepped to Kitty. "You have been quiet. Do you want to go to school?"

She peered to everyone in the room. Jane nodded vigorously as well as Elizabeth, who prayed she would accept. "You could ask Miss Darcy what it is like," said Jane.

"I am certain Mr. Darcy would help me to put you in the same establishment," said Elizabeth. Hopefully, she would not wish to be with Lydia! "Georgiana would accept you, and she has a few friends too. You would not be alone."

"That does not sound terrible." She gave a sort of half-shrug. "Lydia would go to a different school?"

"Yes, she would," said Nicholas with an unwavering tone. "Do you mind?"

"No." She peeked at Lydia and moved to a chair away from her younger sister. "I believe I would prefer it."

Lydia stuck her tongue out at Kitty. "Your tedious company is a bore anyhow."

"And you are a petulant little girl," said Mr. Bennet. He took Lydia by the arm and hauled her up. "Mrs. Bennet, come. You must accompany this child on her return to Longbourn."

"I do not care." Lydia ripped her arm from her father. "I shall walk to the Lucases or to my aunt and uncle Philips."

"You will not leave the house, or I will put you to work in the scullery."

"You would never," gasped Mrs. Bennet. "She is a gentleman's daughter!"

"And it is time she behaved like one." Mr. Bennet turned and gave a curt bow. "I shall return once I have given instructions to the Hills."

Elizabeth reached for her father's hand. "Papa, you cannot simply send Mama home without explaining why." Her mother might not be bright, but she would never learn if he did not take the time.

After he followed his wife and youngest daughter from the room, Mary entered. "I saw Papa take Mama and Lydia to the carriage. Are they departing?"

"Papa is," said Jane. "Mama and Lydia are to remain at Longbourn. Perhaps you could tell Georgiana she may return."

"I shall fetch Darcy," said Nicholas.

"What a scene!" Elizabeth collapsed into a chair and put her face in her hands. "I am mortified."

Jane sat beside Elizabeth and grasped her hand. "Well, Fitzwilliam saw our family at its worst." Her sister's voice remained low while Kitty followed Mary. "If this did not frighten him away, I doubt much will."

"'Tis not amusing in the slightest."

"Oh, Lizzy," said Jane. "You find humour in everything."

"Perhaps tomorrow or the next day, or even next year. Not today."

That evening, Elizabeth had arranged with Lalande to sneak into Fitzwilliam's rooms. After everyone had retired and Alexander had eaten, Elizabeth took Alexander and a small pouch and followed Lalande through the servants' corridor until she reached a door on nearly the opposite side of the house. Elizabeth knocked while Lalande backed away.

His valet opened the door and started. "Your Grace?"

"Forgive me for taking you unawares. I needed to speak to Mr. Darcy for a short time."

"You can allow her in, Bishop. 'Tis not like she has not been in my rooms before."

His man opened the door, and she stepped inside. Fitzwilliam stood by the fire in his shirtsleeves and breeches. "I did not mean to disturb you."

"You are always welcome." He held out his arms for Alexander. "Particularly when you bring our son."

"Ah, I see where your loyalties lie." She laughed while he held up Alexander and made him giggle. "You should know he only just ate."

Fitzwilliam brought him to his shoulder and kissed his head. "What was so important to bring you to my bedchamber rather than waiting until morning?"

"I wished to give you this." She held out the pouch with a shaky hand. "I hope you like it."

His forehead crinkled while his eyebrows knitted together. He took the pouch and manoeuvred so he could open it and remove its contents without relinquishing their son. When he held the miniature in his hand, he smiled so wide it lit his eyes unlike she had seen in so long. "This is wonderful."

"Miss Geddes also painted a larger portrait that has been sent to Worthstone. I asked her to paint a miniature with me wearing a colour other than black." She does not typically paint something so small, but I believe she did an admirable job.

"'Tis splendid. I shall keep it with me always," he said, setting it on the mantle. He reached out and took her hand, pulling her closer to him. "Why were you so nervous to give this to me?"

"My family made the worst of spectacles of themselves today. I am embarrassed, and I suppose afraid of what you might think of me."

"You are being silly."

"I beg your pardon?" she asked with a high tone.

"You are always worried I shall change my mind. Even had your mother committed a hanging offence, you could not be rid of me. You are stuck with me. All you need to do is say yes at the proper time."

Something inside her settled, and she shifted into his arms. "I suppose I am a silly girl, but we have been apart more than we have been together. I try to remember the past as it gives me pleasure, but it does not mean I do not fret about the future."

His large hand rubbed up and down her back. "Stop fretting."

She drew away and held out her arms for Alexander, whose head now rested on his father's shoulder. "I should return. He needs to be put to bed."

"Do not go so soon," he said, pulling her back into his arms. It had been difficult enough to leave his embrace the first time. How would she do so again? "I do not expect anything. I simply desire some time with the two of you."

"He should go to sleep. Perhaps if we lie down with him between us?"

When they were settled, they spoke of Kitty attending school with Georgiana, which in turn shifted to a conversation on Alexander's inheritance, which shifted to a talk of London. When Elizabeth woke the next morning, she could not have said when she fell asleep. She only knew that Fitzwilliam slept on his side facing her, and Alexander was still dozing between them, having slept completely through the night.

# Chapter 25

January 20<sup>th</sup> 1811
Darcy House
London

*Dearest Elizabeth,*

*Georgiana is settled back at school, and Miss Catherine, though scared, kept her wits about her when she met the other girls. Georgiana assures me the young lady who shares a room with your sister is kind, so your sister should be well. You have said she has always been one to follow Miss Lydia. Perhaps this will give her the confidence to be more independent and make decisions for herself instead of following her younger sister.*

*I hope Carlisle has had similar good fortune in placing Lydia. The school he told me of came highly recommended by several of Lady Matlock's friends, so I am certain she is in capable hands. You were correct to insist on her change. I know Christmas eve was difficult, but the conversation was desperately needed. Better now than after it was too late.*

*I hope Alexander is well. Though the girls needed to be brought to school by a certain date, I hated leaving him ill with a fever. I know the apothecary indicated fevers are sometimes nothing more than teething, yet I do not find comfort in his words. Teething is considered a dangerous part of growth by many physicians, yet I would not have them bleed Alexander or lance his gums. Georgiana and I did well without such interventions. I hope Alexander will behave similarly. Pray write and let me know he is well. I shall not rest easy until I am certain.*

*Tomorrow, I depart London for Pemberley. I know it is for the best, but I am pained by the distance the journey will take me from you and Alexander. I have missed you from the moment I kissed your hand goodbye, and I shall not be whole again until I kiss your hand once again in greeting. We are so close, my love. I promise to return should you or Alexander have need of me. I keep the miniature you gave me close to my heart. I shall likely ruin it, yet I cannot keep it anywhere else. I anticipate your next missive with bated breath.*

*Yours most faithfully,*

*Fitzwilliam*

*February 8<sup>th</sup> 1811*
*Pemberley*
*Derbyshire*

*Dear Carlisle,*

*I received word from the investigator Thomas and I had trailing James. He is keeping company with none other than Richard. Neither has money to squander, so I do wonder what they are about.*

*Darcy*

*March 11<sup>th</sup> 1811*
*Netherfield*
*Hertfordshire*

*Dearest Fitzwilliam,*

*I know you cannot help but worry, you dear man. Alexander is well. The fever was mild—as they have all been since he began growing teeth. These illnesses have become a bit of a routine. He runs a fever for a night or two, and within a few days, a new tooth appears. I promise you he is healthy and happy. He is sitting up and has even pulled himself to stand once. At this rate, he will be walking long before I am ready!*

*Millie has taken to giving him pieces of bread to suck on and feeding him a thin pap. I do have concerns he will choke, yet she assures me, he is fine. He has certainly grown since she started. If he continues, he will have to walk for I shall not be able to carry him.*

*I miss you dearly, my love. I know you must go since it is too great a temptation for you to remain so close, but I cannot help but hope for time to pass so we might be together once again. You have said you will come for Easter, and I am eagerly awaiting your arrival. I long for us to walk the gardens with Alexander, and I would be happy to merely sleep in your presence once more. If you can find the time to come, then please do, regardless of whether it is easier or not.*

*All my love,*

*Lizzy*

Elizabeth rolled the ball to Alexander, who sat on the floor. He loved playing ball with her. He always pumped his arms up and down and giggled when she rolled it towards him. His next favourite part was attempting to put the toy in his mouth.

"Alexander, give me the ball." She bent forward and held out her hands while he gave her a huge smile.

Jane laughed and knelt to take the ball from his mouth. "Here," she said, handing it to Elizabeth. When Jane stood, she cupped her hand over the bulge that had just begun to show. Elizabeth had been rather jealous of how easy the first few months had been for Jane. Her sister felt only a slight amount of nausea, and though Elizabeth's illness was not terrible in comparison to some ladies, she had been sick on several occasions. Jane had not. She was just as serene and beautiful as always.

Her sister sat behind Alexander and pulled him onto her lap, but he fussed and reached for the floor. "He is as active as you."

Elizabeth shrugged and rolled the toy towards them. "Fitzwilliam is hardly idle."

A commotion from the hall made Jane look to the door and her forehead crinkled. "I wonder what that is about?" She shifted Alexander back to the floor, rose to her feet, and opened the door. "Graham, please inform Lord Carlisle that his brother has arrived." Her words were quite loud, whether to give Elizabeth advance warning or simply due to the butler's distance, she did not know.

Elizabeth's stomach jumped into her throat. She picked up Alexander and held him to her as Jane disappeared into the hall, closing the door behind her. "Come, let us go to the kitchens. I have a feeling Aunt Jane does not want the colonel to know we are here."

She slipped into the servants' corridor and down the stairs, the warmth from the kitchen growing the farther she travelled. A maid bustled by as she stepped through to the cook's domain.

"Your Grace, did you need something?" asked Mrs. Nicholls, who exited the larder with the cook.

"No, thank you. Lady Carlisle was receiving a guest, and I did not wish to be in the way. Do you know if Lalande is here?"

"She only just returned to your chambers. Do you need help finding it through the servants' passages?"

"I would, thank you. I am certain Lady Carlisle will seek me out when she has finished."

Mrs. Nicholls gestured to a maid. The girl curtseyed and held her arm out towards a different set of stairs. "If you will follow me, Your Grace."

When Elizabeth stepped into her dressing room through the servants' entrance, Lalande ceased hanging Elizabeth's freshly laundered gowns and frowned. "I beg your pardon, Madame, but is something amiss?"

"Colonel Fitzwilliam arrived, and Lady Carlisle closed the door to the hall behind her. I do not know more. It was time Alexander ate and took his nap anyhow, so I searched for you in the kitchens. Since you were already in my chambers, one of the maids brought me here."

"When I am done, I shall see what I can discover."

"Thank you." Elizabeth settled on her bed and opened her gown. Alexander, never one to forgo a meal, latched on quickly and took his usual long draws. He was always a good eater, and after she swapped him to the other breast, his eyes began to droop as they usually did. When he finally slept, she took him to the adjoining room he and Millie used as a nursery and placed him in his cot.

Millie smiled while she sat in a chair near the fire knitting. Today had not been as cold as winter, yet the mist that settled around the fields had a slight bite, making it feel cooler than it probably was.

When Elizabeth returned to her bedchamber, a knock upon the door made her jump, and Lalande hurried in to answer it. She did not hesitate to allow Jane inside.

"Nicholas and I need to speak to you in your sitting room when you are able."

Elizabeth knew the colonel's visit would cause some anxiety, yet she did not think it should cause quite this much. "Alexander is napping. Should we talk now?"

Jane led the way through to the sitting room, allowing Nicholas inside. Elizabeth sat near the fire.

"If you are concerned over my reaction to your brother's arrival," started Elizabeth, "you need not be. I shall take every precaution. I shall not be caught unawares and alone with him again."

"'Tis not just Richard." Nicholas sat across from her and rested his forearms on his knees. His expression was so serious. He held her eye without blinking and his shoulders remained stiff. "Darcy wrote me a fortnight ago to let me know Leeds's nephew James had released the investigator he had hired from his employ. James's creditors were demanding money, and James could not afford to pay for a groom. The man lingered as close as he could until a se'nnight ago when James disappeared in the middle of the night, leaving behind a staggering bill at the inn where he had been residing."

"I thought he was with Prinny in Brighton." Why did she sound so pathetic? She was not the young, naïve girl Richard cornered in the library. She could manage and keep her son safe from both of them. She had no other choice.

"James fell out of favour with the Prince Regent. He lacked the funds to go far, so he found a small inn at Worthing. I can only assume he relied on challenging the naval officers and ships' crews coming in and out of the ports to cards, giving him a greater opportunity to gain funds than at a country establishment on the road to London. He managed to win just enough to get him to Portsmouth and then Southampton. For a man who typically loses at the card tables, he managed to win again then headed north to a small inn in a town called Alton north-east of

Winchester, which is where he remained. Soon, he began losing at the tables there. He also stayed too long since he had no further funds to travel."

He cleared his throat. "I imagine his creditors would not threaten him while he kept company with the Prince Regent. Once they learnt he journeyed alone, they tracked him to that small town in Hampshire. That was when he released the investigator and fled. The man we had trailing him indicated he met up with Richard in Alton. We believe Richard helped him flee."

Elizabeth closed her eyes and swallowed hard. "Do you mean to say James was with Colonel Fitzwilliam? Here?"

"Yes, he was."

At Carlisle's affirmation, she clenched her hands together. Jane sat beside her and wrapped an arm around Elizabeth's shoulders.

"Nicholas sent them to the inn," said Jane.

Elizabeth looked back and forth between them. "Is that a wise idea? The two of them might bleed you dry."

"I have sent my personal secretary with them. He is giving the innkeeper specific instructions. I shall pay for their rooms and their meals. I shall not pay for their liquor or any losses they have at the card tables. He will also warn the innkeeper not to extend them any sort of credit. I do hope with those restrictions they will return to London within a few days."

"Does James know I am here?" Elizabeth immediately wanted to slap herself on the forehead. What a stupid question! Anyone in Meryton could tell James and the colonel where she lived. "Forget I asked."

"Richard knew from my mother. He apparently indicated by letter from Southampton that he desired to visit us. My mother penned a letter in return ordering him to stay clear of Netherfield and you. She had the best of intentions; however, she only confirmed what he likely suspected when he heard of Leeds's death."

Elizabeth rubbed her hand across her forehead in an attempt to cease the pulsing that began behind her eyes. "Fitzwilliam did send James a letter informing him of Thomas's death and Alexander's birth. We had to tell him lest he arrive in expectation of claiming his inheritance."

"He had the Prince Regent's favour and naught to fret over at the time." Nicholas shook his head. "Now, he is desperate. Since James departed Alton, the investigator has been attempting to track him by following several men attempting to claim money from him. James has hidden well."

"We should alert Fitzwilliam," said Jane. "He would want to be here."

Nicholas had steepled his hands in front of his mouth with a furrowed brow, but removed them. "No, I was supposed to keep it a secret to surprise you, Lizzy, but Darcy is planning on visiting us for Easter. He needed to fetch Georgiana and Kitty from school before arriving, so he has journeyed to London. He arrives next week. I was to go to Reading for Lydia, but instead, I shall notify your father that I cannot. He must fetch her himself."

While Elizabeth appreciated Jane's support, her sister's fingers were beginning to dig into the top of Elizabeth's arm. As it was, her head was swimming in information and possible scenarios and reasons for James and the colonel to be together, making that infernal pulsing turn into a pounding. She did not need the bruises as well. She took Jane's hand and pulled it over her head to hold it in her lap. "I do not understand why we cannot tell Fitzwilliam," said Elizabeth.

After shaking his head again, Nicholas sat straight in his seat. "I am afraid my cousin will panic. Georgiana and Kitty's school will be closed during the Easter holiday. My mother could fetch the girls, but I know Georgiana would much prefer spending the holiday with us to my mother."

"And Kitty does not know your mother well at all," said Jane.

"No, she does not. There is also the matter of Darcy taking off the moment he receives word of James's whereabouts. If he receives that letter at night, I do not doubt he will mount the fastest horse in that stable of his and ride like the devil to get here. I shall take responsibility for not making him aware. I simply do not want him injured or killed when we do not even know my brother's intentions or those of James."

Elizabeth closed her eyes and squeezed Jane's hand at the idea of any injury happening to Fitzwilliam. He was so dear to her. He could not come to harm. She would never forgive herself if he killed himself while trying to reach her. "I agree with you." She reopened her eyes and looked Nicholas straight in the eye. "But what do we do in the meantime? I do believe we must remain watchful."

"Indeed," he said, nodding. "I have spoken to Mrs. Nicholls, and we are to make a few changes within the house. While the servants will believe you remain in this suite, you and Alexander will sleep in a different wing. Lalande and Mrs. Nicholls will ensure your passage through the servants' corridor when you retire.

"Fortunately, the weather has not been conducive to your walks with Alexander, so until it improves, we need not fret on that account. If you desire a walk, you must remain within the gardens around the house and we must have more than one footman on guard. I have sent for two of your footmen, Jonathan and Matthew. I am certain Matthew will arrive first since he only travels from London. Both were loyal to Leeds. Colin informed me they were trained as a sort of guard for Leeds, which is why Matthew typically joined the duke at the theatre."

"And also explains why Thomas always insisted Jonathan follow me when I walked."

"Precisely," said Nicholas. "Colin mentioned them before he departed Worthstone. He had concerns over James making some attempt at Alexander's inheritance and did not want to see Thomas's legacy turned over to the wastrel.

"I shall pen a letter to the investigator later. If he knows of any good, reliable men we can use as guards, I shall pay the expense. I do not want you harmed under my roof."

Elizabeth propped her hands upon her hips. Nicholas was as bad as Fitzwilliam when it came to ensuring the well-being of those in his care. "The dukedom should pay for our protection. You and Jane have a child to consider."

"I have a fortune set aside for a girl should it be required. I have never spent my allowance as my brother did. Darcy counselled me to set aside a certain amount when we were at Cambridge. We both invested our savings and continued to put the profit back into the investments in order to see a greater return. I can easily take thirty thousand from the investment for a daughter's marriage portion."

"But 'tis not necessary." She looked to Jane. "Tell him. We can pay for our own protection."

"Whatever is necessary to keep you safe, we will do," said Jane. "You are residing in our home."

Nicholas smiled at his wife. "Even within the house, I want someone with you. That person need not be a man, even Jane will do." He exhaled and ran his hands through his golden-brown hair. "Since the two of you are from Meryton, do you know any in service here who might not be trustworthy?"

Jane pressed her free hand to her chest. "No, I could not imagine any of them betraying us." It was interesting that Jane could think poorly of Colonel Fitzwilliam, Nicholas's own brother, but not the servants. Nicholas levelled a steady gaze on Elizabeth.

"I cannot think of anyone, but I believe Mrs. Nicholls might be a better person to ask. A number of the servants are different than when I married Thomas. The colonel and James do not have much to give them. That is a consideration."

"You must remember Alexander's inheritance," said Nicholas. "James could promise a fraction of its worth and still be a very rich man—even after he paid his creditors."

Elizabeth closed her eyes and bit back a groan. Nicholas was correct. James could have any number of people at his disposal, and Colonel Fitzwilliam was likely counting on a portion of that inheritance. Why else would he journey to Netherfield and bring James along with him?

"I do not mean to frighten you, Lizzy."

She opened her eyes and gripped Jane's hand while she regarded her sister's husband with a mind that screamed "run."

"I do not know what he has planned, but you are better off with us than on your own. Darcy will be here soon, and you know he would protect you with his life."

"Unlike you," she said, with a tight laugh.

"Lizzy! What a thing to say!"

"I was only teasing, Jane. I do trust Nicholas, and I know he would protect us as he would you. I simply needed a bit of humour, even if it was a poor attempt."

Nicholas smiled, though it was tight and flattened his lips. "I understood. He would be an addlepate to attempt to harm you under this roof, but he might not be interested in harming you at all. He could attempt to force you into marriage."

"I should as soon marry a toad," said Elizabeth. What a disgusting notion! As if she would put herself or her son in that position!

"Darcy would solve that dilemma. Regardless of James's actions, Darcy would marry you. He would never allow James to gain that sort of power over you or your son."

He was correct. She only had to rely on Nicholas and Fitzwilliam, and all would be well. She had to believe all would be well, or she would start having fits of nerves. Her father would be so disappointed when Elizabeth began calling for her salts like her mother.

"We will need to talk to Millie. As much as we need to keep these events secret—even from the servants—I do not know how to keep her unawares."

Nicholas frowned and took a deep breath. "For the next few nights, Alexander can sleep with you. When Matthew and Jonathan arrive, they can move a cot in the new suite for him. I would prefer Lalande help with Alexander for the time being."

"You do not trust Millie?" said Jane in a gasp.

He held up his hands, palms out. "Millie is newly employed. As much as I want to trust her, we need to minimize how many people are involved. Her mother is in poor health, is she not?"

Elizabeth drew her eyebrows together. "Yes, but how is that important?"

"We can pay her for the time she is gone, but insist she help care for her mother for a time. Hopefully, this will all have been sorted by the time she is ready to return."

The plan seemed a sound one. The problem would be gaining Millie's acceptance. She and her family were proud—in the best sense of course. Nicholas was correct again. This conspiracy needed to be as small if not smaller than James's or word could leak out.

Lord, but she hated this! Why could the year not be over and her wed to Fitzwilliam? They would be at Pemberley raising Alexander together and not thinking of who wanted to gain

371

control over Thomas's fortune. A part of her was tempted to hand it all over, but as much as the idea had merit, too many people relied on her and Alexander to protect the dukedom and the Osborne holdings.

# Chapter 26

"Why did you not message me?" Fitzwilliam's voice echoed from the walls despite the study being quite small.

Elizabeth grasped his biceps and held him still to cease his pacing. "We did not want you rushing here and harming yourself in the process. You still needed to retrieve Georgiana and Kitty from school. You would have forgotten all about them if Nicholas had sent you a note informing you that James was in the area."

"Not just James, but Richard as well," growled Fitzwilliam. "The two of them together will wreak all sorts of havoc."

"I am well aware." Nicholas sat behind his desk with his hands together on the work surface. "Lizzy is correct. We thought it best to tell you when you arrived. In the meantime, we have taken every precaution."

Elizabeth clutched his arms tighter. "I am going out of my mind from being cooped up indoors and never having one solitary moment, but I am well and so is Alexander."

Fitzwilliam closed his eyes and tried desperately to concentrate on what was before him. Elizabeth safe and sound. "Where is Alexander now?"

"He is with Lalande, napping."

His eyes opened and took in every inch of her beloved face. "What of the woman you hired?"

"I do not suspect her of even having a passing acquaintance with James, but Nicholas had concerns over the timing of her hiring. She is with her ill mother, though I am still paying her wages."

"'Tis a good idea. I noticed Jonathan and Matthew here as well. Did you send for them?" The last was directed at Nicholas, who nodded.

"I remembered Colin's advice from that morning we departed Worthstone," said Nicholas. "They also moved the cot for Alexander into the bedchamber in the other wing."

"Lalande has also always insisted on cleaning and caring for my bedchamber herself, so there has been no change. Jonathan and Matthew are stationed outside of the doors to my old rooms to give the rest of the servants the impression I still reside there."

"Where is Mrs. Nicholls putting me?"

Nicholas laughed and leaned on the desk. "I knew you would desire to remain close to Lizzy, so you are in the adjoining bedchamber to hers. Pray remember you have months before you can wed. We simply could not overlook your ability to protect them during the night. I dearly hope I am overreacting, but I do not believe I am. They arrived four days ago, and Richard has visited daily. He asked about bringing James yesterday, so I do expect them this afternoon."

"What do you do while Richard calls?" He searched her expression for any hint of disquiet—especially in her eyes. He could usually see so much in her eyes.

"I spend time in my sitting room with Alexander, or I pen letters to your aunt or Laura. At the risk of sounding like Lydia, 'tis excessively dull."

He could not help but smile when that one eyebrow lifted and the wry grin he adored appeared on her face. Lord, he had longed for her since he had left after Twelfth night! The days dragged by while he attended to business or went to his club. He did manage to assiduously avoid balls and dinners—except when his aunt had insisted.

Lady Matlock had ceased her talk of him marrying, which was an improvement, but the ladies she invited did not know he held no interest. Thankfully, his aunt had taken to helping him escape the unwanted prattle of those ladies while still attempting to pry the identity of his potential intended from him. He had given nothing away, simply informing her that she would not be disappointed.

"I am certain no duller than London without you."

"You are such a flatterer, Mr. Darcy," she said with a slight smile.

"I think it is time I found Jane." Carlisle stood and departed the study without looking back.

As soon as the door closed, Fitzwilliam tugged her into his arms. "Forgive me if I overstep. When Carlisle said Richard and James in the same sentence, I thought I might explode. I cannot think of you in the same room with either of them. The idea makes me want to whisk you to Pemberley."

"I do wish the year was up, and we could."

The longing tone made him hold her closer. "We have but four months."

"Why does it seem a lifetime?"

His lips pressed against her hair. He dared not kiss her on the lips or he would not know how to stop. He had stayed away because he did not trust himself. After so long a separation, he had a sore lack of control. As it was, he had no qualms about sneaking away during the night for Gretna Green. If they were wed, the threat James posed would not disappear, but it would be diminished to a certain extent. Yet, the problem remained of how desperate could James be? That alone would determine whether he was a true threat.

"I should go tend to Alexander. He will wake soon."

"And I should like to speak to Carlisle. As soon as I am done, I shall refresh myself and rest from the journey. Would you mind if I knock on the door? I would like to see Alexander. I cannot imagine how he has changed."

She cupped his cheeks in her small, soft hands. "He is the dearest little boy. He giggles and gives kisses, though they are rather messy. He has grown so. I believe he will be as tall as you one day, despite my shorter influence."

He turned his face to kiss her palm. "I shall be up shortly."

After she slipped through the door to the library, he poked his head into the corridor where Jonathan stood. "Would you please find Lord Carlisle and tell him I wish to speak to him?"

"Yes, sir." The footman stepped closer. "What of Her Grace?" He spoke in quiet tones so as not to be overheard.

"She departed through the library only a moment ago. She needed to care for her son. Matthew remained in the library, so he will ensure she makes it safely to her chambers."

Their thoroughness settled that part of his gut that had been roiling ever since he first stepped foot into the study. "Thank you for your diligence. Pray, thank Matthew as well."

"Sir," said Jonathan with a quick bow. He hurried off, and no sooner had Fitzwilliam closed the door than Carlisle reopened it and stepped inside.

Before Fitzwilliam could utter a word, Carlisle poured them both a large glass of brandy. "I saw Lizzy heading upstairs from the library. We need to talk."

"So this is not as cut and dried as you made it seem?"

"When it comes to Richard, is it ever?" His cousin sighed and sank into a chair by the fireplace. "He brought James to Netherfield two days ago. James requested an audience with Lizzy."

"Did he?" Fitzwilliam took a sizeable gulp of his brandy and bared his teeth as he swallowed. "Did he say what he wanted?"

"Unfortunately, no. I can only assume he wants money." He grimaced and sipped his own drink. "I have yet to tell Lizzy. I wanted you here before I did so. I do wonder if we should not eschew the mourning period and allow the two of you to wed. You could apply for a special license, and we can have the local vicar perform the ceremony in the drawing room. Because it has yet to be a year we would keep the ceremony private."

"What of London?" said Fitzwilliam. He wanted to burst from his skin. He expected he would have to wait until August to wed Elizabeth, but instead, he could have all he wanted now. He would prefer the motivation to be otherwise, yet he could not argue when he was to gain his most fervent desire.

"What of it?" A crooked grin lit Carlisle's sombre expression. "My mother can handle the *ton*. After a mere few days of calls, all of London will be speaking of the poor Duchess of Leeds, who was forced to marry due to a threat to her and her son. Men wed if they have children in need of a mother. Women of lesser status marry if they have nowhere to live. Why should this be any different?"

Fitzwilliam stared into his glass, watching the fire reflect in the golden liquid. He would be required to propose to Elizabeth and request her father's permission, but that could be done today. He would also need to ride back to London for the special license.

"You want me to meet James on Lizzy's behalf—as her husband."

"I do," said Carlisle. "I know Lizzy would handle herself admirably, but I would prefer to keep her as far from him as possible. Your marriage would also keep her presence with you in the same suite from causing scandal."

"Until new fodder for the rumour mill presents itself."

"That is true." Carlisle gave a tight chuckle. "At least to those who call themselves well-bred yet thrive on the trials of others."

Fitzwilliam threw back the last of his drink, wincing at the burn that scalded as it went down. "I need to speak to Lizzy, and I want to see Alexander. As long as she agrees, I shall ride to Longbourn and speak to Mr. Bennet."

"Thankfully, he returned from Reading and retrieving Lydia yesterday."

"A lucky coincidence indeed," said Fitzwilliam. "In the meantime, I can take care of the license if you will set a time with the vicar. Your mother still has a connection to the archbishop, does she not?"

"She does. You would do well to take her to Doctor's Common. When she learns who you intend to wed, she will likely drive you herself."

With a laugh, Fitzwilliam looked into his now empty brandy. "I only require Lizzy's consent."

"Do you truly believe she will say no?"

"I promised to court her." He rose and set his glass on the tray. "While I could never regret taking Elizabeth for my wife, I do want her happy."

Carlisle tipped his glass as if toasting. "I believe if you simply ask and seek her opinion, she will not refuse you. I daresay she has longed for you as much as you have longed for her. Lizzy might not display a morose countenance, but when she is sad, she is quiet—too quiet."

He could not help a small smile. "I do not doubt her feelings. At least this time, she will wed for love and not duty. In that, I hope she can be satisfied."

"You do not have cause for concern, cousin." Carlisle waved him away. "Go, propose to your lady, but do let me know when you intend to depart. I shall accompany you to Longbourn in the event Mr. Bennet decides this is a laughing matter."

"Lord, I hope not."

Carlisle shrugged and stood, placing his glass with Fitzwilliam's. "He is a bit eccentric; finds humour in the oddest of things. Legally, you have no need to request his permission, though I understand why you want to do so."

With a nod, Fitzwilliam opened the door. "Let me ask her first." He departed the study, took the stairs two at a time, and strode down the corridor until he reached the rooms he had on his last visit. Bishop awaited him inside.

He pulled away his topcoat and waistcoat to wash from the water his valet had already set out. When he was in clean breeches and a shirt, he dismissed Bishop and knocked on the door that connected his chamber to Elizabeth's.

Lalande smiled when she allowed him to enter. "'Tis good to see you, sir," she said.

"Thank you."

She quickly excused herself as he turned and set eyes on Elizabeth in a pose he had not seen since Worthstone: reclined against pillows on the bed with Alexander at her breast.

"He has not ceased to nurse yet?"

"Oh, no." She smiled down at him like a Madonna in a painting. "Cook prepares apples for him, and he eats bread and some potatoes, but he still loves to nurse."

As he stepped closer, Alexander released his mother's nipple just long enough to smile before he began suckling again. Elizabeth had been correct when she had said he had grown. When he had last departed, Alexander could still be cradled in one arm, but now, Elizabeth held him in both, which, even curled, he filled.

"You are too quiet."

He looked at her wide eyes watching him. "I am merely fascinated by how much he has changed."

"I know." Her gaze returned to their son and softened. "He becomes less of a baby every day." She removed an arm to pat the bed. "Sit and talk to me. I have missed you, and we so rarely have this opportunity. Tell me what you and Nicholas spoke of."

"I want to wait a moment to tell you of that." He sat upon the bed, facing her, and slid closer until he touched her leg. "I need to ask you a question first."

Her head hitched back a bit. "A question? That sounds ominous."

He laughed and shifted his hand to the other side of her knees, so his arm straddled her, and he could look her directly in the eye. "I hope not." He cleared his throat. Why was he suddenly shaky and full of nerves? "Elizabeth Bennet—"

She arched that eyebrow he adored but remained blessedly silent.

"You must allow me to tell you how ardently I admire and love you," he said quickly. He took a deep breath and exhaled while Elizabeth's eyes widened. She had to know, which necessitated an extremely short pause else she would ask a question and he would never have the opportunity. "You must know that I have loved you since the first moment I saw you. While I may not have known it at the time, you struck me dumb with your beauty and your fine eyes. As much as I attempted to deny my feelings and keep my distance, all of my efforts were for naught. What began as a strong affection and friendship has grown deeper and more robust as time has passed. At this moment, I love you so strongly that I cannot imagine my life without you. In my heart, you have been my dearest friend, my lover, and my wife since that fateful night at Worthstone. I have never desired anything more than to have you as mine—by my side for the rest of our lives. I beg you to relieve my suffering and consent to be my wife."

Alexander sat up and grinned at him, his two bottom teeth and two top teeth displayed prominently.

"I believe our son is pleased with the idea. What of you?" He took Alexander and brought him to his shoulder while Elizabeth tucked her breast back in her stays and fastened the front of her gown.

"As much as I want to be with you, what of my mourning period?"

"You have observed most of it. I have known a few women who remarried earlier than they should have and did not suffer for it. We also have Lady Matlock and Lady Vranes to help us. A few well-placed whispers and calls would alleviate any worry."

A low laugh came from her chest, and she covered her mouth with her hands, letting them slide down until they paused on her chin. "Could it really be so simple?"

"I wished to court you before your family and friends and treat you as you deserve—"

"I was such a child that day. I beg you not to repeat what I said. Two years of frustration at my lack of control over my life and being a pawn of Thomas's schemes were to blame. I assure you that I have long been most heartily ashamed of it."

"What did you say that I did not deserve? You deserve to be courted and have a proposal of marriage borne out of love. I let my wishes run away with my rational mind." He kissed his son on the cheek, making the baby turn and place his chubby little hands on Fitzwilliam's face. The next he knew, Alexander's open mouth was over his while the babe said, "Ah!"

Elizabeth burst into gales of laughter, Alexander began to giggle, and Fitzwilliam followed. After, she handed him a towel so he could wipe his face. "He has always been comfortable with you—as if he knows in some way that you are his papa." She scraped her teeth along her bottom lip. Lord, he had to restrain himself when she did that. How did such a simple gesture undo him so easily?

"Nicholas believes this to be the best solution?"

"Our marriage might not eliminate whatever threat James poses, but as your husband, I can insist he deal with me."

"You could do that anyhow."

"I could, but I think this to be more effective." He reached out and took her hand. "You must know I would wed you regardless."

She scooted forward and cradled his cheeks in her palms. "I do, and were I able, I would have married you the moment Thomas passed from this world. If circumstances allow us to forgo a certain amount of my mourning, then I would wish to do so." She pressed her lips to his and inhaled as they lingered. When she drew back, her beautiful eyes were glassy and bright. "Yes, I would be honoured to marry you, Fitzwilliam Darcy."

# Chapter 27

In the end, marrying Elizabeth had been blessedly simple. Carlisle sent a note to Richard, saying Jane was unwell, to keep him from Netherfield for a few days while they arranged the wedding plans. Mr. Bennet, once he understood the love Fitzwilliam harboured for Elizabeth and the potential danger she and Alexander were presently in, gave his consent without question. How much the older gentleman realised, Fitzwilliam was uncertain, yet he did not care to elaborate on how long-standing his feelings were.

The special license took no time at all, and the vicar, who had known Elizabeth since she was a small child, was more than willing to conduct the ceremony once they explained the necessity to forgo the final months of the mourning period. The worst part was the travel to and from London for the license.

Now, as he stood in his bedchamber, Elizabeth fed Alexander in hers. Tonight, Lalande was to sleep in Elizabeth's bedchamber with the baby while Elizabeth joined Fitzwilliam for their first night as man and wife in his rooms.

He took a deep breath in and blew it out lest he embarrass himself. Bishop had yet to depart, and to say that Fitzwilliam was an eager groom was a massive understatement. He walked over to the fireplace, resting both of his hands on the mantel and leaning into it. "Bishop, I do not require anything further this evening."

His valet surely started—not that Fitzwilliam was looking at him to know. He simply had never insisted his valet leave him before he had completed his task, so the sudden request was surely enough to make the man raise his eyebrows. Bishop had been his valet since he was sixteen. He could only be surprised.

"Yes, sir." Bishop, no doubt, bowed. He always bowed before departing. "Congratulations on your marriage. I am pleased you and Mrs. Darcy can finally be together as you ought."

"Thank you," he said, closing his eyes and resting his forehead against his arm.

The door closed behind him, and he gave up his attempts at self-regulation. Hopefully, Elizabeth would be more flattered than appalled at his state. After all, he could not help it. At times, parts of his body had a mind of their own.

"Fitzwilliam?"

Her sweet voice bid him to pivot quickly. She stood near their adjoining door, her hair in loose curls around her shoulders and a thin muslin gown that did nothing to hide her nipples straining against the fabric. A groan escaped, and she lifted one side of her lips.

"Have you been thinking of me?"

His fingers raked through his hair, clenching the longer locks in the back. "Do not tease me, Lizzy. I have not been able to truly touch you since before Alexander was born—nearly ten months. I fear I have very little control now the possibility of having you again presents itself."

"And I thought you appreciated me for my liveliness of mind." She pressed her lips together, stifling a laugh.

"You wicked woman," he growled, lunging forward and pulling her into his arms. "I love you for the quickness of your mind and for your generous and kind heart. Those traits make you the most beautiful lady of my acquaintance."

With bright eyes, she untied the ribbon on the front of her shift and drew back enough to let it drop to the floor. "My body is not the same as before Alexander."

His eyes roved over every inch of every curves. Her hips had widened a little, and she now bore a few faint scars on her lower abdomen. Those had appeared in the last fortnight before Alexander was born. "I see nothing disagreeable. These reminders only serve to render you lovelier than you were. They are the remnants of your love for me, and for Alexander, and that you brought him into this world. I could never think of them as anything but an embellishment that adds to your beauty."

"You are full of pretty words this evening." She helped him pull away his dressing gown. He had not worn a stitch of clothing underneath, but since he never had in the past, she had not been shocked.

"Not any longer," he said, taking her lips with his own. He lifted her into his arms and carried her to the bed, releasing her from their kiss long enough to drop her directly into the middle of the mattress.

"Fitzwilliam!"

He laughed and covered her body with his, savouring the feel of her soft breasts as they flattened against his chest, the slight sting of her fingernails as they dug into his arms, and the strength of her legs as they wrapped around his waist and held him tight.

As his lips trailed along her neck, suckling that spot he had once marked and wished to mark again, her breathing hitched. "I want you. I need you. Pray do not make me wait."

His teeth gritted together at her pleading. He had done no more than touch her breast, but his body was begging even more than she was. "Are you certain?"

"I am not a fearful maiden, my love. I have given birth to your son."

He certainly could not argue with her. He slid home while he blinked back tears. She was his—finally and truly his in every sense of the word. He had always been consumed by Elizabeth when they loved one another, yet that strength of passion was nothing to tonight. He could not prevent it from completely enveloping him—not that he had any intentions of trying.

"I love you," she whispered with her hands on his cheeks.

"I love you so much." He kissed her and pressed his forehead to hers. It was too good, and it had been too long. "I cannot wait for you. 'Tis too much."

"Then let go." Her hands found his rear and pulled him in hard.

Her words and actions tipped him over the edge. With a cry, he found his release, his eyes squeezing shut as he nearly floated outside of himself, rushed back, and collapsed. His breath came in pants as he recovered. "I wanted you to find your pleasure too."

Soft lips trailed along his neck before she lightly bit where his shoulder and neck joined. "This will not be the one and only time we shall love each other. You will simply have to ensure you think more of me next time."

He nipped at the side of her breast, laughing at the arch tone she used. "Trust me. The problem was that I have thought of you for too long without being able to touch you." He kissed her soundly. "How are you, Mrs. Darcy?"

"Quite well, Mr. Darcy."

He admired how she looked right after they made love, her hair tousled, her eyes soft, and her cheeks a faint pink. It only made him want her again. His lips claimed hers and lingered, savouring her as he had not been able for what seemed like years. With no need to rush, he caressed and stroked her mouth and tongue until his jaw ached and he hardened once more.

"Well, Mrs. Darcy?"

She smiled and stroked him from base to tip. "I hope Alexander sleeps late in the morning. I suspect we shall be rather tired on the morrow."

He laughed and returned home. This was perfect—Elizabeth was perfect. He only needed to take care of James, so they could return to Pemberley and be together without worry or the possibility of some threat looming. The problem remained of what he could do to ensure his desires became their reality. They had just been granted their ultimate wish. They merely needed to clear the path to their long and happy future.

After eating a late breakfast with Elizabeth, Fitzwilliam answered Carlisle's request for his presence in the study. Elizabeth needed to feed Alexander, so she remained within their chambers, which suited Fitzwilliam well because he had business he wished to complete without disturbing her equanimity.

He entered Carlisle's study, but did not pause at the sight of James Osborne standing by the fireplace. On the contrary, he and Carlisle had summoned him. "Good morning, Mr. Osborne." As soon as Fitzwilliam bowed, he clasped his hands behind his back.

"I am at a loss as to why *you* are here," said James before pressing his lips together so his face was pinched, rather resembling a rat. "I requested an audience with Elizabeth."

Carlisle stepped beside Fitzwilliam. "Your address of my sister is rather familiar considering you have never made her acquaintance. You do not have the particular acquaintance that would bestow the privilege of addressing her so intimately."

Fitzwilliam hardened his expression. "I agree, Cousin."

James's expression only became more pinched. "I do not have a care for what the two of you think. I requested an audience with her, and she is not here. If you do not produce her, I will not sit by idly. I will have my say."

"Why do you wish to see her?" said Fitzwilliam, who stepped to position himself in front of the door.

"'Tis no business of yours." The words came out spat rather than in the congenial tone one would expect when making a request in the home of another.

Fitzwilliam shrugged as casually as he could manage. "On the contrary, any request made of Her Grace is of the dearest concern to me. I was appointed in your uncle's will to ensure her well-being as well as that of her son's—" He had no wish to reveal their marriage yet. Without that knowledge, James might reveal his motivation for seeking out Elizabeth sooner than he would otherwise.

"As if that old prune fathered a child." His chuckle was harsh and dangerous. "I do not know who she bedded—probably some footman—but it was not my uncle."

"I always thought Leeds favoured his Darcy heritage more than the Osborne," said Carlisle, as though he were commenting off-hand to his mother or father or even Jane. "What say you of his son's appearance, Darcy? Does Alexander resemble the Darcys as much as Leeds?"

"Most certainly," said Fitzwilliam. "I believe there are few who would deny the connection once they have set eyes on the boy. Thus far, Mr. Osborne, you have neglected to tell us what you want with Her Grace."

Carlisle crossed his arms over his chest and thrust a leg forward. "You will not set one eye on the lady without telling us, so you may as well give up any notion of privacy. She does know of your desire to speak to her and has intimated that she will not do so without knowledge of your intentions. She has enlisted our aid with that endeavour."

"She has no reason to distrust me." James's eyes darted back and forth between Carlisle and Fitzwilliam, making Fitzwilliam's insides tremble. If they discomposed James enough, would he reveal his intentions?

"She has every reason to be suspicious of you," said Fitzwilliam. "You have amassed a considerable debt that, on your income, will take you a lifetime to repay. Your uncle knew of your habits. He informed his wife of them as he learnt them. Before his death, I also helped my cousin hire an investigator to follow you, so we knew your every movement. If you are here to apply for money, she will not pay for your mistakes. You had best look elsewhere."

"She and her brat have robbed me of my birthright." The words were uttered through clenched teeth with his hands in tight fists at his sides. "I would not be living hand to mouth if she had kept her legs closed for whatever imbecile she bedded."

"Your birthright? Before Alexander, you only would have inherited the ducal properties since my cousin did not want you to completely destroy his legacy. He knew once the reins of his estate were handed over to you, you would have used whatever funds were on hand to pay your gambling debts, then squandered the remaining at the card tables and on horses." Fitzwilliam stepped closer but held fast to his hands behind his back lest he strike the man. "You have no one to blame for your present circumstances but yourself. If you had listened to Thomas years ago when he attempted to warn you regarding your manner of living, you would likely still have an allowance or had some money provided in his will. As you well know, he withdrew his support of you when he wed. I know your father provided you some money. After all, an admiral in the Navy does well enough. Perhaps you should follow in your father's footsteps. I believe Thomas would have been happy to purchase you a commission. I could perhaps persuade Her Grace —"

"A commission?" James cried, his face turning a crimson colour as though he held his breath before he shouted, "Why would I wish to do such a thing when I could simply wed that whore he left behind? She parted her pretty legs for someone. I could bed her at night *and* pay my debts!"

Fitzwilliam's hands flew from behind his back and grabbed James by his lapels, forcing him across the room until his back rammed against the wall. "You can hardly wed the lady when she has already married me. Carlisle and I suspected your motivation.

Did you think either of us would allow you to harm her in such a way—harm Alexander in such a way?"

James struggled against Fitzwilliam's hold, yet the man was smaller and considerably weaker. "She is a bunter—a filthy doxy who has stolen what was mine!"

"The estate was never yours," said Fitzwilliam, knocking him back against the wall while he said it. "You should mind your tone. I shall challenge you if you continue to speak of her thus. Her conduct and demeanour are worth more than one thousand times your degenerate, filthy soul." Fitzwilliam's voice was dangerously low. His blood simmered while his pulse pounded mercilessly in his ears. He could not allow James anywhere near Elizabeth lest he harm her. No doubt existed in his mind that James would do so if afforded the opportunity.

"Do you not know that I have naught to lose." James's laugh was high and maniacal. "I cannot say I am surprised that laced mutton refused to honour her mourning, but like my uncle, you probably do not know one end of a woman from the other." He smirked and leaned his face into Fitzwilliam's. "You were always too much of a prig at Cambridge, were you not?"

"Sabres or pistols?" A hand squeezed Fitzwilliam's shoulder, but he only shrugged it off. He would ensure Elizabeth and Alexander's safety once and for all. James had never been much at fencing and his aim had always been dreadful. His laziness meant he would choose pistols.

"Pistols," said James with a sneer.

"Very well. Tomorrow on the field by the bridge heading towards Meryton. You must have a second. I select Carlisle. Who will be presiding officer?"

After a groan, Carlisle put his hand on Fitzwilliam's shoulder. "Perhaps Mr. Bennet will consent."

As Fitzwilliam released James, shoving him firmly against the wall one more time, the wastrel straightened his topcoat. "I do not object."

"Then leave," said Carlisle, "and do not return."

"Oh, I shall return." James practically sauntered towards the door. "Once I have won, I *will* return for Elizabeth."

Carlisle grabbed Fitzwilliam's arm and held him in place. "Do not do it. You have already risen to his bait. Do not give him further satisfaction."

The door closed, and Fitzwilliam still shook.

"Are you a simpleton?"

Fitzwilliam blinked and shook his head. "I beg your pardon?"

"After all of this time, you finally marry Lizzy, and the day after your wedding, you challenge James to a duel. You must be daft." Carlisle gave a high-pitched bark and covered his face while he shook his head.

"James would not hesitate to harm them." He turned on the spot and began to pace across the carpet. "Did you not hear him? I have no doubt he would marry Lizzy, then kill them both. They would disappear, and he would claim some travesty or another. I cannot allow that."

Carlisle scrubbed his face with his hands and shoved his fingers through his hair. "Yet, you have married Lizzy, which means he cannot implement that plan unless he wins this duel. You have played right into his hands." He sighed and dropped into his chair. "I shall send for Mr. Bennet. I do not wish to make this request by letter. I shall need to find a surgeon."

Fitzwilliam paused in his pacing and pointed at Carlisle. "You must not tell Lizzy. I do not want her to know."

His cousin's lax jaw showed how he felt about such a request. "How is that fair to her? She might never forgive me for keeping such information from her."

"She will fret. If he does kill me, I would prefer she not be waiting for it."

"If you return," said Carlisle with his eyebrows lifted, "she might kill you herself."

"She very well might, but at least, she will be safe."

"How is that?" Carlisle raised his eyebrows before he stood and began pacing himself. "You cannot kill him lest you be charged with murder. Is wounding him or making him cower truly going to prevent him from further mischief? I do not doubt he would kill you." He paused for a moment before he groaned. "I believe his humiliation would only make him worse."

"I must try," said Fitzwilliam.

"I do not trust him or Richard, who is likely to be his second. You do realise this?"

Fitzwilliam sat on the sofa and propped his elbows on his thighs. "I expect no other to be his second. Richard is nearby, he has always resented the two of us for being first sons, and they are friends."

He watched as Carlisle sank into the chair facing him. "As much as I want to throttle you for this, a part of me does understand. Go spend time with your wife and your son. I do not want to see you before the morning."

They both rose and Fitzwilliam stepped forward to hug Carlisle, slapping him on the back. "Thank you, brother."

"Do not do this or I will cry."

With a smile at his cousin's melodramatic tone, Fitzwilliam turned and headed for the door. "I shall tell Bishop to wake me early. Thank you."

"Do not thank me unless you have survived. Otherwise, I shall tell Lizzy everything that was to be done was done by you."

"James is a crap shot."

"He might get lucky. Do not discount him."

Fitzwilliam opened the door and glanced back at his cousin one last time. "I have to believe the luck will be mine. He cannot win."

His cousin's voice carried through as Fitzwilliam began ascending the stairs. "He had best not, or I shall kill you myself!"

# Chapter 28

Mist clung to the ground, creating a haze that likely carried for miles if one could see that far through the gloom. The sun had just broken the horizon giving that ghostly white blanket an almost eerie glow. A horse blew noisily from his nose, breaking the silence that in all probability stretched as far as the mist.

Fitzwilliam's rigid muscles pulsed as though they might almost burst from his skin. The hardest part of this was dragging himself from the bed he shared with Elizabeth—separating himself from the warmth of her naked flesh, curled under the coverlet, only to stand in the cold to wait for James and Richard.

"You picked a damned of a morning for this, Darcy," said Carlisle.

"I simply wanted it done." He stepped forward and pivoted around to Mr. Bennet, his cousin, as well as the former army surgeon Carlisle had located in a neighbouring village. "It is sunrise. How long do we give him?"

The surgeon glanced around at his companions before he cleared his throat. "I would give him an hour, or he could call you a coward."

"I must give you credit." Mr. Bennet snickered. "You thought of a solution not many would consider. You claim to love my daughter beyond reason, yet you challenge the man the day after the two of you are wed. One might think you wish to be free of her." The three men stared at him with their mouths slightly agape. He waved them off. "If only I had thought of this solution years ago. Alas, no one would challenge me for Mrs. Bennet, and she is so fearful of the hedgerows, she might fight the duel for me."

Carlisle rolled his eyes as a faint rhythm gradually gained in volume until they turned at a horse's gallop across the hard

394

ground. Another mount followed close behind. Richard wore his uniform, though he had not been with his regiment for some time.

James dismounted and pulled away his gloves and greatcoat. Fitzwilliam followed suit until they were both standing in their waistcoats and lawn shirts.

While he prepared himself, Carlisle and Richard spoke, examining the duelling pistols and preparing them. Mr. Bennet watched, his face rather pale and suddenly more serious than Fitzwilliam had ever seen him.

"James has no wish to concede," said Carlisle as he approached. "And the blunderbuss insists upon firing the weapon before the duel to ensure we have not given him a faulty pistol." They both jumped at the crack of the matching flintlock firing. James handed his pistol to Richard, who began reloading it.

Nicholas handed Fitzwilliam his pistol and slapped him on the shoulder. "Do not step off your mark. As long as he misses, your honour is satisfied."

Fitzwilliam nodded, swallowed hard, and strode over to stand nearly back to back with James. Before he was truly ready, they stepped from their starting point away from each other and marched fifteen paces. The entire process was like an odd dream. He could not help but think of Alexander, and how he almost seemed to know Fitzwilliam was his true father—how he was never frightened of him despite their separations over the past months. His mind then turned to memories of the night before with Elizabeth, how petal soft her skin felt under his fingers, her high intake of breath when he found that certain spot when he loved her, and her sweet voice whispering her love for him.

At fifteen paces, he turned but kept the muzzle of his pistol down while he waited for Mr. Bennet, who would drop a handkerchief to signal them to fire. What in the hell was he doing? Yes, he needed to rid Elizabeth of James, but was Carlisle correct and there was a better way? He was not afraid of death, yet he was not ready to die. He had too many reasons to live.

The white scrap of cloth in Mr. Bennet's hand suddenly was free, floating in a dreamy fashion towards the ground. "Darcy!" screamed Carlisle, causing him to flinch and raise his weapon. A crack sounded, and he flinched again as it echoed through the fog. James had gotten off his shot first. He tensed, waiting for a searing pain to rip into his flesh. He closed his eyes and dragged in a breath, picturing Elizabeth and Alexander. He would wish for no other image in his mind when he died. He had failed. Now he had to pray Carlisle would do as he had promised.

The air was heavy and difficult to inhale. He opened his eyes as a bright light pierced the mist in front of him.

Elizabeth's eyes fluttered and she snuggled further into the coverlet. She was not ready to wake, yet Alexander would need to be fed at some point. A drawn-out yawn took over her body as she rolled to her back.

Fitzwilliam must have awakened early. His side of the bed was cold to the touch and the quilt had been tucked securely around her. How was he not as exhausted as she? Last night, he had been positively insatiable. They had loved one another twice on their wedding night as well as once the next morning, but the night before, every time her eyes began to drift closed, he was caressing her or kissing her awake, not relenting until she had found her release. Her body still hummed though it had been hours since he finally let her rest.

The clock on the mantel chimed, and she took note of how many times it rang; however, before she could finish, a knock came from the adjoining room.

"Yes!"

Lalande bustled through with Alexander propped on her hip. "Forgive me, Madame, for disturbing your rest, but the young master wishes to nurse. He keeps rubbing his nose in my chest. I have told him over and over mine do not work in the same fashion, but he refuses to listen."

Once Elizabeth pushed herself to a seated position, she held out her hands for her son, who reached eagerly for her. "Come here, sweet boy." He latched on swiftly, and as he always did, gulped steadily. "You would think he never eats."

"I think he has missed you some too. Usually, you fetch him when he awakens in the morning."

"Perhaps." A knock sounded from the outer door, causing them both to start. Her maid bustled over and allowed Jane inside. Elizabeth adjusted the sheet she had covering one of her breasts, though it revealed nothing.

Her sister sat on the edge of the bed and stroked Alexander's little curls. "He is the most beautiful child."

"Wait until you have your own. You will think him beautiful too."

"I do not doubt you." Jane's eyes moved from Alexander to Elizabeth's face and settled while she bit her lip.

"What do you need to tell me?"

Jane startled and placed her free hand over the small swell at her waist. "Pardon?"

"You never look at me in such a way or bite your lip unless you are nervous about revealing some nonsense. What is it? I would prefer you simply dispense with the unpleasantness so we can move on with the day."

A deep breath was sucked into Jane's lungs and blown out. "Nicholas confided that yesterday, he and Fitzwilliam met with James."

Without paying heed to the sheet, Elizabeth sat straighter and clutched Alexander more securely to her middle. "They did?"

"Yes. Fitzwilliam pressed and baited James until James revealed the nasty nature he originally tried to mask. He insulted you by calling you several variations of whore."

"That does not shock me."

"He also insisted Alexander was not the natural child of Thomas."

A small smile tugged at her lips. "Before you and Lalande, I shall not lie on that score, yet he cannot prove it."

"Lizzy, Fitzwilliam challenged him to a duel."

"What?" A chill overspread her body, penetrating deep into her soul. "No, he would never." Suddenly, last night's activities played within her mind—how desperately he strove to bring her as much pleasure as possible, how he never seemed satisfied, and how he constantly told her he loved her, that he could never live without her. "Oh, God."

She was going to vomit. The sparse contents of her stomach burned at her throat, and her head spun. Her legs itched to spring from the bed and dress, but she could not simply leave without feeding Alexander. Before she could speak, Lalande set a basin on the mattress beside her.

"You must breathe, Madame. You appear a little green.

Elizabeth glanced between the two of them. "Why would he do this?"

"He thought it the best way to rid you of James." Jane placed her hand over the quilt onto Elizabeth's calf. "He did not want you to worry, but he and Nicholas departed before sunrise. It has been hours, and they have yet to return. I did not know what to do when they failed to walk through the door. I could not keep this from you. When I spoke to Lalande, she insisted you slept soundly. I simply prayed you would wake soon."

L.L. Diamond

Alexander released her nipple so she swapped him to the other breast. "Lalande?" she called loudly. "Please ready my habit!"

"You cannot be serious. What of James and the colonel?"

"I have no other choice. I must know what has happened, and I cannot sit here helpless while I wait. Do you know where?"

"In the field by Harper's bridge."

As soon as Alexander released her, she handed him to Jane and hurried to don her chemise, petticoats, and stays. Once Lalande had her completely outfitted, she kissed Alexander on the forehead and Jane on the cheek. "I shall return soon."

"Be careful," said Jane, her tone pleading.

"I shall have someone accompany me."

"Matthew or Jonathan can go. I notified both of them in the event you insisted on following after Fitzwilliam."

"You know me too well," said Elizabeth as she slipped out of the door.

When she reached the kitchens, Jonathan was dressed and ready to ride out to Harper's bridge. She strode to the stables, hoping they had a suitable mount else she be forced to walk to Longbourn and beg the use of her father's horse.

Without delay, they climbed atop the two steeds Jonathan must have requested from the grooms before their arrival. Elizabeth had not ridden since before Alexander's birth, but after a few moments of unease, she fell right back into that rhythm, giving the stallion his head as she tore across the grass towards Harper's bridge.

Her blood rushed through her ears and mixed with the wind in a noise that was nearly deafening. How could he do this? Did he not know how much she needed him? If she had not been tearing across a field at a gallop, she would have closed her eyes and prayed. Fitzwilliam had to be well! He had to be!

When they reached Harper's bridge, the fields surrounding it were empty save a few sheep to the north side. Where were they? Granted, it had been a few hours since daybreak, yet Fitzwilliam had not returned to Netherfield. He had to be somewhere.

She once again swallowed down the burn in the back of her throat. Something was dreadfully wrong. Neither Nicholas nor Fitzwilliam had returned to Netherfield, yet they were not here. Where could they have gone?

"Should we try Meryton?" asked Jonathan. "If someone was injured, they might have brought him to the apothecary for the surgeon to treat him."

Her head whipped around to regard Jonathan. "I had not considered that. Yes, we should."

Harper's bridge was only a mile from town, so the ride was not long to reach the first of the cottages where they slowed to a trot. Mr. Jones's home was on the far side of High Street. Elizabeth turned her horse towards the old stone cottage along the opposite end of the town.

Several men stood outside, gathered by the horses. One turned and lifted his leg to mount his horse, and a sob caught in her throat. "Fitzwilliam!"

He returned his foot to the ground and approached her horse, taking the reins as she came to a stop. "How did you know?"

"Nicholas told Jane, who told me. When Jonathan and I reached the field and you were not there, he suggested here." While she spoke, her eyes roved over every single inch of him. Nothing appeared out of place or torn like he had been shot or stabbed. A small part of her released a portion of the tension in her body, but her mind would not allow the rest to become complacent yet. Had he shot James? He could be tried for murder and hanged if he had.

"Before you say anything, I did not wound James. I would prefer, however, to return to Netherfield before we speak further."

She nodded and waited for him to mount his horse. Nicholas stepped from the building, his eyes widening when he noticed her, yet he simply walked towards his own horse. When they were all ready to depart, they rode for straight Netherfield.

Every hoofbeat that passed on their return only saw more and more of Elizabeth's restlessness return. How could Fitzwilliam have put himself in such jeopardy? No matter the danger to her, she would never want him in harm's way.

She gripped the leather in her hands tighter and tighter as they grew closer and closer. By the time she dismounted at the stables, she could barely keep herself from trembling violently. Fitzwilliam approached and held out his arm, but she gave him her best withering glare and walked from the stables to a path through a grove of cherry trees. She had roamed this way often since living at Netherfield.

The orchard was currently in bloom, their soft blush petals in puffs that rained pink droplets when the breeze rustled the branches. Normally, she would lift her face and feel the wind while thrilling in the falling bits of colour, but today, she strode straight through to the stream on the other side, crossing where rocks emerged from the water to form a sort of bridge.

"Lizzy! Pray, stop!" She came to a halt and squeezed her eyes shut. She was so angry with him. How was she not bursting from her skin?

It was the strangest thing. When Jane told her of the challenge, Elizabeth could think of nothing but reaching Fitzwilliam. She needed to know he was well, and if not, to be near him while he was treated for whatever injury he had incurred. At the sight of him hale and whole, she was relieved, yet as the minutes passed since, her relief turned to this shaking mess of nerves or some such affliction she had to rid herself of by walking. Riding would have worked too, but she would have required Jonathan to ride with her. Fitzwilliam would not have appreciated her venturing off with the footman when he had mentioned them talking.

"You are angry," he said softly. He was not far behind her, but she kept her back to him. She would have to look at him eventually, but she needed to keep her wits about her. She could not do that while she gazed at his dear face.

"Why?" It was the most pressing question.

"Because you and Alexander would never have been safe."

She inhaled deep gulps of air while she clenched and released her fists. "Did you kill him?"

"No," he said. "He fired his pistol first, but it did not discharge correctly, instead the pistol exploded."

"What?" Curiosity won out, and she whirled around on her heel. "How does a pistol explode?"

"When a flintlock pistol is fired, sparks fly from the muzzle and more out of a hole on the side. James insisted on firing his pistol ahead of time to ensure we gave him a properly functioning weapon. Once he discharged the pistol, Richard examined it and reloaded it immediately. Nicholas and I believe there must have been a spark remaining inside the chamber that escaped Richard's notice. James mumbled and mumbled that he had never pulled the trigger, but the back of the pistol was gone as was the bullet. Splinters of wood and metal from the pistol had struck him in the face."

"Will he recover?"

"He was alive when I left him, but infection is always a concern."

She stared at him for a while, tracing every feature she feared might be lost to her. Yet he stood before her after embarking on one of the most foolhardy, idiotic . . . She stepped forward and started beating his chest with her fists. "You could have been killed or maimed like James! How could you? We finally have the chance to be together, and you do this?"

For a few moments, he allowed her to pummel him before he took her by the wrists and drew her into his arms, holding her tight against him. "Shhh, I am here. I am well." He rocked back and forth, continuing to croon in her ear.

Her knees gave way and a sob tore from her throat. "I cannot lose you!" She gained control of her legs and pulled herself away. "Do you not understand? You were beside yourself when I gave birth to Alexander, which was a natural part of life. This was not natural or normal. You put yourself in danger when we could have hired someone to ensure James left the country or at least stayed away."

She brushed away her tears with rough fingers. "When I realised the truth of my marriage to Thomas, I thought my life would be devoid of the love I had always dreamt of knowing. I simply cannot fathom that we meant so little to you that you ran off to get yourself killed at the first opportunity."

He stepped forward, his hands grasping her face. "Do you not see? I could not rest easy until you and our son were safe from him. He would never leave us be until he either had Thomas's estate or enough funds to satisfy him. I do not want to die when I have so much to live for, yet I would die to protect you—to protect Alexander."

"You are the most infuriating man! I do not want you to die! I want you to live out your life with me instead. Not squander it away on some ridiculous field of honour." Every last bit of her shook as though she were standing in the bitterest of cold weather. The cool mist of the morning had cleared and the sun shone brightly as it crossed the sky, warming the day.

"I would not consider it squandering my life," he said, his voice low.

"If you had died, you would have left Nicholas to keep James at bay. What would that have accomplished? It was a risk you need not have taken."

He took her hand, drawing her back into his arms. "I simply wanted you safe. Pray do not be angry with me. If I promise to never do it again, will you forgive me?"

"Can you not understand how terrified I was when Jane told me? How would you have felt if I had decided to run out and fight a duel with Miss Bingley over your honour?"

A deep laugh shook his chest. "I would not like the risk, though I would enjoy watching you defeat that lady. I think you could do so easily. I predict she would turn and run the moment you took aim."

She hit his shoulder and attempted to pull away, but he wrapped his arms around her waist and kept her close.

"Lizzy, I love you beyond reason and at the risk of my own sanity."

"Are you implying that I might drive you to Bedlam?" She arched that one eyebrow as her eyes rested upon his dear face.

"No, but ensuring your safety from fortune hunters as well as your mother's nerves just might."

She hit his arm again, and he flinched. "That hurt."

"You deserve it." This had to be the saddest argument ever. How would she ever stand her ground on anything if he wore her down as he had today?

"How was Alexander this morning?"

"Hungry and happy, though he missed his Papa."

"Then accompany me back to Netherfield so I can play with him before he naps." He took a step back, his hands sliding from her waist to her hands, tugging her towards him.

She did not fight him while he led her back to the house and up to their rooms. When he entered the adjoining room, Alexander sat on the floor chewing a wooden block. At the sound of the door, their son turned and a wide grin broke upon his face at the sight of them.

Elizabeth's eyes burned and blurred with tears as Alexander dropped the block, crawled to Fitzwilliam, and lifted his arms to be held. "Ba, ba!" he cried as he was lifted into his father's embrace. When Alexander pointed back toward the blanket on the floor, Fitzwilliam kissed the side of the child's head.

"Do you want to play some more?" He set Alexander's feet on the carpet and helped him walk to where he played. Once he was settled, Lalande took their coats and hats so they could join their son on his blanket.

After a few moments, Fitzwilliam looked up from the stack of blocks he and Alexander had been making. "We should remain a few more weeks to be certain of James's future, but once we know of his fate and return Georgiana and Kitty to school, what do you think of travelling to Pemberley?"

Those tears that had been threatening to fall finally forged warm trails down her cheeks. "I think it sounds absolutely perfect."

# Chapter 29

Fitzwilliam stretched his feet towards the foot of the bed and blinked, his eyes adjusting to that stream of light that filtered through the gaps in the draperies. A familiar humming and gulping made him roll over to Elizabeth, who sat against the headboard with Alexander nursing.

"Good morning," she said with one side of her lips tugging upwards. "I did not realise travelling to London would tire you so."

"Perhaps my exhaustion was due to my demanding wife, who kept me awake until the early hours of the morning." His voice was deep and scratchy as it usually was first thing in the morning.

"I heard no complaints." That one eyebrow arched, and he had to fight the impulse to drag her back down to the mattress and have his wicked way with her.

When he pulled himself to sit, Alexander let go of the nipple he had thus far been engrossed with and sat up in Elizabeth's lap, a wide grin adorning his face. "Someone is happy this morning."

"He is quite pleased with himself. Millie fed him a large bowl of pap, and he decided to follow it with a hearty helping of milk."

Fitzwilliam held out his hands, making Alexander lean forward to reach his father. "Is Millie pleased to be back?"

"Very," said Elizabeth as she closed her dressing gown. "She knew more was afoot than simply our benevolence to give her paid time to visit her mother. We spoke of it before I joined you last night, and she insisted she understood the necessity—that ensuring our safety was of the utmost importance."

"I am pleased she has been so agreeable."

"Well, you did cause a scandal in Meryton. I cannot remember a duel ever being fought in the villages around Longbourn during my lifetime."

"We have naught to worry over from now on." His son held his thumbs in his fists while he lifted them up and down, beating his lap with raucous giggles.

"I do feel for him. The infection was a terrible way to die."

"Richard attempted to dissuade him from firing the weapon before the actual duel. Flintlock pistols typically do not have such grievous faults, but if a spark remained inside when it was reloaded, the gunpowder can ignite without pulling the trigger. James refused to trust Carlisle's weapons and insisted on testing the weapon for himself. He caused his own injuries."

They sat quietly for a several minutes, watching Alexander as he now shoved Fitzwilliam's thumb into the corner of his mouth and gummed it. His pleased expression proved he understood little of his parents' discussion.

Fitzwilliam lifted the baby over his head and made silly faces at him. "What do you have planned for the day?"

"I penned a letter to Laura upon our arrival. Since we do not plan on remaining in London for long, I would be surprised if she does not call."

He laughed low in his throat as he brought Alexander down to his lap. "I sent a note to Matlock house. My aunt may call as well. I know she has been eager to meet Alexander, so hopefully, you will not be inundated with callers when she arrives."

"The knocker will be up, yet our arrival is not well-known. I doubt many will even consider us a possibility."

"Those were always the days Miss Bingley and her sister would come to call."

She cringed and situated her coverlet. "I do hope Nicholas gave her enough of a set down in Hertfordshire that she thinks twice."

"She and Mrs. Hurst fled Hertfordshire with their tails between their legs. If you remember, Mrs. Nicholls indicated they departed early the next morning for London."

Elizabeth rolled her eyes and angled to the side to face him. "The Bingleys have attended several social engagements about town since departing Hertfordshire. Laura happened upon Miss Bingley at the Earl of Coventry's ball and gave her the cut direct. I know not of your aunt."

"Perhaps you will discover that today." He cuddled Alexander close, closing his eyes and kissing his son's soft cheek, letting that peace he so required to spread throughout his body. "I cannot tell you how happy it makes me to wake to the two of you every morning. I thank God every night before I sleep that both of you are now mine."

Her fingers combed through his hair and she kissed his cheek, though he was unable to resist and turned so their lips met. "I know we needed to return Kitty and Georgiana to school, but I would have been pleased to simply journey to Pemberley. I have missed Laura and your aunt's company, but I am eager to enjoy the solitude of home."

"A fortnight, dearest. Then we shall go to Pemberley."

Elizabeth shifted and rose from the bed, holding out her arms for Alexander. "I should dress and speak to the housekeeper. I need to send a note to Madame Bonheur. I require a few gowns for when the mourning is officially over." While they had wed, Elizabeth still adhered to the dress requirements for mourning Thomas. She always wore the half-mourning colours of dove grey and lilac, which were a vast improvement over black, yet did not suit her as well as the bolder colours she had worn in the past.

The baby happily fell into her arms and bestowed a wide, open-mouthed kiss to her cheek when she brought him to her shoulder. "Thank you, dearest," she said when he pulled away with a giggle.

Darcy sighed and peered at the bed covers. He would have been content to spend the day here with Elizabeth, but too many duties called him. "I suppose I should make myself ready. I have an appointment at my solicitors before I return Kitty and Georgiana."

"I am glad that falls to your lot and not mine." She wore an impish grin that made leaving the bed even harder, though he followed her to her side of the bed and swung his feet over the edge of the mattress.

He drew her by the hips between his legs and leaned his forehead against her stomach.

"Are you well?"

"I am. I know we have our entire lives, yet I do not want to be away from you. I suppose it is nonsensical, but I would be well-pleased to remain within these rooms for the rest of the day."

"Eventually, I would need to get out." The fingers of her free hand caressed his scalp, while Alexander's tell-tale hand hit him in the head. "Poor Papa," she said as her lovely ministrations ceased followed by Alexander's pats. He lifted his face, and she bent forward to bestow a kiss to his lips.

"Go ready yourself for the day," she said. "The sooner we take care of our business, the sooner we can be together again. We do not want Pemberley to fall into a terrible state from your distraction." He rolled his eyes at her gay laughter. She was inordinately fond of making sport of him.

Sooner than he was ready, she pulled from him and disappeared behind the door of her bedchamber where she would hand Alexander off to Millie and dress. If he summoned Bishop now, he could meet her in the breakfast room before he needed to leave. That was all the inducement he required to spring from the bed and stride to his own dressing room.

"Lady Vranes to see you, Mrs. Darcy," said the butler as he shifted aside to allow Laura to pass.

Elizabeth rose swiftly, and as soon as the door closed behind her friend, the two clasped hands and kissed cheeks before Elizabeth gestured to a chair. "I am so happy you could come."

While her friend settled, she placed her hands with her reticule in her lap. "Of course, I received your letter explaining your marriage, but it shall take some time to become accustomed to the appellation. Do you miss being 'Her Grace'?"

"Not in the slightest," said Elizabeth with a sigh. "I am more than content simply being Mrs. Darcy, and I would prefer to be Mrs. Darcy to even being a princess or a queen. I never dreamt I would have a title much less that of duchess, so Mrs. Darcy suits me very well indeed."

Laura's eyes darted to a maid who entered with tea. "You certainly look well." As soon as the maid departed, Laura relaxed into her seat some. "Forgive me for speaking freely, but I always assumed your marriage to the duke was one of convenience. He required an heir, which you provided. The two of you seemed friendly, yet your interactions lacked a certain intimacy which is borne of deeper feelings. I suppose the point of this is that I hoped, if you married again, you could do so for love. With my own felicity in marriage, I do feel it a shame when one is wed to someone they merely abide."

Elizabeth shifted to a chair closer to her friend and clasped her hands. Laura, at times, did behave much as an older sister and in quite a bold manner. Yet she cared so for those in her circle. "Do not feel distressed. I would prefer you speak your mind rather than keep thoughts to yourself. I did not love the duke as a wife should love a husband, but I love Fitzwilliam dearly. Pray, do not fret. While I did not wish for Thomas's death, I would not be this happy were I still married to him."

"Then I am relieved," said Laura, removing a hand to place it to her chest. "When you wrote me of the circumstances of your marriage, I did worry that you wed again for convenience, this time for protection. A great weight has been lifted from me to know your heart is engaged."

"Fitzwilliam is the best man I have ever known. He loves me, and he loves Alexander as though he were his own son." While she did not mind confiding in Laura, some secrets were better left to as few people as possible. "When you see us together, you will know. He may not be a perfect man, but he is perfect for me."

She tittered and clasped her hands. "I would have given my right eye to have been witness to Miss Bingley receiving the news. That is my only regret in cutting her."

"How spiteful of you," said Elizabeth with a bit of a giggle.

"Only to those who deserve it, dear girl—only to those who deserve it. That so-called lady has been one of the most spiteful of society since her coming out. She belittles all who she believes inferior, whether they are or not. I have heard that Lady Matlock cut her at a ball last week, though I do not know the circumstances. That lady is done in London society. She had best return to whence she came and marry someone in her home county. No one of importance in London will so much as look at her now."

"When she was in Hertfordshire, she would try my nerves, yet now I only pity her."

"Do not feel sorry for her, my dear. She has had this coming to her for some time. Regardless of your birth, you were a duchess when she first belittled you. You were a gentleman's daughter before that. She has always given herself more consequence than she truly possesses."

At a knock on the door, Elizabeth paused before she spoke. "Come!"

The door opened, and Millie peeked her head in. "I beg your pardon, ma'am. The young master has been a bit fussy. I thought perhaps . . ."

"Of course, bring him in."

As soon as Alexander set eyes on Elizabeth, he reached his chubby arms for her. "Ma!"

"Oh, look!" Laura clasped her hands in front of her. "He is perfectly adorable."

He nuzzled his forehead into Elizabeth's neck for a moment before he lifted his head and smiled at Lady Vranes.

Laura gently ran a finger down his soft cheek. "He resembles the Darcys, just like his father. I remember my own father commenting that the duke and George Darcy could have been twins if George Darcy had not been two years younger than the duke." She leant against the arm of the chair in a casual manner. "When do you depart for Pemberley?"

"We leave in a fortnight. We shall pass through Hertfordshire on the way and break our travel at Netherfield to visit Lord and Lady Carlisle once more before we head north." Lady Vranes opened her mouth to speak, but the door opened again, startling them both.

"Thank you! Pray do not stand," said Lady Matlock as she passed the butler, who had never so much as had the opportunity to announce her. "Lizzy, I am so glad you have come to London!" She kissed Elizabeth's cheek and curtseyed to Laura. "Lady Vranes, I am happy to see you again." She suddenly stopped and pressed her hands to her chest. "Oh, Lizzy, he is beautiful. He looks so much like his father. It is well-known that the duke always favoured the Darcys. If I had not known the connection, I would have assumed he was Fitzwilliam's, the resemblance is so striking."

Her son lay his head on Elizabeth's shoulder, and she rubbed his back. "I believe he is teething again, so Millie brought him to me. I hope you do not mind." It was probably better to ignore Lady Matlock's comment.

"Heavens, no! I am pleased to see the poor dear." She sat across from them primly. "With your mourning, I have not seen you for ages, so I was eager to visit when I received my nephew's note."

"I am pleased you have called. If you had not come, I would have called upon you. I might have even sent a note since I need a few gowns for when my mourning is over. You always have such a keen eye for fabrics."

"Lady Matlock does have beautiful gowns," said Lady Vranes. "I patronise Madame Bonheur, but mine never turn out as well as yours."

Elizabeth placed a hand on Laura's. "Madame Bonheur will even claim her success is Lady Matlock's choice of fabrics. She does have a wonderful eye. Perhaps you could join us? Unless you have no need of a new gown."

Her friend turned her head so her chin touched her shoulder in a cheeky gesture. "Oh, I *always* need a new gown."

After they dissolved into laughter, Lady Matlock pressed her hands together. "I also cannot tell you how thrilled I am to call you niece. My nephew was so stubborn before Christmastide, insisting he had his eye on a particular lady. He was quite mysterious, I tell you. I can only assume he meant you."

With a shake of her head and a quick, nonchalant shrug, Elizabeth did her best to answer calmly. "I cannot say how long Mr. Darcy has held a *tendre* for me. I can only tell you that I was greatly moved by his ardent proposal. I am content to say my high regard for him has grown a great deal since our marriage. He is a wonderful man."

Lady Matlock took a deep breath and sighed dreamily. "I am beyond happy to hear it. He is indeed a good man. Nicholas told me of Richard bringing that cretin James to Netherfield. I cannot apologise enough for his interference into your affairs. Last we had heard, he was in Southampton." She shook her head with tears in her eyes. "I wish we could understand why Richard has turned out as he has. He was such a lovely boy. He adored puppies, and my husband took great pride in how swiftly he learnt to ride a horse."

"I am certain it was nothing you did," said Elizabeth. How terrible to love your child with all you have in you, and for them to be a disappointment as Richard was to Lord and Lady Matlock.

The door opened again and Fitzwilliam strode in with a smile as great as one of the peaks in Derbyshire. "Good morning, Aunt," he said in a cheery voice. He kissed Lady Matlock on the cheek and stood tall. "'Tis agreeable to see you, Lady Vranes." Both ladies stared at him with wide eyes and eventually grins.

Laura peered over to Elizabeth with a giggle. "I can see marriage certainly agrees with Mr. Darcy. Lizzy, what have you done to him?"

Lady Matlock tittered and leaned back in her chair. "I can only agree with Lady Vranes. What have you done to my nephew? I do not believe I have seen such a smile on him in ages."

Fitzwilliam laughed and took a seat beside Elizabeth. Alexander reached for him, and he happily took their son while the ladies continued to watch him with incredulous expressions. He nibbled Alexander's fingers and kissed his cheeks while his aunt practically glowed.

"I must say, Lizzy. The tirade my husband suffered when Lady Catherine learnt of your marriage was well worth the misery when I witness this spectacle. I wonder how devoted he will be to your own children if he is this way with his cousin's."

"Aunt, as far as I am concerned, Alexander is as much mine as he was Thomas's. I shall be the one to raise him, and I have no care for who his father is to the rest of the world. I love him as my own, and shall always love him the same as any future children. Do I make myself clear?"

"Yes," said Lady Matlock, a bit pink. "Forgive me. I did not mean—"

"I know you meant no offence." Fitzwilliam made a silly face at Alexander, who laughed and clasped his father's cheeks, planting an open-mouth kiss to Fitzwilliam's lips. When he released him, Fitzwilliam took out his handkerchief and wiped his face. "As I was saying, I know you meant no offence, but I am the only father Alexander will ever know. I would never want him to feel as though he is loved less than any siblings who happen to come along—not that I ever would."

"You are an excellent father, Mr. Darcy," said Laura as she stood. "I must be going. Pray, send around a note to let me know when you plan to shop. I truly would enjoy joining the two of you."

"I should probably depart as well." Lady Matlock rose. "I promised to call upon Mrs. Chamberlain before returning home. Let me know when you have Madame Bonheur's appointment, Lizzy. I shall be pleased to accompany you."

Elizabeth stood and walked them to the door while Fitzwilliam continued to play with Alexander. Once they departed, she returned and closed the door behind her. "You did not have to set down your aunt as you did, especially in company."

"I shall not have people say Alexander is less to me than my own children. Even if he were not my own flesh and blood, I would still take offence to the notion that I care for him less than any brothers or sisters. In my mind, he would still be mine."

She sat beside him and cuddled to his side, kissing Alexander's palm as it pressed against her cheek. "I do love you so. You have the biggest heart of any man I have ever known."

"You have not known that many men, dearest."

"Quite true, but why should that matter?" She arched that eyebrow in his direction, and he answered with a passionate kiss to her lips, leaving her breathless. What had she ever done to deserve that?

# Chapter 30

**Christmas 1810**

The grand staircase at Pemberley was festooned with boughs of holly, a kissing bough hung in the drawing room, and a yule log burned merrily in the grate as laughter filled the house as it had not in years.

"So, you will not be returning to Netherfield after Christmastide?" asked Elizabeth. Nicholas and Jane had arrived the day before, bringing Georgiana with them. Mr. Bennet had been good enough to retrieve Kitty and Georgiana for their break and brought them to Meryton, allowing Georgiana to join Nicholas and Jane on their journey to Pemberley.

Elizabeth had spent a prodigious amount of time with Jane, speaking of happenings since they had last been together, but neither Jane nor Nicholas had revealed their intentions of avoiding Hertfordshire until that evening.

After a sigh, Jane leaned into Nicholas's arm. "I love Mama, but I made her leave the room during my lying in. After five hours of her lamenting her nerves, I required peace. Thank goodness for Lady Matlock."

Nicholas smiled softly and wrapped his arm around his wife. "To be honest, I had to put an end to Mrs. Bennet's calls. After two days of her insisting Jane incorrect on every minute detail, I told the butler not to admit her. The daily visits after Edward was born were enough to make me seriously consider turning Netherfield back to the owner."

Fitzwilliam's low, warm laugh rolled through Elizabeth and made her want to cuddle to him. In the months since their marriage, they had grown closer, despite the occasional arguments. With two such stubborn individuals, the clashing of the minds was certain to happen on occasion. Elizabeth did love how they made up after. Just the thought made her toes curl in her slippers.

"No, we shall journey to Matlock," said Jane. "Nicholas has told me many stories of the home where he grew up, and I anticipate seeing it for myself."

After wrapping his arm around his wife's shoulders, Nicholas glanced down at her. "You will also be mistress there one day. I know my mother is eager to teach you as much as she can."

"I know Lady Matlock mentioned she would be pleased to have you closer," said Elizabeth. "But I never considered that you would move to Matlock so soon after Edward's birth."

"I now understand why you needed to rid yourself of that housekeeper," said Jane, shaking her head. "Mama despised that I wanted to feed him as you did Alexander, and she would not let the baby sleep. She either spoke too loudly or insisted he needed to be held." At least in Lady Matlock's letter, she was beside herself with excitement, and in a drastic change of plans, decided not to journey to London for the Season. She intended to visit them at Netherfield, but she would not need to now.

"I still cannot understand how you laboured without a friendly face in the room. I believe I would have cried inconsolably."

Elizabeth peered toward the door to ensure it was closed while Fitzwilliam's shoulders shook from his amusement. "I was not alone, Jane."

Her husband's voice still rumbled with laughter. "I was so furious with you that day. You scared me to half to death." Nicholas, who had known since nearly Alexander's birth, joined Fitzwilliam's laughing.

With a gaping expression, her sister glanced to each of them with a high-pitched "Pardon?"

"She refused to allow Lalande to send for the midwife," said Fitzwilliam with a squeeze of Elizabeth's hand.

"Fitzwilliam delivered Alexander."

Jane's expression of shock did not disappoint before Nicholas blew out a noisy breath. "You are a brave man. I still do not know how you did it. Father drank brandy with me in the study."

"I am thankful you were not in your cups when you first viewed your child," said Jane to her husband.

"My mother would have throttled me."

Jane suddenly slapped his arm. "And you knew Fitzwilliam delivered Alexander and never told me. How could you?"

Before he could respond, the door creaked open, and they all turned as Georgiana entered. "Alexander and Edward were both asleep when I looked in on them."

"Alexander has enjoyed today immensely," said Fitzwilliam. "He also missed his afternoon nap. I am not surprised he fell asleep so early. I only hope he will sleep through the night and not awaken during the early hours of the morning."

Elizabeth sighed and laid her head upon his shoulder. "Do you remember when Millie kept him from his afternoon nap? He fell asleep before supper and woke at midnight. We all took turns with him through the night."

"I shall care for him if it is needed," said Georgiana eagerly. "He is such a sweet child, and I see so little of him. I have missed so much of his growth. He has almost become a little boy in the time I was away."

Fitzwilliam's lips caressed the top of Elizabeth's head. "You must finally accept he is walking and says more words every day. I daresay he will be as outspoken as you before he is five."

Jane, Nicholas, and Georgiana laughed and shook their heads, but her husband was probably right. Alexander was much more like Elizabeth in demeanour than Fitzwilliam.

Her only response was to swat him on the arm. "Georgiana, I should like to hear some Christmas music. Would you mind terribly?"

"Oh, of course not." She clasped her hands as she walked towards the instrument. Soon, a familiar melody filled the air. Georgiana's playing, as well as her singing, had improved greatly during her time at school, and while she performed, the family did not talk but appreciatively listened and watched. As she progressed through to the final verse, her lilting voice gave life to the words.

As soon as Georgiana played the final chord, Elizabeth clapped before she wrapped her arm back through her husband's. "You played that beautifully."

Their younger sister, who in the past year had begun to behave with more of the famous Darcy reserve, particularly when in company, pinked in the cheeks at the praise from not just Elizabeth, but the rest of their party as well.

Jane rose and pulled Nicholas behind her. "Tonight has been lovely, but I may fall asleep where I sit if I do not retire."

"We have no wish to keep you from your much-needed rest," said Elizabeth with a smile. "I do remember those days well. I often startled myself awake while Alexander suckled at my breast. It was disconcerting, but I do not know how many times I inadvertently fell asleep while I nursed. It was a relief when he was old enough to lie in bed with me and eat."

Her husband's hand grasped hers and their fingers entwined. She cherished every one of those small gestures. "We shall depart for church at nine." He rose and clasped Nicholas on the shoulder. "Unless you cannot rouse your wife."

"I shall be awake for services." A small lift to one side of Jane's lips let on that she was amused by Fitzwilliam's attempt at humour.

"I shall retire as well," said Georgiana. She hugged her brother then Elizabeth. "I confess playing with Alexander all day has exhausted me. He is such a dear boy."

Elizabeth glanced up at Fitzwilliam, who smiled widely. Where he had always been so stern in appearance, he now smiled more than ever. Those who met Alexander always attributed his similarity to Fitzwilliam to Thomas's resemblance to his Darcy mother, but Alexander was much more like Fitzwilliam in looks than Thomas ever was. They were fortunate no one considered the differences as much as the similarities—even Georgiana's suspicions had never been aroused.

"Yes, he is," said Jane with a slight upturn of her lips. "He could not be anything but, could he?" Jane kissed Elizabeth's cheek. "Merry Christmas." After she did the same to Fitzwilliam and Georgiana, she pulled Nicholas towards the stairs. Georgiana followed suit and departed behind them.

"You are looking tired yourself," said Fitzwilliam quietly. "You worked so hard planning the holidays. I hope you did not overdo." His hands took hers, he kissed the backs of both, and let them fall to their sides, still clasped together.

"I did not overdo. As you well know, Mrs. Reynolds did the bulk of the work. I simply made the plans."

He pressed his forehead to hers with his eyebrows raised. "You helped decorate. I still cannot think of why you would climb that ladder to hang a garland. My stomach dropped when I found you thus. You could have fallen."

She pulled her hand from his and set it on her hip. "I enjoyed decorating the house. I was also not high. I simply stepped up a few rungs to reach the mantel better and would not have gone further. Do not forget that Jonathan stood at my feet in the event I lost my balance."

After Netherfield, Fitzwilliam had hired Jonathan and Matthew to work for them rather than the dukedom. Now, rather than serving as mere footmen, they were more accessible to serve Elizabeth and Alexander as they had Thomas. The two of them had not truly been footmen since. Instead, on those rare occasions Fitzwilliam was unavailable, they accompanied Elizabeth on rides or trailed behind her and Alexander when they walked.

He drew back but pulled Elizabeth into his arms. "Next time, you will request me. I should be the one to catch you." His bottom lip protruded much like Alexander's did when he pouted.

"Very well. I shall keep your chastisement in mind."

His lips claimed hers and cradled them as though they were fine china, sending a pleasant shiver through her body. How she hoped his kisses would always invoke such reactions in her. She clung to the back of his topcoat to anchor herself lest she dissolve into a puddle at his feet.

As he stepped back, his hands slid along her sides, one grasping her hand and pulling her from the drawing room, up the stairs, to their chambers, where he closed the door behind him. Before he could draw her into his arms again, she scooted towards the nursery, opening the door and slipping inside. Millie knitted in a chair by the window, but she smiled and stood. "Miss Darcy certainly tired him out. He has not made a peep since she laid him down."

After Millie departed, Elizabeth leaned against his cot and placed her hand to his back, letting the even rhythm of his breathing relax her.

"He is well." Fitzwilliam's arms wound around her waist, and she pressed against his solid warmth.

"I know. I simply needed to be with him."

"Do not let Georgiana's comments of his growth bother you. He will continue to need you for some time to come. He is not ready for Eton or Cambridge yet."

A sharp pang travelled through her chest. She did not want to think of him going away to school or Cambridge. "I know it will come. I just do not want to miss a moment of this time. I suppose it is nonsensical."

"Perhaps you are more sensitive than usual since it is Christmas. I have missed my mother and father more during Christmastide than at other times of the year. My memories of holidays when I was young come to mind when I see the kissing bough hung once more with fresh holly and mistletoe. I caught my parents under it on Christmas Eve nearly every year."

She wound her arms around his neck and stood on her tiptoes, planting a soft kiss to his lips. "Perhaps I am more sentimental because of Christmas, but I am more inclined to believe it is due to our second child."

"Second child?" His forehead wrinkled in the most adorably confused manner. How had he completely missed the absence of her courses? They loved one another often enough that he could easily know, yet he had not noticed.

"I believe it happened when Alexander finally ceased nursing. This child has not quickened yet but give him another month. I daresay he will make himself a nuisance before long."

The moment realization hit, he gasped and turned her to face him. His forehead touched hers as his shoulders heaved in with a massive breath and relaxed. "You truly think . . .?"

"My breasts are sore, and I eat, though I rarely have a huge appetite. The smell of Nicholas's kippers this morning made me want to run for the rose garden."

"In winter?" he said with a laugh.

"Even if they were fertilizing them, the plants would smell inordinately better than kippers."

With a deep laugh, he lifted her in his arms and carried her back to his chambers, where he set her on her feet. Once he helped divest her of her clothes, he lowered to his knees and pressed his lips just above her navel. "I am your Papa, little one. You have the best Mama in the world, so you must not give her too many problems. I do not think your Uncle Nicholas would appreciate Mama becoming sick during his breakfast."

She ran her fingers through his dark curls, loving the gentle tone he used while he spoke to their unborn child. It was so like how he spoke to Alexander when he was still in her womb, and even how he spoke to him now when they played.

Fitzwilliam always had time to spend with his son, taking him for walks or playing blocks. Even Mrs. Reynolds praised her master's skills as a father. She never failed to comment how few would take such an interest in a child so young, yet he made a point of setting aside generous amounts of time not only for Alexander but also her.

"I am cold, dearest," she said after a few minutes of him speaking utter nonsense.

"Forgive me." He helped her under the coverlet, removing his own clothes before crawling in beside her and drawing her close. "I cannot tell you how I feel at this moment. I missed so much with Alexander."

"We could not help that." She turned onto her side so they faced one another.

Fitzwilliam tugged her closer. "I know. When you still carried him, I remember how my chest ached every time I would see you and your body had changed. I felt the same with his growth during your mourning."

"At least we did not have to wait the entire year." Her voice held a bit of a higher tone.

"I would have survived, but it would have been so difficult to return to London for that last separation."

"I know. You will be with me for the entirety of this child."

"Except the birth," he said, his head hitching back a hair.

424

"Especially the birth." She kissed his lips. "I promise not to make you deliver him this time, but I want you with me."

"The midwife will object." He whispered as though someone might hear.

"Then we shall find another midwife."

"How many midwives do you think are in this part of Derbyshire?" He finally smiled rather than being so serious.

"Enough that we can find one to do as we ask. Else you will be delivering this child." She arched her eyebrow, and he grasped her by the back of the head and kissed her hard. He rolled her beneath him, only releasing her lips when she was breathless and wanted more. "What was that for?"

"I want to do that whenever you lift that one eyebrow. Most of the time we are in company, and it would be wholly inappropriate. You simply made the mistake of provoking me while we were in the perfect place."

"You are saying this," she lifted her eyebrow again, "provokes you?"

He claimed her lips again until she started laughing and pressed him back.

"You have given me a wealth of power. Do you realise? I shall be able to disturb your equanimity wherever we go."

"Be kind," he said in a warning tone.

"Perhaps I shall be kind to us both." She lifted her eyebrow, and he dove back for more not stopping until he had collapsed atop her, his breathing in gasps.

"I believe I enjoy provoking you," she said with a giggle. Her body still tingled from their lovemaking, and she cherished the heaviness of him against her. She loved him so much it was frightening at times.

"What did you think when you first saw me?" His question surprised her. He had never asked her of it before. He lifted onto a forearm while his fingers trailed along her face. "I can tell you what I remember. I remember your eyes being what I first noticed. They sparkled, and I could tell you were amused by the proceedings."

"I was so uncomfortable with the attention of the entire room upon me. The notoriety was ridiculous. I laughed at their fascination with a country nobody—at why I was such an oddity."

His fingers combed through her hair. "You had these beautiful curls piled on top of your head with jewelled pins that glimmered in the candlelight. You charmed me."

She took his hand and pressed a kiss to his palm. "When I gazed down from the stairs, I saw you standing beside your father—so tall and handsome. You were so dour. I wanted more than anything to see you smile."

He rolled them both to their sides as they held each other close. "I smile a great deal now."

"You do, and the sight makes me content. I like to believe it is because of me."

"It is because of you," he said with a frown.

"You are also happier because of Alexander. I cannot claim all of the credit. I still wonder how I became so fortunate. After I wed Thomas, I never thought I would be joined to a man I love with my entire being, yet here I am. As much as people could scorn how we began, I cannot regret it. I can never regret what brought us together, and what gave us Alexander."

He brushed a tear from her cheek with his thumb. "I thank God every morning that I am blessed to spend the rest of my life with you."

"We shall have another baby to join the family this summer. Do you want another son, a son to inherit Pemberley, or would you prefer a daughter?"

"A daughter can inherit as well as a son. I have no care as long as you and the baby are well. I confess a petite little girl with long mahogany curls streaming behind her sounds about perfect."

"You desire a girl who resembles me?" She laughed and shook her head. "My father always says I am why his hair turned grey. I am inordinately fond of your lovely dark hair. It would be such a shame for it to turn silver."

He feathered his fingers along her ribs, making her squirm. "Are you saying you would not love me with grey hair?"

"No," she said with a gasp. "I do love your dark hair, but nothing time alters will change my feelings. I shall love you with all that I am until my dying breath."

"Good." He kissed her long and tortuously slow before he finally drew back, pressing his forehead to hers. "My feelings— well, I do not know how to love you by halves. You, Elizabeth Darcy, are my world. I would give you all I owned if you only asked."

"I do not want your possessions. I only want you."

"And that is why you are perfect."

What could she do when he spoke so sweetly? Well, all she could do was kiss him as passionately as he did her. After all, he said precisely what was in her heart as well.

# Epilogue

Alexander Osborne stood on the steps of Pemberley watching his father walk towards the old chapel near the river. Fitzwilliam Darcy had built the small structure before the birth of Alexander's younger brother Bennet, in honour of their mother, who was inordinately fond of sitting across the river and enjoying nature. The structure had only been used for family events such as christenings and churchings, so it was small and always quiet.

His father no longer bore the dark curls that could be seen in the youthful portraits in the gallery, but now wore a crown of silver-grey that shone brightly against the autumn reds, browns, and oranges that decorated the Derbyshire peaks.

"What is it?" came a light voice from behind him. Aunt Jane always knew when he needed to talk. Even when he was young, he could tell Aunt Jane whatever he wished. She never judged and gave infinitely wise counsel. Not to say that he never trusted his mother or his father with his problems, but his aunt knew how to reach him when no one else did.

"He is so different."

"Of course he is. He could not lose your mother without losing a part of himself." Alexander's mother, Elizabeth Darcy, had passed from this earth while she slept a fortnight ago. She had been interred in that tiny chapel by the river—the chapel where his father walked. As of late, he spent his days either in her favourite spot where she sat and read or inside where he could trace his fingers over the stone that covered her final resting place. A new rose appeared there daily.

After a shaky breath, he drew a cluster of letters from his pocket, tied neatly with a pink ribbon. "I wanted to ask him about these. Grace found them in her dressing table at Worthstone. They were tucked behind one of the drawers. She was searching for a comb I gave her for our anniversary and they fell."

L.L. Diamond

He had read the contents of a few of them, but quickly set them aside. They conjured too many questions that he had planned to ask his mother when they visited at Christmastide. His mother and God apparently had other plans.

His aunt did not open the correspondence but flipped through them briefly. "How much did you read?"

"I do not know what to think. I . . ."

"We should not speak here. Come." She led him down into the rose garden and took a seat on a bench in the centre. When she could not be down by the river, his mother loved to sit in the midst of the roses in the summertime. Today, no one lingered about since the gardeners were working in the orangery and on the south lawns.

When he sat beside her, Aunt Jane handed him the letters. "Your mother first met the Duke of Leeds in Meryton . . ." He listened as his aunt told him of his real father, Thomas Osborne. They rarely spoke of the former duke. As far as Alexander was concerned, Fitzwilliam Darcy had always been his father—he was, after all, the only father Alexander had ever known. Thomas Osborne died a mere nine days after his birth.

While he listened, Aunt Jane spoke clearly and even paced in front of him for part of the story. When she finished, she stopped and faced him as though waiting for something. He could only stare at her as his entire body trembled.

"You are teasing me, are you not?" He swallowed hard and glanced around him. "My mother and . . . I do not believe it."

"You hold the proof in your hands, Alexander. I daresay if you read enough of those, your father will confirm my story in his own handwriting."

"But why would they never tell me?" His voice echoed from the front of the great house as he sprang from the bench and ran both of his hands through his hair. "Why would they allow me to believe the duke is my natural father?" He lowered his voice for the last.

"To protect you and the dukedom. You were born to save the duke's estate and the people who relied on him. Do not ever doubt that you were conceived in love, because you were—a deep, abiding love. But you possessed a great inheritance because your mother was wed to the duke. If they wanted to keep any question of what was yours from society as well as prevent a hellish scandal, they had no choice but to hide their past." She clasped his shoulders. "You have children. Would you not give all you own to do what was best for them? Even if this came to light now, the scandal would be great."

"But do I not deserve to know?"

Aunt Jane's head tilted a fraction. "You might consider their perspective. They would be telling you of their affair—of how they sinned in the eyes of the church and most people. Such a conversation would not be so easy with one's child." She watched him for a moment. "Now that you know, does it change how you feel about your father, about Fitzwilliam?"

He paused and closed his eyes. Thomas Osborne had never really been more than a name to him, only mentioned when the past of Worthstone came into conversation. Fitzwilliam Darcy had been the man who taught him to ride, who held him when he fell from his first pony, and who taught him all he knew about managing the Leeds dukedom. His father had always told him that being a duke was nothing more than an embellishment to his name. The title was not what mattered. Instead, your character and your behaviour made you a man worthy of respect—not a title.

"I love him as I always have, though I suppose I feel more connected to him than before."

"That is understandable," said his aunt. "Perhaps your perception makes you feel that way."

"I always thought my mother and father to have the highest morals. I do not know how to reconcile this."

Aunt Jane smiled and took his hand in hers. "Do you think they never had any guilt? In the beginning, they attempted to deny their feelings. You must remember the duke orchestrated the beginning of their intimate relationship. Once the affair began, they saw no reason to deny themselves what they desired more than anything—to be together."

He sighed and hugged his aunt. "Thank you. After finding these, I suspected, yet I had no idea how to confront my father."

"He will not be pleased with me. I must find Nicholas so we can hide in the orangery."

Alexander smiled and squeezed her hand. "I shall claim I forced you to tell me."

She laughed and cupped his face in her palms. Her laugh was so different than his mother's, yet it still resembled her in a way that made his chest ache. How was she gone? How was he to go on without her? When he considered his own feelings, he could not help but think of his father. How would he continue? She was his entire world.

Aunt Jane kissed his cheek before he set off in the direction of the river. The chapel was set close to a small bridge where the stream narrowed and twisted into the forest. As he cleared the wooded pathway, his father sat on a bench by the water, his head tilted up. How many times had he seen his mother in the same position, her face towards the heavens and her eyes closed? She always loved the feel of the breeze against her face.

As he approached, his father turned and opened his eyes. "I did not expect you to follow."

"I . . ." He tapped the bundle of letters against his hand. "I wanted to return these to you." His father's eyes flared when he reached for them, his fingers curling around them gently as though they were made of a delicate crystal.

"Where did you find them?"

"Grace found them. They were in mother's old dressing table."

His father's fingertips, weathered by the years, traced the heavy lines of his own script. "She always wondered what became of them."

"I suppose they fell behind the drawer."

He nodded, and his eyebrows drew down while he stared at them. "Did you read them?"

"A couple," said Alexander. "I confess that by the dates, my curiosity was piqued. I thought it would be a conversation about Aunt Georgiana or of Thomas Osborne. I did not expect . . ."

"You did not expect to find our love letters."

"No." He shook his head as though the word needed emphasis. "I knew you and Mama wed before her mourning was completed, I knew that you loved each other deeply, but I suppose I thought you grew to love each other."

"You and your mother did require protection from James Osborne, but our union was *never* a marriage of convenience—ever."

"Thomas Osborne is only my father in name, is he not?" His heart beat madly against his ribs. Why? He already knew the answer. People always commented on his resemblance to the Darcys, but they claimed the duke resembled the Darcys. The truth held a certain amount of convenience to hide their sins. "You are my true father."

"Did you learn that from the letters or have you spoken to your Aunt Jane?"

"Does it matter?"

"No, it does not, though I had reconciled myself to the fact that you would never know."

"Regardless of what the world believes, I have always considered you my father. You never failed to ensure I knew how much I was loved by both you and Mama."

His father stifled a sob and shook his head. "Forgive me. I loved your mother so much, and I loved you from the moment I knew of your possibility. I mourned that you would never know I was not only your father in the sense that I raised you, but also by blood. I certainly could not explain how I had an affair with your mother, and I know she did not relish the idea of revealing her indiscretions to her son."

"Do you regret it?"

His father's head whipped around and his brilliant blue eyes shone, glimmering with the moisture welling along his bottom lid. "Never! In the eyes of God and society, we may have been wrong, but I could never, ever regret that time with your mother or with you. When we wed, we made our peace with our lives and our past, and continued forward. Your mother always preferred to think of the past—"

"As its remembrance gave her pleasure."

"Yes, and we did just that. We have five wonderful children. Bennet has run Pemberley for these past ten years, allowing me to travel some with your mother—to show her Paris and Rome. I still remember the look of awe in her eyes at her first glimpse of the Colosseum." He cleared his throat. "Your sisters have all married men they love and have families of their own. We took great joy in watching all of you grow and spread your wings. Now I simply wait to be with your mother again."

A chill flooded his heart, and he stiffened. "You will not give up?"

"No, I could not," said his father in a weak tone. "Your mother would never forgive me if I did."

Alexander reached over and put his hand over his father's. "I love you. Even had I never discovered the truth, I could never consider anyone but you my father."

His father choked back another sob as Alexander wrapped his arms around him and held him tight. The feeling was so different from what he recalled from years past. The last time he had held his father, he was much younger and his father was so strong. He never thought anyone could be as tall and strong as Fitzwilliam Darcy. Time changed everyone, his father included.

Alexander took a long, deep breath and closed his eyes, lifting his face into the breeze. With his father in his arms, he attempted to commit the memory to his mind—to create an indelible imprint so he would never forget.

People live their lives and have so many experiences, but how many did they remember with the clarity of a portrait, how many of those precious remembrances kept them company in their later years? Memories and love were a person's wealth—money meant nothing.

Alexander was a fortunate man. He had a beautiful wife who he loved, and three children who held his heart as well, but he would never have appreciated what he possessed if his mother and father had not taught him what it was to love.

Regardless of what people believed or what a piece of paper said, in Alexander's heart, he had always been the son of Fitzwilliam Darcy. As it turned out, what he had always believed and desired was actually truth.

The breeze shifted a few tendrils of his curls as he wrapped his arms tighter around his father—the best man he had ever known.

## The End

L.L. Diamond

**Acknowledgements**

To tell the truth, this story has always given me fits of nerves worthy of Mrs. Bennet!

I first started writing the story of Elizabeth, Darcy, and Thomas right after we first moved to England five and a half years ago. I closed myself into my room in temporary housing and typed away, but became derailed when we moved into our actual house. When I finally was able to continue writing, I started *An Unwavering Trust* instead. I think it's fitting that I finally finished it several months before we move back to the United States.

It's been at least six or seven years ago now that I first read the history of the Duke of Cumberland and the mysterious late-night murder of his valet. The question of what occurred that night will never be truly known, but the theory of the valet being the duke's lover stuck with me. If they were indeed lovers, it was an ingenious method of hiding their affair, and was the trigger for Thomas to be born inside my mind. What if you had a duke who needed an heir but couldn't bring himself to actually do the deed—well, with a woman anyway?

Thomas is a tricky character. His actions are despicable, but I wanted him to remain a sympathetic character, which I struggled with and probably why I shied away from finishing this five years ago. Despite Thomas's trickery and deceit, I hope you still care for him. After all, if it wasn't for Thomas, we wouldn't have a happy ever after for our dear couple.

As always, I so appreciate my family. I get a great deal of support from them whether it's my son, who wants to stay in the room with me, but has to play his video games with headphones or everyone giving me some time to finish what I've been working on, they're willing to do what's needed.

Brandon always does as much as he can and is definitely a second half. Is it bad that we can finish each other's sentences or go to ask the other the same question at the same time? Sometimes I wonder if our brains have partially fused together over the past twenty odd years. He took me to see the new *Emma* recently and has even taken me to Bath for a day to see the promenade. Perhaps I will convert him completely one day!

I've had a number of betas along the way, but Carol S. Bowes has stuck with me from the beginning, or nearly the beginning and was my wonderful copy editor for this go around. We finally met in person this past summer, and we had a blast talking and seeing *Pride and Prejudice* in the only remaining Regency theatre in England.

Thanks to Brynn for her editing and her help with the JAFF community. We always love to get our books out there for those who have yet to find the genre.

Thanks to Debbie F. for proofreading and those who were my fabulous ARC readers!

A huge thanks to my friends both in the military community and outside of it. Friends are precious and a good friend is priceless. I thank my friends for every willing ear and every laugh that's gotten me through a rough day. With the current trials we are experiencing, I wish for everyone to have friends to rely on and love. Love is always the most important consideration!

JAFF has a huge online community which has been extremely supportive and helpful over the years—whether from a fellow author or the fan base, I appreciate it all.

Thank you to everyone who has purchased my books, left me wonderful messages, left an amazing review, and followed me after reading one of my stories. I wouldn't be able to have this much fun without your support and encouragement.

L.L. Diamond
## About the Author

L.L. Diamond is more commonly known as Leslie to her friends and Mom to her three kids. A native of Louisiana, she spent the majority of her life living within an hour of New Orleans before following her husband all over as a military wife. Louisiana, Mississippi, California, Texas, New Mexico, Nebraska, and now England have all been called home along the way.

Aside from mother and writer, Leslie considers herself a perpetual student. She has degrees in biology and studio art but will devour any subject of interest simply for the knowledge. Her most recent endeavors have included certifications to coach swimming, certifying as a fitness instructor and indoor cycling instructor, and she is currently studying to be a personal trainer. As an artist, her concentration is in graphic design, but watercolor is her medium of choice with one of her watercolors featured on the cover of her second book, *A Matter of Chance*. She is also a member of the Jane Austen Society of North America. Leslie also plays flute and piano, but much like *Pride and Prejudice's* Elizabeth Bennet, she is always in need of practice!

Made in the USA
Coppell, TX
08 May 2020